First to the Cape

by

Hugh Chare

Publication Data
First to the Cape © Hugh B. Chare 2023

Book and cover design by Hugh B. Chare
ISBN: 978-1-940012-08-7

www.kilihune-books.com

Other books by Hugh Chare
The journal of Jan Englebrecht
British Spy in the Bushveld
Federica
First to the Cape

The James Martin series
African Encounter
Across the Zambezi
Just off the Great North Road
Well, there you go!
Return to Africa
We don't make glass
The Sagitta Mishap
Carbon Copy
Flight 5 to Johannesburg

Marieke Englebrecht mysteries
Death in the Mopane
Revenge after twenty years

Preface

It is amazing to think that in the short time between the first well-advertised and documented powered controlled flight in 1903 to the outbreak of war in 1914, that aircraft development moved so rapidly. Obviously, people saw the benefit to the military from having flying machines and early on their flight tests, the Wright brothers approached the US Army about their machine. The US Army was interested, but the Wright brothers and their company seemed to spend more time on lawsuits than aircraft development, so when the United States entered the Great War, there was a paucity of US-built aircraft that were adequate for combat, and they used many French aircraft. In contrast, the French, British and German inventors kept developing new machines, and by the time the Great War broke out, the opposing forces each had a number of models to choose from. Post the Great War, the aviation industry took off, and passenger and freight services expanded. All metal planes were first built by Junkers in Germany, but their development and use were hampered by the restrictions imposed upon the Germans by the victors of the Great War. There was a marked difference in the amount of support granted to the fledgling aviation industry by the British government, which seemed to do everything in its power to hinder the development of the industry, and the French government, which actively supported the industry.

There were never as many aircraft builders as there were car builders, but the number and variety of planes built are still surprising. Not many of the early builders survive; those that do are typically now part of some large enterprise or quasi-government entity. The same is true of airlines, the longest surviving airline with the same name being KLM, or Koninklijke Luchtvaart Maatschappij N.V., founded on the 7th of October in 1919.

This is a work of fiction. Any resemblance in the featured characters to actual persons, living or dead, is purely coincidental. Some of the terms used were in common usage in the 1920s, but would not be used today. Historical accuracy has been maintained, but the author would not use such terms today.

Contents

29th June 1914

From the Franco-Prussian War of 1870-1871 and subsequent events, including the accession of Wilhelm II to the throne of Germany, the Russo-Japanese War of 1904-1905, the Moroccan crises of 1905-1906 and 1911, the annexation of Bosnia and Herzegovina in 1908 by Austria Hungary, the Italo-Turkish War of 1911-1912 and the Balkan Wars of 1912, Europe was ripe for some form of conflict with two major blocks, the Triple Alliance of Austria Hungary, Germany and Italy on the one hand and the Triple Entente of France, Great Britain and Russia on the other hand.

"Did you see the paper?" Federica asked her husband, George.
"Not yet, why what's in it?" he replied.
"Archduke Ferdinand of the Austro-Hungarians was assassinated in Sarajevo yesterday," she explained. "What will this mean?"
"This will mean war," he said. "The Austrians won't stomach such a thing and will demand retribution from the Serbs, probably with terms that the Serbs cannot and will not give. So it will be war. After all, they have all been positioning themselves for shifts in power for some time, and it only needed something like this to set things off."
"Will it affect us?" she asked.
"Undoubtedly," he said. "The Germans will support the Austrians, the Serbs won't like that. The Russians, although they don't have the best of relations with the Serbs, will stand by them. Then the other players of the Triple Entente will get involved, so expect war sooner rather than later."
"When do you think?" she asked.
"Not long," he thought. "Perhaps a month and then we'll see the first shots fired."
"I wonder why it is that ambition of a few leads to wars?" she thought.
"I think it's just that, ambition," he replied. "Each of the major powers would like to see more territory under their sway, and if that cannot be done peacefully, then start with implied threats and if that doesn't work, look for a pretext to wage war and conquer."
"I suppose you saw that in the war in South Africa?" she asked.

"I did," he agreed. "And in India, got to expand the Empire, you know, or hang on to it at least. In India, there was money to be made through the trading companies, and we were afraid we would lose it to Russian influence that could come in through Afghanistan. In South Africa, it was gold, gold that we as Britain did not control, so we found a pretext and went to war."

"And look what that cost," she commented.

"Wars are expensive," he agreed. "If we go to war with the Austrians and the Germans, we will be paying for it for years to come."

"It's official," George said at breakfast on the morning of the 4th of August. "We've declared war on Germany for not leaving the Belgians alone. The French are now moving men and supplies as quickly as they can to counter the German moves, and we will be sending men and equipment to France to help them."

"Will they want you?" she asked.

"Probably," he thought. "Though I'm not sure in what capacity. In the last war, I was attached to Field Intelligence, but Europe is not South Africa; I'm not sure how this will all transpire."

"What can we do as the Sirius Car Company?" she asked.

"I think we should take a look at reworking our Antares wagon and offer it again to the War Office," he suggested.

"I didn't think they were that interested the last time," she commented.

"They weren't," he agreed. "But, circumstances have changed and they may well see the value now, but whatever happens, they will need many lorries, buses and ambulances."

"What do you suggest?" she asked.

"For Antares, put in one of the new engines that William has developed and take a look at the gearboxes and axles and perhaps incorporate the larger petrol tanks you developed for that Australian friend of Nastia's," he said. "And, add a large water tank for the people using the car."

"I think that could be done fairly quickly," she agreed. "If I wanted to add mounts for a gun, what should I do?"

"I think the Lewis gun," he replied. "The Vickers is heavy and a little cumbersome. I will get the details from BSA, and we can experiment."

"What else?" she asked.

2

"I'm not sure how progressive the War Office will be," he said. "But, I think they will start out by commandeering as many buses and lorries as they can, then they will look to acquiring more, so expect some demand for our Arcturus and Regulus vans and lorries."

"I'll talk to Nastia and William today," she said. "I imagine that as we go to war, the demand for cars will go down, but perhaps we will see an influx of orders for lorries and vans."

"We should also look to how this may affect our people in Orly," he said, referring to the French subsidiary, FAS, *Fabricant Automobile Sirius*, they had set up in Orly to build cars, vans and lorries for the Continental market. "I expect some will volunteer, some may get conscripted, but perhaps not if the French government orders from the Orly factory and decides that they would better serve their war effort by building lorries and vans."

"I'll contact Yves later today and find out what he thinks," she said.

"I think we should also expect some orders at Abbey Biscuits and for uniforms at Windsor Garments, and I would think that the Somercotes lead mine in Derbyshire will be asked to increase production," George added, referring to three of the other businesses that they owned. "I would also expect, as things progress, that men will volunteer for military service, and that eventually conscription will be introduced. Either way, we are likely to lose some of our workforce here as well as in France; we should be looking to replace those losses, probably with more women. For Abbey and Windsor, I don't see that as a problem, but for Sirius and Burnham Castings we might need a training program to help women with the processes of casting, machining and assembly, I would imagine that the War Office would be reluctant to take men from the mine, so wouldn't expect to see much change there."

"Anastasia and I will take care of the training programs," Federica assured him. "We will also have to look to the future, when all the men come back and want their old jobs back, do we just throw the women out onto the street?"

"They may depend upon how the businesses are doing then and how the general economies of France and here are," George thought. "If things go well, perhaps we will be in a mode of increasing everything and may not have to put anyone out. Only time will tell."

"At least we don't have a sales office in Germany to worry about," she commented. "The South African and Australian offices will be fine. I will contact Franco and see what we should do with the office in Italy."

"I suppose it will depend on how involved the countries get embroiled in the war," he thought. "But, I agree, that at the moment it looks like most of our offices will be on the same side, except Italy. I wonder what Italy will do, stay with the Triple Alliance or try and sit it out?"

"That would be interesting," she said. "I have seen a lot of diplomatic moves by the Italians to get closer to Britain and France, perhaps the Italians see the Austrians more as traditional enemies than allies and are beginning to wonder whether or not the supposed Triple Alliance was ever truly a defensive agreement."

"I think the Italians are looking at the lie of the land and are calculating how to get back territory in the Alps from the Austrians and some along the Adriatic, so don't be surprised if they switch sides," he said.

On Friday of that week, George was in the Horse Guards building on Whitehall, summoned to discuss his role and his reactivation to active duty. While he was cooling his heels in the corridors, he heard his name called and turned to see an old acquaintance, now Major General David Henderson.

"Wheelwright, what brings you here? You are being reactivated?"

"I am, Sir," George replied. "Congratulations, Sir, on the Royal Flying Corps. I am sure that it will be of great value in the coming conflict."

"Did I hear that you have a pilot's licence?" Henderson asked.

"I do Sir," George confirmed.

"Many hours of flying time?" Henderson asked.

"I have probably flown twenty hours a month for the past six years," George replied,

"Splendid, what have they talked to you about?"

"They seem to think that I might be of use to Callwell in Military Intelligence," George explained. "But, I cannot pose as a German, and I think I might be better used gathering wider intelligence about general troop movements to guess at intentions."

"Quite," Henderson said. "Look, I'll talk to Callwell, but I think you should go to Egypt. Take a squadron of aircraft and keep a close eye on the Ottomans; we cannot afford to lose Suez."

"Do you think the Ottomans will get involved?" George asked.

"Don't you?" Henderson asked. "The Ottomans are more likely to side with the Germans and may see this as an opportunity to recoup some of their recent losses and, at the same time, help their friends by denying us the use of Suez. We need Suez to move oil and, if needed, to bring in troops and supplies from India and Australia."

"Is that within the purview of the RFC?" George asked.

"Certainly," Henderson confirmed. "We are ideally suited to gather intelligence from the air and can see over the wider scope of battlefields, so keeping an eye on the Turk by flying up and down his border and peeking in is just what we need. Just don't provoke a war!"

"I will try not to," George promised.

"I'm not sure where the best place for you to base is, Henderson said. "The Turk is the other side of Sinai from the canal, so you'd have to fly over the Sinai and then work out where the border is, runs from Aqaba to the Med, maybe you could push into Sinai a bit and establish a base forward from the canal, just don't get yourself in a position where you'd be vulnerable to attack from the air."

"I'll look into that," George said.

"I see they've reactivated you as Major, you held that rank in South Africa as I recall," Henderson said.

"I did at the end of the war," George confirmed.

"For services rendered in the field in South Africa," Henderson said. "I was disappointed when you resigned your commission. I would have liked to see you stay on."

"I had a family estate to take care of and a new business enterprise of my wife's that I also helped with," George explained.

"Your wife's business?" Henderson asked.

"We own the Sirius Car Company, among other things," George explained. "My wife and sister are the designers and run the business; we even built an armoured car and tested it for the War Office a few years ago, but at that time, there was little real interest."

"Perhaps we should look again, I can see an armoured car being of value in Sinai and around the canal," Henderson mused. "Well, Suez will be a little different, but keep a close eye on the Turk; we don't want any surprises."

"No, Sir," George said.

"Well, must be off," Henderson said. "You'll get your orders next week, and I'll expect you in Egypt as soon as you can arrange transport. You'll need to requisition planes and recruit pilots, observers and ground crew. I'll assign who I can, but I'm going to need most of the people we have in France. I'll give you written authority to accept qualified pilots as volunteers and give them commissions as lieutenants, but the support crews you will have to either get from whatever we can offer from the RFC or transfers from other units. Your orders will give you authority to requisition whatever you need to form the regiment and get it to Suez ready to operate, and I'll give you a good adjutant to help."

"Very good, Sir," George said.

Henderson was as good as his word, and George received his packet of orders on Monday morning. Henderson or his staff must have worked through the weekend to get it all done. The orders sounded straightforward enough, put together a squadron of twelve planes together with the appropriate pilots, observers and ground crew, arrange transport to Port Said, select an operational base location somewhere east of the canal and start sorties as quickly as possible to keep an eye on the movements of the Ottoman Empire with regard to safeguarding the Suez Canal. What was vague was what he would need to do that. Fortunately for George, he was given a Captain Henry Anderson as his adjutant and Anderson was already well established within the Royal Flying Corps and brought with him the schedules of men and materiel that went with a squadron of planes, everything from the aircraft themselves to the knives and forks they would need in the mess tent. One of the first things George did was check what kind of aircraft the Ottoman Empire had, to see what he might possibly encounter in Egypt. As far as he could tell, it was a small collection of Blériot and Deperdussin craft left over from the Balkan Wars. He was happy to note that they were even slower than most of the British types in production.

He did not doubt that, as the war progressed that the Germans would probably help out the Ottoman Empire, either with equipment or pilots or both, but for now, things did not look too bad.

For the next few weeks, George was kept busy organising staffing. He needed three captains, eighteen pilots, who would be lieutenants, another eighteen second lieutenants who would be the observers, three senior sergeants and a total of 140 other ranks. Added to this, he also needed aircraft. All he could get was Royal Aircraft Factory model BE-2, a slow, stable aircraft that might be good for intelligence gathering, but which George saw as less than desirable if someone started shooting at you. The ground support lorries he could do something about, instead of the usual Crossley tenders, he asked Federica if she could give him ten Antares wagons. For the larger tenders and repair lorries, he decided to stick with the Leyland lorries that the RFC used and acquired twelve heavy tenders plus trailers for each. Henry Anderson pointed out that this was well over establishment for both light and heavy tenders, but George argued that they would need to transport everything themselves once they got to Port Said. He also found and acquired a Holt tractor and a piece of machinery called a land leveller. This was amusing to most of the men until he pointed out that it was likely to be either the land leveller clearing a runway for the aircraft or men with shovels. That made it suddenly very popular. Lastly, there were motorcycles from Phelon and Moore for use by despatch riders and other functionaries.

Everything was collected at the Sirius Car Company factory near Slough, and the aircraft were disassembled and crated for shipment to Port Said. The men were accommodated in tents, and George took the time to get to know them. Henry Anderson then addressed all the other supply items they would need to set up operations in Sinai: tents, mobile kitchens, tools, petrol, food supplies, rifles, machine guns, ammunition, bombs, cameras, binoculars, compasses, and other sundries. Anderson also organised the new uniforms they would all need in Egypt, khaki drill shirts and trousers, not the heavier woollen kit they would have needed if they had been going to France. While their Antares wagons were being built by Sirius, George had some of the mechanics follow them through the assembly operations so that they knew the vehicles really well and would be able to service them in the field. Henry Anderson suggested that they also use the time to make sure everyone could drive both the light and heavy tenders, so that they would never be stuck for drivers. They received notice of a sailing date and were told to have everything at the Southampton docks by the 17th of September for a sailing date of the 18th.

Some of the pilots George found by going to the Royal Aero Club and eliciting volunteers. As many of them knew him, they were willing to sign up, though some were a little disappointed that they would be going to Egypt to fly reconnaissance missions rather than France, where the action was likely to be. While he was busy with pilots, George was visited by his brother-in-law, William McIntosh.

"George," William said. "Are you still looking for pilots?"

"I am," George confirmed. "Are you interested?"

"Of course," William said. "I've talked things over with Nastia, and she and Fede can manage the business well enough without us, and if I don't volunteer, my estimation is that before long conscription will be imposed."

"I'm afraid you're right about that," George agreed. "I don't hold to the view that this will all be over by Christmas, I think we're set for a much longer war."

"What planes do you have?" William asked.

"BE-2s," George replied.

"Slow," William said. "But, perhaps we can modify the engines a little and get some more speed out of them, or just replace them."

"Have you looked at the engines?" George asked.

"I have," William confirmed. "Renault V-8, air-cooled, only gives about 70 to 80HP, but the damn thing weighs almost 500lbs. I think we could take one of the engines we have for the Regulus or Arcturus vans and do a better job. We'd have to adapt the fuselage for water cooling, but I think we could get over 100HP for much less weight."

"Why don't we take some engines with us, and when we're in Egypt, we can experiment?" George suggested. "And we should also take one of our own planes with us and see how it fares against the BE-2."

"What's the name of that officer you have with you?" William asked.

"Captain Henry Anderson," George said. "I'll introduce you, and then we can get the paperwork done to get you commissioned."

"Do you have enough pilots?" William asked.

"The RFC gave me four, I got twelve volunteers from the RAC, you make seventeen, so I need one more unless I fly myself, or get one of the captains to fly a plane and not a desk," George replied.

"Could we go and meet Captain Anderson?" William asked.

"Of course," George said. "In fact, he's coming to dinner tonight, so why don't you and Nastia come along."

Henry Anderson duly presented himself for dinner at the Wheelwright house that evening and was introduced to Federica, Anastasia and William McIntosh and Giovanna McIntosh, who, being only two, was taken off to bed by a nanny once the introduction had been made.

"Delighted to meet you all," he said. "I'm given to understand that Mr McIntosh will be joining us in Egypt, did I hear correctly?"

"You did," George confirmed. "That brings us to seventeen pilots, so perhaps we will be lucky and get one more pilot, or perhaps we'll teach someone when we're there."

"Will tells me that you are going to take one of our planes," Federica said. "Which one?"

"I'm sorry," Anderson interrupted. "You have your own planes?"

"We've actually built quite a few," George explained. "My wife decided some time ago that she wanted to branch out from building cars and lorries into building aircraft, so we started in 1907 and have built probably twenty since then, five of which we still have."

"What happened to the others?" Anderson asked.

"We pulled them apart," Federica explained. "After we would build a plane, we would test it and see how it would fly, then we would make improvements, and quite often we scavenged parts and materials from the older ones to build new ones. We looked at all the planes that had been built before 1907, including the one by Gustave Whitehead and that of the Wright brothers, and many more and borrowed, copied, modified and adapted until we got what we wanted."

"So what kind of aircraft are they, have I ever seen one?" Anderson asked.

"At the moment, it's still a conventional biplane," Federica explained. "But I'm working on a design for a monoplane using Duralumin instead of fabric coverings. I have a wing design that I think will be perfect for the monoplane, and I'm currently looking at the fuselage to reduce drag and waiting for William to give me the engine I would like."

"Is your biplane a single-seat, two-seat?" Anderson asked.

"We have a two-seat, the Aquila, that would be equivalent to the BE-2," Federica replied. "But, it has the pilot forward of the observer and has a larger, but lighter, water-cooled engine giving us a top speed of about 120 mph, and it has a range of about 500 miles. We have a second type, the Auriga, that is larger with two engines that I was thinking of for passenger service before this war came along; it would carry twelve passengers. That is also a biplane but is a little slower than our Aquila, only reaching just over 100 mph, but it also has a range of about 500 miles and can carry quite a few bombs if we want that."

"Why doesn't the RFC have these planes?" Anderson asked. "It sounds as if they have much better performance than many we have."

"Well, mainly because we've been fairly closed-mouthed about the details," Federica explained. "We were looking to build a plane for a commercial service of some sort and didn't want to disclose too much too early, lest someone copy our designs. I am not sure how well the designs would adapt to the rigours of military service."

"My wife has an ambition to have an aircraft that would run on a London to Cape Town air service," George commented.

"That's a tall order," Anderson said.

"We know," Federica agreed. "Unless we can do it in well under two weeks, there is no advantage to travel by sea; in fact, there are serious drawbacks. One cannot take much luggage on a plane, but on a ship, there is practically no limit."

"Do you have everything you need for your expedition, Captain?" Anastasia asked.

"I think so," Anderson replied.

"You have aircraft, guns and ammunition, I presume," Anastasia said. "What about a field kitchen, sun goggles, a wind sock, camouflage netting, tents for the planes, spare parts for the aircraft and the lorries, spare tyres, which I imagine you will need a lot of?"

"I'm sorry," Anderson said. "Sun goggles and camouflage netting?"

"Sun goggles, or glasses if you prefer, have been used in Venice for years to reduce glare from the water. I imagine that they would be useful in the desert sun," Anastasia explained. "And camouflage netting and tents to cover your planes when they are not in use, one to keep them cool and two to hide them from an enemy."

"I confess I had not thought of that," Anderson said. "It's not in the manual would be the standard answer, but perhaps it should be."

"While we are talking about such things," George said. "I want to be sure that every man in our squadron has a rifle and a pistol. That may not be to regulation, but if it comes to the point of having to defend ourselves, we should be prepared, and I also want to take enough Lewis guns to have one for each plane and one for each tender, can that be done? Also, could you arrange for all the men to be mustered tomorrow at eight, we're going to Bisley for some rifle training."

"All the men?" Anderson asked.

"All of us, officers and men," George confirmed. "We will all be able to shoot when we get to Egypt, one day it may be necessary."

"Fede, could we get six of the engines we used in the Regulus lorry to take with us?" William asked.

"Of course," she agreed. "Will six be enough? If you have twelve planes, shouldn't you take twelve plus perhaps another six for spares?"

"I'm sorry," Anderson said again. "What engines?"

"William is our company engine designer," Federica explained. "He has been working on engine development since he joined us, particularly with a view to my ambition to fly London to Cape Town."

"We have developed an engine with a very high horsepower-to-weight ratio," William explained. "We were thinking that we could modify the BE-2s with new engines and get a better turn of speed and more range."

"Does the War Office know about this?" Anderson asked.

"Not really," George said. "They have their hands full at the moment getting people to France. We wouldn't want to bother them with all these details. When we have performance data, then we'll let them know what we've done."

"You're confident, then, that you can do this?" Anderson asked.

"Quite," William stated. "We may have to do a little balancing of the aircraft, because our engine is so much lighter than the Renault, but we can do that with extra petrol tanks and by moving a few other things around."

"Well," Anderson commented. "When the General assigned me to this squadron, I thought I was going to a backwater with little or no chance of anything really interesting happening, but now I'm thinking I may have an opportunity to see real development done in field conditions. I presume that, as we learn, it would be acceptable to pass our knowledge onto the other squadrons?"

"I would insist," George said. "If we can make improvements that help our people, then we should make sure they can all take advantage if they choose. But, they may not listen as much of what we do is not quite the norm, and we may be regarded as crackpot inventors."

"Where are you going to build your landing field?" Federica asked.

"We have to select a site," George replied.

"Well, it seems to me that as the BE-2 has a range of 200 miles or so, then you should build your landing field somewhere in the middle, perhaps east of Ismailia. If you build it at Port Said or at Suez, then you will be at the limits of the range of the aircraft to fly the full length of the canal, and you'd be nowhere near Aqaba," Federica suggested.

"An excellent point," George conceded. "What do you think, Henry?"

"I think we should change our destination from Port Said to Ismailia," Anderson replied. "Perhaps on the trip out to Port Said, we can look at the maps that the War Office does have and pick out a likely spot somewhere east of Ismailia."

"If I may make a suggestion," Federica said. "Land at Ismailia, then push east along the coastal road to Katia, set up base there, then perhaps go south and see if you can't find a suitable spot close to Aqaba. Katia is probably far enough back from the Ottoman stronghold at Rafa that you'd be less likely to be attacked from the air."

"That would take some doing," Anderson said. "There aren't any roads that I'm aware of south on the eastern side of Sinai."

"Perhaps fly and scout it out," Federica suggested. "If the Turk wanted to attack Suez, what would be their route?"

"From the sea would be difficult because we have the Navy," Anderson said. "From land, the only practical route I can see is the coastal road, I suppose it would be possible to take an overland route that is not the road, but with a large, or even medium-sized raiding party, that would be a challenge and spotting it from the air would be easy."

"How far up the Gulf of Aqaba can the Navy take you without coming in range of the guns at Aqaba?" Federica asked.

"A long way, I should say," Anderson thought.

"Why not send a small force that way too and fly north from there and south from Katia," Federica suggested.

"Let's do this," George suggested. "We take everyone to Katia, set up operations there, then we send a team to the Gulf of Aqaba to set up a landing field and bring in fuel and supplies, then we can fly down the length of the border, which can only be 120 miles or so, land and refuel, then come back, perhaps stay overnight on occasion and make the first flight north in the morning so that Johnny Turk doesn't see too much of a routine."

"That sounds like a good plan," Anderson agreed. "If we have a plane scout the coastline south of Aqaba, they can pick out a likely landing spot for the Navy, and we can organise to get supplies in. We'd need to leave a detachment there to guard the supplies."

"We'll do that," George agreed. "And leave them with enough arms and ammunition to protect themselves."

"I wonder if we can get the Navy to leave a small gunboat in the area," Anderson pondered.

"I'm sure we could," George said. "We are blockading the gulf anyway, so putting something small up into the gulf to take care of small boats that might put out from Aqaba makes sense."

"Do you have water carts and petrol carts?" Anastasia asked.

"No," Anderson said. "Normally, supplies and water would come under the Army Service Corps."

"Water will be a big issue," George said. "When I was in South Africa, it was the limiting factor on many operations, horses need a lot of water, and so did the men. Without it, I could see the difference in a day or two; we should plan for a gallon a day per man."

"That's quite a lot," Anderson said. "Perhaps we should find a drill and drill for our own water if we can't find a decent well. Where do Suez and Ismailia get their water from?"

"Isn't there the Sweet Water Canal that takes fresh water to Ismailia?" Anastasia asked.

"Of course," Anderson said. "I'd forgotten that. "But it's a long drive from there to Katia, we'd need to try and find a source of water close to the town, as there is a town there, there must be water somewhere. Down at the bottom of Sinai on the Gulf, I don't know, we'd have to rely on the Navy for a while until we found local water, then we'd need to look at filtering it."

"There is always the Berkefeld filters," Federica said.

"We will give you three water wagons and two wagons for petrol," Anastasia promised. "We have just developed our Spica lorry, which we can fit with 350-gallon tanks. For the water wagons, we'll add large versions of the Berkefeld; you just need to make sure that you can get a supply of the diatomaceous earth. The tanks are baffled internally to stop the effects of water or petrol movement impacting the lorry. Where are the fueling points for the BE-2 aircraft? Perhaps we can provide a hose and nozzle to make it easy to fill."

"The two tanks are mounted in the upper fuselage longerons," George explained. "They both can be filled from the top through brass screw caps. The main tank is sixteen gallons, and the secondary tank is just over eleven gallons."

"So if we put some kind of boom on the petrol trucks, then the hose and a filling nozzle can be taken to the tanks," Anastasia suggested.

"I think two of the planes have the main tank under the observer's seat," Anderson said. "I seem to recall reading that somewhere."

"So, what do you do, remove the seat and then fill the tank?" Anastasia asked.

"Exactly," George confirmed. "So the hose and nozzle should be able to be extended down inside the fuselage."

"We should add a couple of Antares armoured cars so that you can take them to Aqaba," Anastasia suggested. "That way, people you leave down there will have more than just small arms, and perhaps a mountain gun or two."

"I'll see what I can do about Lewis guns and mountain guns," Anderson said.

"And what about tools for servicing and repairing the planes and the lorries?" Anastasia asked.

"We have what we need there, unless your lorries have to have special tools," Anderson said.

"We'll provide four sets for the lorries," Anastasia said. "What about cooking and eating?"

"That's part of the basic establishment," Anderson said. "We have all we need there, bar the food itself, which we'll need to arrange to get on a regular basis."

"As we're talking about food, perhaps we should go in and eat?" Federica suggested. "I'm sure that Captain Anderson would like some respite from the work of getting an expedition to Egypt together."

"There's an American company from Ohio, Star Drilling Company, they have portable drills," Anastasia said. "They're powered by steam, but as water is an issue, perhaps that could be replaced by a petrol engine."

"I'll look into that," Will said.

"Anything that we might have forgotten?" George asked.

"I've got a fairly long list," Anderson said. "I'll get some of the supply sergeants on it right away."

The following day, the squadron went to Bisley to the rifle range and were put through their paces by George. George had not forgotten how to shoot; he had won prizes at Bisley competitions in the past, and during the Second Boer War, he had proven himself in the field as well as on the range. George had a new rifle that he wanted to try; it had been given to him by Federica. It was a Westley Richards .318, slightly larger than the Lee Enfield .303, and in George's opinion had the better action. However, the Lee Enfield was really good for high rates of fire, with no problems from heating and with jamming occurring only very rarely. He concluded that he would take both rifles with him to Egypt and hope that he did not have to use them too quickly and too often. Some of the officers and men knew how to shoot, and some did credibly well, but there were quite a few who had no idea, so basic instruction was called for. Fortunately for George, six of his sergeants had seen service before in South Africa and were familiar with the rifles and pistols and took charge of drills to teach the men the basics. By the time they finished, every man in the regiment had test-fired a pistol and rifle and knew how to field strip the weapons, clean them, load them and fire them. George asked the sergeants to put together classes to hold on the boat, to reinforce what they had just taught, so that the lessons would not be lost. In Egypt, he planned to hold live-fire drills regularly and told Anderson to make sure that they had an adequate supply of ammunition that could be replenished.

On the drive back to Slough, Anderson had questions.

"Is it true that your wife designed the aircraft that you have?"

"She did," George confirmed. "She and my sister make a formidable team, whether designing cars or aircraft."

"Isn't that a little unusual?" Anderson asked.

"I suppose so," George agreed. "But, for me, it has become so much part of our normal life that it is hard to understand why more women are not designing cars and other machines."

"Where did they learn?" Anderson asked.

"My wife had excellent teachers in Hong Kong, and my sister went to university in London," George explained.

"Is that where she met McIntosh?" Anderson asked.

"It was," George confirmed. "They were in the same class, and after they received their degrees, they both came to work for Sirius, Nastia as the chief designer and Will as the engine specialist."

"What did you do in South Africa?" Anderson asked.

"I was attached to Field Intelligence in the latter part of the war, which is where I met the General who at that time was Kitchener's intelligence chief," George explained.

"When did you learn to fly?" Anderson asked.

"We taught ourselves, then we went to the Blériot Flying School near Rouen in 1909, then got British certificates from Brooklands after it opened in 1910," George replied.

"So, Mrs Wheelwright is a pilot as well?" Anderson asked.

"We all are," George said. "We had intended to build aircraft for commercial enterprises flying people, but this war has rather upset the apple cart for a while. Perhaps when it's over, we can get back to our dream."

"You don't think this will be over by Christmas?" Anderson asked.

"No," George said. "This will go on much longer, and it's hard to know how things will go. Are we ready for our voyage to Port Said?"

"We are," Anderson confirmed. "We just need to crate up the engines that your wife said she would give us and take delivery of the tanker wagons that your sister mentioned, and we're ready. We must be the only squadron that is as well equipped and is almost self-contained."

"Well, when we get to Egypt, we need to get an airfield site selected quickly and get the planes assembled and in the air," George said. "I presume you have details of to whom we pass information to in Cairo?"

"I do indeed," Anderson confirmed. "General Maxwell has just been given the command of the Egyptian forces, replacing Major General Byng. I know Maxwell's adjutant."

The next day, Federica received news from Yves in Orly. The French government had indeed placed orders for numbers of vans and lorries and had put most of the staff on the reserved occupation list for the moment. That meant they were secure from any immediate risk of conscription, but that could change as the war progressed. Yves himself had thought of volunteering and was proposing to name his factory manager, Philippe, as his successor for the duration of the war. Federica was happy with the choice of Philippe and told Yves that he should follow his heart, and if he felt that he should volunteer, then he should do so. She asked him to let her know his decision as soon as possible so that she could make sure that Philippe got all the help he might need from England as he built the lorries and vans. Yves did not wait long and telegraphed her his decision to volunteer that evening. He was accepted into the French army as a captain and assigned to an artillery division. Philippe had no immediate desire to volunteer and was instead focused on his job to get vehicles built for the war effort.

There was one more thing that Federica wanted to get done before George and William went off to war, and that was to ensure that she had the appropriate powers of attorney to execute agreements, sales or acquisitions for the family. The companies that they owned were jointly owned by George, Anastasia, William, and herself, so with George and William gone, she needed to be sure that whatever might occur, she could take care of things. Mr Baker of Baker, Fielding, Higginbottom and Watts, solicitors from Chancery Lane in London, was duly summoned to come and prepare and witness the execution of the appropriate documents. Federica's first dealings with Mr Baker had been frosty as he had indicated that women were perhaps not capable of running a business or managing stock portfolios. Since that time, their relationship had changed, and now he was an ardent follower of her stock purchases and was more than happy to do her bidding with the various businesses that the family owned.

"Good morning, Mr Baker," Federica said as he was ushered into their office by Alice White, their office manager.

"A very good morning to you, Mrs Wheelwright, Mrs McIntosh," he replied. "Such a troublesome time we now live in."

"It is indeed Mr Baker," Federica agreed.

"I understand that Mr Wheelwright and Mr McIntosh will be leaving soon for Egypt," Mr Baker said. "I trust, gentlemen, that you will be circumspect in your actions and return to us here safe and sound."

"That is our hope," George agreed. "I have managed to live through two wars and had foolishly thought that we would see an extended period of peace with no conflicts."

"I am not of the age where I may be of much service in the field," Mr Baker commented. "But, I have volunteered some of my time and services to the War Office. They are considering how best I may serve. Now, I understand that you have need of powers of attorney?"

"That is so," George agreed. "While we are away, Fede and Nastia will continue to run the businesses, but from time to time, there might arise circumstances that require a company action. We need to have all in place such that Fede and Nastia may execute any documents that are required."

"Quite," Mr Baker agreed. "That we may do very expeditiously. I have forms of power of attorney already made out. If you gentlemen could just sign here, then I will witness them."

"Is there anything else we need to do before you leave, Mr Baker?" George asked.

"I also brought copies of your last wills and testaments. Are there any changes that you would like to make?" Mr Baker asked.

"May I?" William asked. Mr Baker handed him his will and William quickly read through it. "No, I see nothing that I would change, George?"

"I suppose I should check," George said. "If I may, Mr Baker?"

"This is the latest," Mr Baker said, handing him the document.

"No, the changes that I had thought about, I see we already took care of," George said. "This is fine Mr Baker."

"Very good, Sir," Mr Baker said. "In that case, I will bid you all a good day and return to London. I will pray for your safekeeping and look to see you here again when this unpleasantness is passed."

On the 15th of September, a large convoy left the premises of the Sirius Car Company bound for the Southampton docks. They had the aircraft in crates, all the personal gear of the officers and men and the supplies they needed for operations. Buried in the mountains of supplies were tins of biscuits from the Abbey Biscuit Company, gifts from the employees of the company. In Southampton, they found their ship and watched as the lorries and crates were loaded on board. The loading went on through the night and all the next day, and by the end of the 17th, all was aboard, and they received word that the ship would sail at six the following morning, with a new destination of Ismailia. Federica and Anastasia said their goodbyes and left to go back to Hedsor and to the factory that now would likely be receiving orders for lorries and vans to support the war effort. For them, running the factory was business as usual, but they would have to recruit and train more people, mostly women, to replace the men from the factory who had already volunteered for service either in France or with the RFC squadron that George had charge of.

"Well, they're gone," Anastasia said to Federica as they were driving home from Southampton. "When will we see them again?"

"That is a question to which I have no ready or good answer," Federica replied. "The last time George went away it was three years before we saw him again."

"How did you manage?" Anastasia asked.

"Letters, prayers, keeping busy with your education, anything to keep my mind occupied," Federica explained.

"It seems such a shame that Will will miss Giovanna growing up," Anastasia commented. "If he's away for three years, she'll be five when he gets back. There must be huge changes in a child between two and five."

"We should take photographs at least," Federica suggested. "That way we will have some record and perhaps could even send some to Will while they are away."

"Will they be safe?" Anastasia wondered.

"I have faith in George," Federica said. "He came through conflicts in India and South Africa with scratches and scrapes, but he came through without major injury."

"I don't want Will to get hurt," Anastasia said. "I hope he doesn't take any unnecessary risks."

"I'm sure that he'll be circumspect," Federica assured her, not wanting to point out that in war, men take risks and put themselves in harm's way as a matter of course.

"How do I explain to Giovanna that her Papa is not coming back soon?" Anastasia asked.

"I think show her a map of where he is and tell her that he will be back as soon as he can be," Federica suggested. "What about the other wives and sweethearts that we have in the companies that we have, we should do something for them while the men are away."

"I will talk to Alice and ask her to organise something," Anastasia promised. "I suppose misery does love company, and it may help some of them just to know that many of us are in the same boat. Just having you here with me helps me; all I want to do now is go and sit in a corner and have a good cry. Perhaps I will go and visit Mama for a few days, I miss her now that she has moved away to Windermere. But, I could only do that for a few days, I would not wish to leave you with all that will need to be done."

"One thing more we need to do," Federica said to Anastasia as they set about replacing men who were volunteering. "Many of the women we may employ will have families, some of them quite young, so we need to set up care centres at each of our factories so that they may leave their children in safety and know that they will be well tended to."

"I'll talk to Alice about that," Anastasia said.

"We should find young women who can run the centres and make sure they have some training in child care and nursing. I presume those of school age will be off to school as normal, but what about in the school holidays?"

"We should plan for that as well," Federica agreed. "When we employ women, we should ask if they have children and if they want to leave them with us, or with a relative or friend. This war is going to lead to all kinds of turmoil. I agree with George, it won't be over by Christmas. I see a much longer conflict."

"I wonder how much it's going to cost," Anastasia pondered. "Untold millions, I should think. We should look to taxes being higher in the future, we will have to pay our debts eventually."

1916

The war had been raging for almost two years, and the great powers were locked in a land battle for France and Belgium. The Battle of Verdun waged on for months, followed by more action at Somme. In the Near East, the British started to advance on Baghdad, and T.E. Lawrence, with Faisal's army, was attacking targets in the Arabian Peninsula. In the air, new planes were being introduced with models from Airco, Armstrong Whitworth, Martinsyde, Bristol, de Havilland, Sopwith and Morane-Saulnier. On the ground, the horse still ruled for transport, but lorries from Dennis, Leyland, AEC, Thorneycroft, Maudslay and Daimler were fast being introduced. 1916 also saw the first use of tanks on the battlefield.

"We have another contract from the War Office," Anastasia reported to Federica. "Another two hundred lorries, as soon as possible, and another order for uniforms and from the Red Cross an order for twenty more ambulances, and we have a couple of new subcontracts for artillery carriages. I thought we would add five more ambulances to the order as a donation."

"That would be fine," Federica said. "Here's something else, the Aircraft Manufacturing Company has asked us to take a subcontract to build the new de Havilland DH-5 aircraft. I was thinking that we could expand the building we have at Handy Cross and take some of the staff from Sirius, take on a few more and set up a production line there."

"I'll talk to Mr Stuart and Mr Coates about that," Anastasia said. "When we expand the hangar, why don't we build some long trusses and use them to give us a clear 150 feet under the roof, that way we won't be hampered by columns in awkward places."

"Good idea," Federica agreed. "I'll leave that to you, you're the structural engineer. The contract also calls for us to build the Le Rhône engine for the aircraft. I thought we'd just do that in the engine shop at Sirius and move them to Handy Cross when we need to. For the people we have working there, I thought we would arrange a charabanc to take them there from Sirius."

"I'll talk to Mr Fox about getting castings for the Le Rhône engines," Anastasia said. "So much to do!"

The Handy Cross building was what was left of an old business they had had, which had been traction engines, both for ploughing and for transport. They had sold the engines but kept the land and buildings and had used them to build their own aircraft over the years. Federica had also built a runway topped with Tarmacadam that she had acquired from a road building that had extra from a contract and was looking to dispose of it, so now they had a hard runway, fully 2,000 feet long and 100 feet wide.

"Will this war never end?" Federica complained. "The government was foolish when they suggested that it would be over by Christmas. Now it's trench warfare, and from what I've read, conditions are horrible."

"I'm heartily glad that George and Will are flying, at least they're not on the front lines, sloshing around in the mud and water of the trenches," Anastasia commented. "I wonder if they'll get moved from Sinai to France."

"I suppose that's possible," Federica said. "Anyway, do we have all that we need for two hundred more lorries and twenty ambulances?"

"We have most, we may have to queue up for some forgings, but at least we know we can get the castings. I'll talk to Mr Fox and tell him what we need," Anastasia said. "I wonder if we shouldn't look to some kind of artillery tractor, I have seen pictures of men and horses trying to move the guns around the battlefields in Flanders."

"Perhaps adapt one of our lorries that has all its wheels driven," Federica suggested. "Or perhaps something like the Holt tractor that George took with him to Sinai."

"If the conditions are as poor as I think, then perhaps the Holt tractor type would be better," Anastasia said. "But to move that around, quickly adapt one of our lorries to tow a trailer to carry the tractor."

"How do they move the new tanks they have?" Federica asked.

"I believe they use the railways," Anastasia said.

"How much do these tanks weigh?" Federica asked.

"About nearly thirty tons, I believe," Anastasia said.

"No wonder they have to go by railway," Federica marvelled. "Is it possible to design a lorry to carry that much?"

"It might be," Anastasia said. "If we took the Knox-Martin tractor idea and used our Arcturus wagon, increased the engine size, strengthened the chassis and built a trailer with quite a few wheels, it might work. Why don't we build a prototype and see?"

"I read somewhere that the Foster-Daimler tractor can tow up to 35 tons," Federica said. "So it might be possible. How much does the heavy artillery weigh?"

"I think about four to five tons," Anastasia replied. "I think the standard horse team is twelve for the 60-pounder gun."

"Twelve horses can pull a lot," Federica said. "But I suppose a lot has to do with conditions, if it's muddy, there could be a problem with the horses, better to have a Holt tractor."

"I was thinking that the trench warfare in Europe is more about getting supplies and guns to the front," Anastasia said. "It may be more to our advantage to look to see what we could do in Mesopotamia, it's more open warfare there, no trenches, but more mobile armies, there Antares armoured cars would be good, tanks are too slow."

"We're probably fighting an uphill battle against the establishment in the Army," Federica said. "Perhaps for the nonce, we should concentrate on producing the lorries and ambulances as quickly as we can and make sure that they all run properly."

"We need to start thinking about what we will do with all the women we have working for us when this war does end," Federica said to Anastasia one day. "We know that as soon as the men come back from the war, then they'll want their old jobs back, which I don't begrudge, but it still strikes me as unjust that we should cast aside those who are doing such a good job for us."

"I agree," Anastasia said. "We're fortunate, we have money, so no matter what, we have no concerns with feeding and clothing ourselves. Perhaps we should look to our Windsor Garments to see what we can do there, and to Abbey Biscuits. I imagine that the foundry will very quickly switch back to men, as will Sirius Cars. It's so frustrating that societal attitudes dictate that working-class women slave away for the benefit of the upper classes, and upper-class women are just supposed to marry well. I am concerned that when the war does end, there will be a period of low growth in the economy, and that will lead to unemployment."

"I suppose that's inevitable," Federica said. "Everything we do now is for the war effort, and when that demand stops, what will be there to replace it?"

"We could think about more food production," Anastasia suggested. "No matter what happens, people will still need to eat."

"I'll talk to Mr Forester about acquiring some more land and starting a market garden," Federica thought. "And I'll talk to Mr Robertson from Abbey about more basic baked goods, so that if people cannot afford biscuits, we can at least provide bread."

"How much longer do you think this war will go on?" Anastasia asked.

"I wish I knew," Federica said. "I read all I can, but it seems to me that the Western Front is a stalemate, elsewhere in the world, in East Africa and Mesopotamia, things drag on, and I suppose in the end it will be who can produce and supply the most who will prevail."

"I wish we could vote and have some say in what our government does," Anastasia said. "Sometimes it seems that all men do is get us into conflicts, old men sending young men to war."

"I agree," Federica said. "I think what will happen is that one party will look at the horrific loss of life in this war, think about all the voting men who died, then come up with a plan to give certain women the vote, women they think will vote for them."

"So you see the Conservatives as proposing certain women get the vote for their own ends?" Anastasia asked.

"I see it as possible," Federica said. "Think about the appalling losses in the recent actions at Verdun and Somme, a lot of officers died, officers who they think would vote for them, so those votes need to be replaced."

"That's quite cynical," Anastasia laughed.

"I know," Federica agreed. "Anyway, enough of that for now, it's time to get our regular parcels put together for all our employees who joined up and are in France or wherever, and we need to reply to the letters we've received from George and Will."

"I saw the other day that the army now has a pipeline for water running from the canal to Arish in Sinai," Anastasia commented. "Apparently,

Allenby shares George's concerns about water. The pipeline should make it easier for those at Arish to get water, and as Katia is between the canal and Arish, it should make it easier for George and Will, too."

"Just as long as they filter it and clean out what they can," Federica said. "I don't want them to get dysentery or anything else unpleasant."

The hangar at Handy Cross was enlarged and now boasted a clear span of 150 feet, which made moving planes around much easier than it would have been if there had been columns in place. Federica set up a production line, and wings were made, fuselages built, the parts mated, and then engines were fitted and the rest of the controls installed. It all went surprisingly well, but then perhaps not, they had been used to production lines with Sirius cars, vans and lorries and had worked out over the years how to improve things. They started turning out planes at the rate of three a week, so Federica could see them fulfilling their contract quite quickly. Perhaps their performance would lead to additional contracts, which would help to keep the workforce busy. The greatest challenge was delivering the planes. They were flown to Stag Lane, the aerodrome used by de Havilland, and just getting pilots to fly them was a challenge. Federica finally trained some of the workforce how to fly and had them ferry the planes, then find their way back on buses.

The war proceeded, with more men being called up, more casualties, more demand for arms, ammunition and supplies, such that it seemed that the whole country had one focus. The Military Service Acts 1 and 2 had created some chaos, but it was recognised by the local tribunal that men working in the foundry and the Sirius works were busy making equipment for the War Office, and conscription from their ranks was limited, but still there, the only enterprise not touched by conscription was the lead mine in Derbyshire, those jobs were all deemed to be reserved occupations as the War Department needed lead for bullets. Federica and Anastasia had to make more adjustments to the workforce and had to bring in more women and give them the training they needed to do the jobs. Those on the farms were exempt by statute, but still some volunteered anyway. Federica was eventually asked to sit on the local tribunal that judged whether a man's appeal for exemption was justified. That was difficult work; some of the men claimed to be conscientious objectors driven by religious or moral beliefs. Not many of those appeals were actually granted, but there were many granted related to the work the men did and the need for those skills to supply the war machine. The tribunal kept in mind that hundreds of Welsh coal miners had had to be recalled from the front to go back to work in the mines and supply the iron and steel industries. Without skilled foundry workers and machinists, companies like Sirius could not get the parts needed to build the lorries and ambulances needed by the army and the aircraft needed by the RFC.

The child daycare centres were a success, so much so that Federica thought that she would keep them going even after hostilities had ceased. She did note that not many companies provided the care; in fact, it was only really the munitions factories that did. The other thing that had arisen was the popularity of women's football teams. The munitions factories had started them as a way to improve the health of the workers, not surprising really as the conditions were awful and the side effects of the TNT and gun cotton were not truly understood, the only obvious effect was to change the colour of the skin to yellow, giving rise to the nickname canaries for the women who worked as artillery shell loaders. Alice took on the task of organising teams, and they soon had one from each factory. The women played teams from other factories, and they usually came with their fierce supporters, and the games were surprisingly popular. Federica did not doubt for one minute that when the war was finally over that the FA, the Football Association, the governing body of football in Britain, would find some lame excuse to ban women from playing on any of the FA grounds.

"I'm getting tired," Federica confessed to Anastasia one day. "This everyday push to produce, keep up morale and manage without George and Will is draining. I cannot imagine what it is like for them, camped out in the desert somewhere, flying up and down Sinai and whatever else they do over Mesopotamia."

"It is wearing, isn't it?" Anastasia agreed. "We are rather stuck with being akin to ladies of the manor, got to show pluck, what, keep our chins up and don't let anyone see our frailties."

"I had hoped when George came back from South Africa that we'd seen the last of conflicts for a while, how disillusioned I have become," Federica said. "I dare not write to George and tell him my feelings, lest he worry and put himself in danger because his mind is elsewhere."

"I have the same fears for Will," Anastasia said. "I have enlisted the help of Mama to look after Giovanna; she travels down from Windermere tomorrow."

"How many of our men won't be coming back?" Federica asked.

"The last count I had was three from the foundry, four from Sirius, two from Abbey and one from Windsor. We're doing what we can for the widows and their families," Anastasia said. "I'm sure there will be more before this is all over."

"George told me that in South Africa, as many died from disease as from injuries, if not more. I suppose that will be true again, especially with the awful conditions in the trenches," Federica observed. "Where do the War Office and the Red Cross get their supplies for the hospitals?"

"I don't know," Anastasia admitted. "I'll try and find out."

"I've been following the development of new large aircraft," Federica said. "Handley Page has a new one in testing, it has two Rolls-Royce Eagle engines, we'll see how it does. Kennedy is using ideas from the Russian Sikorskii to build a new craft, Kennedy designed it and Gramophone and Fairey are doing the actual construction, it sounds to me as though the limitation will be the engines, the only ones the government will release to him are Salmson 200 hp ones and there will be four, not enough horsepower I think for the size of the aircraft. It is huge with a wingspan of 142 feet. Then I also saw that Vickers is working on a new bomber, I think they call the Vimy."

"Perhaps we should do something just to take our minds away from the daily challenges," Anastasia suggested.

"I'll see if I can't get details of the Sikorskii aircraft from somewhere. I think I read that Sikorskii had made his drawings available to our War Office, perhaps I can get copies from them and we can see what we could do," Federica said.

"George has been promoted," Federica told Alice one day in December. "It's been gazetted, so it's official, Lieutenant Colonel Wheelwright, and Will also got promoted to Major. How is your fiancé doing?"

"He's safe enough," Alice replied. "He's organising the movement of ammunition and supplies from the French ports to the lines. It sounds like a never-ending job."

"We should think about some sort of Christmas gathering, I hesitate to say party, because we don't have much to celebrate, what do you think?" Federica asked.

"A children's party, perhaps?" Alice suggested. "I have lists of how many we have at each factory and their ages. Should we provide presents?"

"I think so," Federica said. "There's not much joy in the world at the moment, so anything that will bring smiles will be good."

"What about teddy bears, toy cars, letter blocks, marbles, dolls and games like snakes and ladders and draughts," Alice suggested. "There are lots of toys and games out there that focus on the war, which I suppose is good in that it makes the children part of the war effort, but perhaps some respite from the war is good too."

"We should have a Father Christmas like Selfridges in London has," Federica thought. "He can hand out the presents from a sack, or sacks."

"Who do we get for that?" Alice asked.

"Could we persuade your father?" Federica asked. "He strikes me as a sort of Father Christmas person."

"I'm sure he'd be delighted," Alice said. "I'll get some fabric from Windsor and have Mama make him a costume. I wonder how long it will be before they raise the age for conscription, so that he'll get caught in the next lot."

"Too soon, I expect," Federica said. "I don't think the War Office is getting as many as they had hoped. If they do raise the age, I think your father would best serve the country by using those ideas he has and inventing things to make the lives of our soldiers more bearable."

"I think he would enjoy that," Alice said. "Anyway, back to our Christmas parties, I'll organise people to help with food, and I presume we'll pay for the food?"

"Of course," Federica replied. "I suppose we'll have to buy all the toys, we can't really make any ourselves. I wonder if we shouldn't make toy cars that are our own. I should talk to Mr Fox and see if he has any ideas. That brings up another issue: do our people have enough to eat?"

"I think most do," Alice said. "We pay quite well, and Mr Forester has been setting up stands by the factories each week and selling vegetables at a good price, good for the buyer that is."

"Well, I don't expect to make a profit off everything," Federica laughed. "So, as long as our farm income meets or slightly exceeds our expenses, I'm happy with that."

The Christmas parties were a great success; the children all overate and were then delighted with the presents they received. Mr White as Father Christmas was an instant success and well-received by all. Federica then set about preparing for their own Christmas. It was going to be the third Christmas without George and Will, and she tried to put the best face on it all. Sophia, Anastasia's mother, had come down from the Lakes to help with Giovanna and was enjoying her granddaughter immensely. Federica told the household staff to take off Christmas and Boxing Day, and that she would attend to all the cooking required. Letters arrived, and she was concerned with one. It was from George.

"Dearest," it began. *"Just to let you know that we are being redeployed to Flanders. There is a new detachment here already, and we are packing up to go. We are getting new Vickers planes, which will be much better for us than the old ones we have been flying. I have insisted with the generals that we be given enough time, well behind the lines, to become accustomed to this new plane and how it handles and behaves. So, we spend some time at St Omer before moving forward. We leave for Ismailia next week and then take the boat to Dieppe, and then we make our way to St Omer and then to Beele. It is so unfortunate that we will be so close and yet will not have the opportunity to see one another."*

Federica digested this, then looked at the map she had and found Beele. She was concerned because the casualty rate amongst pilots above the

Western Front was really bad. But she had quietly obtained some reports, and they showed that most of the losses were from individual problems with the pilots, from training to health, from mechanical issues with the aircraft and last, and actually least in numbers, by enemy action. She had read some comments by pilots who had become aces, that the most common error new pilots made was opening fire on their opponent too soon and by not being expert enough in aerobatics to outmanoeuvre the other. She took comfort in that George and his squadron had been flying regularly for the past two years or so, but that had been mostly against the Turkish Air Force and only recently against experienced German pilots.

"I received a letter from Will," Anastasia said as she joined Federica. "He tells me that they're going to France."

"I know," Federica replied. "I just received a letter from George with the same news."

"What do you think?" Anastasia asked.

"I trust in George's judgement, I can do nothing else," Federica said. "He has pilots who have been flying for some time, so they are not new to the air, so I suppose the challenge will be to see how they adapt to the new machines."

"What do we know about the Vickers?" Anastasia asked.

"It's not a bad machine," Federica said. "It can climb quickly, has a machine gun that will fire through the propeller with an interrupter gear and has seen service on the Western Front. I think the move to France is driven by the need to counter German offences."

"I hope they'll be safe," Anastasia said.

"At least our letters and parcels should get to them in less time," Federica commented. "I wonder how often they will be grounded by the weather, it won't be like flying over Sinai, and I hope the RFC is going to give them some warm clothes for the winter that is coming."

"Should we put parcels together and send them some?" Anastasia asked.

"It might be sensible," Federica said. "I'm sure they'll have their flight suits, but they can't live in them all the time."

"I wonder where they'll be billeted, in houses or in tents," Anastasia pondered.

"I suppose that will depend on how many are already there and if, in fact, there are any houses left," Federica said. "I imagine that living in a tent is only a small step up from the trenches, subject to the cold, the wet, the rats and all the other unpleasantness."

Thinking about Kennedy and his efforts to build a large bomber, Federica one day took herself off to London and presented herself at the offices of the War Office and asked to speak to someone in charge of aircraft development.

"Really, Madam, and what would your interest there be?" the orderly at the door asked.

"My husband, Lieutenant Colonel Wheelwright, has asked me to get some information for him," she replied. "Lieutenant Colonel Wheelwright is currently with the RFC in Flanders, recently transferred there after two years in Sinai."

"I see, Madam, well perhaps you could try the Major in Room 41, that way one floor up," the orderly said.

"Thank you," Federica said. She made her way to Room 41 and found a clerk there sorting out a pile of paper.

"Madam," he said as she entered.

"Good morning, my husband, Lieutenant Colonel Wheelwright, has asked me to get some information for him," she said, stretching the truth more than a little as this was her own venture.

"That would be Lieutenant Colonel Wheelwright, lately in Sinai and now Flanders?" he asked.

"It would," she confirmed. "He told me that he had learned that the Russian Sikorskii gave us copies of the drawings of his craft, and George, the Colonel that is, wants to review them to see if he can do something with them."

"Like Mr Kennedy is doing?" he asked.

"Indeed," she said. "George has some notion about improving things, so I am tasked by him to gather whatever information I can."

"I could get you copies of the drawings if you would care to wait," he said.

"If it is more convenient for you, I can come back at a later hour," she offered. "It looks as if you have more than your share of work there."

"That would be most helpful," he said. "Perhaps three?"

"I will be here then," she agreed. "If there are any costs for the copies, then I am instructed to pay them."

"Any costs will be minimal, Madam," he said.

"Morning, Henry," a major said as he entered the office.

"Good morning, Major Wilson," the clerk said. "This is Mrs Wheelwright, her husband is Lieutenant Colonel Wheelwright of the RFC, recently transferred to Flanders from Sinai."

"Good morning, Madam," the major said. "I trust Henry has been of service."

"Henry has been most kind," Federica said. "I should leave and let you attend to the volume of work that I am sure you have."

Federica left and wondered what she would do with the rest of the morning and the early afternoon. London was still busy, for all they were at war, but there were signs everywhere that things were not as usual. There was evidence in places of the German Zeppelin bombing raids that had occurred in 1916. Federica wondered how soon it would be before Britain retaliated and raided the German cities. She was reminded of something George had said about the war in South Africa, it had become a war against a whole population, with concentration camps, scorched earth policies and such all aimed at reducing the will of the people to fight. She supposed that some of the bombing raids were intended to hit military or transportation targets to hinder Britain's ability to wage war. But bombs went astray, navigation was not always the best, and most of all, the weather did not cooperate. Federica saw the searchlights that had been installed to hunt out the Zeppelins in the night skies and recalled reading about successes that British pilots had had shooting them down. To her, being bombed from the sky would be a horrifying experience, and she wondered if there was a way to detect the raids early and track them so that they might know what the intended targets were, and then what could be done to protect from bombs falling from the sky. She resolved that the first thing she should do when she returned home was to organise painting the roofs of the factories so that they were less obvious from above and to shield lights at night so that the raiders could not use their own lights to target them.

Lunch Federica took at the Ritz, an extravagance she knew, but she felt like doing something for herself. She was seated quickly, and she looked about and noted the number of senior army and navy officers and wondered how they reconciled their eating in the height of luxury with the eating conditions in the trenches.

"Excuse me, Madam," one officer said. "Have I had the honour of meeting you before?"

"I don't think so," Federica said, wondering what this was all about, a line used to start a conversation that in his mind might lead somewhere or a genuine enquiry.

"I'm sure we have met, Mrs Wheelwright, is it not?" he asked. "I should introduce myself, Brigadier Harris. I was with your husband in South Africa, and we met very briefly in London four years ago at a soirée. This is my aide, Captain Hill."

"Now I remember, General," she said. "But you will forgive me that my attention was rather focused on George that day."

"Of course," he said. "If I may ask, where is your husband now?"

"He's with the RFC in Flanders," she said.

"As I recall, you have a factory making cars?" he asked.

"We do," she confirmed. "We have contracts at the moment to make lorries and ambulances for the army and a subcontract to build aircraft for the Aircraft Manufacturing Company."

"And how is that going with your husband away?" Captain Hill asked.

"We're doing very well," she said. "We have had to add more women to our workforce as men have volunteered or lately been conscripted, but we manage."

"You say you are building aircraft, which one?" General Harris asked.

"The de Havilland DH-5," she replied.

"Your company, the car company, what is the name again?" he asked.

"The Sirius Car Company," she replied. "We are still building some cars, but most of our production is lorries, 3.5 and 5 cwt, 1 ton and 2 ton."

"Would it be possible to mount searchlights on the back of your lorries?" he asked.

"I imagine that would be fairly simple," she said. "You would also want a power supply for the light?"

"Quite," he agreed.

"What do the lights weigh, and what do they need in terms of light source?" she asked.

"About five hundredweight and acetylene," he replied.

"We could do that," she said. "We'd modify the chassis a little, then add an acetylene generator for the light and position the light on a turntable so that the crew could aim it anywhere."

"How long before we could get lorries with lights?" he asked.

"You get us the lights and we'll have the first lorry to you in under a month, it would take that long as we would have to do some testing to make sure things worked well, after that deliveries could be quite quick," she thought.

"Excuse me, madam," Captain Hill interrupted. "How is it that you know this?"

"Necessity," she replied. "We have to learn, adapt and invent. So, my sister-in-law and I have become accustomed to the terminology and the mathematics involved."

"I will send you an order soon," General Harris said. "If you deliver it to the AA battery at Hyde Park, they'll run it through its paces and give me a report. What about guns on the back of your lorries?"

"Again, how heavy are they and how is the recoil managed that they don't destroy the lorry they sit on?" she asked.

"Nine hundredweight for the 13-pounder gun," he replied. "Plus, the lorries are equipped with blocks and jacks to hold them while the gun is being fired."

"Isn't there a Thorneycroft three-tonner that already serves?" she asked.

"Quite," General Harris said. "Could you produce those under a subcontract?"

"I'm sure we could," she said.

"Would it be possible for Captain Hill and me to visit your factory?" he asked.

"Of course," she said. "Just let us know when, here is my card with the telephone number of our office. Do you wish to see the aircraft factory as well?"

"If that would be possible," he said.

"We will arrange it," she said. "Forgive me for asking, General, but what is your position in the War Office?"

"The Army Service Corps," he replied. "We're tasked with getting everything that is not a bullet, shell or grenade. So that includes food, clothing, transport, gas masks and all the ancillary items a modern army needs."

"We do supply uniforms through our Windsor Garments company," she said. "Both to the Army and the Red Cross. We had wondered where the medical supplies come from, bandages, field dressings, beds, linens, stretchers, all that is needed in a field station and a hospital."

"We have a number of suppliers," Captain Hill said. "We have a department dedicated to that."

"Yours must be quite an organisation and enterprise, General," Federica commented.

"It keeps us busy and the demand is never-ending," he replied. "War goes through materiel remarkably quickly."

"George noted that from his time in South Africa," she said. "He told me that the veldt in places was littered with discarded saddles, food tins, and other detritus, apart from rifle and shell casings."

"Your husband was in South Africa?" Captain Hill asked.

"He was, in the latter part of the conflict he was assigned to field intelligence and spent many weeks in the veldt himself," she replied.

"I heard a story about an RFC unit in eastern Egypt that came equipped with sun goggles, camouflage nets, their own water well drill, and even a Holt tractor, and they had over the establishment in lorries and tenders, even down to their own water and petrol tank lorries, the officer in charge was a Major Wheelwright, is he your husband?" Captain Hill asked.

"He is," she confirmed. "We decided that if he had to go to Sinai, we would send him with the best we could provide," she said. "We took what the RFC gave us and added our own."

"Well, Mrs Wheelwright, we have imposed long enough," General Harris said. "It was good to make your acquaintance again, and I will be in touch regarding a visit."

"Thank you, General, I await your call," she said.

At three, Federica went back to the War Office and announced that she had an appointment with the people in Room 41.

"You know the way, Madam?" a different orderly at the door asked.

"I do," she confirmed. She went up the stairs to the office, and Henry the clerk had a roll of drawings ready for her.

"What do I owe you?" she asked him.

"Five shillings, Madam," he said. Federica dutifully handed over her five shillings and took possession of the drawings and the chit that Henry gave her to give to the orderly at the door. She noted that it was signed by Major Wilson, and she wondered if he had actually signed it, or if Henry had become skilled in just signing documents as needed. Whatever the case, the orderly at the door took the chit and saluted. She made her way back to Paddington and the train home. On the way, she could not resist but unrolled the drawings and took a quick look. The units confused her a little, but fortunately, someone had provided a key to convert the Imperial Russian units to English units. An older man came to the compartment, so she rolled the drawings back up and secured them with an elastic band. He nodded, grunted a quick greeting, then sat down and buried his head in the Times.

"I see that we've finally pushed the Turk out of British Egypt," the man said, putting the paper down. "About time Rafa was taken, can't imagine what took so long."

"Have you been there?" Federica asked.

"No, but Johnny Turk is not much of a soldier, so can't see why this took so long," he said.

"Isn't Rafa quite a long way from Cairo?" she asked innocently.

"Only 120 miles from the canal," he said. "Don't know why the colonials didn't take it sooner, in my day in South Africa, we made short work of Brother Boer."

"My husband was in South Africa," she said. "His recollections are a little different."

"When?" he asked.

"From 1899 until the cessation of hostilities," she replied.

"Well, once we had taken the cities, there was only mopping up to do," he said. That was rather at odds with what George had told her, but Federica allowed the old man to have his fantasies.

"Excuse me, I must leave here," she said. "Good day to you, Sir."

Federica left, shaking her head. The old man probably lived in the past, and if he had seen action, he would have forgotten the horror of it all and only remember the adulation when the triumphant returned to London. At home, she called Anastasia, who came over to see what she had brought home.

"What are these funny units?" she asked as she pored over the drawings.

"Imperial Russian units, fortunately, there is a key here that tells us what they convert to," Federica said. "I see that as my first task, write in all the dimensions we can understand."

"It's huge, isn't it," Anastasia said. "This is the same one that Kennedy is trying to build?"

"It is," Federica confirmed. "It seems to me that there is a lot that can be done to reduce drag, which in turn will increase speed and give us more lift."

"Do we have room at Handy Cross to build this?" Anastasia asked.

"I think so," Federica said. "We'll tackle the wings first, then we'll look at the fuselage and then mate it all together. Which engine gives us the most horsepower for the least weight?"

"The Polaris engine," Anastasia replied. "350 hp for only 900 pounds, so four of them should do the job for this aircraft."

"As big as this is, it will need more than two wheels to land on, and we should provide some form of shock absorber on the wheel struts," Federica said. "Looking at the wings, it seems to me that the simple design of the wings is for ease of manufacture, not the best necessarily for flying conditions, so I propose we redesign the wings for flight and accept that manufacture will be more complex."

"I agree," Anastasia said. "I think instead of simple plywood, we should use the sandwich panel materials we developed for the cars, lighter and stronger than simple plywood. I wonder if there is a way to use better struts between the wings that can be streamlined, to reduce all the wires we would normally use, even though the wires are thin, there must be a drag effect."

"We'll investigate that," Federica said. "I was thinking for the wing design, we would set up a loft for the drawings and spar assembly, like marine buildings do. Oh, I forgot to mention, I met a General Harris from the Army Service Corps, and he wants to come and make a visit at some time. He's also asked us to look into fitting a searchlight on the back of one of our lorries, I was thinking of the the Arcturus."

General Harris and Captain Hill came for their visit towards the end of January. It was a cold, dreary day, but inside the factories, it was at least warm and dry.

"Good morning, General, Captain," Federica said as she greeted them. "This is my sister-in-law, Anastasia McIntosh, who runs the businesses with me, and this is Mr Ian Stuart and Mr Andrew Coates, who run the Sirius factory."

"It's good to meet the people who are building what we'll need to win this war," General Harris said. "Mrs Wheelwright, you've been hiding your husband's light under a bushel, DSO in the Boer War and now a DFC and another DSO in the current war. So, please, what do you all do here?"

"Mr Coates builds the bodies of the cars, vans and lorries, and Mr Stuart puts it all together with the chassis, engine, gearbox, axles and such," Federica replied. "Anastasia and I focus on the designs of the cars. Perhaps we could start at the end of the line where we deliver vehicles and work our way back. Ian, if you would please."

Ian Stuart led them to the dock of the factory and showed them lorries being loaded onto railway wagons.

"You don't deliver by driving them?" Captain Hill asked.

"We can, but this load is booked on a ship to leave Dover on the fifteenth of next month, so we'll send a trainload," Ian explained.

"Do they get tested before delivery?" Hill asked.

"They do," Ian confirmed. "We occasionally find something amiss when we do that, but as late, not often. We have taken pains to make all the parts interchangeable, so things fit together well. Mrs Wheelwright and Mrs McIntosh have created brilliant and easy to build designs."

"You did not design these lorries?" Hill asked.

"No, all the design work of the cars, vans, lorries, factory buildings and even production layout is done by Mrs Wheelwright and Mrs McIntosh," Ian replied. "We are part of the team and make our contribution, of course, but the impetus for the designs comes from the ladies."

"Extraordinary," Hill said.

"These are our assembly lines," Ian said, leading the way back into the factory. "All the parts are brought to each vehicle as it moves along the lines. We had to create more than one line as we added lorries; the fixtures needed to move them were larger, so needed more space."

"What are those papers the ladies are referring to?" General Harris asked.

"The assembly line has workstations, and at each station, certain things are installed," Ian explained. "The papers tell them that for that vehicle, they will need such and such parts. When they've installed them, they have a little stamp that they use to show the work has been done."

"I see that everyone has the same overalls, men and women," Hill commented.

"We thought it would be better if we provided work clothes," Ian said. "We provide two sets and launder weekly. We also provide work boots; we don't want toe injuries from things being dropped."

"That lorry is not the same as the one before or after," General Harris commented.

"When we start something in the line, it gets its own work packet, so we can assemble different models," Ian explained. "We have weekly production meetings and go through all we're going to do and what parts we need."

"Where do the engines come from?" Hill asked.

"We have a side shop where they're built," Ian explained. "We get the castings from our foundry, machine them here and build up the engines here."

"What is that monorail there?" Hill asked.

"That comes from the body shop," Andrew explained. "We know what vehicle is next, so we build up the right body on a fixture that ensures that it will mate properly to the chassis, then we move it over, and it gets secured in place."

How many lorry models do you have?" General Harris asked.

"We've got the Procyon, Regulus, and Spica cars, vans and small lorries, then we have the Arcturus, Castor and Altair larger vans and lorries, and finally we have the Antares and Capella cars and light lorries that have all wheels driven," Federica replied.

"And you can accommodate all those on the same lines?" Hill asked.

"We can," Ian replied. "The work packets tell the people which one it is, and they start with an assembly fixture to build the chassis, then all else gets added as it does down the lines."

"How are the car bodies built?" General Harris asked.

"We found that using ash for frames took too long, and there is a huge demand for ash that the foresters have difficulty meeting, so we went to steel frames made of angles and tubes and clad that with the patented materials we use for the bodies," Andrew replied. "We also bake the paints to speed up the drying process. If we did not do that, it would take weeks to make a body. We have looked at heavy presses for forming mudguards and bonnets like Fisher does. If we do that, we would probably extend the idea to whole body sides and roofs, so we are investigating what it would take, and how much it would cost to put in the appropriate presses."

"What about axles and wheels?" General Harris asked.

"We purchase wheels, and we build our own axles. We used to buy axles, but we decided to acquire that company and run it ourselves," Federica explained.

"How many cars and lorries are built in a day?" General Harris asked.

"We are currently making ten a day, but we're confident that if the demand is there, we could make twelve, or even fifteen a day," Federica replied.

"Fascinating," General Harris said as they wandered the line and watched men and women attach parts. "How is all the paper put together?"

"We have a small department that works a week or two ahead of the main production, and they know what goes into each vehicle, so they put the packets together and also check that we have all the parts we need," Ian explained. "We work hard to improve efficiency everywhere we can, and we have cut down to very little the extra time we have to spend correcting parts that don't fit. This factory was built with the idea in mind that we would have a moving production line, making sure that we have all the parts when they are needed, so there is no standing around waiting for a part, unlike many factories that grew from existing buildings that were put up for very different products, also we knew from company experience we had in the carriage business, that we needed something far quicker and less expensive than hand panel beating and forming."

"How many engine models do you have?" Hill asked.

"We standardised on engine type, so all ours are now Vee type engines, with 4, 6, 8, 10 or 12 cylinders," Federica said. "Anastasia's husband, Will, now Major William McIntosh of the RFC, is our engine designer and has worked hard to get us high horsepower, low weight engines."

"May we see where you build planes?" General Harris asked.

"It is a little drive there, would you care for lunch before we go?" Federica asked.

"That would be delightful," General Harris said.

"This is the company cafeteria," Federica explained. "We provide lunch for all the people from food we grow ourselves. Shall we join the line?"

"Of course," General Harris said, clearly enjoying himself. He got in line behind two ladies and struck up a conversation with them. He got his lunch and joined Federica and the others at a table shared with some workers.

"Such a shame," General Harris said. "Esme was telling me that her husband was killed at Verdun, and Nellie told me that her husband is still at Verdun. Have you had many losses here?"

"We have lost ten from here, three from the foundry, two from Abbey Biscuits and one from Windsor Garments," Anastasia enumerated.

"And how many do you have volunteering or conscripted?" General Harris asked.

"Early volunteers were 22 from the foundry, 528 from here, 12 from Abbey Biscuits and six from Windsor," Anastasia replied. "Since then, we've had six more conscripted from the foundry, 180 from here, four from Abbey and two from Windsor. We've made up the numbers with women. The only company we have unaffected by war losses is the Somercotes Lead company we have in Derbyshire, there all the men are in reserved occupations, so none went off to war but remained toiling below to extract the lead ore."

"Some of the parts we saw look quite heavy. How do the ladies manage that?" Hill asked.

"We use a lot of lifts and hoists and jigs and fixtures," Ian replied. "We found that it also gave us less injury with the men, so they will be retained even after all the men come back."

"You have many employees here, where do they all live?" Hill asked.

"We draw from Slough, Maidenhead, Windsor, some as far away as High Wycombe, the more local ones walk or ride bicycles to work, for the farther afield we provide bus transportation to get them here and home again, there is competition for workers in this area, so we have to draw from where we can and also look carefully at the work to see that it is useful and not duplicated and that we organise things well enough that people are not standing around waiting for parts," Ian replied.

"How many men and women work here?" General Harris asked.

"Two thousand four hundred and twenty-three," Federica replied. "Of that, we have one thousand eight hundred and ten men, and the balance are women."

"That is a lot of women in a factory that one would have imagined was a place where only men worked," Hill commented.

"It's a question of availability," Ian said. "Apart from the volunteering and conscription, there are only so many people living in the area, so we take what we can get and do a lot of training."

"Thank you, Ian and Andrew, for the tour and your time," Federica said, "Shall we go, gentlemen?"

They drove to Handy Cross in the drizzle, and when they arrived, there were three planes on the Tarmacadam waiting.

"Those aircraft there, is there an issue with them?" General Harris asked.

"No, it's simply the weather," Federica said. "We might be able to fly in it, but Stag Lane is not always that visible, so they've asked us not to deliver for a few days. They will call when conditions there are better."

"This is a huge building," General Harris commented.

"The arch span is a little larger than that of Paddington," Anastasia said. "But it is quite sound. It gives us the freedom under the roof to move aircraft about as we assemble them. We build the engines in the shop at Sirius and bring them out here. Wings are done over there, and we use the same kind of moving assembly line here that we do at Sirius."

"I must say, ladies, that this has been most instructive and altogether heartening that British industry is so well run," General Harris said.

"We do what we can," Federica said. "We would like to see our husbands home again and those who have gone from our factories, so if we can give them the materiel to hasten the progress of the war, we will. Oh, I forgot to point it out, did you see your first searchlight lorry in the line at Sirius?"

"I did," General Harris said. "I shall certainly keep this all in mind when we are looking for contractors to supply lorries and such. How do you do it all?"

"Long hours," Federica laughed. "And Anastasia and I have been fortunate to find very competent factory managers who do such an excellent job and are always ready to discuss and consider improvements to the way we do things."

"Forgive me for suggesting this, but they have no issues working for you?" General Harris asked.

"Because I'm a woman," Federica laughed. "We weeded those out in the interview process, and we have learned to rely on one another."

"Well, as it is said, keep up the good work, and perhaps this conflict will finally be over," General Harris said.

Back from the War

On the eleventh hour of the eleventh day of the eleventh month of 1918, the guns fell silent as an armistice was put into effect by the warring parties. The war had dragged on for over four years in many countries and had culminated in a stalemate in Western Europe, the balance of which had been tipped by the entry of the United States into the conflict. Germany recognised that the United States brought men and materiel in numbers and amounts it could not hope to match, it also was plagued by the effects of the Spanish Flu that was ravaging both sides in the war, and by internal strife that led to the overthrow of the Kaiser. For those involved in the actual fighting, the cessation of hostilities was a blessed relief, and their focus was now going home and returning to their lives and loved ones. The RFC and the RNAS, Royal Naval Air Service, had been combined to form the new Royal Air Force.

"Nastia, are you ready?" Federica asked.

"Nearly," Anastasia replied. "I'm just getting Giovanna into her winter coat."

"Do you think she will remember her father?" Federica asked.

"Perhaps, but I doubt it," Anastasia said. "Will left in the autumn of 1914, and Giovanna was only two at the time. It's been just over four years, and I have no idea how much six-year-olds remember. Where do we need to go?"

"The dispersal centre is in Crystal Palace," Federica said. "It should take us about two hours to get there. Do you remember when we went to the first car show there in 1903?"

"I do remember those days and the next year when we exhibited. When did Will and George arrive?" Anastasia asked.

"George sent me a telegram a week ago," Federica said. "I suppose just getting that many men back from the war and through the process of demobilisation takes time. I had thought he might telephone, but I suspect that the dispersal centre has only one telephone and that its use is restricted to whatever some petty functionary considers official army business."

"There, we're done, we're ready to go," Anastasia announced.

"Where are we going?" Giovanna asked.

"We're going to pick up your Papa and Uncle George," Anastasia replied.

"They've been away at the war, haven't they?" Giovanna asked.

"They have," Anastasia confirmed.

"Do you remember your Papa?" Federica asked.

"I think so, Auntie Fede," Giovanna said. "But not very well."

"Perhaps after you see him, you will remember more," Federica said.

"Is Grandmama Sophia coming with us?" Giovanna asked.

"She is, I think she is waiting for us by the car," Anastasia said. "We thought we would take the large Daimler, it will be room enough for all of us."

"Do we all have our masks?" Federica asked. "This influenza epidemic is really bad, and I wonder how many more will suffer before it is over."

"I wonder what it really is?" Anastasia thought. "We know so little about these diseases and how they are transmitted."

"Well, if we wear good masks and practice good basic hygiene, we may be able to avoid catching it," Federica said. "That seems to have worked in our factories."

Crystal Palace was busy, men coming and going, those going happy to be out of the war finally and on their way home, those coming anxious for the process to be quick and over, so that they too could go home and those going thankful that they were finally on the last leg of their journey home. Federica saw George and William and waved. She and Anastasia were thrilled that their husbands were finally home after an absence of over four years, during which time they had had to rely on letters and newsreels to assure themselves that they were well. In the latter part of the war, their squadron had been moved to France and they had seen out the last year of the conflict in the skies over Belgium, France and Germany. That most of the squadron had survived the war was credited to George, but he gave credit to the determination of the whole squadron not to lose anyone, and those few that they had lost had been to actions in the skies over Germany, mainly among new pilots sent to fill vacancies that resulted from promotions.

"George," Federica called. He saw her, and he and William came over, masked against the influenza as were most people.

"Fede," George said. "I'm happy to see you finally. How are you?"

"I'm happier now that you're here," she said. "How are you, Will how are the rest of your people?"

"I'm fine, Fede, no influenza," William assured her. "Nastia, I cannot tell you how much I've waited for this day. Sophia, how lovely that you came as well. Giovanna, do you remember me?"

"A little, I think," Giovanna replied. "Are you coming home with us?"

"I am," he replied. "Will you tell me all about things at home while we go?"

"I will," Giovanna said gravely. "Mama and Auntie Fede have managed everything while you have been away, and Grandmama has been with us as well. Are you Uncle George?"

"I am," George replied. "I am so sorry we have been away so long, we have missed you and your Mama and Grandmama and Auntie Fede. How are you, Sophia?"

"As well as can be expected," Sophia replied. "I'm just glad that you and Will are back safe and sound. It has been a hard four years."

"Is the war finally over?" Federica asked.

"Probably," George replied. "An armistice was agreed upon late last year, and now they are negotiating a peace treaty. That is taking some time, but will eventually get agreed upon, but I suppose until it is signed, then there is a faint chance that hostilities will resume."

"Are they bringing all the planes and lorries back as well?" she asked.

"We loaded everything onto a boat before we came back," he replied. "It has probably already been offloaded at Southampton, and now I suppose the War Office will be looking to sell as much as they can to begin to defray the cost of this war. Our own Aquila plane, I have arranged to have returned to us."

"Such a waste," Federica bemoaned, "all because of the ambitions of a few men."

"Did you know that Yves was killed in the last days of the war?" George asked.

"No," she replied. "I'm so sorry, I really liked Yves, and he was doing such a good job for us before the war."

"How has Philippe done?" George asked.

"Well," she said. "He has been good to work with, and he has built up the Orly company very nicely. I would like to visit the factory there soon and see all the people again. I suppose cross-channel ferries with more normal service will resume again now."

"I would think so," he agreed.

"So, what else should we think about?" she asked.

"Perhaps we could look to see what they do with planes and engines," he suggested. "We might get some useful equipment at reasonable prices."

"Can we get back the lorries we provided?" she asked. "I would like to have them back. Are they in reasonable condition?"

"They have seen four years of service in the desert and on the Western Front," he said. "We took care of them as best we could, but one could hardly call them in good condition; they might be better for parts."

"I was rather thinking of tearing them apart and seeing what stood the rigours of service and what may need to be corrected in the design," she explained.

"I will get onto Harry tomorrow and see what can be arranged," he promised.

"Have you all your luggage?" Federica asked.

"I do indeed," he confirmed. "Such as it is. I turned in my service rifle yesterday, so only have my own and this small kit bag."

"What about the others in your squadron?" she asked.

"Harry and the rest left yesterday," he explained. "Will and I stayed on to make sure everyone was discharged properly and on their way home. Those from our factory who volunteered or were conscripted should be home already."

"Nastia, Will, are you ready?" she asked.

"We are," Anastasia replied.

"Shall we go then, we may talk more on the drive home?" Federica suggested.

The drive home was filled with conversation about what they could see from the car, for the benefit of Giovanna, and what life had been like in France in the latter stages of the war, for the benefit of Federica and Anastasia. As George remarked, as hard as some things may have been for them, it was nothing like life in the trenches, where mud, disease and generally appalling conditions were the norm, and where in the latter months of 1918 the influenza epidemic had made more of an impact than the actual fighting. Federica, Sophia and Anastasia wanted to know all about Egypt, Belgium and France, and George and William wanted to know how things were with the business and how Federica and Anastasia had fared during the long years of separation. Obviously, it was going to be some time before all questions were answered and before life returned to some measure of what it was before the war began. When they finally reached home, the domestic staff were there to greet them. The staff had changed from the last time that George came back from a war, Beatrice, who had been the maid, was now employed at the Windsor Garments company as a supervisor, Jane, the cook, had retired and had been replaced by Christine, who was working out splendidly, according to Federica. Eleanor, the housekeeper, had retired, and Federica had decided that she had no need of a replacement. William Forester, the farm manager, was still with them and had worked hard during the war to grow as much as possible to support the war effort, and his efforts had been recognised by the Ministry of Food. Forester's two daughters both worked as supervisors for the Abbey Biscuit factory. Last, but certainly not least, Federica and Anastasia had been recognised for their efforts in building planes and lorries for the war effort and both had been awarded the Order of the British Empire, a new honour created in 1917 by King George V, particularly to recognise those who had contributed to the war away from the front lines of combat.

After dinner, the Wheelwrights and the McIntoshes went their separate ways to rediscover each other and start the process of putting the war past them. Sophia excused herself and went off to her room for an early night. Federica, recalling the last homecoming that she had welcomed George back from a war, led him off to the bedroom and a shared bath.

"So, are there any new scrapes and scars?" she asked.

"Not one," he replied. "I spent much of the war behind desks, or at least away from the actual fighting."

"Did you see any of the fighting?" she asked. "Your letters were vague in the extreme."

"A little," he admitted. "In Egypt, we spent most of our time flying up and down Sinai looking for evidence that the Turk was going to attack, which they did on a few occasions. Two even tried to chase me when I was flying once, but by then Will had fitted new engines to the BE-2s and I lost them quickly, which I think really surprised them. Will and his wingman were behind me a little and came up behind the Turks and shot them down."

"What about France, wasn't there much more activity there?" she asked.

"There was," he agreed. "But we were given the job of spotting for the artillery and we had others flying above us to protect us from the Hun."

"How did you avoid this awful influenza?" she asked.

"We were fairly isolated from the greater part of the army, and we took steps to quarantine ourselves and restrict access to us," he said.

"Well, I'm glad it's over," she said. "I don't like you going off to wars like this; it is most distressing."

"What about you, how have you fared?" he asked.

"I have been worried about you a lot," she said. "But, I occupied my time and thoughts with running the companies, and we have done well. I am sure there are those who will say that we profited from the war, but we just did what was asked of us. We had problems with the influenza epidemic; six of our ladies at Windsor died, and two at Abbey. We provided for their families as best we could. We had to do quite a bit of moving things around so that our ladies were not working quite so close to one another, but it seemed to help, and we let anyone who was not feeling well stay at home, but we still paid them, it cost us a bit, but I think it was worth it."

"You had no deaths at Sirius?" he asked.

"No, we had about twenty off sick for a while, but they all recovered and came back to work after a month," she replied.

"I suppose the people at Sirius were just more spread out than at Windsor or Abbey," he mused.

"That's true, and it was easier for us to spread the line out a little more at Sirius," she added. "We did have more problems in our factory in France, there we had many more people off sick and we lost six who died in November."

"And you, you did not get the influenza?" he asked.

"No, none of us did, nor anyone on the farm, perhaps because we were so careful about getting too close to other people and to wear masks when we were out and about," she said.

"Did you know that the RAF has sent three parties from Cairo to select a route and prepare aerodromes for future flights to Cape Town?" he asked.

"I had heard a little," she said. "But, enough of that, we will talk more of it tomorrow, now, we have four years to make up for!"

"*Mia stella*," he said. "I have been waiting since we got off the boat from France."

"You're remarkably frisky for a man of 48," she said, commenting on his current condition.

"Age has little to do with desire," he commented. "It has been a while, and I must say that you are as desirable now as when I first met you."

"I have tried to stay active," she said. "I think I have kept my figure well, don't you think?"

"Very well," he agreed enthusiastically.

"Good, so show me how much you have missed me," she commanded.

At breakfast the following day, George was surprised at how Sophia had seemed to age. His father had married her when he was still quite young, after the death of his own mother. His father had died in 1902, but Sophia, although still quite young, had not remarried. Now she lived in the quiet of the English Lake District on their estate on Windermere, but she had come south during the conflict to spend time with Giovanna and relieve Anastasia of some of her burdens. Now, to George, she looked as though she was ageing. But then, when she heard him come in, she brightened up, and the years seemed to fall from her. Perhaps he had caught her in a moment of private reflection which gave the appearance of age, but was it really something more personal and emotional and less physical.

"Sophia, how are you? We hardly had time yesterday for any conversation," he asked.

"I am relieved that you and William are back safely," she said. "It has been difficult for Fede and Nastia. I think I may stay a few more days, then leave you to your homecoming and go back to the quiet of the Lakes."

"You are happy there?" he asked.

"I am," she confirmed. "I have a nice cottage that overlooks the lake, and the farm people are most kind. I have no wants there and have taken up writing."

"Writing, writing what?" he asked.

"My great novel," she explained. "It is about a man who goes to Africa and comes back to England to start a new life."

"You base it on Papa?" he asked.

"He is the inspiration," she agreed. "But, my fiction is probably rather more melodramatic than his actual life."

"Perhaps," George said. "When may we see some of it?"

"She hides it," Federica announced as she came into the dining room. "We have both asked to see and we have been fobbed off with excuses."

"When I am ready, you will see it," Sophia protested.

"Sophia, George tells me that there are survey teams looking at a route to fly from Cairo to Cape Town," Federica said, changing the subject.

"Will that help you in your dream?" Sophia asked.

"I believe so," Federica confirmed. "As I understand it, the teams are also building aerodrome facilities along the way, which would be most beneficial. Where are the teams going, George?"

"As I understand things, the Number 1 Party is checking from Cairo to Nimule in the Sudan. The Number 2 Party is looking at Nimule to Abercorn in Northern Rhodesia, and the Number 3 Party has Abercorn to Cape Town."

"The Number 2 Party sounds as if it has the biggest challenge," Federica said.

"Either them or the Number 3," he agreed. "Up to Nimule, you have the Nile, but south of Lake Victoria, there is not much, and over Northern Rhodesia, there is probably even less. I know Shortbridge, who has been given the northern part of the Number 3 Party, so between Abercorn and Broken Hill. Looking at whatever maps there are, he will have a challenge; there are few roads and no substantial infrastructure at all, just miles of bush and local villages and very few major landmarks."

"Have you had the chance to tell George of your new aircraft?" Sophia asked.

"Not yet," Federica said. "I was saving that for later."

"How did you manage to build a new plane with the war going on?" he asked.

"It was not easy," Federica said. "It took quite a while because we did it slowly, but I am happy with the result."

"When may I see it?" he asked.

"When we have finished breakfast," she promised.

Breakfast was quickly disposed of, as George was keen to see just what Federica had invented. She and Anastasia had designed aircraft before the war that had flown, the later ones very successfully, as he had proven in Egypt and France with the Aquila, so he wanted to see what improvements she had made. They had also gained considerable experience building aircraft as a subcontractor for the Aircraft Manufacturing Company. They drove to Handy Cross and the new hangar.

"This building is immense," George said as they arrived.

"Nastia designed it, and we built it when we took on contracts to build planes," Federica replied.

"Which planes did you build?" he asked.

"The de Havilland DH-5, de Havilland DH-10, the Royal Aircraft Factory S.E.5, the Sopwith Camel, the Handley Page O/400 and the Vickers Vimy," she replied.

"You did a lot," he said. "This runway is new, too."

"I excavated a little then built it up like the Via Appia, but instead of granite setts on the surface I acquired a load of Tarmacadam that a contractor had left over from a road job and was looking to dispose of," she said. "It has meant that we have had to look more at brakes because the aircraft rolls out much farther on landing than on grass. It does make the takeoff roll shorter as we can accelerate more quickly, less drag than on grass."

"May we look inside?" he asked. She led him to a side door and they went in.

"This is huge," he said. "Does it fly?"

"Of course, it flies," she said. "Let me tell you a little about it. In 1912, the Russian Igor Sikorskii invented a large aircraft that he called *Bolshoi Baltiskiy*, which had two engines, but it was underpowered. Then he modified things and went to four engines, and in 1913, he built the *Russkiy Vityaz*, which was amazing. Imagine it was built as a passenger aircraft with a passenger cabin, washroom and toilet. It too was underpowered, so he changed the engines and the new aircraft was called the *Il'ya Mourom'etz* and first flew in 1914. In February, it carried 16 people, and a dog of all things, as well as the two pilots. In June and July of 1914, they flew from St. Petersburg to Kiev, about 800 miles with only one stop for petrol, and then they flew back again."

"Didn't the Russians have a bomber that looked like this?" he asked.

"They did," she confirmed. "They converted the passenger aircraft to be a bomber, we in Britain are now going to try doing things the other way around by converting the Vickers, de Havilland and Handley Page bombers into passenger planes, like the Handley Page Air Cruiser that will carry 40 passengers."

"How did you get the details of the plane?" he asked.

"The War Office," she replied. "Apparently, the Russians offered the details and the drawings to us and the French, but our War Office and the Air Board were just not that interested. I went to see them and some clerk probably thought he was humouring a stupid woman wasting her money when he gave me all the details for just the small cost of reproduction."

"What have you changed from Sikorskii's design?" he asked.

"Well, we learned that the Kennedy Giant that was essentially designed around the Sikorskii craft, but they could only get 200 hp Salmson engines, which proved to be underpowered to even get it off the ground," she replied.

"I heard something about that," he said. "So what did you do?"

"We added our own engines, the Polaris 350 hp ones, and then had to check the engine mounts to see that they were adequate," she replied.

"We enlarged the fuselage and changed the shape by making it taller and adding a floor, below which we can store luggage in a hold. We also changed the nose to look more like that of the Sundstedt Hannevig flying boat. I like the way the pilots are enclosed, but they still have a clear view of what is ahead, and I also like the shape. We changed the outside covering of the frame to be a rigid laminate similar to the low-weight materials we use for our cars. Can you believe that he had it insulated and heated, and that he had electric lights in the cabin, and there was even a toilet? We used another layer of our wood honeycomb laminate on the inside as well as insulation; it was the lightest thing we could find."

"Have you changed the wings at all?" he asked.

"We have," she confirmed. "Nastia and I looked at the wing shape and did some calculations, and modified the section and the shape. We went with tapered wings that vary in chord from almost 15ft inboard to 8ft outboard, we also adopted the K-Bar cellule truss that Martin designed in the United States, the wing taper made manufacturing more complex as we had to change the ribs as we went outboard and change the shape of the spars, but we think the performance gained is worth the effort. We used the ideas that Fairey came up with for flaps, which change the wing camber and lower the landing speed. We went with all tractor engines, so we did not have to concern ourselves with problems at the wing trailing edge. Now we have a plane that will fly, will carry 40 people with their luggage for over 700 nautical miles without stopping for petrol, with a reserve of fuel for another 40 minutes of flying."

"So, you changed almost everything, from the wings, to the engines, the fuselage and by the look of it, the wheels as well. How fast will it fly?" he asked.

"We have yet to conduct complete trials, but our calculations suggest a maximum speed of 125 knots with a cruising speed of 110 knots. We've taken the weight down so much that it takes less power to keep it aloft and running, so we've got speed and range," she replied.

"So, you've actually flown it that fast?" he asked. "We had nothing in the war that would fly that fast, I think the fastest plane I heard of was the Martinsyde Buzzard that was supposed to reach 125 knots. How did you manage to get that kind of speed?"

"We've taken it out on several flights," she confirmed. "We believe we reached our calculated speeds, but we need to check again. We added sacks of potatoes in the back to simulate passengers. We achieved the speed with the more powerful engines, and by being meticulous about everything that might cause drag, which to some extent accounts for the shape, and by weighing everything that we used and looking to see if we could find alternates that were as strong and durable, but lighter."

"How did you get around the ban on non-military flying?" he asked.

"We took several RAF officers and two Air Ministry inspectors with us," she replied. "Ostensibly to test the viability of our plane as a bomber. We flew one day from here to Windermere and back without stopping; it took about four and a half hours, so we probably averaged close to 115 knots."

"I'm sorry to come back to this, but 125 knots, that sounds almost not possible. Tell me again how you managed to attain such a high speed?" he asked again.

"We used the Polaris engines that William designed, which have a very high power-to-weight ratio, and if you look at the way we built the plane, we have tried to reduce drag as much as we can," she replied. "If you look, you can see how we built fairings around the engines and even the wheels, so they won't create that much drag, if you look at photographs of the plane as Sikorskii built it, the drag caused by the engine radiators must have been tremendous, which probably contributed to the slow speed of the craft. We also stayed away from any open cockpit for the pilots; the turbulence caused around the opening for them is significant. It took Nastia and me quite a while and a lot of testing before we were able to get this result. We changed the shape of the struts, the shape of the fuselage, the shape and type of heat exchangers for the engines, everything to reduce drag. I read a study that said that even the struts and wires between the upper and lower wings, if not done well, can make over a three-knot difference, so every little thing adds up. We even built a small wind tunnel and tried all kinds of shapes in it to see which would give us the least turbulent flow as the air passed over them. That helped a lot."

"Did the Air Force officers that you took up know that you intended this only as a passenger plane?" he asked.

"I think they guessed as much," she admitted. "But they were happy for the ride, and they liked the idea of flying fast over the countryside. It was late in the war when we took them, so I think they knew that we could never get a bomber operational quickly enough to make any difference; they were more interested in the Handley Page bombers and were focused on the new V/1500 model that was going to be able to reach Berlin. We were not that far advanced at that time. We set up two redundant sets of controls for the pilots and put in instruments from Smiths, but we also added some extra altimeters from Richard and De Giglio to see if the different systems give different results. So, we have for each pilot an altimeter, a rate of climb indicator, a turn indicator, a clock and a compass, and between the two sets of flight instruments we have the engine gauges, tachometer, oil pressure gauge, oil temperature gauge, and above them the fuel gauges. It was not that expensive, now that the Aircraft Disposal Company is in full swing, you can pick up a Bristol fighter for only £800, or a Siddeley Puma engine for £400, and parts cost much less. We got most of the instruments from Smiths, except the turn indicators, which are the new ones from America, made by Sperry. Our own experience with Sirius Cars has taught us a lot about gauges, like fuel gauges, but things like the turn indicators are new to us. Do you know when the government will lift the ban on non-military flights?"

"I am guessing only, but I think probably May or thereabouts," he said.

"It cannot be soon enough," she complained. "Bossoutrot flew from Paris to London last month with 12 passengers. I know they got around the ban by saying they were all military officers under orders, but this country will get left behind. Our own air force just started a mail service by air between Folkestone and Cologne. The Germans have already started flights for commercial purposes, but we sit waiting for the government to act, or at least get out of the way."

"It still is amazing to me that something this large flies," he said.

"It is, isn't it," she agreed. "We were more fortunate than Kennedy, who built his Giant in 1917, which looks very similar to Sikorskii's plane. Kennedy says that he worked with Sikorsky for a while, but perhaps not for long enough, as his plane just about got off the ground, it was so lacking in power."

"What engines did he use?" George asked.

"Four Salmson 14-cylinder engines, but they only put out 200HP each, and that was just not enough for the size of the craft," she explained. "I have seen photographs, and I believe the engines were arranged in pairs, one tractor and one pusher per wing. Unfortunately for Kennedy, where he built the craft at Northolt, there were no hangars large enough to accommodate it, so they had to build it outside. That is also one of the reasons I spent the money on this large hangar that we now have. That was actually quite a challenge as the roof trusses have to give us a clear span of over 150ft."

"What kind of seats did Sikorsky use?" he asked, bringing the subject back to the plane they were looking at.

"Wicker chairs," she said. "I wonder if that is the best idea, but for the moment cannot think of a better solution. It seems odd to me that the pilots' seats are fixed, but I see nothing that tells me whether or not Sikorsky secured his wicker chairs to the floor. Nastia and I looked at chair design and have a wicker shape that is comfortable, and, of great import, is light in weight, and we have affixed them to the floor, oh, and the floor is the same kind of laminate we used for our cars. The last item we are working on is a lavatory. Five hours in the air at a time may be more than many people can endure without some use of the lavatory. What we are trying to decide is what kind of lavatory, shall it flush and if so, where do we store the flushed material, and for ground servicing, how do we quickly and cleanly empty that tank and refill the flush supply. I cannot imagine following the railway practice of simply allowing the effluent to fall freely onto the tracks below. Imagine being bombarded from above with human waste. How horrible. I cannot find anything that tells me what Sikorskii did and how he managed those issues."

"Is there anything that I missed?" he asked.

"We thought a lot about the comfort of passengers," she said. "We put silencers on the engines and have tried to insulate the fuselage as best we can to reduce noise. We do need to go back and look at seats again. The wicker will work for short trips, but I'm not sure how well it would be for four to five hours."

"Something to research," he said. "Anything else?"

"We added brakes to the wheels," she said. "We took Lanchester's idea of a disc brake, then we took the friction materials that Frood has developed, added to that the hydraulic system that the American Lougheed has invented and built a brake, we also put oleo struts on the landing gear to reduce the shock when we land. We borrowed and copied shamelessly, and I'm hoping that no one works out what we did and considers legal action, so this plane will never be flown in the United States, they seem so set on lawsuits over there, if you look at the endless suits between the Wrights and Curtiss, it's no wonder the Americans had to use French aircraft when they finally entered the war, they were so far behind is all but engine development."

"So, as runways are paved and rolling resistance is lowered, we can still stop?" he asked, coming back to the brakes.

"That was the idea," she confirmed. "If you think about it, takeoff is a lot easier on a paved runway than on grass; the rolling resistance is less, but with no soft ground to provide the resistance to stop, we might run off the end of the runway, which would not be good."

"How do the brakes actually work?" he asked.

"We have a hydraulic pump and lines to each wheel and pistons on each brake that clamp the friction materials onto the disc," she explained. "We have run taxi tests at the field and they seem to work well."

"How much did it cost?" he asked.

"With the hangar improvements, the runway and the plane itself, we've spent £10,235 over the past four years," she replied. "We've been able to expense it all as we've gone, so we have no debts associated with it. We used materials from the cars, we bought where we had to, we adapted things, we did, I think, a good job of managing costs, and I must confess we did better than had anticipated with the aircraft contracts, so they paid for much of this."

"Do you give the type a name yet?" George asked.

"This one will be the Andromeda series," Federica replied

"So, we had the Aquila, then Auriga, now Andromeda," he mused. "I suppose constellation names are good for planes. Does this particular one have a name, or just the number?"

"I've decided to call it the White Nile," she said. "If we build more and use them on the London to Cairo to Cape Town route, then I was thinking of naming them after the major rivers we would see along the way."

"What other rivers will we cross or encounter?" he said, half to himself. "Let's see, there'll be the Blue Nile, the Zambezi, the Limpopo, the Orange, what others?"

"My researches also show the Luapula, the Kafue and the Vaal," she added.

"I'd forgotten about the Vaal," he said. "You'd think I'd remember that one, I was in South Africa not that long ago. Where are the Kafue and the Luapula?"

"Both run between Northern Rhodesia and the Belgian Congo," she explained. "The Luapula runs north from Northern Rhodesia into the Congo and into Lake Mweru, and the Kafue rises close to the Congo on the Northern Rhodesian side, and runs south through Northern Rhodesia, becoming a tributary to the Zambezi."

"That gives us eight," he said. "I suppose if we need more, we could always add smaller rivers that we would cross, or else major African rivers that we would not cross, but that which people would recognise."

"That would give us the Niger, the Congo, the Volta, the Senegal, the Gambia, the Shire, the Rufiji, the Ruvuma, and I'm sure many others that I cannot name today," she said.

"When do we get a flight?" he asked.

"Well, we probably need to wait until the ban on non-military flights is lifted," she said. "So, let's look at business issues first, then in the next month or so we'll take a flight when we can."

"Those are our aeroplanes at the back of the hangar there?" he asked.

"I wondered when you were going to ask," she said. "While we were working on the Sikorskii design, we made modifications to our own smaller craft. We found that by changing the wings and improving the fairings that we could get more speed with the same engines."

"So, if we were to make improvements to the engines, they would be even more capable?" he asked.

"They would," she agreed. "The Aquila will now reach 150 mph and the Auriga 130 mph, with a better engine, I would expect more."

"You've really been busy," he said.

"It kept me from worrying too much about what was happening to you," she said. "We heard shocking things about pilot deaths."

"Much of that was the rush to get pilots to the Front," he said. "So, sadly, I think many came with the minimum of training and flight time. Against more experienced Hun pilots, they were outmatched. That is not to say that the Hun did not have the same problem; we all were trying for mastery of the skies and putting up as many planes as we could."

"Well, I'm very glad that you went to Egypt first and were able to get lots of flying hours before going to France," she said.

"So am I," he agreed.

Federica and George met with Anastasia, William and Sophia and went through each of the family businesses. Federica told the rest that she had taken George to Handy Cross and shown him the new hangar and the plane. Federica then went on to discuss the rest of the family businesses. Abbey Biscuits was down a little in sales, but only because they were still recovering from the effects of sugar rationing imposed by the Ministry of Food late in the war. The workforce was already mainly women, so there was no great impact from the return of men from the war; in fact, of the ten men who had volunteered or been conscripted from Abbey, only six came back. The same workforce issues were generally true for the Windsor Garments company; most were women anyway, and of the four men who had gone, three came back. At Windsor, the emphasis was now going to be away from uniforms to fashionable clothing that had a broader appeal. Federica expected a dip in sales as the general economy recovered from the war effort, but she expected to see better days in the 1920s. The biggest problem they had had to face had been the effects of the influenza epidemic, they had had some people off sick in July and August of 1918, then a few more in October and November, but by then they had worked out how to separate the people at work, they had provided masks to wear and had installed more facilities for the washing of hands. Then in early 1919 the influenza seemed to come back again with more cases, and Federica put that down to men and women returning from the war and bringing the infection with them, so they had instituted a policy that anyone could have their old job back, but they had to go into quarantine first, forty days seemed a little too severe, so she had settled on two weeks.

The Burnham Foundry had been busy during the war and had had to make many changes in their employment base as men had volunteered for military service or had been conscripted. Those men had been replaced with women, and now the men were coming back looking for their old jobs, or at least most of them were coming back; of the thirty who had gone, twenty-three returned. Anastasia had had the idea of splitting the business into two parts, one for large castings, such as were used in railway wagons, car engines and such, and smaller investment castings, used in all manner of machines, like sewing machines, novelties and devices. Her idea was to move many of the women into that operation and bring the men back into the part that dealt with the larger pieces. The small investment castings were a new venture for them, but she had every expectation of success. For some peculiar reason, the foundry had just not seen the number of cases of the influenza that the other businesses had, and Federica was at a loss to explain why.

The final business was the Sirius Car Company, which had seen the greatest losses of men to the war. Of the forty who had gone, fully twenty did not return, a tragic statistic. For the latter two years of the war, Sirius had not been building many cars, but had been fulfilling contracts with the War Office for vans, lorries and ambulances for the war effort. Those orders were expected to discontinue forthwith, so would leave a gap in sales that they would have to try and fill by selling to enterprises around the country and abroad. George commented that they had had many comments from the ANZAC and South African contingents about their wagons, and he felt that they should focus their efforts on exporting the smaller wagons that came with four-wheel drive. The Australians and the Africans had all remarked that their lack of paved roads made travel difficult and that the Antares and Capella wagons had appealed to them. He also pointed out that the versions produced at Orly were left-hand drive and would be saleable in Francophone Africa. Federica agreed and promised to talk to Philippe as soon as she could to see how they would distribute their vehicles into French-speaking Africa. William said that he would contact his father and brother and see how they could broaden their distribution network in southern and central Africa. George had had some dealings with people from Egypt and the Sudan, and he felt that he could get distributors set up in those countries fairly quickly. Lastly, there were the Americas. The United States had a burgeoning auto industry, but Canada seemed to be lagging a little, with some local companies, such as McLaughlin, Grey-Dort and Bartlett, but also with locally built American cars from Ford and REO. Perhaps there they could also make a mark and set up some distributors. For South America, none of them had any specific contacts, but Federica recalled that her brother, Franco, had been busy setting up a network of distributors for olive oil and other Italian commodities and was also looking for products to import into Italy. She thought that he had set up a network in Brazil and in Argentina. Perhaps, they could use the same network. She undertook to contact Franco forthwith and have him look into the issue. As Franco had inherited their father's import-export trade, including the distribution of Sirius cars in Italy, he should jump at the chance to expand his territories and product offerings, and now that hostilities had been concluded, it was back to business as it had been before the war. One thing they went through in detail was the improvements and changes they had made to their line of cars over the past four years. While the demand for cars had been down, driven by the need for vans and lorries, they had taken the opportunity to change the engines to the new Vee-four or Vee-six configuration, with the V-eight going in the Capella wagon and the Altair lorry. They had also modified the bodywork to be easier to manufacture and also to improve the looks of the cars.

For the present, as with the foundry, they had those men who had come back from the war, all wanting to return to the jobs they had held before the war and then the problem of what to do with the women who would be displaced. Some had already said that they wanted to go back to their previous roles as mothers and housewives, but there were some who enjoyed the work, the pay and the freedom that financial independence brought. Federica's plan was to accommodate the increase in the workforce with the return of the men by bringing in-house some of the parts that they had been sourcing from other companies, but perhaps if they could generate enough sales, then that might not be necessary. For the moment, at least they had the financial wherewithal to withstand a period of reduced sales, provided that did not drag on too long. They had also learned quite a lot about workflows as they had spaced things out to avoid close contact while the influenza epidemic swept through the country in its various waves.

Last, but not least, were the properties in Scotland, Derbyshire and the Lake District. As those in Scotland and the Lake were essentially hill grazing properties with tenant sheep farmers, Federica saw not much change there, particularly as the farmers had all been classified as reserved occupations and had stayed farming throughout the war. The Somercotes Lead Mining Company had been extremely busy during the war, but Federica expected that with the cessation of war that the demand for lead would decline and that the mine would no longer be profitable and therefore would likely close within a year or two. The lead mine had been hard hit by the influenza epidemic, and some 52 men had been off sick, and four had died. They had done what they could for the families, but they were waiting to see what the government would do, if anything. There was also an extensive portfolio of stocks and shares in many and varied companies, and Federica and Anastasia both expected some degree of volatility in values as life returned to a more peaceful mode and companies sought to adjust from wartime production to peacetime products and services. They had decided to not immediately try and do too much buying and selling, but to take a longer-term approach and see how market trends went in the next year. They still had cash and gold reserves that they had not had occasion to tap, which was of great comfort to them all.

The current business issues covered, Federica turned to her new project, air flight service from London to Cape Town, via Cairo.

"George has told me of the RAF teams that are currently in Africa setting out a route from Cairo to Cape Town and even preparing some aerodrome facilities and emergency landing fields," she said. "If we are to start up an air transport service, then we need to know what else we need apart from a plane that will serve."

"Well, we will obviously need pilots, navigators and mechanics for each of the planes," George added. "And, I would think that we will need some people on the ground at certain locations. I would not want to leave everything to the crew."

"I think that may depend on what the Lloyd-George government decides to do, if anything, about supporting commercial air traffic," Anastasia commented.

"I wonder what the government will do?" William said. "I see the French are actively promoting air travel and travel companies, I wonder if our government will do the same?"

"Something tells me not to expect too much," Federica said. "The government has always struck me as parsimonious at the best of times, and at the moment, they are probably trying to work out how to pay for the war. It is of interest to note that George Holt Thomas incorporated Aircraft Transport and Travel Limited two years ago, which suggests to me that he, at least, has some confidence in the notion of air travel."

"Thomas has his own money to fund the venture," George commented. "I wonder what will he do and where will he fly?"

"Paris would be my guess," Anastasia said. "It offers the most possible traffic at this time. But, then again, perhaps New York would be better."

"The Atlantic has not yet been flown," Sophia protested.

"True, but there are a number of teams on their way to Newfoundland to try and win the Daily Mail £10,000 prize, if they can get back here in under 72 hours, without stopping," William said.

"Did you not think of entering the competition?" Sophia asked.

"I thought of it," Federica replied. "But Nastia and I decided that we would rather spend time with George and Will, and we wanted to do more testing of our plane before we attempt such a long overwater crossing. The restrictions on non-military flying have meant that we really have not had enough flight testing. I would imagine that most of the entrants in the Daily Mail challenge are going to be using converted bombers from the war."

"What issues will we face across Africa?" George asked.

"First, we have to cross the Channel, then the Mediterranean, but that has been done already, so most of the issues are known. The recent flight of the Handley Page aircraft to India should be instructive if we can get hold of the logs and flight reports. Once we reach Cairo then the real problems begin. Over Africa, I think the heat, the weather and the altitude will be the challenges," Federica said. "It will generally be much hotter than here, and air density will change with heat; you must have found that in Sinai."

"We did," George confirmed. "We noted that it took longer to take off than it did in France."

"Altitude, especially in Central Africa, will also affect that," Federica said. "So we will need power reserves in the engines to get off the ground within a reasonable distance."

"I presume that whatever route the RAF picks will avoid mountains," Sophia commented. "Are there not some tall mountains in the area of Uganda? What are they, the Mountains of the Moon?"

"They are," George confirmed. "I am presuming that the RAF teams will follow the Nile south to Lake Victoria, one can use the river as a navigational aid, but Lake Victoria must be over 3,500ft above sea level and to the west of the lake are the Virunga Mountains that go as high as 16,000 feet, so we should avoid them. I think Pretoria or Johannesburg will be our greatest challenge for landing and takeoff, it must be about 6,000 feet above sea level, and on a hot day, that will need a long runway."

"We would need to stay away from the Virungas," William laughed. "Even I cannot get an engine to give us enough power reserves to get over them with a full load, not yet, at least, but I think we can manage Johannesburg. I would also think that at extreme altitude, breathing would be difficult."

"We should stay away from extreme altitudes then," Federica said. "I was also thinking that reliable supplies of good, clean petrol may be a problem, but that all comes back to how much support the present government gives to the air transport and travel business. We may have to set up a system to get our own supplies of petrol to the aerodromes."

"One other thing we need to think about is static electricity," George said. "We noticed it a lot in Sinai, especially when the wind blew and it was dusty. We had some issues with petrol and sparks when we were filling the planes from the lorry. In the end, we earthed them all together to a large iron stake we hammered into the ground."

"That is something else I'll add to my list of things to think about at the aerodromes," Federica said.

"I know that you and Nastia have flown the plane from here to Windermere and back at almost 115 knots, but even if we can fly at 115 knots all the way, it will be many hours of flying time to get from here to Cape Town," Sophia said.

"About 57 hours of actual flying," Federica said.

"Well, as we probably will have to do most of the flying in the day, we will need hotels to accommodate our passengers between flight stages," George said.

"Why cannot we fly at night?" Sophia asked.

"We could," George said. "There is no problem with flying at night; in fact, the weather conditions are generally better, so it's no problem except for navigation. We can use the stars to give us an accurate fix on where we are and which way we are going, provided of course that we can see the stars, but if it's cloudy then we would have a problem as compass variation is enough that it would be less than prudent to rely on them entirely."

"You really need better instruments then?" Sophia asked.

"We do," George confirmed.

"Here we are often beset by fog and rain," Sophia commented. "Does that also occur over Africa?"

"Fog, not so often, except perhaps over areas with much water, like the Sudd, or by the Cape," George thought. "But, weather, certainly. There are rain storms and dust storms, and odd winds that we would have to contend with. We would need to be flexible with schedules to allow for inclement weather and associated delays."

"Did you get dust storms in Sinai?" Anastasia asked.

"Sometimes," George confirmed. "Then we did not fly, but then neither did the Turk. But, we did not have passengers, mail or goods to deliver."

"Perhaps you should think of creating a French company," Sophia said. "The French government seems to favour such enterprises, are there not already companies that were founded by people like Farman, Breguet and Latécoère?"

"There are," Federica agreed. "We have La Lignes Aériennes Farman, the Compagnie Générale Aéropostale and just this month Compagnie des Grands Express Aériens flying from Le Bourget to Lausanne. I think that they are all looking at short flights within Europe, but we have to assume that they will be looking at how to fly to their African colonies."

"So if we start a British company and a French company, what will they be called?" William asked.

"I think Sirius Air Lines for the British concern and Ligne Aériennes Sirius for the French, and we'll also create the Sirius Aircraft Company to build planes, if we ever get to that stage," Federica suggested.

"That sounds reasonable," George agreed. "Do we provide equipment to both the airlines?"

"We do," Federica confirmed. "I know that Farman has a good plane with the Goliath, but I think our Andromeda is as good, if not better. Sikorskii is a brilliant designer, and we only had to make changes and improvements to his concepts to have a viable commercial aircraft. Most of the work we did was to get it to go faster by reducing drag and weight everywhere."

"What else do we have to think about?" Anastasia asked.

"Hotels, meals, petrol, spare parts, local agents, ticket sales," Federica reeled off.

"Perhaps it would make sense to take a trip along the route that the RAF finally maps out and make those kinds of arrangements," George suggested.

"I think you and Fede should go," Anastasia said. "Will and I can manage things here while you are away, and we can telegraph you if necessary if anything arises that we cannot manage."

"What's your best guess for the route?" William asked.

"Up the Nile from Cairo," George replied. "I think it likely that the RAF will lay out stations at points along the way, but particularly at Aswan, Wadi Halfa, Khartoum and somewhere south of there. In the upper reaches of the Nile, I am not certain where they will go, but Lake Victoria seems a good guess, which means Jinja. Between there and the railway in Northern Rhodesia, I am not sure which way they will go. But on the railway, I think they will look for fields at Livingstone, Bulawayo and either Pretoria or Johannesburg, and after that, it's the main line to the Cape, so possibly Bloemfontein, Kimberley, Beaufort West and on to Cape Town."

"So, from here, we have to decide whether we start from Hounslow Heath or Lympne, then we would fly to Paris and beyond that, I was thinking of Marseille, Rome, Brindisi, Athens, then Alexandria before stopping in Cairo at Heliopolis," Federica said.

"So, you could actually make a start and find agents in France, Italy, Greece and Egypt," Sophia suggested. "And, while you do that, you can make arrangements with hotels for the overnight accommodation you will need, unless you can work out how to fly safely at night."

"I'll start planning that," Federica said. "Meanwhile, we have things to do here and need to get our concerns back to a peacetime regimen. I am going to go to Orly as soon as I can to see Philippe. Perhaps Nastia, you will come with me?"

"That would be fine, Mama, would you mind staying a few more days to help Will with Giovanna?" Anastasia replied.

"I would be delighted," Sophia confirmed. "But, don't be away too long, I have my opus to return to."

"Ah, yes, the great work," George said. "I await the opportunity to see it with great anticipation."

"Only because I will not let any of you see it before I am satisfied," Sophia laughed. "But, another few months should see me done."

"Is there anything else that we need to discuss today?" Federica asked.

"I don't think so," George replied. "We should get our managers in soon as a group and review each business so that we all know how we will make the transition back to operating in a time of peace. I think our greatest challenge will be weathering the lack of orders for a while until life returns to a more normal mode."

"I will have Alice make the arrangements," Federica said.

Alice made the arrangements, and in short order, Winston Fox from the Burnham Foundry, Henry Robertson from Abbey Biscuits, Ian Stuart and Andrew Coates of Sirius Cars came to the house and met with Federica and the other family members. George chaired the meetings and listened as each of the business managers discussed their current situations and the challenges they faced in the near and longer terms. They talked at length about the losses of men from the war, and all were of the mind that they could manage with the men that they had and the women who had filled in during the war. They also were in agreement that if some of the women wanted to go back to their domestic life, then they would not replace them with new employees, men or women. Each of them could see problems ahead as the country went into the post-war years and dealt with the realities of the huge debts that had been incurred to fight the war and the uncertainties of the markets that they served. There was little in the way of surprises, which was good as it meant that the family had a good grasp of each of the businesses. At the end of the meeting, Federica asked Ian Stuart if he would go with her to the Orly factory to meet with Philippe. That he was quite happy to do, but first he had to obtain a passport, but that was something that could be done quickly, so Federica set a date and then asked Alice to make travel arrangements.

Back in the air

The Air Ministry lifted the ban on non-military flying on the 1st day of May, 1919. It was supposed by then that the peace negotiations that were still underway had reached a point where the end was in sight and peace would soon be signed by all the warring parties. The flight ban may have been lifted, but there were still restrictions, restrictions that were peculiar at best. Aircraft were limited to service aircraft, and pilots had to be within three miles of an airfield in case of an emergency. That constrained flying to a great extent, as there were not airfields at three-mile intervals scattered across the country. However, the fledgling airlines of the time took the opportunity and started to fly goods and people within the United Kingdom. The two that made the greatest splash were AT&T, Aircraft Transport and Travel, and HPTL, Handley Page Transport Limited. The planes used were converted bombers from the recent war and were notoriously slow, but proved to be very safe and reliable.

"Did you see this news item?" Federica asked George at breakfast.

"No, which one?" he asked.

"The Tarrant Tabor aircraft crashed while they were trying to take off," she explained.

"Wasn't that the latest bomber?" he asked.

"It is, was," she confirmed. "It was a large triplane with six engines. It seems that they started off with just four engines, then started up the other two, then it nosed over and crashed. The two pilots were injured, probably fatally."

"As I recall, that was a really large craft," he said.

"It is, was," she confirmed. "They were making design changes to use it as a commercial aircraft. It was planned for a passenger load of 9,000 lbs, with a fuel load of 10,000 lbs, which would give them 12 hours of flying. It wasn't that fast, with a maximum speed of only 110 mph."

"Nine thousand lbs, that must be close to 40 people or so," he said.

"It would, that would work out to 225 lbs per person, so an average person plus some luggage," she added. "I wonder what the problems really were?"

"I'm sure we'll find out in time," he said. "Why did they go with six engines?"

"As I understand things, they had planned on four Siddeley Tiger engines, but they are not ready, so they went with six Napier Lion engines and mounted the extra two between the middle and upper wings," she explained. "I'll wager that the problems had something to do with where those two engines were placed."

"I wonder how the Felixstowe Fury will fare on their attempt to Cape Town?" he said.

"Well, the craft flew well enough last year, and the recent crossing of the Atlantic by the United States flying boat is encouraging," she thought. "I am not sure if I really like the proposed route to the Cape, first to Gibraltar, then Malta, Alexandria, Khartoum, Victoria Nyanza, Lake Tanganyika, Lake Nyasa, Beira, Durban and then on to the Cape. I would prefer to use the French base near Istres, add stops near Rome and Athens, then past Lake Victoria I would like to fit in Victoria Falls, but past that, I cannot see where a flying boat would go, except to the coast, which is quite a way from Livingstone, either east or west."

"So, you think we should stay with our land craft rather than look at a flying boat?" he asked.

"For now," she agreed. "I would also be concerned with finding clear water to land on in the upper Nile, if we had to, there may be problems with the Sudd."

"I wonder why the Fury went with five engines?" he said.

"I think it was like the Tabor, the engines planned were not ready, so they had to go with the smaller Rolls-Royce Eagle and add another to get the horsepower they needed," she replied.

"All the more reason to have Will really work on our engines," he said. "It would be disastrous to have an underpowered aircraft, particularly if we fly through Johannesburg and have to deal with the altitude and high temperatures."

The forming of Sirius Airlines, Ligne Aériennes Sirius and the Sirius Aircraft Company was duly done, and George set about hiring the first recruit. It was likely that the government would insist on properly qualified navigators to be aboard on long flights, so there was probably going to be some demand in the future for those same navigators. He contacted some whom he had known in Sinai and France and found quite a few that had left the Air Force and were deciding what to do next with their lives. He contacted two of them and brought them to the Sirius offices for discussions. When he told them what was planned, they both wanted to sign on. Terms were agreed and Richard Collins and Stephen Walker became the first full-time employees of Sirius Air Lines. George gave them the task of following the progress of the Royal Air Force teams mapping the Africa route and of collecting what maps there were, plus whatever meteorological data there might be. He set up an office at Handy Cross at the back of the main hangar and left them to their own devices. The other two people he transferred to the airline were John Edwards and Thomas Manning. They had worked for the Burnham Foundry when Federica was building her first car and had been assigned by Mr Fox, the manager, to help her. Subsequently, they had transferred to the Sirius Car company, and now George was moving them to the airline. They had gone through apprenticeships and had gone on to further education, done service in the war in the Flying Corps and were slated to be flight engineers on the service to the Cape. Federica had liked them as apprentices, and they had responded by learning as much as they could about the cars and lorries that Sirius built, and then by helping Federica and George build their planes before the war. They were knowledgeable about all the systems on the new plane and had helped build it, and were capable of field diagnoses and repairs, just the kind of people both George and Federica wanted as flight engineers.

Just over two weeks later, on the 15th of June, the first non-stop Atlantic crossing was made by Alcock and Brown, flying a converted Vickers Vimy bomber. They left Canada on the evening of the 14th of June and flew through the night into the dawn and early morning, finally making landfall over Ireland and crashing in a bog near Clifden in County Galway. The Daily Mail prize of £10,000 was awarded to the pair who had made the flight in a little over 15 hours at an average speed of some 115 mph. Federica and George studied reports on the flight with great interest, looking for the things that went wrong so that they could look to their own plane and see what might need changing or improving.

"It looks like their air turbine failed early in the flight," George said. "That would have meant no heat in their suits and no wireless."

"I think we need to look at small generators run from the engines," Federica said. "If put one on each inboard engine we should have enough power for lights in the passenger cabin, the wireless and perhaps heat if we cannot work out how to use the exhaust gases to heat the air coming into the cabin, I don't think we should issue all our passengers with Sidcot suits and big flying boots."

"How are we going to manage heating the cabin air?" George asked. "We cannot just have air blowing in from the outside, at 115 knots, that would be very uncomfortable as well as noisy."

"I'm sure we can conjure up some mechanism that allows us to bleed air in from the outside, without having a gale blowing through the cabin," Federica said confidently. "Perhaps we can invent some sort of heat exchanger, to use the exhaust gases to indirectly heat the cabin air. Are you coming with me to Orly to see Philippe?"

"No," he replied. "Giovanna and I were going to drive Sophia back to the Lakes while you and Nastia were in France."

"Of course," she said. "It had slipped my mind. How long will you be gone?"

"Only four of five days," he thought. "We'll drive up to Windermere, stopping perhaps in Stoke for the night depending on the weather and the road conditions, stay for a day or two, then come home."

On the 16th of July, Federica was delighted to learn of an Italian plane that had landed at the Kenley Aerodrome. It was a Fiat and had been flown over from Paris that day, but the flight had started in Turin. What impressed her most was that the flight from Turin to Rome, a little over 360 miles, had been done at an average speed of 161 mph, or almost 140 knots. Now, that to her was the kind of performance she was looking for on the trip to Cape Town. The rest of the journey had not been at such a pace, but then she read that bad weather had slowed the flight from Rome to Paris and Paris to England across the Channel was plagued with weather issues. Perhaps, once they got over Africa, she

74

reasoned, they might be able to achieve higher speeds than she was currently planning.

"Did you see this item about the Fiat flying between Turin and Rome?" she asked George.

"I did," he confirmed. "The speed that they quoted was that in any way due to following winds?"

"The article doesn't say," she replied. "I wonder if they really did do the trip at 161 mph due only to the engine, or were they helped along by the wind?"

"How can we find out?" he asked.

"I'm not sure that there is much information yet that tells us what the winds are at altitude," she said. "It may be quite different to what we see on the ground. Perhaps the Meteorological Office can answer those questions. It may be really important to us over Africa. If we are flying at an air speed of 115 knots and the winds at altitude are 50 knots in the wrong direction, our travel times are going to be really long, and we will need to be sure of alternate landing sites, where we can also buy petrol."

"We need to keep a close eye on whoever makes the flight first to see what we can learn about winds and from which direction they blow at different times of the year," he commented. "So much to think about."

"Maybe we should send some people to Africa, and have them fly small balloons with weather instruments attached," Federica suggested. "We might learn a little more about the winds."

"I'll look into that," George promised. "But, maybe kites may be a better idea. If we took a couple of large lorries and attached windlasses to them, we could fly kites and get measurements directly. If we flew balloons, we'd have to work out how to get the instrument package back to the ground safely and somewhere that we could find it. I'll get the papers of Teisserenc de Bort and Gold and see what I can learn about balloon flights and how they collected the data, and I'll have our navigators talk to the Met Office and kites and data collection."

A few weeks after the Fiat flight, flights from England to France were started, and the first scheduled commercial flight from London to Paris left Hounslow Heath at ten past nine on the morning of the 25th of

August and landed at Le Bourget two and a half hours later. There was some controversy at the time over whether or not the first commercial flight had really been that of Aircraft Transport & Travel, AT&T, or Handley Page Transport, HPTL, but certainly on that day, AT&T landed before HPTL. The controversy centred around whether or not the AT&T flight had in fact been in the published timetable of AT&T, or whether it was essentially a charter flight. This cross-Channel service looked good, but it was expensive and was eclipsed by the efforts of the French who with a Farman Goliath plane, had attempted to fly from Paris to Dakar only a few days before, a distance of some 2,597 miles, the first leg of the journey being a non-stop flight from Paris to Casablanca in 18 hours and 23 minutes, which meant an average ground speed of a little over 60 mph, or a little over 50 knots, something that Federica felt that they would need to improve on dramatically if they were to have a viable air service. Thereafter, the plane flew on to Mogador and Tiznit before heading off across the desert to Port Etienne. Somewhere in this leg, things went wrong and contact was lost with the plane. The crew managed to put the plane down on a beach short of their destination and were eventually rescued by local people near Koufra in Mauritania. Even though they did not make their final destination, the singular achievement of flying non-stop to Casablanca was amazing. Federica and George followed all this activity with great interest and tried to learn from each of the airlines and the endurance flight record attempts. If they were to succeed with the Cape Town route, then they would need to know what the pitfalls might be and what others' experiences were.

The RAF teams were still labouring across Africa, but it was generally believed that their report and the facilities that they were constructing would all be ready by January of 1920. This gave Federica and George a few months to continue testing their plane and making whatever modifications they determined would be required. Federica had some of her fears confirmed, that one of the challenges was going to be just crossing the channel. During the first two weeks of the cross-Channel service, two of the scheduled 56 flights were cancelled because of bad weather. By the time the end of August rolled around over ten per cent of scheduled flights had been cancelled, due to weather and during that period, only about 60 days had been considered fit for flying, and that was in the summer months. Flying in the period from December to March was likely to have even more delays and be more of a challenge. Their schedules would have to allow for delays and cancellations, the effects of which could well be magnified by similar delays along the rest of the route. One of the other issues they faced was navigating. The compasses they had were the best they could find, but still had the reputation for being somewhat unreliable, which meant that pilots often flew low enough so that they could follow the railway lines. That meant that the flights were often bumpy as the planes flew in turbulent air. The days of soaring above the weather to find smooth air were yet to come when pressurisation of the fuselages was developed. Federica became a student of the weather and spent much time poring over weather reports, not only for the cross-Channel part of the route, but reports that came in from the colonial outposts and gave her a sense of what to expect along the way. George consulted with his navigators and created a model on a large sheet of paper, in which he input various flight times to better understand how to break up the journey into reasonable daily travels. His first proposed route would have them stopping overnight in Rome, Athens, Cairo, Khartoum, Jinja, Broken Hill, either Pretoria or Johannesburg, then on to Cape Town. The challenging legs of the route were crossing from Athens to Alexandria, then flying south of Lake Victoria to Broken Hill. Between Cairo and Khartoum, there were likely to be plenty of emergency fields along the course of the Nile, even above Khartoum. George anticipated some fields, but south of Lake Victoria, he was not sure what route the RAF party would select and where they might put landing fields.

While Federica and George pondered the route and the schedules, William was busy with engine modifications, specifically supercharging. He was working hard on this modification, as it would mean that they could maintain airspeed even as they flew higher. His reasoning was that at least over much of Egypt and the Sudan, the Nile was visible from great heights, so there was no need to fly close to the ground and perhaps the air would be smoother higher up. He doubted that they would routinely fly that high, which would introduce possible breathing problems as the air thinned out, but 10,000 feet might give a better ride than 1,000 feet and might be needed for short periods to get over mountains. The supercharger added some weight, but he reasoned that the improved output would more than counter that effect; in fact, his horsepower-to-weight ratio was looking really good. William also spent quite some time looking at propellers, deciding whether he would use ones with two or four blades. Sikorskii had used two-bladed propellers, but William was testing a four-bladed propeller to see if he could get better performance. In the war, many of the BE 2 aircraft had used four-bladed propellers, but most of the more agile, faster aircraft had used two-bladed propellers. The issue came down to propeller loading, size, tip velocity and a variety of other considerations. He was currently leaning towards a four-bladed propeller, similar to the ones used on the Vickers Vimy machine. He knew that the Handley Page V/ 1500 craft used both two and four-bladed propellers, the two blades as tractors and the four blades as pushers. Even given that, he was still inclined to follow the lead of Vickers and go with all four-bladed propellers. His other modification was to fit electric self-starters to the engines. They had put them on the Sirius vehicles and had had success, even modifying them for more reliability and greater power, so he had taken the largest one they had for their lorry and had adapted that for the aircraft engines. His bench tests had all worked perfectly, so it meant that starting the engines in African fields would not now require either teams of men or a Huck's Starter, which also required at least one man to operate.

On the 1st of September, Federica announced that she was ready to start test flights again. William had finished with his engine changes and wanted to see how the superchargers had changed performance in the air. Bench tests had been fine, but bench tests were done close to sea level, not at 10,000 feet. William strung instruments on the engines to measure temperature and oil pressure, and fitted extra pitot tubes on the fuselage for airspeed indicators and added an extra two barometers for altitude measurements. He wanted to gather as much flight data and engine data as he could, so he could be sure that everything was running to his satisfaction. Federica had other concerns. Before she flew across the Channel, she decided that a run up to Scotland would be a good test of the engines and the plane, so James telephoned one of his acquaintances in the Air Force and made arrangements to land at the East Fortune station in Scotland. That would be a flight of almost 320 miles each way. The others were also eager to go, so it turned into a family outing. The weather was forecast to be sunny and dry, which was good. The longer-range predictions, such as there were in England, full of uncertainty and variability, were for cooler weather later in the month, so Federica wanted to get some test flights in as quickly as possible. The navigators were asked who wanted to go on the first trip, and both jumped at the chance. George asked them to draw straws to see who would actually do the navigating and who would be along for the ride. Richard Collins drew the short straw, so he busied himself acquiring the appropriate Ordnance Survey maps of England and Scotland, so that he could plan their route. Also joining the party were John Edwards and Thomas Manning, to get their first real taste of what it would be like to be a flight engineer. Lastly, Federica handed out her version of clothing for flying. There were trousers and shirts for all, and short jackets to go over the shirt, all in a fawn colour, with the Sirius name embroidered on the chest of the shirt. Lastly, there were nice-looking black boots. She reasoned that she was definitely not going to try and fly in a skirt, so trousers it was.

"Are we ready?" Federica asked on the morning of the 2nd. "Let's tow the plane out of the hangar, fuel it up and get aboard."

"I'm ready," Will replied. "I have as much instrumentation as I can string."

"We're ready," Anastasia said. "Giovanna and I are along on this trip as passengers and observers."

"Ready when you are," George said, said after the tanks had been filled and they were all aboard. "When you take off, head towards the Parmoor Manor and we'll turn north there."

"Fine," Federica replied. "What about you, Richard?"

"We're fine," Richard replied as the spokesman for he and Stephen.

"I've got the log book filled out, so let's start up the engines then," Federica said. She went through the procedures and was gratified that the new engine starters worked well, and each engine started. She then ran through the controls and tested each, and when she was satisfied, she advanced the throttles and taxied out onto the runway. She told George to deploy the flaps, and then, after a last cycle through of the controls, she pushed the throttles all the way forward and accelerated down the runway. Well, before the end, she pulled back on the stick and they climbed out over the Chiltern Hills towards the West. Over the manor house of Parmoor, she stowed the flaps and then made the requisite turn to the north and headed towards Stokenchurch.

"This plane is fast," Richard said. "I'm not used to having to change maps so quickly. I think I should switch to a larger scale. We do have a nice day, though, no problems at all seeing landmarks. We should be coming up on Princes Risborough any minute, come two degrees to your left, and we should be lined up for Buckingham next."

"Richard gets the easy navigation," Stephen said from the back. "Wait until he has to take you across southern Sudan."

"I'm sure we'll manage," Federica said. "Shall we climb a little higher?"

"Why not," George said. "Will, how do the engines look?"

"Temperatures are coming up nicely, oil pressures are good, things seem to be fine at the moment," William replied. "Thomas, are you getting all these readings down?"

"Yes, Sir," Thomas said, then John read out another series of readings and Thomas noted those as well. They were taking them every five minutes. That might work out to be too many, but too many was better than too few.

"I see no change in airspeed," Federica said. "It looks like those changes you made to the engines are working well. I am having difficulty believing the airspeed. Are we really going that fast?"

"We'll find out when we get there," George said. "We know it's 320 miles airport to airport, so we just divide the distance by time. Which direction are the winds from, Richard?"

"According to the Met Office people, they are generally from the West, so crosswinds as opposed to head or tail winds."

Buckingham passed, as did Leicester, Derby, Sheffield, then Leeds, after Leeds, they passed over the Yorkshire moors, and landmarks became more terrain items than buildings, roads and railways. Not long after they passed Middleton-in-Teesdale, Richard suggested a turn of one degree to the left that he said would take them right over the Roman fort at Housesteads. Giovanna and Anastasia craned their necks to see out of the windows to the ground, and then Giovanna announced that she could see it and a small lake to the North.

"That will be Bromlee Lough," Richard said. "Next will be Jedburgh, and after that, we should start thinking about our descent into the East Fortune airfield."

"Richard, see if you can raise the airfield on the wireless," George suggested. Richard managed that and established that the wind was from the northeast, so he quickly set up the approach so that they could land upwind. Federica deployed the flaps, made her approach and landed. The field was grass, so the landing roll was much shorter than it would have been at Handy Cross, and Federica did not have to use the brakes until the last minute when she brought the plane to a stop by the main buildings. Air Force personnel came out to greet them, and George opened the door and lowered the stairs they had built in.

"Good morning, George," a familiar voice said, and George saw that it was Harry Anderson.

"Hello, Harry, I didn't know you were stationed here," George said.

"I'm not," Harry said. "I'm just visiting. I landed a short time ago and heard that you were coming in, so I waited for you. How was your flight?"

"Good," George replied. "Uneventful, and surprisingly short, we made it from Handy Cross in two hours and fifteen minutes from takeoff roll to stop. That means cruising speeds of over 120 knots, and the winds were mainly cross, so no tailwind."

"Really?" Harry said. "That's amazing, this is your wife's latest plane?"

"It is," George confirmed. "She modelled it after Sikorskii's behemoth."

"Any issues, oh, hello Will, I was just asking George if there were any issues on the way north," Harry said.

"I saw the temperature start to climb a little on the number two engine," William replied. "I'll have to take a look at that. Otherwise, the supercharging works wonderfully. I'm still having a difficult time with the speeds we're able to get; if I had not logged our departure time and arrival time, I would have said it was not possible. I think it's all the work that Fede put into streamlining and the extra power from the supercharged engines."

"Harry," Federica said as she climbed down from the plane. "So nice to see you again. When can we recruit you to be one of our pilots to take this plane to Cape Town?"

"In about six months," Harry replied. "If I'm not employed by then."

"Hello, Harry," Anastasia said when she left the plane. "Giovanna, do you remember Mr Anderson?"

"Yes, Mama, good morning, Mr Anderson," Giovanna said. "Mama told me that you spent a lot of time with us before you all went off to the war. I think I remember that."

"I did indeed, I'm surprised you remember me," Harry agreed. "Fede, George, this is Squadron Leader Barnes, he runs this station. Freddy, this is Federica and George Wheelwright, Anastasia, William and Giovanna McIntosh. I'll let the others introduce themselves."

"Thank you for letting us land," Federica said.

"It is our pleasure, Mrs Wheelwright," Freddy replied. "Do you need anything, petrol, or anything else?"

"No, thank you," Federica replied. "We've enough petrol to get us home, I was thinking of finding our way into Edinburgh and getting some lunch."

"It's only twenty miles," Freddy said. "Look, we've got a charabanc here, if you don't mind me riding with you, we could all go into Edinburgh and get lunch."

"That sounds delightful," Federica said. "Lunch will be our treat."

"I say, splendid," Freddy said. "While we go, tell me all about your plane, Harry tells me that you and your sister-in-law actually designed it."

Lunch in Edinburgh was fun, flying was most of the conversation, and Federica recruited Freddy as another pilot, also to start in about six months. On the trip back to the airfield, Freddy asked Giovanna when she was going to learn to fly.

"When I'm old enough to reach all the controls and pedals," she replied.

"Did you enjoy the flight up here?" he asked.

"It was jolly good, thank you," she replied. "We saw the Roman fort at Housesteads, and all the houses look so small from up there."

"They do, don't they," he agreed. "I have tried to get my wife to take a flight with me, but she says that she's too nervous to do so. I'll tell her that I met you today and that you flew all the way from Bucks to get here."

"I'm looking forward to the flight home," Giovanna said. "I think Auntie Fede is going to try and beat her time for getting here."

"How long did it take?" he asked.

"Two hours and fifteen minutes," she replied. "For 320 miles, that's quite fast, isn't it?"

"It is indeed," Freddy said. "I hope that she'll beat that time on the way home. Well, here we are. Are you sure there's nothing you need?"

"Thank you, Freddy, but I think we're set, Will, anything?" Federica asked.

"No," William said. "I need to keep an eye on the number two engine, but that may have just been the trip up here."

The return trip was uneventful until they passed Sheffield, then William, after a discussion with John and Thomas, asked Federica to shut down the number two engine.

"What's wrong?" she asked.

"It's running too hot," he explained. "We need to take a look at it when we land. You can increase the RPMs on the other engines a little, and we'll maintain our airspeed."

"I'll have to watch the rudder a bit," she said. "It'll be interesting to see how much the loss of the one engine makes to the balance of thrust. Have you any idea what the problem is?"

"Not yet," he admitted. "We'll have to take a look when we're on the ground."

"Is there a problem, Daddy?" Giovanna asked.

"Only a minor issue," William assured her. "That's why we're taking these flights, to find and solve all these little issues before Auntie Fede makes the long flight to Cape Town. We also have three other engines, and my tests show that if we have to, we can fly and land with only two."

"That's Derby," Federica said. "Not too far now, and we're still making very good time."

"I wonder how long it will be before we have to start really watching out for other planes?" George mused. "We've seen four other planes on this trip, but they were all well below us."

"I suppose that in time there will be a need to have some kind of traffic directions as we do now on the roads and railways," Federica said. "The wireless will help because then we can talk to people on the ground and they can tell us if it's safe to land and that there's no one else in the way."

"We've already adopted some of the sea rules," George remarked. "We've got navigation lights, port red, starboard green and white fore and aft, we use knots for airspeed and nautical miles for distance, just like ships, and the latest air navigation rules talk about main routes."

"I wonder if there'll be flight lanes overseas as there are shipping lanes?" she said.

"Possibly," he thought. "But, there may be mountains in the way of a direct path, and countries may not want planes flying over some places, like military camps and such."

"Prohibited areas, like the 71 the Air Navigation Act names," she laughed. "Well, here we are at Buckingham. We should start descending soon. Richard, which direction is the wind on the ground, and how do we land?"

"I've been on the wireless to Handy Cross and they tell me that the wind is from the west southwest, so come left fifteen degrees, we'll pass over Aylesbury, then turn to the west over Amersham and make a straight in approach from there," Richard instructed.

Once on the ground, William and the engineers immediately set about examining engine number two to find out why it was overheating. They removed the engine cowlings and started their examination. It was Thomas who noticed the crack in one of the water lines, so they had been losing coolant. Replacing the broken pipe would be simple enough, but that did not really answer the question: why had it cracked in the first place? They decided to remove the cowlings from engine number three and start it up, and watch it as it ran. William finally worked it out; the way the line was mounted, it vibrated, and obviously, vibrated enough that in time it would fatigue and crack. He shut down the number three engine, and then he and the others then sat down and worked out a better mounting system that would reduce the degree of vibration transmitted through the pipes. The design done, they went to the workshop at the back of the hangar and made up four new pipes and fixtures and then changed them out on all four engines. As far as this test went, there were no other mechanical issues to resolve, so they were happy with the flight.

George went back to his tables of times and distances for Africa to see what difference an air speed of 120 knots would make. Obviously, that would not always be possible, particularly if the wind were against them, so he needed to look at prevailing wind directions for the route to see how that would vary throughout the year. He had fuel consumption to think about as well as the wind. Higher fuel consumption might generate more horsepower and thereby higher speeds, but it came with the cost of weight. Their engines each needed about 200 lbs of petrol per hour, so a total of 800 lbs per hour for petrol and another 32 lbs per hour for oil, so for a flight of six hours, they would need almost 5,000 lbs of fuel and oil. A lot would depend on where the British set up the landing fields and what services would be at each. William had told George that he was especially concerned about fuel quality. During the war, the British planes had done well with the petrol provided by Shell, but the French had had problems when they had been unable to obtain the same fuel and had had to buy from America. The octane rating of the American petrol was lower than that from Shell, which sourced their oil in Sumatra. The lower octane content played havoc with engine performance, and that was something they could not afford. So much to think about!

The next trial flight was delayed a day because of bad weather. It had been hot and sunny, even reaching 80°F, then the wind direction changed, and there was rain and thunderstorms, with one poor soul in Finsbury Park even being struck by lightning and dying. Federica and

George spent the day discussing how they would accommodate delays due to weather when they started up the commercial service. Simple cancellations could lead to even more problems if the number of passengers on the cancelled flight exceeded the spare seats on the next flight. Then they got to discussing developments in the industry that had recently been reported upon.

"Did you see the piece on the Grahame-White Aero-Limousine?" George asked.

"I did," Federica confirmed. "Nice looking plane and well fitted out in the cabin, but too few passengers and too slow for us."

"What about the American Lawson aircraft?" he asked.

"Now that has promise," she said. "Twenty-six passengers is good, but again, it's slow, 100 mph is not what we want."

"The report on the Lawson craft did say that the seats were finished with green leather. I wonder what's under the leather," he said.

"Some kind of frame," she thought. "We really should experiment with seat design. Travelling for five to six hours at a time could be a numbing experience with a poor seat. I doubt that we would want the passengers wandering around too much, so better make the seats as comfortable as we can."

"I'll look into that," George promised. "Maybe I'll start with a wicker frame and then add cushions and a covering."

"I see that the report on Lawson said that they are planning a New York to San Francisco service. How far is that?" Federica wondered.

"I think about 2,600 miles," George replied. "So about a third of the way to Cape Town."

"When we planned out the route, where did we make pilot changes?" she asked.

"Well, we planned an overnight stop in Rome and one in Cairo, then the third night would be in Khartoum. There I had planned to turn the pilots around and have them fly the northbound home and let the Cape Town boys take the southbound," he explained.

"Is that too many hours of flying at one time?" she wondered.

"I don't think so," he said. "I flew more than that in the war, and I didn't have the luxury of hotels for the night. The flight times are such that the crews should get a good night's sleep at each stop."

"Providing they stay out of the bar," she said. "We'll have to make that a rule, no drinking and flying. I know you probably did a lot in the war, but now we will be flying passengers who have paid a fare and should consider their safety above all else. I think between each round trip between here and Khartoum, or Cape Town to Khartoum, we should allow a couple of days of complete rest."

"That's going to cost in extra crews," he said.

"True," she agreed. "But we'll factor it into the fares."

"Well, perhaps tomorrow the weather will have improved enough that we can fly to Paris," he said.

The rain did indeed pass through fairly quickly, and behind the front, it was clear and dry and much cooler, so the trip to Paris was back on. The two navigators drew lots to see who would do the way-finding this time, and it was Stephen who won. He had maps ready of England and France, and the latest weather forecasts. They had been keeping track of the AT&T and HPTL flights to see how many had to be delayed or cancelled because of weather. So far, September had been a good flying month, and the prospects looked good for an easy crossing. The actual distance to the Le Bourget airport was only 244 miles, so less than it had been to Scotland. They all assembled at the airfield at six in the morning and got the plane ready for the flight. George had made arrangements with the Customs Service to have an officer present when they departed and returned, which would save them the necessity of putting down at Hounslow Heath, then making the ridiculously short hop over the Handy Cross. All the officer wanted to know was when they would be returning. George promised to send a telegraph as soon as they knew to give him at least two hours' notice.

"All set?" Federica asked.

"All set," came the reply from each of the others in the plane. Anastasia and Giovanna would not be along on this trip, Giovanna had school to attend and Anastasia had some issues with the Sirius Car company to sort out. She did, however, ask them to take along some parts that had been requested by their French subsidiary, so the plane was loaded with crates, giving them a pseudo passenger load of 30 people, with a crew of 10. The crew numbers were well over the expected norm, but they were taking as many as they could, both to simulate a full load and to learn as much as they could about the way the plane flew, and what would be the navigation issues. Federica started up each of the engines and then taxied out onto the runway. The takeoff roll was longer than it had been when they had gone to Scotland, but now the plane was much heavier than it had been then.

They took off towards the west, then quickly turned and came around to aim themselves at Paris. It was a clear day, and they had a good view of the coast before crossing the English Channel and making their way over to France. The Channel crossing was short; it only took thirty minutes, and then they were crossing the French coast over Dieppe. From Dieppe, they followed the main roads, which now all led to Paris. Federica used the wireless to call ahead and talked to the people on the ground at Le Bourget. Fortunately, she spoke French well, which made life easier, but did raise the question in her mind of how countries were going to handle communications with aircraft from other countries. Pilots could not be expected to know half a dozen languages, so perhaps a standard would be set by international agreement. When they landed, they were met by French customs staff and by their own staff from their French factory. The customs officers quickly cleared the crates of parts, and then the question, what was next.

"We go on to Istres," Federica suggested.

"I think so," George agreed. "It's only 8:30 in the morning, so we have time still. Say three and a half hours to Istres, that gets us there just before lunch, we buy some lunch, fuel up and leave at one thirty and are back at Handy Cross at 8:00 tonight, it will still be light, the sun sets at 7:20, so there'll still be light enough to see by."

"That's cutting it fine, don't you think?" Federica said.

"Maybe," George agreed. "But, let's see how we do, we can always stop here for the night on the way back, if we don't think we can make it in time."

"All right," Federica agreed. "But, if I don't think there'll be light enough at Handy Cross, we will be stopping here for the night."

"Fine, let's get going then," George said. "We've filled up with petrol, and all the gauges looked good on the way over here. Stephen, any mountains between here and Istres?"

"Just south of Saint-Étiènne, the ground rises to about 3,700 feet, but otherwise there's little to be concerned about," Stephen said.

"Good, all set?" Federica asked. "George, you take this flight."

"All set," George said. "You know, the barometers we have are useful for indicating altitude, but they don't take into account where the ground actually is, so we could be happily flying along in Africa at 10,000 feet only to run into a mountain, we need something better, particularly when we're close to the ground."

"I know," Federica agreed. "Let's look into that when we get home."

Without the crates of parts, the takeoff roll was much shorter than it had been early that morning, and they were soon off on their way to the Mediterranean coast. As they flew south, the conversation turned to recent long-distance flights and what had gone wrong. With the Farman plane over Africa, the problems had been with a propeller, starting with overheating, then eventually cracked bolts and a loose propeller. After the engine had been shut the second engine had started to overheat, and they had had to put down on a beach and had eventually been picked up. That led to a long discussion about bolts and why they cracked, was it incorrect tensioning, or a latent defect in the bolts that showed itself with stress, or even the incorrect kind of bolt. The conclusion was that they just did not have enough information to form a definite opinion, but that they should use the best bolts they could find for the propellers out of an abundance of caution; bolts were cheap compared to propellers or even the plane. The discussion of potential latent defects in the bolts led to other discussions about detection of such defects. Perhaps X-ray pictures would show cracks or inclusions in the bolts? There were a number of papers that had been recently published that dealt with the examination of metals and metal parts, with some talking about using the Coolidge tube for the detection of defects up to 55 mm deep. That would be more than adequate for the examination of bolts, so the consensus was that they would look into that.

Conversation then switched to the present, and Federica remarked on how pretty the French countryside looked from the air.

"It does," George agreed. "But you should see the mess that was made on the Western Front, there are artillery craters and trenches all over the place, it'll be years before much of that land is usable again."

"I'm glad you were in the air and not down in a trench," Federica said. "I can't imagine what conditions were like in the trenches."

"From what I saw, it was really bad," George said. "We took pictures from the air, of our side and the other side, it just amazed me how far the trench systems ran and how much work was put into digging them. It didn't help when the influenza epidemics hit, conditions were awful, wet, damp, muddy, rats and fleas everywhere, and the men were just exhausted, so probably a breeding ground for all sorts of disease."

"What a waste," Federica sighed. "So, Stephen, how long to Istres?"

"Another thirty minutes," he replied. "I've had them on the radio and they told me that the wind is out of the Southeast at eight knots, so we should be able to go straight in and not have to overshoot and turn over the Med to come back in."

"Good," she said. "Take us down when you're ready, George."

"I'll wait a few minutes, then drop down to 5,000 feet, then I'll line us up for the approach. Any landmarks that will help Stephen?"

"When we clear this line of hills, you should be able to see it straight ahead," Stephen replied.

"I have it," George said. "Let's go down a little lower and make our approach." They touched down seven minutes later and taxied over to the buildings. French military aviators came out to meet them, intrigued by the size of the plane.

"*Bonjour,*" Federica said as she climbed down onto the ground.

"*Bonjour,*" an officer replied. "*Je suis Colonel Montclair, bievenue à Istres.*" Federica thanked the colonel for his welcome, introduced herself and everyone else and explained that they wanted to buy petrol and some lunch. The colonel surprised them by telling them that Philippe had called earlier that day to let him know of their visit, so he had lunch ready for them, all he wanted in return was to be shown around the aircraft. Federica was happy to oblige and took the colonel and several of his officers on a guided tour of the plane, starting on the outside, then on board. The colonel was intrigued by the design of the plane, and it took quite a bit of explaining by both Federica and George that the designer was, in fact, Federica.

"Mon Dieu," was all the colonel could say. He was fascinated by the plane, and over lunch, he asked question after question, all of which Federica or George answered, depending on who was not eating at that moment. Finally, Federica made their excuses to the colonel and said that they should be leaving as they hoped to be back in England before dark. He understood and extended an invitation to visit at any time. She did dictate a telegram and asked the colonel to send it to the Customs officer in England. The plane had been refuelled while they were at lunch, but Federica still checked the fuel levels and walked around the plane looking for anything amiss. Finding nothing, she waved farewell to the French aviators and climbed aboard. Stephen Walker was to navigate back, and Federica said that she would take the controls.

"Ready?" she asked of the rest in the plane. "Good, let's start, engine number one." She pressed the starter button and was gratified that all worked as it should. It would have been embarrassing in the extreme to have failures in front of the French audience. She started the rest of the engines, then waved to the ground people who pulled out the wheel chocks. Then they were on their way. Federica taxied to the end of the runway, then took off towards the sea, turning when she had reached a suitable altitude to head back towards Paris, then the Channel. Stephen gave her a heading, and she set her compass accordingly and climbed out to their cruising altitude. They were enjoying afternoon sea breezes that were blowing on shore, so started out with a tailwind, which would help with the travel time.

"Shall we try a little higher?" George suggested.

"Why not?" Federica agreed. "Shall we go up to 12,000 feet?"

"Let's try it and see," George said. They climbed up, and Will took down readings from the various gauges.

"It's a little colder up here," he said. "I suppose as we go higher, it'll get colder still, just as well you insulated this Fede."

"I just did what Sikorskii had done," she said. "When will we lose the sea breeze?"

"I would guess very soon," Stephen said. "This mountain range will block winds coming in from the Med. Can we get a guess of ground speed?"

"Difficult to do without markers," George said. "Let's see if we can spot a railway line and then count the telegraph poles."

"At the speed we're going, that's going to be a challenge," Will laughed.

"Maybe, but if we try slowing a little and then speed up, perhaps we can see the difference in how fast the poles seem to pass," George said.

"We'll try, Stephen. When do we see the first railway line?" Federica asked.

"We'd have to detour from a direct route to do that," Stephen said.

"Why don't we take a test flight in a few days' time and fly down the Great Western Railway and time travel between stations?" Federica suggested. "We can get from the railway the distance between stations, then we can also look at how fast the telegraph poles seem to be passing and then establish some guides for ground speed."

"I'll look into that," Richard said.

They flew on, passing over Clermont-Ferrand, then did a quick check of time and concluded that they had more than enough daylight left to get to Handy Cross, so set a course for Orléans and Rouen, bypassing Paris. Across the Channel, they saw the Brighton Pier, then looked for other landmarks to confirm their compass heading. Over Farnborough, they started down and crossed the Thames just outside Henley, flying at about 5,000 feet. From there, it was a short trip into Handy Cross and they landed to the west, into the setting sun.

"Well, that was very good," Federica said as they shut down the engines.

"It was," George agreed. "Will, any issues of note on the engines?"

"Not that I can see," he replied. "We'll look through the numbers and see if anything crops up, but so far all looks well. I wonder if we shouldn't drain the petrol tanks, then see how much we used between Istres and here. They were filled at Istres, so we should get a sense of gallons per hour, that I can quickly convert to pounds, so that we can start to get some information on fuel loads."

"Let's do that tomorrow," Federica suggested. "All I want now is a hot bath."

"We'll take care of the petrol tomorrow," Richard promised. "Stephen and I can do it with the help of Thomas and John."

"Good, I'll leave you to it then," Federica said. "Can I leave you to set the chocks and cover the engine inlets?"

"Of course," Richard said.

"I'll deal with Mr Single," George said, referring to the Customs officer.

"What's next?" George asked Federica as they drove home from Handy Cross.

"Apart from your Great Western Railway check?" she asked.

"I was thinking of perhaps Rome, Brindisi or even Athens," he said.

"Let's do Rome first and see how that goes," she suggested. "Where can we get good weather charts for the Med?"

"We should ask the Met Office and perhaps ask Philippe to contact the French met people," he suggested.

"I think that's going to be one of the biggest issues we'll have, getting good weather information," she said. "I doubt that there's very much south of Cairo. Have you any idea if the RAF plans to have petrol at any of the strips they create up the Nile?"

"I believe they plan some stations with petrol, oil and water and some strips that are essentially emergency strips with just water," he replied.

"Do we need to provide our own petrol?" she asked.

"We'll have to ask the RAF whether or not they plan to put in a system to replenish stocks," he said. "We might think about putting our own lorries in some places to make refuelling easier."

"How do we get the lorries there?" she asked.

"We can probably use the railway as far south as Assuan, after that, I'm not sure," he said. "It may just be easier to drive them there."

"Who do we have to see about getting permission to operate an airline across Egypt?" she asked.

"I'll check," he said. "So, next trip, Rome?"

"I think so," she said. "We should find out if Franco needs anything so that we can fly there faster than sending it by sea."

"Okay, we're home. If you want to go and have a bath, I'll start dinner," he said.

"You mean, you'll talk to Christine about dinner," she laughed.

"No," he said. "I told her that we weren't sure when we'd be back, so to go home at five and I would get dinner for us when we came in."

"That was considerate of you," she said. "Just don't give me any army bully beef."

Rome wasn't built in a day

The European nations took quite different approaches to the new mode of transport, all supporting except the United Kingdom. In 1920, in the words of Winston Churchill, then Secretary of State for War and Air, the civil aviation industry had to stand by itself. That led to the collapse of all the early attempts to set up the fledgling air transport business. The route from Cairo to Cape Town was finally flown by Lt.-Col. Pierre von Ryneveld and Flt. Lt. C. J. Quinton Brand and Mr Burton, a mechanic, replaced during the attempt by Flight Sergeant E. F. Newman of the RAF and Mr F. W. Sheratt of Rolls-Royce, with support from the South African government. They actually used three aircraft, as two crashed on the way. Another attempt by a Times-sponsored team had ended in a crash, allowing the South African team to overtake them in Tanganyika. Another attempt in a Handley Page DH14 sponsored by the Daily Telegraph had also crashed. In February of 1920, the first Control Tower was built at the Croydon airport and pilots, who had them, used their radios to call in and identify themselves.

The weather did not cooperate for the balance of 1919, so Federica and George applied themselves to the business of running their enterprises, all of which seemed to be adapting well to the new era post the Great War. Cars were back in demand, but Federica saw problems in the future as the pent-up demand caused by the war was satisfied, causing early confidence in the economy that would be replaced by a drop in demand in the later years. So, she and George sat down and put plans together that would let them weather the storm that she saw coming. The secret would be not to expand by investing, but to husband cash and look for ways to better run the various businesses to satisfy the short-term increase in demand. Federica was confident that they could put together a plan to run an air service to the Cape, but was growing less confident that there would be any support from the government. All they heard from the Air Ministry was negative, so if they were to succeed, it would have to be off their own bat. That did not preclude them from continuing the trials of the plane, to prove its capabilities and give them greater experience of flying something so large. They did achieve one major milestone, and that was to get the aircraft certified for airworthiness one brilliantly sunny but cold day in early January of 1920. The Ministry inspector and test pilot came to Handy Cross and did his examinations and made his test flight, and pronounced that the craft was very airworthy. They were also issued a registration number, or really a series of letters.

"Did you see this item about *The Times* charter for the Cairo to Cape Town route?" George asked Federica.

"Them and the *Daily Telegraph* flight and the South African sponsored flight, the race was on," she said.

"But it looks like crashes are the order of the day," he said.

"I did, I wonder what caused the crash of the Vimy at Tabora?" she asked. "Their route of flight was interesting: Manston, Villemont, Lyons, Istres, Rome, Naples, Catania, Malta, Tripoli, Benghazi, Sollum, then Cairo. It took them from the 24th of January until the 3rd of February just to get to Cairo. That hardly bodes well for an effective route from London to Cape Town. As I recall, after Cairo it was Luxor, Assuan, Khartoum, Jebelein, Mongalla, Nimule, Jinja, Kisumu, Mwanza, then Tabora. I wonder what took them so long to get to Tabora; they only got there late in the month."

"Then there was this, the South Africans sponsored a plane and another Vimy was tried until it crashed at Kurusku, just short of Wadi Halfa on the 11th of February," George said. "Their route was a little different: Brooklands, Turin, Taranto, Sollum and Cairo, then up the Nile to Kurusku. Then they got another Vimy that was flown from Cairo to Wadi Halfa, Khartoum, Mongalla, Kisumu, Shirati, Abercorn, Livingstone and Bulawayo for the next crash. Then the South Africans lent them a de Havilland D.H.9 and flew that from Bulawayo to Pretoria, Bloemfontein and Beaufort West to Cape Town, arriving on the 20th of this month, 45 days in all, quicker to go by boat. So the route has been flown all the way, and we won't be the first to the Cape. Knighthoods were handed out to van Ryneveld and Brand, but I haven't seen any mention of what they might have done for the mechanics."

"We may not be the first to fly all the way, but I'll wager that ours will be the first plane that goes all the way, with no crashes. I wonder what it is about the Vimy that three of them crashed, two on takeoff, how do you crash a plane on takeoff," she wondered. "Their route is interesting, dropping down to North Africa on the shortest overwater crossing, I still think our proposed route is shorter, and didn't I read that Cairo to Khartoum was at night, I suppose cooler then."

"I wonder what the problem was with the Daily Telegraph Handley Page, why did it crash after leaving Assuan?" he mused.

"I suppose that we'll see some kind of report in time," she said.

"Do we continue?" he asked.

"I was thinking of this as a commercial venture, not a record-breaking attempt," she said. "So let someone else take the glory of being the first to actually get there, no matter how many machines you break up on the way, I want something to be far more reliable. Can we get accident reports to find out why these crashes occurred?"

"I'm already looking into that," he assured her. "But, according to *Flight*, it was engine trouble."

"What engines does the Vimy have?" she asked.

"The latest version, which I presume they used to fly Cairo to the Cape, has Rolls-Royce Eagle 360 hp, two of them, very reliable engines normally," he replied. "The report in *Flight* of the *Times* team was that it was magneto problems, and the report in a later issue of Flight about the van Ryneveld flight was underpowered for the altitude and the temperature at Bulawayo. Lt Col van Ryneveld also reported all kinds of weather issues on the flights, from thunderstorms over the Med to sandstorms over Egypt, so we'd have to be alert. The crash near Wadi Halfa was because of engine overheating, and it seems that coolant leakage has been a problem. I read a report that a radiator drain tap vibrated to the open position, and they lost coolant. Perhaps we should look at air-cooled radials instead of in-line water-cooled."

"So no wonder they had to put down somewhere," she said.

"No wonder, it also points to the potential advantage we would have with the four engines, unless all have the same fundamental problem, we can shut down one with only a small reduction in performance," he commented. "It would really be of use to get complete trip reports with the crashes as well. I'm getting what we can from Flight, but I'll look to see if there are official reports as well. Interesting to note that the van Ryneveld trip was held up at Victoria Falls because of heavy rain. I wonder why they picked the rainy season to go. Why fly to Southern Africa in the middle of their summer. September or May would have been better months."

"That may be true, but if we are to offer a commercial service, we would have to operate all months of the year, not just those months when the weather was more clement," she said. "We really do need some more speed if we're going to succeed."

"There is another problem as far as commercial ventures go," he said. "The British government and the Egyptians still haven't come to any agreement as to who controls commercial air traffic."

"I was reading something about that," she said. "I read that there are moves afoot to try and get a monopoly for Vickers. If that succeeds, then we're out for any route that takes us across Egypt."

"I also read that the French and the Germans are making noises about wanting to fly over Egypt as well," he added.

"So, the route may be flyable, even for us, but politics may get in the way of actually set up a company," she said. "So much for my naive dreams of just picking a booking agent, hotels and providing ground support, it may all come to nought while politicians argue about who actually controls what. Still, for now, let's press on and at least prove to ourselves that we can fly the route."

"So, Rome the day after tomorrow?" he asked.

"If this weather holds," she replied. "But I think we'll go to Firenze instead, then Franco won't have to motor down to Rome to meet us."

"What do we do, fly to Orly, then Istres, then Firenze?" he asked.

"That's what I thought," she confirmed. "I thought we'd hug the coast from Istres to Nice, then cut over the sea to Livorno, then go inland to Firenze."

"We should find out if Franco needs any parts," he said.

"I was going to send him a telegram telling him that we were coming and asking if he needed anything," she said.

"This is so much more enjoyable than flying in Flanders, wondering who might be trying to shoot you down," he said. "One thing I think we should get when we do fly down Africa is some clothes, light clothes for the heat and perhaps something to wear on board for when it gets cold. I thought the insulation did quite well on our runs to Scotland and the Med, so perhaps we won't need too much, certainly not Sidcot suits."

"I wanted to stay away from open cockpits," she said. "They create a huge amount of turbulence and drag. I know some pilots like them so that if there is a problem, they can get out quickly, but that hardly engenders confidence with paying passengers."

"Quite," he said. "Personally, I like flying enclosed, no prop wash, no oil spray, not freezing to death as I climb higher."

"Have you looked at the weather forecast?" she asked.

"It's looking good early next week, supposed to be warm and dry, even hot, so should be a good time to fly," he said. "I got data from Will and we've been burning less fuel than we thought, so our range is extended, we can do about 550 nautical miles and still have some reserve of petrol left, so we could do here to Istres in one go, if we don't have headwinds. If we do, then we should plan a stop

Federica heard back from Franco, and there were parts that he asked for, so she had Anastasia box them up, ready for shipment. The day they decided to go, George said that he would stay at home and trust in John Edwards and Thomas Manning to keep an eye on the engines and record data as they went. Both navigators, Stephen and Richard, wanted to be along, and Richard drew the straw for the duty of navigating to Florence. They all assembled at Handy Cross at six in the morning, met with Mr Roberts from His Majesty's Customs Service, called into Croydon with their intentions, and were soon off with George piloting the plane. Their route took them straight from Handy Cross to Istres, a distance of 538 nautical miles, well within the limit of their safe flight. In the event that they felt that headwinds were an issue, then they would stop at Clermont-Ferrand, which had a hard runway and had petrol.

"Coming up on Clermont," Richard said. "Fuel levels look good, we've actually got a bit of a tailwind, so we're doing about 140 knots over the ground. Should be in Istres in just over an hour."

"I'll see if I can raise them on the wireless," Stephen said. "No, not yet, I'll try again in thirty minutes."

"It all looks so peaceful down there," Federica commented to George as they flew over the French countryside.

"I think this part of France was well away from the fighting," he said. "The Germans bombed Paris, but never got this far south."

"How far is it from Istres to Florence?" she asked Richard.

"About 275 nautical miles," he replied. "So, with no headwinds, two and a half hours."

"Good, that should have us there by tea time," she said. "We'll stay overnight in Florence and go home tomorrow."

"I've got Istres," Stephen said. "They tell me that the winds are light off the Med, so recommend dropping down over the Camargue and coming in from the west."

"Okay, I'll set that up," Richard said. "Come right three degrees, that should take us right to where we should turn east and descend into the airport."

"I see the Med," George said.

"Time to turn east and start down," Richard said.

"I see the field," George said. It only took him a few more minutes, and they were on the ground. The same colonel who had met them before came out to greet them and offer lunch and petrol. Federica paid for the petrol and checked how much was loaded. She knew they did not need full tanks for the two and a half hours to Florence, but better to be safe than trying to find somewhere to land because fuel had run out.

Federica flew them from Istres to Florence, following the coast of the Mediterranean until they got to Cannes, then cutting straight across the sea to Pisa.

"Did you see that the FA banned women from using any FA football field?" she asked George.

"I did see that," he confirmed. "Does that put an end to our factory teams?"

"It does, rather," she said. "We've nowhere to really play, except school pitches. I knew there would be a lame excuse for a ban, but I never expected them to say something as idiotic as it would affect women's health and their ability to have babies. If anything, it improved it because the players were generally quite physically fit. I think the real reason is that the women's teams were drawing bigger crowds than the men's teams, can't have men being shown up by mere women."

"Not everyone is as comfortable as we are with women who are talented and capable," George said.

"That's right, Mrs Wheelwright," Thomas piped up from the back. "The stories I heard in France, listening to some of them, it's amazing that some women even know how to cook, let alone manage the household money."

"Well, now we can vote, at least some of us, so watch out," she joked.

"How long before we get a woman MP?" George asked.

"Well, we could have had one if Markiewicz had taken her seat," Federica said. "That would have been interesting, an Irish Nationalist in Parliament."

"Look at that boat down there," George said, changing the subject. "It looks as if it's in trouble; it's listing badly."

"Let me see if I can get anyone on the wireless," Stephen said. "I've got someone, but it sounds like Italian to me."

"Let me talk to them," Federica said. She reported what they could see and gave their best guess for position, then George dropped down and circled the ship. They could see lifeboats being launched and the crew making haste to abandon ship before they went down with it. He waggled the wings a couple of times and then flew on towards Pisa.

"The Italian navy has sent a ship out to look for the survivors," she said. "It'll be a few hours before they get there. I wonder if the crew had enough lifeboats?"

"I thought after Titanic that commercial ships and freighters were all supposed to have enough lifeboats for everyone on board?" John asked.

"Supposed to and do are quite different," Federica said. "I've no idea what the registration of that ship was, but not all countries will be that diligent in ensuring that there are enough lifeboats. That brings up a point, what do we have in the way of life rafts and life jackets?"

"Nothing at the moment," George said. "But, you're right, to get to Alexandria, we're going to have to cross the Med, so we should have something."

"I'll look into that when we get back," John said. "I can't swim, so I want something I can hang on to."

"It seems to me that life rafts are cumbersome after they are inflated, and how do you get them inflated if the plane is in the water, and isn't there something we can do for each person?" Federica wondered. "If you would look into that as well, John, we need to take some precautions. I wonder what Alcock and Brown did when they flew the Atlantic. Oh, and I think we should put a first air box somewhere in the main cabin."

"There's Pisa," George said. "I can see the tower, so Florence shouldn't be far now."

"I wonder what the people on the ground think when this great big lumbering giant flies overhead," Federica said.

"Probably wonder how it stays in the air," George said. "I know I did until I read all that was to be had about flight. Now I understand the theory, but it is still a marvel to me each time I see a plane of this size actually fly."

"I suppose in time planes will get even bigger and even this behemoth will look quite small," she said. "When we do fly over Africa, should we take a firearm?"

"Definitely," he replied. "If we were to have to put down in the Sudan or parts of Central Africa, we might have marauders to contend with, or even wild animals, so a rifle and a pistol, and a Very pistol in case we have to shoot off flares, either in the water or in the wastes of Africa."

"So much to think about," she said. "Look, there's Florence. Stephen, can you raise the airfield yet?"

"I can, but again it's Italian," he replied.

"Let me talk to them," she said. "Right, George, they say to land towards the northwest, so come around to the south side of the city and we'll go in that way."

"I wonder how long before Florence decides that planes flying right over the old city is not a good idea," Richard said, coming forward and staring out of the windscreen at the city.

"If I were them, I'd build an airport somewhere that had better approaches," Federica said. "Nice landing, Dear."

"Thank you," George said. "It looks like they want us to go over there."

"Buon giorno," an Italian official said as they climbed down the stairs onto the hard stand.

"Buon giorno," Federica replied, then she launched into a stream of Italian that left the rest of her crew just gaping. They were joined by Franco, who had come to meet them and to collect the parts they had brought for him. They unloaded the parts and Franco attended to customs quickly, then he escorted them to the cars that he had brought to take them to the house. There, they were allotted rooms and then given dinner. They slept that night and then took the next day off to visit the sights of Florence, new to all except George and Federica. On the return journey home, they decided to stop at Clermont-Ferrand, which was a better division of distance than Istres. After picking up petrol there, they flew straight back to Handy Cross, then sat down to analyse all the data they had gathered.

"So, on the way there, we averaged a ground speed of 130 knots and on the way back, 110 knots, that must be due to the wind conditions," Federica said as she looked at the numbers. "What does fuel look like?"

"We burned 180 lbs per hour of petrol and 21 lbs per hour of oil per engine," John replied. "The burn rate was a little higher coming back, but then the engine rpms were up a little to counter the slight headwind."

"Do you think that burn rate will change as the engines get older?" George asked.

"That I don't know," John admitted. "And data from the war experience is hard to find. We do know that we should look to overhaul our engines every 150 hours or so, so if it's 57 hours flying to the Cape, then I would keep spare engines there in case, but at the end of each return flight, swap them out and overhaul the recently flown engines at our leisure."

"Before we make our next trip, would you pull these engines apart and give them a good going over," Federica said. "Take measurements as you go and tell us what is wearing and how fast."

"I've been reviewing routes again," George said to Federica about a week later. "I think it would be safe for us to do Hounslow Heath to Paris, Marseille, Rome, Athens, Cairo, then set off up the Nile. Given no wind then that would be one and a half hours to Paris, stop in Paris say for one and a half hours, then three hours to Marseille, stop overnight in Marseille, then on to Rome, three hours, one and a half there, then five to Athens, overnight there, then another five and a quarter to Cairo. If we were to encounter severe headwinds that would slow us considerably, then alternate landing spots at Brindisi and Sollum."

"The longest overwater would be?" she asked.

"Athens to Cairo, actually Crete to Cairo as we would fly over the island," he replied.

"So we need to establish relationships with hotels in Marseille, Rome and Athens and Cairo to start with," she said. "Then look at what might be available in Brindisi and Sollum. From Cairo, then what?"

"I think Cairo to Assuan, fuel up there, then on to Khartoum," he replied. "Just over four hours to Assuan and then another four plus to Khartoum."

"So, lunch at Assuan, what's there?" she asked.

"There is the Thomas Cook Cataract Hotel," he replied. "It serves those who journey up the Nile by steamer. By all reports, it is a most elegant place, so would be a good stop for us."

"What about Khartoum?" she asked.

"There is the Grand Hotel run by the Sudanese Railway," he replied. "Another hotel that would serve us well."

"And south of Sudan?" she asked.

"Then it gets a little more spread out in terms of landing places, I'd make a stop at Mongalla, then overnight at Kisumu, stop at Tabora and overnight at Livingstone, then overnight at Pretoria, stop in Bloemfontein and make the last run to Cape Town," he replied.

"So, seven nights in hotels in all, quicker than the boat, but will it be quick enough to command the fare?" she wondered.

"I was thinking that we'd switch crews in Khartoum," he said. "Have one crew fly from here to Khartoum and back, and another Cape Town to Khartoum and cross over there."

"Hotels in Kisumu and Livingstone?" she asked.

"In Livingstone, there's the Victoria Falls Hotel, a railway hotel built to see the bridge over the river, in Kisumu, there's the Kisumu Hotel, largely serves the railway and the lake steamers," he replied. "In Jo'burg take your pick, there's quite a few there, maybe we should try and develop a relationship with one."

"Why not get Will's family from Kimberley to organise that for us," she suggested. "Not much point in having family in South Africa if you can't call on them to help."

"So, what do we need to still address with the plane?" he asked.

"The seats and the toilet," she said. "I'm not satisfied that I would want to sit for five hours in a wicker chair, plus I found that the seats we have on the cockpit weren't the most comfortable after a while, plus we still need to decide exactly how we will do the toilet and the tanks required."

"Let's give the seat problem to Andrew Coates and see what he can come up with, and the toilet challenge to Mr White," George suggested.

"Good idea," she agreed.

The engine overhauls showed some wear in predictable areas, and Will went off the think to see what he could do in the way of metals and lubrication. Andrew Coates came up with a seat suggestion in a remarkably short time, but then admitted that he had been working on the issue for some time and had been studying what had been done for trams, buses and trains. The train journeys could be the longest, and he knew from his own experience that sitting in one place for hours on end got tedious, to say the least. His design was novel. He had wooden slats that were slightly rounded at one end, and they were grouped together to form a natural curve with the highest point behind where the knees would be, and falling off sharply in front of the knees and sloping gradually back behind the knees. The back of the seat was actually hinged to the base, so that it could be tilted back and forth and reach up to the shoulders of an average man, providing good back support. He had a prototype made, and the whole of the Sirius flight staff tried it out. He said that for the actual ones for the plane, he would cover in some light fabric with a little padding. Federica had to agree that at first trial felt more comfortable than the wicker chairs. The new seats were a little heavier than the wicker, but Federica felt that they would not seriously impact the passenger load. George wanted to know how easy they were to make and if they could do it in the body shop. Andrew assured him that they could and had already worked out a production scheme that would mean a seat built in only twenty minutes, given pre-cut and shaped slats, and side and back frames. He was seriously considering a similar design for all their cars, vans and lorries, the only difference being the use of leather to cover them. He had thought about steel springs inside a cushion, but had decided against that. The furniture industry had been using steel springs for well over 80 years, so their use was well understood. Cushioning materials were also changing, but horsehair was still probably the most used.

Mr White came up with a solution for the toilet. He formed a bowl from stainless steel and had two tanks made, also of thin-gauge stainless steel, one for flushing water and one for flushed materials. He also worked out how to have valves easily accessible from the outside of the plane to empty and fill the respective tanks. His flush mechanism included a non-return valve for the flushed material that he thought would be highly desirable. The whole system was quite expensive, and the bowl and tanks took some making. In fact, he made twenty bowls before he was satisfied, scrapping the rest, so Federica wondered about the practicality of including it on any future aircraft builds.

"Are we ready to make our next flight?" Federica asked George.
"This time to Athens," she replied.
"Could we make Rome in one day and not stay in Marseille?" she asked.
"Still stop at Istres for petrol, but then on to Rome," he thought. "Then it's a shorter run to Athens, stop in Brindisi before flying over the Ionian Sea."
"I thought Franco could run down from Florence and arrange a hotel in Rome," she said. "In Athens, where do we stay?"
"Thomas Cook will make a booking for us at the Grande Bretagne," he replied. "I was wondering if we should risk taking a reporter with us."
"A reporter?" she asked. "Which paper?"

"Flight," he said. "It might be beneficial to us to get some publicity about the proposed route and the plane itself."

"I remember the first newspaper article written about our cars," she said. "Not the thing designed to make me benevolent to the press."

"He doesn't have to know who designed the craft, and none of us will tell, we'll just leave the question unanswered and let him decide himself what he thinks of the plane," George suggested.

"Have any of the other long flights taken reporters along?" she asked.

"Not that I'm aware of," he said. "I also rather think that whoever we may persuade to come with us would style themselves a contributor rather than a reporter."

"Who do we take on this trip?" she asked.

"I think as before, but we should ask Will and Nastia if they wish to come," he said.

"I feel guilty about flitting off to parts afield and leaving Nastia and Will the job of running Sirius and the other businesses," she said. "I must talk to Nastia about that and perhaps devote a little more time to the mundane and daily and less to the romantic notions."

"I was thinking that when we do make our final attempt to the Cape that we try and go straight there with no side trips, but on the return, perhaps spend at least a day at Victoria Falls, stop in Kenya to see animals and Cairo to see the pyramids," he suggested.

"I like that idea," she said. "I saw in an advertisement the other day that Thomas Cook is offering trips to Assuan by rail or steamer. Perhaps we might suggest to them that a trip that is flying down from Cairo to Assuan and then taking the steamer back to Cairo might be an adventure people would undertake."

"Along those lines, perhaps train to Victoria Falls from Cape Town and fly back," he said.

"But first, we need to prove we can fly there and prove to ourselves that we can do it without draining the purse," she said. "We have spent enough already on this venture; it is time for us to add to the coffers, not keep taking."

"What do you suggest?" he asked.

"Well, we have the foundry that is doing well, Abbey and Windsor do well, Sirius has exceeded my dreams, but perhaps we could add electrical items to our companies," she suggested. "Perhaps all the parts needed for cars, we could produce and sell to others as well as Sirius."

"So, starting motors, generators, alternators, lights, switches, and such?" he asked. "Like Lucas?"

"I think we could do better than them," she said. "We have our own Sirius to supply and we could learn how best to make motors, generators and the like, and then improve on them and how we make them, and perhaps also sell motors for other industries including our own machine shops where I would like to see the back of all those belts coming down from the ceiling, and replace them with electric motors at each machine. Those belts terrify me. I can imagine someone being caught up in one and injured."

"Then we should look to modernise our machine shop," he agreed.

Federica sought out Anastasia and sat down with her.

"Nastia, I have been selfish and have spent time and money on my hobby and have neglected my duties," she confessed.

"I want to see us succeed in the air as much as you," Anastasia said. "I have no regrets or complaints about the time and money you have devoted to the air."

"Thank you," Federica said. "But it is time I spent some more of my energies on enterprises that will give us more of a return in the immediate, not in some far-off day."

"You have a plan, I know that look," Anastasia said.

"I am proposing that we start a company to make electric motors, generators, alternators, switches, and the like that may be used in cars and in other machines," Federica said.

"As Lucas does?" Anastasia asked.

"Similar," Federica agreed. "If we succeed, then we can use products in our own cars and sell to others, and I would also like to make motors of a size to replace all those belts in the machine shop. I hate those things."

"That would be good," Anastasia said. "The belts constrain how we lay out the shop, with a motor on each machine, we could place them as we wish to make a better pattern of work in the shop."

"I have identified a building in Taplow, not far from the station and well away from the river and any flooding that may occur, that would be quite suitable and would like to purchase it and modify for our needs," Federica said. "The housings for motors and generators we would make ourselves in the new part of the foundry that makes small parts and we would employ people, mainly women I think, to wind the armatures and assemble the motors, we need to find engineers who can design the motors and someone to manage the company."

"You have already thought of a name?" Anastasia asked.

"I had thought of something like Burnham Sirius Armatures, but realised that that would be too close to BSA and Birmingham Small Arms, so instead propose Star Electrics," Federica suggested.

"That fits with us using the name of stars for our cars," Anastasia said. "Good, I like the idea. Where do we get copper wire for the windings?"

"Boltons of Birmingham have been around for many years and are a good source of wire," Federica said. "But first, we need a manager and some engineering and design skills. I am thinking of asking Richard Collins to step in as the manager; he did sterling work managing Handy Cross."

"He would be a good choice," Anastasia agreed. "What do we give Stephen to do?"

"I think expand the maintenance business we have," Federica thought. "We have the repair shop in London and the one here, but perhaps we should set up a chain of garages to repair, overhaul and maintain the growing number of cars and lorries in the country."

"Are you sure you should not be making your next test flight?" Anastasia asked.

"I'm sure," Federica confirmed. "The route to the Cape has been flown, after a few mishaps, which we should learn from, so the most I want to do at the moment is fly to Cairo until we fully understand all the failures, beyond Cairo, getting repairs done will be difficult, so reliability is our prime concern. I will take a weekend at some point and fly to Athens, would you come with me on that trip?"

"That would be lovely," Anastasia said. "Fly to Athens, what a thought!"

"I will proceed with the building then and transfer Richard and advertise for some engineers," Federica said. "I think when we interview them, we will have Mr Fox and Mr Stuart with us as well as Richard."

Federica acquired land and buildings in fairly short order. The place she bought was not in Taplow but in Slough. During the war, Slough had been the site of a huge repair depot for mechanised transport for the military, and at the end of the war, vehicles by the hundreds were auctioned off, and a group of business leaders, all men except her, set up the Slough Trading Estate. The site was close enough to Burnham to make the movement of parts simple, and it was also well situated to serve the growing number of new industries, many of which were driven by the growing use of electricity in industry, housing, lighting and such. The advertisements for engineers yielded good results, and she, Anastasia, Richard, Mr Fox and Mr Stuart finally picked several to take on. They were immediately tasked to design and make the products, which they did in fairly short order. All this took until late June, and by July, they were actually producing parts, something that Federica thought was nothing less than remarkable. She set two main tasks for Richard: produce all the electrics required for their cars, vans and lorries, and then motors, controllers and switches to power all the tools in the machine shop.

The people for the new electric products factory included all those from the Handy Cross works, where production of aircraft had ceased as soon as the Armistice was declared and contracts were cancelled. There had been pressure from the government to take on more men, rather than women, particularly those laid off as the heavy industries slowed down as production of steel, ships, tanks and munitions dropped back to pre-war days, but most of those heavy industries were a long way from Slough and relocating workers was just not something Federica was prepared to do and something the government, for all its push to employ people, was certainly not going to pay for. So unemployment in Glasgow, Newcastle, Belfast and other cities that boasted basic heavy industries stayed fairly high, but in the area around London that had more light industry, particularly associated with electrical and automotive products, unemployment was fairly low.

Richard and his team soon had electrics for the cars that were tried, tested and proven, and a switch was then made to move away from the purchased parts to their own parts. Then Ian Stuart started on the machine shops. He took electric motors that Richard was now producing in quantity and affixed them to the machine tools, replacing the overhead belts that Federica so detested. It also meant changing the electricity supply to the machine shop, and that took a little work as cables had to be laid, switches installed, and the connection to the power company improved. However, overall, their power consumption went down as the belts had not been the most efficient way to transmit power.

Meanwhile, Stephen had not been idle and had already set up three more garages in areas where they knew there were reasonable numbers of their cars and was already taking in business. He ordered parts by the score from Sirius and was actually turning a profit. He did spend time with the Sirius engineers going over repairs he had had to do, and worked with them to devise improvements in the designs that would lead to fewer failures.

"Is your goal to make your job obsolete?" Federica joked with him one day.

"That will never happen," he said. "Even with the best designs, things just wear out and must be replaced, and motorists have this habit of running into things, which gives us a steady repair business."

"I suppose the difference between maintenance and repair," she said.

"Indeed," he agreed.

"I have made agreements with the tyre people that we will also stock and fit new tyres, so that if one is not inclined to replace tyres oneself, we can do it, for a fee, of course," he said. "I'm also negotiating with two petroleum companies for the best prices for petrol and oil."

"Do we make any margin on the sale of petrol?" she asked.

"A few pennies per gallon," he said. "But it gets customers in and has them returning for oil changes and the like, so we build a loyal base."

"Splendid," she said. "Thank you, Stephen."

The situation at the Somercotes Lead Mining Company was not as rosy. Federica had been right. After the cessation of hostilities, the demand for lead had dropped dramatically, and to cap that, there was a growing trend to switch from lead to copper in plumbing, pushing the demand down even further. They were left with no choice but to shut down the mine and lay off all the workers. George met with them and explained the situation and offered jobs in Star Electrics and at the garages that Stephen had set up, but only ten of the workers decided that they would move to the south and start anew, twelve did find employment with some local quarries that were busy with building materials for new houses, the rest returned to the land and worked in agriculture, either in their own small holdings or with larger farms. The management of the mine looked for similar positions in the coal industry or in the colonies. George stayed long enough to make sure that the shafts were covered and that access was locked up, and then retained four of the workers as caretakers to make sure the buildings were not vandalised until such time as the mine was either restarted or the property sold off.

"I think we should take our Athens trip," Anastasia told Federica. "I've arranged to have two weeks off for a holiday, so let's fly to Athens, then I want to take Giovanna to see her grandmama in Windermere, can we fly there?"

"If we had an aircraft with floats, we could actually land close to her cottage, but for us, I think the closest field would actually be as far away as Carlisle, unless we can find a farmer who has a nice flat field with no stock on it," Federica replied.

"I think good luck with the flat field in the Lakes, unless it's down by the sea," Anastasia said. "So, it will be the train. Has the plane been flown recently?"

"We've been using it to ferry parts to Paris, and we've also been collecting performance data as we go," Federica said. "We now have several hundred hours of flight data and engine data, so we can estimate closely the times it will take for flights, given that we know the winds. That is still the least understood of our challenges; just getting weather data for Africa is hard. We can get surface temperatures, wind direction and speed, but it would be nice to know what happens when we go up a few thousand feet."

"Have the balloons helped?" Anastasia asked.

"They have to some extent," Federica confirmed. "We've used a winch with a long line on it to tether them and collected temperature and wind data. We know that the temperature drops about five degrees for every 1,000 feet we go up. The longest line we used let us hold the balloon at 5,000 feet above the ground."

"I suppose in time the Met Office will work out ways to get us forecasts even in remote areas," Anastasia said. "So, when do we go to Athens?"

"Next week, would that be acceptable?" Federica asked.

"Next week would be wonderful," Anastasia said. "Giovanna will be on holiday from school, so it's a good time to go."

All associated with the aircraft project wanted to go to Athens. Federica suggested that Will pilot them as far as Rome, then George could take the next leg on to Athens. The weather was holding, it was even quite hot, promising to be hotter in Paris, Rome and Athens. Will wanted to try out his new engine. It had a completely new liquid cooling system that he felt was more reliable and improved superchargers that he was sure would give them more speed. He wanted to try two of the new engines and keep two of the old engines, and hang whatever instruments they could onto each engine to monitor performance. He had also taken the lessons of the Cape flights to heart and looked at the magnetos very carefully, and made significant improvements to their reliability. It seemed that the principal lesson from the Cape flights was that reliability was paramount and needed much attention. The party set out early in the morning, actually taking off at seven and flew straight to Istres, bypassing Paris. After a stop there to fill the petrol tanks and also take some lunch, they were on to Rome.

"These data look tremendous," Will said as they reviewed the day's run that evening at their hotel. "It tells us that we averaged 125 knots, part of the way we were running against a headwind and for the last two hours we had a slight tailwind, but it shows me that the new engine configuration and the improvements we've made to the engine cowlings to cut drag even more are really working."

"In a perfect world with no weather delays and no constant headwinds, what would be the flying time to the Cape?" Federica asked.

"Fifty-three hours," George replied.

"Remember that's with only two of the new engines," Will said. "So, I would expect with four to see even more improvement."

"So, the Vimy problems were engine overheating and magneto. Did we see any of that?" Federica asked.

"No," Will said. "All the temperature readings were well within the limits, and I saw no significant variation between the engines, except that the new ones ran about ten degrees cooler than the old ones. Magneto, no issues at all. I'll take a look at them in the morning before we head off to Athens."

"Is not Rome to Brindisi to Sollum, then Alexandria, a shorter route than via Athens?" Anastasia asked.

"It might be slightly," Federica agreed. "But I don't see many paying passengers either booking tickets to Sollum, or alighting there, but I could see people flying from Rome to Athens, or Athens to Cairo, so from a commercial viewpoint I think that's the better route."

"Athens today," George announced as they all boarded the plane. "I thought we'd make a straight run there, not stop in Brindisi unless it looks as if we're running significantly behind the flight plan I have."

"What will we see in Athens?" Giovanna asked.

"Lots of really old buildings," Anastasia told her. "We'll spend of couple of days there, even go to the seaside, the water there will be nice and warm."

"Can we build a sandcastle?" Giovanna asked.

"I'm sure we can," Anastasia assured her. "Hold on, we're off."

"I wonder how high we can go safely," Federica pondered.

"Well, mountain climbers tell us that as we go really high, the air gets thinner and it's harder to breathe," George said. "So, there's probably a limit to how high we can go comfortably. Too high and we'd have to supply oxygen to each passenger and to the crew."

"Can that be done?" Anastasia asked.

"I'm not sure," George replied. "When the American, Schroeder, flew up to 33,113 feet, he had an oxygen supply, but details are unclear as to how it operated, and he also complained about the intense cold that iced up his goggles, coated the oxygen mask and flask and also gave him frostbite. We wouldn't want to do that, but perhaps we'd have a better ride at somewhere like 15,000 feet. Will, will our engines still perform at that altitude?"

"Probably perform, but at what level?" he replied. "I know that at least to 15,000 feet we've seen quite a drop in power output, higher than that we'd have to run tests and see. But, not on this trip."

"No, I agree," Anastasia said. "How high are we now?"

"According to the gauges, 13,500 feet," George replied. "It might be my imagination, but it seems that the ride is a little smoother. How are the engine temperatures?"

"The colder air outside seems to be making up for the lack of cooling caused by the less dense air," Will replied. "So, far things look well within the limits we have placed for safe flight."

"I'm glad we insulated the plane," Federica commented. "What's the outside temperature?"

"Cold, really cold," George said. "Not quite down to freezing, but it's the summer and the ground temperatures are well into the 80s and 90s. If it was freezing down there, it would be really cold up here."

"If we could fly straight from Paris to Rome, how high would we have to go to miss the Alps?" Federica asked.

"We'd have to be at least 11,000 feet to cross without hitting anything, given the margin of error of the altimeters, so 12,000 feet would be a safe altitude," Will replied. "It's quite a long flight, probably about 600 nautical miles, so at least five and a half hours of flying. I think for the nonce, better to stick with Istres, then across the Med."

"There's Brindisi," George said, pointing ahead.

"That didn't take long, we're well ahead of our flight plan," Will commented. "So, now the Adriatic."

"I thought we'd skirt the mountains of Greece and come on over the Gulf of Corinth," George said. "How are the engines behaving?"

"Just fine," Will said. "No problems that I can see, what about petrol?"

"We've enough," George said. "That extra tank we put in really made a difference; it gives us more margin for the unexpected."

They were over the Adriatic quickly, then went up the Gulf of Corinth to Athens. The runway at Athens was at Tatoi, a field the Greeks had used towards the end of the Great War. It was a little way north of the centre of Athens, but the field was good enough and had petrol as well. They found transportation into Athens itself and their hotel, already booked for them by Thomas Cook.

"The writing is all funny," Giovanna commented as she studied the various signs and papers written in Greek.

"They use an alphabet that is similar to the Roman one we use," Anastasia explained. "It's older than the Roman alphabet, but many of the letters are the same; in fact, the very word alphabet comes from the first two letters, alpha and beta, or a and b."

"Why did the Romans change it?" Giovanna asked.

"I have no idea," Anastasia admitted. "Perhaps one of your school teachers might have an explanation."

"I doubt that," Giovanna said. "They teach from the texts they have, and if you ask them anything outside the text, they tell you not to ask silly questions. Not like you and Auntie Fede, who will at least consider the question and give me an answer, even if it is that you don't know."

"Pray, do not bait your teachers too badly," Anastasia said.

"I won't, Mummy, I promise," Giovanna said. "Can we go to the seaside?"

"Let's have dinner and a bath tonight, and tomorrow morning after breakfast we'll walk down to the seaside and see what we can find," Anastasia suggested.

"The water is lovely, it's so warm," Giovanna said as she splashed around in the shallows along the shoreline of the Kalamaki Beach.

"I imagine that in the winter it is not quite so inviting," Anastasia said.

"It's hot here," Giovanna said. "Much hotter than at home."

"The Mediterranean is generally a lot warmer," Anastasia said. "It is so much farther south than England."

"That makes a difference?" Giovanna asked.

"It does," Will said. "As you go south towards the equator, it gets hotter, then on the other side of the equator, it starts to cool off again as you go all the way to the South Pole."

"Does that affect flying?" she asked.

"It can," Will confirmed. "If it gets very hot, then it's difficult to take off, and if the airfield is up on a high hill, then it's even more of a problem."

"Is that why the Silver Queen II crashed at Bulawayo?" she asked.

"That's what we understand," Will confirmed. "The engines did not have enough power to go fast enough to get off the ground with the high airfield and the hot day."

"So when Auntie Fede flies this aeroplane to Cape Town, does it have enough power?" she asked.

"We believe it does," Will confirmed.

"How fast does it have to go to take off?" she asked.

"At Handy Cross, about 75 mph," he replied. "Here. because it's warmer, probably about 80."

"That's awfully fast," she thought. "Faster than our car."

"It is," he confirmed. "The Austro-Daimler Prince Henry car will go about 85 mph, so it won't be long before cars are going really fast. In fact, Dorothy Levitt driving a special Napier car broke the land speed record for women in 1913, doing 96 mph."

"One day, I'll break that record," Giovanna announced.

"You might at that," Will conceded.

"Why cannot a woman go as fast as a man? Surely it is the strength of the car that matters, not the man?" she asked.

"It is indeed all dependent on the car, and betimes the driver," he replied. "Anyway, where shall we build your sandcastle?"

Their time in Athens was well spent, enjoying the weather, the warm sea, the food and the history of the place. They also sounded out various hotels to find one that would be suitable for overnight guests breaking their journey south. When it was time to leave, Will spent some time filtering the petrol carefully, and he was glad that he did. The amount of silt he trapped would have played havoc with the fuel supply to the engines. Their return trip was quick and uneventful until they got within sight of England, then the weather turned sour and the plane was buffeted about. All held on and no one lost their seat, but it did point to something that had not been addressed by anyone: how to maintain one's seat in bad weather. It was also apparent that the seats themselves should be secured to the floor, so that there was, in fact, something to hang on to.

"I'm heartily glad to be back on solid ground," Federica commented to George when they finally landed.

"That was not the most pleasant part of the journey," he agreed. "We do need to look at constraining the seats and being able to secure ourselves to avoid being thrown about by the weather."

"We do indeed," she echoed. "So, what was our time?"

"We averaged 130 knots," he said. "There and back, it would have been slightly better, but for the latter part of the trip from Dover to here. The headwinds were pretty fierce."

"So, with all four new engines, what is your best estimate?" she asked.

"I think look for speeds of 140 to 150 knots, so more room to counter headwinds," he said.

"So, the next step is Cairo," she said. "First, we need to apply ourselves to the new electrical enterprise, and then perhaps in September take a run to Cairo."

"I've always wanted to see the pyramids," he said. "When I was in Egypt, we saw them but only in passing."

Africa at last

The Air Ministry created a competition intended to promote Safety, Comfort and Security in civil aeroplanes. In large aircraft, the first prize was not awarded, but the second prize went to Handley Page for their W.8 aeroplane, and the third prize went to Vickers for their Vimy Commercial. In the small aircraft category, the first prize was awarded to Westland for their Limousine aircraft. The General Post Office issued their first Air Mail Label.

"Do you worry sometimes that someone will steal a march on us and set up a Cape service before we do?" George asked Federica.

"No," she replied. "If you look at the cross-Channel flights from Croydon to Paris and Croydon to Amsterdam, there are enough issues with them at the moment to keep Instone, A T and T, and Handley Page busy and losing money. Mark my words, the whole thing will collapse like a house of cards, possibly as early as next year. The government would need to provide some form of subsidy to get the industry off the ground, so to speak, but Churchill has no appetite for that. That plus the fact that I see no progress in the Anglo-Egyptian squabbles about who's actually going to have authority over air traffic."

"Do you regret that we didn't enter the Air Ministry competition for Safety, Comfort and Security?" he asked.

"Not really, though I think we could have taken the un-awarded first prize, the Handley Page W.8 is a nice enough aircraft, but not, I think, as nice as ours," she replied.

"So, is a London to Cape Town route viable?" he asked.

"It's possible," she said. "Though I'm beginning to doubt the wisdom of my dream. I was banking on there being enough odd business from city to city that even if there are few passengers who want to go all the way to Cape Town, that there will be enough revenue to at least cover expenses, if the Egyptian thing ever gets sorted out."

"So, we'll not build any more planes just yet?" he asked.

"This is not the time to be building more aeroplanes," she said. "The Aircraft Disposal Company is charged with getting rid of 10,000 aircraft and 35,000 engines of all types and models. I trust the RAF keeps the latest so that if there are any more wars in the near future, they will at least have some machines."

"So, we take on no new people either?" he asked.

"Not for the moment," she said. "We can manage those that we have, it costs us a little, but we are learning all the time, and I think we should set up regular meetings with the engineers from all our factories to talk about problems, we never know when a solution from one circumstance may apply to another. Putting Richard and Stephen in charge of things reduced our expenses, and I think we should see if John Edwards and Thomas Manning would consent to new assignments at Sirius, or if they really want to stay with aeroplanes."

"Do you wish to talk to them, or shall I?" he asked.

"I don't mind," she said.

"I'll do it then, with the understanding with Ian that if we need one or both for test flights down Africa, we can borrow them," he said.

"I was wondering how complicated it would be to design a viable monoplane as opposed to a biplane," she said.

"There have been a few monoplanes," he said. "If you think about it, Blériot crossed the Channel in a monoplane in 1909, and before that, there was the Demoiselle, and the Antoinette set all kinds of records in 1909 to 1910, Fokker made a nice fighter in 1915 and Junkers even had an all-metal monoplane in 1915 as well, and the American Cessna made a really nice little machine, the Comet, so it's been done, but only with small machines. The Bristol M.1.C actually saw active service in Palestine in 1917, so they are viable, I'm just not sure how large a one we could build. I suppose it all comes down to engines and power, we need a high horsepower, low weight, very reliable engine."

"I'm sure Will is doing the best he can to improve what we have," she said. "But, perhaps it will be a while before it is commercially viable. I wonder what the Junkers all-metal machine weighed."

"I'm sure we can find out," he said. "I'll make enquiries."

Federica went through the accounts of all the companies and was gratified to see that all were turning a profit, so she could indulge herself a little longer. The Cairo to Cape flight was still a challenge to be conquered. It mattered not to her that the route had been flown all the way; it had been done with three different machines, so it was obviously still quite a risky affair. Night flying appealed to her, but there the risk was something going awry while it was yet dark and having to find somewhere to put down and not being able to really see what was there. It seemed to her that each issue she brought up all came back to the same thing: reliability, that plus some obvious skill on the part of the pilot. Running bench tests of engines told them some things, but it did not tell them what would happen with continued exposure to salt spray from the sea and from sand that they would surely encounter on the way south, particularly over Egypt and Sudan. Making an air route that could survive meant getting the time down well below the 14 or so days it took by ship. There would always be the adventurous who make the trip by air, just to be able to say that they had, but that population could not be relied upon the generate enough revenue to pay for the aircraft and the crews necessary, both in the air and on the ground.

"Anastasia, I'm thinking of flying to Cairo on the fifteenth of next month," Federica told her.

"Good time to go," Anastasia said. "The weather is generally clement, so you should have the minimum of difficulties. Sadly, with Giovanna at school in September, I will be unable to come with you, but take photographs of the pyramids for me."

"I will," Federica promised.

"I will be interested to learn if the engines that we have now fitted perform as well as they have been doing on the trial flights we've been taking," Anastasia said. "It's such a pity that there isn't a field near Windermere; flying up to see Mama would be preferable to the train or car."

"I suppose it will be a while before airfields are created and made usable to anyone," Federica said. "The RAF has fields, but they hardly want us making free use of them."

"Well, take care and come back safely," Anastasia said.

"It is my intention to do so," Federica laughed. "I was also thinking of inviting the people from *Flight* and *The Aeroplane* to visit Handy Cross and show them the plane."

"I'll take care of that for you. Why don't we set a date for the 1st of October," Anastasia suggested. "It's a Friday, so we'll have them down in the morning and then give them lunch after they've crawled all over the plane. If the weather's nice, we can even take them up for a short trip around the Chilterns, say about an hour."

"That ought to be quite long enough," Federica agreed. "We should have basic layout drawings as well, with specifications, and perhaps flight logs so that they can see what we've done."

"I'll attend to that, or should I say, Alice will," Anastasia promised.

Federica went to see Ian and borrowed Thomas Manning for a week. She first had him go through the plane and check all the controls, then she had him check the engines, as far as starting each one and checking that it ran properly. That done, she and George, with Thomas along as the flight engineer, set out for France at six in the morning on the 15th of September as she had planned. She flew from Handy Cross to Istres and they took a short break there, long enough for a meal and to fill the petrol tanks. Then George took them over the water to Rome, putting them in at three local time, so a splendid day's run.

"I like this starting early in the morning," Federica commented to George in their hotel room.

"Less turbulence caused by the heat of the day," he agreed. "We noticed it a lot in eastern Egypt. So, tomorrow, early departure again?"

"I think so," she said.

The next day's run from Rome to Athens went fine as far as Athens, then, crossing the Mediterranean, things turned for the worse.

"I don't like the look of that thunderstorm ahead, it looks really black and threatening," Federica said to George. "Should we try and fly through it, or turn back to Athens?"

"Well, there's nowhere to land in Crete, so it's back to Athens," he said. "Why tempt fate?"

"Indeed," she agreed. "It's coming this way. Can we outrun it?"

"I would think so," he said. "It looks like it goes well into the sky; it must go up to 20,000 feet or more."

"Okay, I'll turn around and take us back," she said. They flew back with the storm at their back and made it to Athens just in time to catch the leading edge of the storm and the rain. On the ground, George sent telegraph messages to Anastasia to tell her of the delay and also sent one to their hotel in Cairo to change the booking, which he did, guessing that they would be late by three days. If it looked longer, he could always defer things again.

"I don't think it would have been wise of us to try and fly through this," he said. "I can't imagine how buffeted we would have been. I flew in some bad weather in Egypt, and it's not at all pleasant."

"Just as well we fixed the seats down," she said. "And put in the straps to hold us to the seats, even just the little of the storm we got was violent enough. I wonder when van Ryneveld and Brand flew from Taranto to Sollum why they didn't go back. Fourteen hours in the air in an open cockpit cannot have been pleasant in a storm."

"Perhaps they were far enough into the flight that it was quicker and more expedient to go forward than back," he suggested.

"I wonder how much buffeting our plane would take before we saw damage," she pondered.

"I suppose the only way to really find that out is to fly into bad weather," he said. "Not a prospect I would relish."

"Should we have some kind of windscreen wipers for rain?" she asked.

"We might look at that," he said. "I imagine that at speed the rain will get blown off anyway, but at low speed, such as at takeoff and landing, windscreen wipers might be useful."

"How do we stop them from blowing off?" she asked.

"I'm sure we can design them to stow out of the airflow," he said. "I'll talk to Mr White about them and see what we can do."

"What about ice?" she asked. "What do we do if the weather is bad and we start to get ice on the wings?"

"Drop down to a lower altitude where it's warmer," he said. "We don't want ice on the wings."

"Do you imagine there would be the possibility on the Cape run?" she asked.

"I'm sure that at the right, or wrong, time of year, then over the Channel and northern France we could see ice and down by Cape Town also, in the middle, I suppose it's possible but at the altitudes, we'd be flying at I don't see it as likely," he replied.

"I wonder how long this storm will last," she said.

"We could check with the shipping people, they might have an idea," he suggested.

The storm actually lasted three days until it blew itself out and sunshine returned. Fortunately, the runway at the Tatoi airfield was paved so it was not a muddy morass. They set off again early in the morning and were rewarded by wonderful views of Crete as they flew overhead. Then it was on to Egypt and Alexandria as a landfall.

"Pity the lighthouse is no longer here," George said as they crossed over the coastline. "It would have made a super beacon to aim for."

"True," she agreed. "How long to Heliopolis?"

"Only a few minutes more," he replied. "Look, it's ahead there, and there are the pyramids."

"They are big, aren't they," she said. "It does make you wonder how the ancients built them."

"We saw them briefly when we were moved from here to France," he said. "But they didn't give us time to linger, so we only saw them from afar. This time I will be sure to go and look and perhaps even climb upon them."

"Well, here we are in Cairo," she said as they landed. "It's warm here."

"Rather more hot than warm," he laughed.

"I hope the hotel has a nice room for us," she said. "What do we need to do to protect the plane?"

"Cover the pitot tubes, the engine air intakes and the windscreen," he replied. "We don't want sand in the engine or the pitot tubes, and sand can abrade the glass and reduce visibility. Other than that, take on a watchman or two to make sure nothing gets stolen. The airfield is supposed to be secure, but people will always find a way."

"Thomas, have you any plans for the next two days before we return?" Federica asked.

"I wanted to see the pyramids also," he said. "Them and the Sphinx."

"I wonder what that is supposed to represent," Federica said.

"I suppose in time someone may work it out," George said.

After the plane was secured, they took a taxi into the city itself and Shepheard's Hotel, the renowned hotel where east was supposed to meet west.

"This is an impressive edifice," Federica said the George as they were dropped at the front door.

"It is," he agreed. "I can see why the British command used it during the war, very posh. Our quarters in the eastern desert were nowhere near as nice."

"So, I think a bath, clean clothes and then lunch," she suggested. "I'm actually quite hungry."

"Good idea," he said. "Thomas, what are your plans?"

"I'm going to take a walk around," he replied. "Get some exercise, then I'll sort myself out for a late lunch."

"Sign for the lunch to the room and we'll take care of all expenses," George said. "Did you see anything that we should be aware of on the flight this morning?"

"No," Thomas replied. "Everything looked good, engine temperatures and oil pressures were right where we want them, so things look very good."

"Fine, we'll stay a couple of days, then go home," George said. "Perhaps we'll try Wadi Halfa and Khartoum another day. Before we go traipsing off through Africa, we want more data on the engines so that we know that we've got reliable power sources."

"They look good, Mr George," Thomas said. "When we get back, I'll pull them apart again and check everything, but I've seen nothing yet that bothers me."

"Good, thank you, Thomas," George said.

Bathed, clothed in raiment not designed for the sky, Federica and George found the dining room and were seated at once.

"You are the ones with the huge airplane?" a voice asked.

"That would be us," George replied.

"Sam Higgins, at your service. I am curious about the design, it is clearly not a Vimy."

"Federica and George Wheelwright, no, the design is modified from the design of the Russian Sikorskii," George replied. "You have an interest in aircraft?"

"I do, I do," Sam replied. "I'm looking at what it would take to fly New York to San Francisco. What's the range of that machine?"

"We have planned for 700 nautical miles," George replied. "Or about six hours of flying."

"So, minimum four stops from New York to San Francisco," Sam thought. "If you ever want to sell it, let me know. Would it be possible to get a flight?"

"We're flying back to Athens, then Rome, then England in three days' time," George said. "You would be welcome to come with us, if that fits with your plans."

"That would be admirable," Sam said. "My business here is almost done, so London would be a suitable interlude before sailing home."

"May I ask what business you have?" George said.

"Sure, hotels," Sam said. "I've got a few scattered across the country, east coast to west coast. I've been looking at investment here, but it looks like the better hotels are already taken by Wagons Lit, and by other French and British interests. What business are you good people engaged in?"

"We have a car company and some other enterprises," George said.

"Which car company?" Sam asked.

"The Sirius Car Company," Federica replied. "We make cars, vans and lorries."

"Lorries, right, trucks," Sam laughed. "I've seen a few around, nice looking."

"We like to think so," she said.

"What about the airplane?" Sam asked.

"We have been investigating the Cairo to Cape Town route," George replied.

"Seems to me with all the backwards and forwards of the Egyptians and your own government that I'll have a coast-to-coast airline flying before they agree on who can do what," Sam said.

"I have been reading about the various lawsuits brought by the Wright brothers and by Curtiss. Is it even possible at this moment to bring an aeroplane into America without being subjected to lawyers?" George asked.

"The government finally stepped in and told them to put an end to the nonsense," Sam said. "So now there is the Curtiss Company and the Wright Aeronautical Company, and they have an uneasy peace."

"Is there a viable route from east to west?" Federica asked. "Are not there some mountain ranges along the way?"

"There are," Sam agreed. "The Appalachians, then the Rockies, Rockies are higher, but there are ways through that don't mean flying too high. Are you engaged for dinner tonight?"

"No," George said.

"Perhaps you'd be my guests at dinner, my wife would be delighted to meet you," Sam suggested.

"We would be delighted," Federica said. "At what time?"

"Shall we say seven?" Sam suggested. "Here's my card."

"These are ours," Federica said, proffering cards from each of them.

"This names you as the Managing Director, Mrs Wheelwright," Sam commented.

"She is," George confirmed. "She's the creative spirit of the company, and the designs of the cars are hers and of my sister."

"Kinda rare," Sam commented. "I bet it's been a struggle to get past all the class stuff and the illusions that women can't do anything that requires brain power."

"It's had its challenges," Federica confirmed.

"I bet. Until tonight," Sam said.

"Flying across the United States might be interesting," Federica said to George later, as they walked along the banks of the Nile.

"A similar challenge to flying Cairo to Cape Town," he agreed. "But for much of the way, more facilities than across Tanganyika and the Rhodesias."

"Anyway, for the nonce, let's stay focused on the goal," she said. "I shall be satisfied when we get to Cape Town with no crashes or breakages."

"I was thinking of the idea of a monoplane," he said. "The wings have to be cantilevered from the fuselage, so have to be designed differently than our wings today. It seems to me that aluminium would be better than steel, if we can work out how to get the strength we need with the shapes we need."

"We need to look at Duralumin," she said. "It has better strength than just aluminium, but we have to watch the corrosion. Didn't the Junkers company produce some machines late in the war?"

"They did," he confirmed. "Both biplanes and monoplanes."

"It seems to me that if we can work it out, then a monoplane offers the chance of a cleaner plane than our big lumbering giant of a biplane," she said. "At least it's not a triplane like the Bristol Braemar, or the Pulman, or the Felixstowe Fury. Those to me are truly hideous."

"Being hideous is not a constraint to flying," he laughed.

"That may be true," she agreed. "But it's often the case that the more complex something is, the more likely it is that something will go awry."

"Shall we return and dress for dinner?" he asked.

"It's as well we brought clothes that are not just for flying," she laughed. "I cannot imagine what the other guests would think of us if we arrived in our flight suits and boots."

Dinner was a success, Mrs Emily Higgins turned out to be quite charming and very down to earth. She told them that she came from a farming family and had worked the fields before meeting and marrying Sam. She was excited about the notion of flying back to London, and clearly she was thinking of what it would be like to fly across parts of the United States. She and Sam lived in New York, but she allowed that she would prefer to live in San Francisco, if only there were not earthquakes. She had been there in 1906 and had seen the destruction and had been horrified by it.

"Did you see service in this past war?" she asked George as they took coffee in the lounge after dinner.

"I did, both in eastern Egypt and in France," George replied.

"How did you manage, Federica?" Emily asked.

"I kept myself busy running the businesses we have, and prayed a lot," Federica replied.

"Our son was a pilot in the latter part of the war," Emily said. "I offer thanks regularly that he came home alive and well."

"And what does he do now?" Federica asked.

"He manages our hotel in New York," Emily said. "It may be a mother talking, but I think he's doing a great job."

"How many cars does your company make in a year?" Sam asked.

"We are not the size of Ford," Federica replied. "We only make ten or so cars, vans and lorries per day, so let's say, 1,500 a year, perhaps a few more, that is in England, in France we produce about as many."

"That's still a respectable number," Sam said. "Could you produce more?"

"We could," Federica replied. "Our production today we constrain to the sales we make; if more people bought, we would make more."

"Do you have a dealer in the States?" Sam asked.

"No," she replied. "If you are interested, I would suggest machines made in France, where we make another eight to nine a day, then there's no issue with the steering wheel being on the wrong side."

"What other businesses do you have?" Emily asked.

"We have a foundry that supplies the castings we need and also sells to the railway companies, we have a clothing company, a biscuit company and an electrical company," Federica replied.

"Biscuits, that's cookies, right?" Emily asked.

"That's it, Honey," Sam confirmed.

"Would you consider shipping your cookies to New York?" Emily asked.

"We would, but you should sample them first to see if they would meet the tastes of your clientele," Federica suggested.

"I will," Emily said. "So, we leave for Athens three days from now?"

"We do," George confirmed. "We would like to make an early start, if that's acceptable."

"I rose early on the farm and was at work at six, so an early start is no hardship for me," Emily said. "We will be ready, you just tell us when."

"Today the pyramids," George announced as he and Federica ate breakfast. "I have retained a guide, a chap I knew in the desert, and he has camels that we will ride."

"What fun," she said. "I wonder how it is to ride a camel."

"A long way off the ground," he said.

"People are looking at us askance," she said.

"That's because of the way we're dressed," he thought. "Here am I decked out as I was in the eastern desert, and there you are in trousers of all things, with high laced boots, topee in hand, not crinolines and dainty shoes and a fashionable hat, which I agree would be quite unsuitable for our excursion, but which I imagine is the dress of most fashionable young women who come here."

"Well, if I'm to go clambering around on the pyramids, I don't want to have to be hitching up my skirts every few minutes," she said. "And, I don't suppose that riding a camel is best done in a skirt."

"Even though that is essentially what the men here wear?" he asked.

"They have learned what works for them," she thought. "And have ways to make themselves comfortable. So, shall we sashay forth and see the sights?"

They took a taxi to a place where they met their guide, Ahmed, his diminutive assistant, Salah, and their camels. There had to be fifty camels all waiting for tourists, all wanting to make the trek to the pyramids. George greeted Ahmed and told Federica more about Ahmed and his service in the eastern desert, that he was well known to him and that he spoke a little English but much better French. Ahmed showed them how to sit on the camel and get them comfortable, then he got the camels up onto their feet and led the way to the pyramids, with Salah trotting along behind. It was hot, not sweltering, but still hot and at times, flies were a nuisance, and Federica did wonder if the flies pestered them as a result of being on the camels. Still, it was a pleasant ride, rather like being in a small boat on the sea. Ahmed brought them to a spot where they could see the pyramids closely, and George wondered at the size of the blocks that built them and just how did the ancients manage to do that. Ahmed couched the camels, and they alit and followed him as he led them up and up until they stood atop the great pyramid.

"The view from here is amazing, isn't it?" Federica said to George as they looked out over Cairo and the Nile.

"It is, we should have brought a camera," he said ruefully.

"No matter," she said. "We will remember. Look down there, those are our camels with Salah."

"Can you see our hotel?" he asked.

"Not through all the smoke and haze," she said. "It must be over there somewhere."

"Here, try the binoculars," he suggested. "Look that way and you'll be able to pick it out. Even with the binoculars, it's still fairly hazy."

"I suppose I can just about make it out," she said. "Well, now we've been to Cape Town, we've been to Cairo, next will be all points between."

"Indeed," he agreed. "Doesn't all this make you wonder how on earth the ancients actually built these?"

"It must have been a massive undertaking," she said. "These blocks must weigh at least two tons each."

"I suppose in time we may learn more about their methods," he said. "So, are you ready to clamber back down?"

"I am," she confirmed. "I rather fancy some coffee, perhaps I'll try Turkish coffee, have you ever tried any?"

"I have," he said. "It tends to be stronger than the coffee we would make, and may be taken sweet or not. It's worth a try."

The climb down the pyramid took as long as the clamber up, but only because there were other climbers to avoid. Salah was waiting with the camels, and Ahmed quickly took them back to where their taxi was waiting. George paid him generously, probably ruining things for subsequent clients. The hotel did offer Turkish coffee taken on the terrace.

"You're right, this is stronger than the coffee we normally make," Federica remarked to George as she sipped the brew.

"It tasted really good after flying around above the desert for an hour or two," he said. "So, tomorrow, an excursion on the Nile?"

"What fun," she said. "What will we do, go up the river, then turn around and come back?"

"I thought we'd take a felucca and just see what we can see," he said.

"Maybe we can see where Moses was put into the bullrushes," she said.

"I'm sure we can imagine that," he said. "Tomorrow, Ahmed and his brother, Karim, will take us on a felucca up the river for an outing. We meet them on the waterfront here by the hotel at nine in the morning. I would wear what you have on now, and definitely bring the hat."

The Nile was fascinating, first past the buildings of Cairo, then past fields of crops, all clustered around the life-giving waters of the river.
"I wonder what Cleopatra's boat looked like?" Federica said as the felucca scudded up the river, driven by the prevailing southerly wind.
"I doubt that we'll truly know," he said.
"When do we stop for lunch?" she asked.
Ahmed pointed to a spot just ahead, and they pulled in, and he and Karim quickly had a lunch table set up with food to eat. Federica noted that they went and sat under some date palms and ate their own lunch.
"They don't eat with us?" she asked George.
"We discovered in the desert that we and they were more comfortable going our separate ways," he said. "We have different customs, and it takes time for each culture to learn the ways of the other. They are not offended by not eating with us, any more than we should be offended by not eating with them."
"Is the Nile as big as this very far south?" she asked.
"I think it has a fair size and can be followed from the air for a long way, even past Khartoum, and even if the water itself is not visible, the green of the fields around it certainly would be," he thought. "Flying south to Khartoum, we would not slavishly follow the river because we know it twists and turns, so we cut across the big turns, which should not be difficult."
"And south of Khartoum?" she asked.
"Then I believe we have to start relying on compasses," he said. "We know the heading for Jinja, the question will be compass variation and wind direction, any wind abeam will influence our actual flight path, so we will have to do some calculating, even guessing at times. Night flying on a clear night would sometimes be better, and navigation would be more certain."
"The problem with that is runways that are not lit, and as happened to the one Vimy, have a failure and have to put down where," she thought.

"Well, we'll address that when we're ready," he said. "For the moment, let's just enjoy our lunch and the peace and quiet away from the hustle and bustle of Cairo."

The journey downstream was just a gentle drift as the lateen sail of the felucca did not lend itself to tacking into the wind. But the current was enough to carry them back to the hotel in good time before the sun went down. They had plenty of time to bathe and change for dinner, and at dinner, saw Thomas deep in conversation with a young woman. He brought her over to see them.

"Mrs Federica, Mr George, this is Esme, she is a teacher who has been on holiday here in Cairo," Thomas said.

"Esme," Federica said, looking her over quickly. She was short, Federica would have said pert, with wild black curly hair.

"Mrs Wheelwright, Mr Wheelwright," she said. "Thomas told me that you flew here?"

"We did," Federica confirmed. "Tell me, Esme, where do you teach?"

"I have a position at a school in Reading that I will take up at the beginning of January," she replied. "I am seeing what I can before I start work. I obtained my degree from the University of London in June. I will be teaching French and English."

"When do you return to England?" George asked.

"In two days' time, I take the boat from Alexandria to Southampton via all sorts of ports, so it will be a slow journey," she replied.

"Would you care to try flying back?" Federica asked. "We leave on the morrow, stopping in Rome overnight on the way back."

"Gosh, really, is it safe?" Esme asked.

"If it isn't, we're being very foolhardy," Federica replied. "If you have an interest, we leave at six in the morning from here."

"Gosh, that's awfully early, but that would be super, thank you," Esme said.

"Thomas can attend to you as we go," George said. "But, Thomas will be busy on the flight collecting data. We will have two other passengers, a Mr and Mrs Higgins, from America."

"I will be packed and ready at six," Esme promised.

"I wonder if she'll be sharing Thomas's bed tonight," Federica said to George after they had left.

"Fede, what a thought," George said in mock horror. "Of course she will, she's struck and he's struck, so we'll see if the teaching job gets thrown over for something else."

"There's Sam and Emily Higgins, we should remind them to be ready at six also," she said. She waved, and they came over to join them.

"Are we still set for six in the morning?" Sam asked.

"We are," George said. "We'll leave here at six, drive out to the airfield, check the plane and make sure the petrol tanks are full, then leave for Athens. We'll stop in Athens for some lunch and a break, then go on to Rome. The following day, it will be Rome to Istres on the Med coast of France, then Handy Cross where we hangar the plane. You are welcome to stay with us before going to London."

"Thank you," Emily said. "We will be up with the larks in the morning, such an adventure."

Everyone was up and about and ready to go at six, so a small procession of taxis took them all to Heliopolis, where Thomas attended to petrol while Federica and George prepared the plane for flight. They left at seven, flying north over the city, then Alexandria and on towards Crete.

"This is lovely," Emily said as Federica went aft to see how they were faring. "I can see so much, we had a wonderful view of Crete just now."

"How are you doing, Esme?" Federica asked.

"It's so amazing," Esme said. "Here we are in the air, flying like a bird, and the ground is rushing past below us. We just saw a ship going into Crete as we passed, and before that, another headed towards the Suez Canal, and now more water before Athens."

"As I said before, if you ever want to sell this, contact me," Sam said.

"Thank you, the Thermos flasks there have tea and coffee if you desire," Federica said. "We should be in Athens in an hour. Thomas, anything of note?"

"Not a thing, Mrs Federica, the engines are all behaving nicely, all Sir Garnet," Thomas replied.

"Good," Federica said.

They landed at Tatoi and found lunch, bought petrol, visited toilets and were off again, destined for Brindisi and Rome. They retraced the route they had used coming, which was down the Gulf of Corinth and over the Ionian Sea.

"I wonder where the Ionian ends and the Adriatic begins," Federica said as they flew over the water.

"I suppose it's the strait off Otranto, between there and Albania," George said. "There's Italy straight ahead. We should be over Brindisi in twenty minutes, things look good, we're making good time, so straight on to Rome?"

"I'll ask," she said and quickly went back to ask if anyone needed to stop at Brindisi.

"I'm fine," Sam said.

"Me too," Emily echoed.

"I'm quite all right," Esme added.

"Thomas?" Federica asked.

"I'll be fine to Rome," he replied.

"We should be in Rome in two hours," Federica said.

"It's interesting," George commented to her as she got back to her seat. "Stops are really driven by passenger comfort. We can put enough petrol in the tanks to fly fourteen or fifteen hours, but we would need breaks in that time. What did Alcock and Brown do for a loo when they flew over the Atlantic?"

"I've no idea," she said. "But a wild guess says that they had some form of funnel and tube that let them pee and dump it out over the sea."

"Pity some poor soul underneath," he said.

"That's why we have all these stops," she said. "Most people can manage four to five hours, but beyond that, discomfort becomes very real."

"So, even though we have the semblance of a system on board, we should still stop every four to five hours or so?" he asked.

"Definitely," she confirmed.

Rome was reached, not in a day, but in an hour and forty-five minutes, which told them that they had had quite a brisk tailwind.

"We're here," Federica told her passengers. "We have a hotel booked with rooms for all, and we'd like to depart from the airfield here at eight in the morning, which gives us a little time to negotiate the traffic in Rome in the morning. Is that acceptable?"

"Fine with us," Emily said.

"Me too," Esme added.

"Tomorrow we fly over the Med to Istres, which is near Marseille, then if the weather holds and we don't run into headwinds, we'll fly straight back to England, otherwise, we'll stop for a break in Paris and then hop over the Channel and home," Federica said.

"Which hotel are we in?" Sam asked.

"The Excelsior," Federica replied. "Have you stayed there?"

"We have," he confirmed. "Very nice, very comfortable."

"Esme?" Federica asked.

"Oh no," Esme replied. "When I came through Rome on my way to Cairo, I stayed in a much less expensive hotel, more like a boarding house than a hotel."

"Well, this will be a treat," Federica said. "We're trying to see which hotels we should partner with for commercial flights to Africa, and I cannot see passengers being content with anything other than the best."

"Probably right," Sam said. "The Excelsior was sold recently by the Swiss to the Italian Grand Hotels. I looked into it, but Grand beat me out."

"Well, here are the officials," George said. "Do we all have our passports ready?"

Formalities were taken care of, and then taxis were obtained to run them into the centre of Rome and the hotel. The rooms at the Excelsior may have been booked, but there was some kind of problem with Sam and Emily's room. Federica took charge and, in a torrent of Italian, demanded to see all and sundry who had any influence or authority. She got what she wanted, probably just to stop the continuous invective that she was heaping on them.

"You speak Italian," Sam said, in rather an understatement.

"My family is from Florence," she explained. "My father is a trader and we started out in Hong Kong but moved back to Florence, where the rest of the clan now live."

"So, do you speak Chinese as well?" Emily asked.

"It has been many years," Federica replied. "But, I still remember a few words."

"Well, after that, dinner is on us," Sam said.

"We don't want to impose," Federica said.

"Nonsense," Emily said. "Shall we say seven, a little early for the Italians I know, but then we are leaving quite early tomorrow morning. I'll make sure we have a table for six of us."

The staff of the hotel carried bags and were as obsequious as they could be, not wanting other guests to hear the tirades that Federica was obviously capable of. George knew that much of it was dramatic for the sake of being dramatic; he had seen her negotiate with her father and would have sworn that they would come to blows, but all had been agreed to and settled, and harmony restored.

After the fiasco at the reception desk, the dining room was very accommodating, and because there were few eating that early, the staff was attentive. Federica carried on quite a long conversation with the maître d'hotel and learned about the change in ownership and what it would mean for the staff, information that she passed on to Sam and Emily. Dinner was excellent, and the chef actually came out to talk to them as he was not yet swamped with a rush of orders. Sam asked him, through Federica, if he would think about a move to New York, and after glancing around to make sure no one was in earshot, he said he would, and Sam passed his card to him and suggested that he write or telegraph what he would want to make the move. Formalities for entering the United States, Sam said, he could take care of. Possibly as a result of that, desserts from the menu were dismissed, and a special dessert was created and served.

"Why is it that we cannot start with dessert?" George asked.

"Tradition," Federica said. "Here, soup is early in the meal, if not the first course, but in Hong Kong, it was towards the end and included much of what had been served as the main course."

"If I eat any more, I will surely burst," Emily said.

"Burst is not very ladylike," Sam teased.

"I could have thought of other terms, but my farming upbringing would show, and it would be even less polite," she said.

"Well, I'm for bed," George said. "Fede and I need a good night's sleep before the flight tomorrow."

"Was it a waste of money to get a room each for Thomas and Esme?" Federica asked George as they took the stairs up to their room.

"Probably," he said. "But must maintain a semblance of propriety, wouldn't look good, you know, even though I'm sure the Italians would be quite understanding, probably even encouraging."

"I wonder which will give up their bed," she pondered.

"He will," George said. "Esme will invite him to spend the night."

"You're probably right," she agreed. "Anyway, it hasn't affected Thomas's work at all, so what he does is his business."

Traffic in Rome was just getting started when they left for the airfield. Horse carriages still dominated, but there were cars mixed in as well, with the two modes of transport existing in an uneasy relationship, both vying to take supremacy on the roads, leading to chaos and much invective as carriage drivers swore at motorists and motorists swore at carriage drivers. They did all make it to the airfield in one piece, and Federica and Thomas set about preparing the aeroplane for the flight, while George took care of formalities. They took off a few minutes before eight and were soon out over the coast and on their way to France, a flight of a little under three hours. It was not long before they crossed Corsica before heading out again over the sea to make landfall near Toulon. The French Air Force welcomed them back to Istres and offered coffee and croissants as the fuel tanks were filled. Federica asked if they knew what the weather was like to the north, and she learned that what wind there was was coming off the Atlantic, blowing east, so it would be abeam of them. That just meant that they would have to allow for the drift caused by the side wind, but they had done that before and knew which landmarks to look for to confirm their compass heading. It did mean that there was no need to stop in Paris; they could go all the way to Handy Cross. George sent the now customary telegram to Mr Roberts letting him know their estimated time of arrival and who was on board, with passport numbers and all. They had found that that made the process a lot easier.

"Esme, would you like to stay with us tonight, or have you made plans?" Federica asked as they motored from the airfield at Handy Cross to their house.

"Thomas has kindly offered to drop me at the station," she replied. "But, thank you for the very kind invitation. This has been a wonderful trip and an experience I will not soon forget."

"I'm glad you enjoyed the flight," Federica said.

"They make a nice couple," Emily said as they watched Thomas drive away with Esme.

"They do," Sam agreed. "But they're not going to the station, there's a detour planned, a detour to the bedroom."

"Sam," Emily giggled.

"Well, it's obvious when you look at them, and why not, they're young, we don't live in the age of Victoria any more, so no more pretence about such things. Let them have their fun," he said. "Mrs Wheelwright, do you think I may take copies of the flight logs home with me to show my son, and specifications of the machine?"

"Of course," Federica replied. "I will provide you with logs for the flights and the engines, and the drawings of the aircraft."

"That would be great," he said. "Tomorrow, Emmy and I should take leave of you and journey to London to start the next stage of our journey home."

Contributors from *Flight* and *The Aeroplane* duly arrived on the 1st of October, along with a photographer each. Federica and George welcomed them and introduced Anastasia and Will as all part of the design team for the aircraft and its engines. Then they took the party to the hangar and showed them the machine.

"This is impressive," Mr Black from *Flight* said.

"What, the plane or the hangar?" Mr Jarman from *The Aeroplane* asked. "I can't decide what to consider first."

"You're right, David," Mr Black said. "This hangar is amazing. Tell me, Mr Wheelwright, where did the inspiration for this aircraft come from?"

"While I was in France, Mrs Wheelwright and Mrs McIntosh took the design of Sikorskii and made some changes and built it," George replied.

"And it has a certificate of airworthiness?" Mr Jarman asked.

"It does," Federica replied.

"I remember from some years ago a chap from *Automotor Journal* writing about a car and saying that he doubted that it had the ability to stand up to long-term use, and then having to eat his words, that was a Sirius car, I note a Sirius badge on this craft, would I be correct in my thinking that you ladies are the same designers as for that car?" Mr Black asked.

"We are," Federica confirmed.

"And you have flown this craft far?" Mr Jarman asked.

"Our last trip was to Cairo and back," Federica replied. "These are the flight logs."

"It has a fair turn of speed," Mr Black commented.

"We're working to improve that," Will said. "We've managed to increase the horsepower output of the engines, while reducing weight, and improving reliability. These are the engine logs from the past trips to Cairo, Athens, Rome, Istres and Scotland."

"For your interest, we also have for your outline drawings of the plane with dimensions and specifications," Anastasia said.

"How is it that we have not seen this enter commercial service?" Mr Jarman asked.

"We've been gathering data from flights to understand the possible issues, and when we're ready, we will undertake a longer trip, probably here to Cape Town. We know that it has been flown by the same two pilots, but with three separate machines, we wish to go all the way with no mishaps and no breakdowns," Federica said.

"Is it possible to take a flight?" Mr Black asked.

"We had planned to do that," George replied. "We'll just pull the craft from the hangar to the runway, then we can board and be off."

"That was a pleasure," Mr Black said when they were back on the ground.

"It was indeed," Mr Jarman agreed. "When do you plan your Cape run?"

"Probably April or May of next year," George said. "We are looking at weather patterns to see what times of year give the best chance for reasonable weather all the way to the Cape."

"I noted two other planes in the back of the hangar," Mr Black said.

"Those are ours as well," George said. "This is the Andromeda model, and those are the Aquila and Auriga models. These are the technical data and line drawings for them."

"I will be sure to forward these materials for inclusion in this year's issue of *All the World's Aircraft*," Mr Jarman said.

"Do you and Mrs McIntosh have pilot's licences?" Mr Black asked Federica.

"We do," Federica confirmed. "We obtained them well before the war and kept our hours up by delivering planes that we built under contract. Now, may we offer you some lunch?"

"Terrific," Mr Black said.

"What do you rate the chances that the cross-Channel flights will continue?" Anastasia asked as they sat down for lunch.

"Not good," Mr Jarman said. "There are three competing from here, and they're up against the French, who have government support, unlike ours. If our government wants to grow the commercial air traffic business, it has to start looking at it differently."

"I agree," Mr Black said. "Flying is no longer just for the adventurous and the military; it offers much more, the ability to quickly go to places that hitherto were only reachable by ship."

"You do not advertise in either of our journals," Mr Jarman commented.

"We've nothing to advertise at the moment," George said. "If we were selling planes, we might, but at the present we are concentrating on Sirius and the building of cars, vans and lorries. So we advertise in *The Autocar* and *The Motor*."

"Mr McIntosh, we understand that you are the engine designer," Mr Black said. "Tell us a little about your engines."

"We have a line of Vee configured engines, from four to twelve cylinders, all water cooled, all twin overhead cam valves, compression ratio five and a half to one, power to weight ratio of point five," Will replied. "We've also looked at supercharging the engines for better performance as we go higher. We're using the same engines in the Sirius line as well, but of course the much smaller four and six-cylinder ones."

"And you're continuing to work on them?" Mr Jarman asked.

"We are," Will confirmed. "More power for less weight gives higher speeds, so more lift and better flying characteristics."

"Are they easy to maintain?" Mr Black asked.

"We designed them to be, recognising that we may need to fix one in the middle of Arica one day where there are no hangars," Will replied.

"Well, this has been a most instructive day," Mr Black said. "I wish you well in your venture. Have you considered taking one of us along with you for the flight?"

"We may," Federica said. "We will contact your editors about a month before we depart and ask them if they would like to send a contributor."

"We look forward to that," Mr Jarman said. "Thank you all for your time and generous hospitality."

"I wonder how we will be portrayed when the articles are written," Federica said after the Press had left. "Just as well you didn't mention the monoplane that we're working on, we would have never seen the back of them."

"How is that going?" Anastasia asked.

"Fede and I are just in the early design stages," George said. "But, we're thinking of a monoplane with the wing above the fuselage and two engines, one below each wing. We're thinking of an all-metal aircraft, so we're looking carefully at how we design the wing and the fuselage to keep it strong enough but also keep the weight down. We'll use a lot of Duralumin."

"Would a radial engine be better suited for this craft?" Will asked.

"It might," George thought.

"I have a concept for a nine-cylinder radial that would give us 500 hp and weigh only 500 lbs," Will said.

"That would be superb," George said. "When might it be ready?"

"I'll need some time," Will said. "But six months and I'll have bench-test data. I've got a prototype already built, and have run it; now I need to get more hours on it to see how it performs. It's the classic radial that's air-cooled with heat transfer fins on the cylinders. There's probably a limit to how much I can get out of it and similar models, unless I do what others have proposed and have one radial behind the other, giving us 18 cylinders in all."

"I look forward to hearing what your bench tests show, and perhaps will take our Auriga and swap the engines on that for trials," Federica said. "Now, home I think and back to Sirius, Abbey and Windsor."

Sale

The first fatal accident on a scheduled air service occurred on the 14th of December when a Handley Page Transport Handley Page 0/400 aircraft crashed near Golders Green on a flight from Cricklewood to Paris; four persons were killed. The Air Navigation Act received Royal Assent. The company, Aircraft Transport and Travel, AT and T, ceased operations, and other nascent airlines had problems with routes not enjoying the passenger numbers they needed for successful operation. Financial difficulties caused the cessation of British commercial air services in early 1921, until the government finally stepped in with subsidies to help British airlines compete with Continental services that received support from their governments.

"Do you think Sam Higgins was serious about buying our plane?" Federica asked George one day in late October of 1920.

"I think so," he said. "You think we should sell it?"

"I do," she said. "The notion of a cleaner-looking all-metal monoplane appeals to me. Biplanes are nice enough, but we know that all the wires slow them down; you can tell that just by listening to the noise they make. So, I would rather we turn our attention to monoplanes that have no wires."

"I'll send Sam a telegram," George said. "If he says yes, then what, we take off the wings and ship it by sea?"

"That might be best," she said.

"How much do we ask for it?" he asked.

"Ten thousand pounds," she suggested. "We have expensed everything we've done, so there's nothing owing on it, but it would be good to get some funds to apply towards the monoplane."

"Have you seen the reports on the Zeppelin Staaker?" he asked.

"I looked at them, it's a behemoth, isn't it, a high-wing monoplane with four Maybach engines, built into the wings, I wonder if that's better than hanging the engines beneath the wings," she recalled.

"Beneath will probably be easier to maintain," he thought. "But if we do that, we have to make sure that the landing wheels keep the engines well clear of the ground."

"I would agree with that," she said.

"There's another one that is a little different," he said. "The Stout monoplane. The wings are really different, no wonder they call it the Bat Wing."

"Why?" she asked.

"The wings go quite a long way back over the fuselage, almost to the tailplanes," he replied.

"I wonder why they did that," she mused. "Anyway, if we could sell the Andromeda, we'd have room in the hangar for a new monoplane."

"I'll pursue it," he promised. He duly sent off telegrams and was surprised to get a response by return that indicated that Sam was indeed interested in buying the Andromeda and even offered £8,000 for it and said that he would attend to shipping and insurance.

"Take the £8,000," Federica said. "And ask him when he wants it shipped."

Messrs Pickford arrived two weeks later with four large lorries to take away the plane. Federica supervised dismantling it and made sure that everything was marked and, where necessary, boxed up. She also made sure that it was well wrapped, as she suspected that it was going as deck cargo. Finally, she provided detailed instructions for putting it all back together again. She watched the lorries leave with mixed feelings. On the one hand, she and Anastasia had spent so much time and energy to design and build the plane that she hated to part with it; on the other hand, it signalled the start of a new era and adventure. Much of what they had learned could be and would be used for any future designs, so no time or effort was wasted. When the last lorry had disappeared from view, she went inside the hangar that now almost echoed as she went in, it was so cavernous and almost empty, but for the two smaller aircraft parked near the back. In time, she thought they would go too, to be replaced by monoplanes, which first though, had to be designed and built, the greatest challenge being the cantilevered wings that had to be structurally sound to support themselves and hold up the fuselage. She drove back to Burnham and talked to Anastasia, and together they hatched a plan to take the design concepts they already had and fill in all the myriad details that would make the difference between success and failure.

"Did you see the item in *The Aeroplane?*" George asked Federica when she arrived home.

"No, were they kind or horrible?" she asked.

"Very kind actually," he said. "The description of the plane is simple enough, that appears in the *Aeronautical Engineering* supplement to the magazine, but the contributor added a long piece in the main section talking about the flight we took, and he is complimentary, to say the least, he talks about the flight with not much noise, nicely heated and with comfortable seats."

"That's good, I wonder do we tell them that we have just sold it to an American interest?" she asked.

"If anyone asks to see it we can tell them to go to New York or wherever Sam plans to rebuild it," George suggested.

"Did we receive the money?" she asked.

"It was here the day after he sent his telegram saying that he would buy," George confirmed.

"I wonder what he plans to do with it," she said.

"Probably boast to his friends that he's got the bigger airplane, as he calls it," George laughed.

"I'd like a break from planes and flying until after Christmas," she said. "Shall we go somewhere for Christmas?"

"That would be splendid, in Britain or parts afield?" he asked.

"Let's go to the Côte d'Azur," she suggested. "We can take the ferry and the train and go in style. I should ask Nastia what she has in mind, perhaps they'd like a break too."

"You do realise that if we go to Côte d'Azur, you are probably going to have to dress for dinner, no pyjamas there, or flying gear," he kidded her.

"I know," she said. "I do know how to dress, and I even have clothes that are still fashionable. You will also have to dress nicely, no tweed jackets and riding breeches."

"You may want to visit Madame Garnier," he suggested. "She might have something for you."

"It's her daughter, Marie, now," Federica said. "But, you're right, a new dress might be appropriate."

Marie Garnier was delighted to see Federica; she had, after all, been a loyal and generous customer for some years. Federica told her what she needed, and Marie made some suggestions, simple dresses that would be elegant but which would not offend the world as being overly opulent, as most were still recovering from the privations of the Great War. After much discussion, Federica ordered three new dresses, an extravagance she knew, but one she could afford. Then she had a thought, Windsor Garments was now branching out more into fashions that younger women would wear and could afford, perhaps Marie would consider a relationship where she proposed designs and Windsor made them.

"That sounds interesting," Marie said after Federica had put the idea to her. "How to be stylish at a price most can afford. That is indeed a challenge. Would it be convenient to visit Windsor Garments and see for myself the pattern, cutting and sewing rooms?"

"Of course," Federica said. "I will take you whenever it is convenient for you."

"Perhaps this afternoon?" Marie asked. "I have no clients this afternoon."

"That would be splendid," Federica said. "Shall I treat you to lunch before we go?"

"Thank you," Marie said. "How exciting, to be part of fashion for the people. I have followed the trends of Coco Chanel, Jeanne Lanvin, Jean Patou and Madeleine Vionnet, and think I can create dresses that emulate the style, but at a cost that a young working woman can afford. What about shoes?"

"We don't have a boot and shoe company, should we?" Federica asked.

"It might be useful," Marie said. "There are companies in Nottingham who did well during the recent war and who are now struggling with profitability, so now might be a time to buy an existing enterprise."

"I will investigate that," Federica said. "Where shall we luncheon?"

"Would you consider the River View?" Marie asked. "It has a wonderful location on the river, even though today is not a day I would want to be out on the river."

"We will do that," Federica said. "I have my car here, so we may drive there in short order."

Lunch was eaten as they looked out onto the Thames and the rain. The restaurant was not overly busy; it was hardly the season for idling on the river or touring. The visit to Windsor Garments was a success. Marie liked what she saw in the various rooms, from patterns to cutting to sewing and talked to many of the ladies working there.

"This is a company that has the feel of happiness about it," she commented to Federica as they left to return to Maidenhead.

"We do what we can," Federica said. "I would not have the people who work with us struggle, so we pay quite well and treat them as people, not just hirelings."

"Your Mr Painter seems well acquainted with the needs of the garment industry," Marie commented.

"He has been with the company for quite some years, and we will soon be looking for his replacement as he nears his retirement age," Federica said.

"Would you consider it too forward of me to put my own name forward as someone who would manage Windsor Garments?" Marie asked.

"Not at all," Federica said. "You would have an interest?"

"I do," Marie confirmed. "The fashion industry is changing, there are still those who can afford handmade couture, but there are multitudes of women who cannot, yet why should they be denied clothes that have style and appeal. There are clothes available at low prices, but the cut and style tend to be simple, easy to make, and of passing attraction, but with a little imagination, clothes can be made for a price that will be stylish and sought after."

"We should talk further," Federica said. "Would you object to also talking to Mr Painter?"

"Not at all," Marie said. "I think he and I see much the same way."

"I will arrange it," Federica said.

"We may have found a replacement for Mr Painter when he retires," Federica told George and Anastasia later.

"Who?" Anastasia asked.

"Marie Garnier," Federica replied. "She came with me for a visit to the factory and went. I told her that Mr Painter was nearing his retirement, and she asked if we would consider her."

"Well, she certainly knows the design side of the business," Anastasia said. "The business and accounting issues, how is she with them?"

"I think when we talk to her, we ask about those things," Federica said. "Are there others in the company whom we should also consider?"

"Possibly," George said. "But perhaps a different perspective would be of value, fashions are changing, more women want to escape the Victorian and Edwardian enveloping modes of dress, and abandon the corsets and the need for help to dress."

"The help to dress was largely with the monied class," Federica reminded him. "Those less fortunate had no need of corsets, pinched waists and all the frippery that the Victorian era had."

"Still, there is a market to be had for the idle rich," he said.

"That is true," Anastasia agreed. "And we should not ignore it, but sell our dresses with the help of advertising in *Vogue* and other journals."

"I will attend to the interview with Marie Garnier," Federica said. "Now, another matter, I was thinking of dragging George off to the Côte d'Azur for Christmas, have you made any arrangements, Nastia?"

"We are going to the Lakes to see Mama," Anastasia replied. "It will be good for Giovanna to see her grandmama again."

"I hope you find her well," Federica said. "Do you know how her epic novel is progressing?"

"She is ready to publish," Anastasia replied. "I am going to help her with the publisher."

"I wish you good fortune with them," Federica laughed. "I doubt they have anyone's interest at heart but their own."

"Of a certainty," Anastasia agreed. "That is why I'm going to lend weight to the negotiation."

Interviews were set and Marie acquitted herself so well that the decision that she should succeed Mr Painter was unanimous; in fact, Mr Painter was quite excited by the notion of her taking over. They agreed terms, and Marie even suggested that they retain her current fashion boutique and use it as a shop for Windsor Garments. She had a very capable assistant who could run the boutique. All that was needed was a date on which she would start and Mr Painter suggested that the first of the New Year would be a good day, and that she should spend time with him in the interim to fully understand the lines they had, the machines they had, their sources of fabric and most of all the people that worked at the factory. That done, Federica turned her attention to the Christmas holiday and their jaunt to the Côte d'Azur. She contacted Thomas Cook to arrange for a booking at a hotel in Cannes and then contacted Wagons-Lits to arrange the trip from Victoria Station to Cannes on the *Calais-Mediterranée Express*, a sleeper train that would take them in comfort through Paris, Lyon and Marseille on their way to Cannes. Thomas Cook made them a booking at *the Carlton Hôtel*, now welcoming back guests after the war. Federica also called Philippe in their French factory and asked him if it would be possible to have use of a car while they were in Cannes. He said that he would make arrangements and have the car at the station when they arrived.

The Wagons Lit train left Victoria station at three in the afternoon for the short run down to Dover and the ferry. The Channel crossing was rough, but the ferry still ran, and they were in Calais in plenty of time to transfer to the waiting train. A sumptuous dinner was served between Calais and Paris, then in Paris, there was all the shunting around to get the sleeper cars from the Gare du Nord station to the Gare de Lyon station. From there, it was an overnight run to Lyon, arriving a few minutes early at eight-thirty in the morning. Breakfast and lunch followed as they travelled south towards Marseille, followed by afternoon tea between Marseille and Cannes. Wagons Lit had taxis arranged and quickly transported passengers to their hotels or other destinations, but Federica and George had their own car. A representative from the local distributor of Sirius met them at the station with a brand new Regulus car and gave them directions to the hotel. *The Carlton Hôtel* was really an imposing edifice and had had a long history with Russian aristocracy, a clientele that was no longer going to grace its doors after the 1917 Revolution. Cannes was not hot, not even that warm, but it was warmer than England, and the chances of frost and snow were very slim. Frost had happened on rare occasions, but there was none anticipated while Federica and George were there. Their room faced the sea and was up on the sixth floor with its own little balcony overlooking the beach.

"This is very nice," Federica said to George as they unpacked.
"A little different to my tented accommodations on the Western Front," he said.
"Was it truly awful?" she asked.
"For us, not too bad, but for those in the trenches, awful is not a strong enough word," he replied. "I'm sure that many more died of disease than enemy fire."
"At least this Spanish Flu seems to have abated a little," she said. "But, we should still be circumspect, too many people suggests to me the possibility of passing the infection on. Do we dine tonight?"
"It's a little late," he said. "And I have eaten so many meals today on the train that I'm not sure I would do justice to any dinner."
"So, bath and bed," she suggested.
"That sounds like an invitation," he laughed.
"It's more of a command," she said. "We're on the Côte d'Azur, romance is supposed to be in the air, so we should take advantage of our situation and be antisocial and just spend time with each other."
One of the benefits of the newer fashions was that there were no corsets to take off, just the simple dress and undergarments, which Federica rid herself of very quickly. The bath was not designed for two, but it was not too difficult for them both to get in and enjoy the moment. Then it was bed and the delights there.

"What do we do today?" George asked Federica at breakfast.

"It doesn't seem too cold, so perhaps a walk along the esplanade," she suggested. "I think it's a little cold for the sea, so I at least will not be going in."

"Don't expect me to brave the waves," he said. "I have had my share of cold days and cold water, so the only water I will be getting in will be a hot bath later."

"Pardon, Monsieur," a man said. "George Wheelwright, is it not?"

"Jacques Pétain," George said. "Jacques, my wife, Federica. Fede, Jacques, was in charge of the French squadron closest to ours. How are you, Jacques? Still in the air force and a colonel now?"

"No," Jacques replied. "At the end of the fighting, I returned to my town and my business, and you?"

"I did the same, I left the RAF and went back to our family businesses," George said.

"What business do you have?" Jacques asked.

"We have a car company, Sirius, and we have a foundry, a garment factory, a biscuit factory and a factory making electrical products," George replied. "And you?"

"We have a textile business," Jacques said. "We weave silk and sell to the makers of clothes."

"Perhaps we might discuss at some time supply that we may use," George suggested.

"That would be admirable," Jacques said. "Ah, Sophie, this is an old friend from the Front, George Wheelwright and his wife, Federica."

"Enchantée," Sophie said. The conversation then switched to French as Sophie spoke little, if any English. The Pétain family were not related at all to the more famous Marshall Pétain, but the name had been useful to Jacques in the war. Their textile mill was in Lyon, and Jacques and Sophie were taking a holiday away from things. Federica did what George should have done and invited the Pétains to join them for breakfast. They traded histories, and Federica and Sophie shared all that they had missed during the war and how happy they were that both their husbands came back alive and well. George and Jacques talked about current business interests, leaving wartime experiences to the history books.

They agreed to meet again for dinner that night, then went their separate ways for the day. Federica wanting to take a drive into the hills behind Cannes, and Sophie wanting to view the shops in Cannes. George drove, and Federica stopped him from time to time to take pictures with her new Zeiss Icarette camera. George had bought it her for Christmas and had given it to her early so that she could document their travels.

"I like this camera," she told him as they stood at one spot looking out over the smaller hills below and the sea beyond.

"Is it better than the one your father had when he drove one of our early cars back to Florence?" George asked.

"We'll see when I develop film and make some prints," she said.

"We need to make a room dark where you can do that," he thought.

"I had thought that we might use part of the cellar," she said. "We can put up a partition to exclude light, and we already put electricity down there."

"You won't be chilled down there?" he asked.

"I don't think so," she said. "So, what do I need?"

"That I don't know," he admitted. "Perhaps you should consult with the chemist in Maidenhead who develops films for people."

"I'll do that when we get home," she said. "Now, let's see if we can find somewhere that sells coffee."

They found coffee at a small café set among the trees and got their coffees and a pastry and sat and watched the world go by, not that there was much activity, the hills were quiet, with no hubbub of noise from traffic, either horse-drawn or cars.

"If we are to do advertisements for Windsor, we should think about a photographic studio that we might engage, or perhaps find our own photographer," she said.

"I like the idea of our own photographer, then we can also use him, or I suppose it's possible, her, to take pictures of clothes, cars and biscuits," he said.

"I'll investigate when we get home," she said. "Shall we go?"

"Back to the hotel?" he asked.

"Or somewhere we might have lunch," she said. "I hate to say this, but I think all we will do on this holiday is eat."

"Well, as long as we're circumspect, then we'll not gain too many stone," he laughed.

"I cannot imagine gaining even one stone," she said. "I'd have to starve myself for weeks on end."

"Don't do that," he said. "So, there is a place I saw on the esplanade, Café Cannes, of all names, perhaps we could try that."

Lunch was quite good, and after lunch, they took a walk along the esplanade toward the boat dock.

"Have you ever thought about a yacht?" Federica asked.

"It has often struck me that if you are in the shipping business, then boats are a necessity, but yachts are a pure luxury and extravagance, even more so than our planes," George replied. "If we wanted to take a voyage somewhere, it might be better to charter one, with a crew to man it, rather than have our own moored somewhere on the coast."

"What about a smaller one on the Thames, that would be closer and probably get more use?" she asked.

"For me, flying holds more attraction than messing about in boats, no matter what Kenneth Grahame says," he replied. "But, perhaps we should take one out one day in the spring or summer and see if we would like it."

"We'll do that," she agreed. "Learning to sail would also teach us more about wind and its behaviour, which I believe may be of use when flying."

"It may," he agreed. "But I venture to guess that winds aloft are quite different to winds on the surface."

"Have you ever given any thought to gliders?" she asked.

"After Lilienthal had his crash, I thought it would be expedient to let others do more development before venturing up in one," he said. "But I grant you gliders would be a terrific way to learn about winds, hot air currents rising and all the things that happen up in the air that we can't see."

"We'll just keep an eye on things then," she said. "Shall we walk back? I can't believe I'm saying this, but afternoon tea is calling."

There was a gala dinner held at the hotel on Christmas Eve, and the chefs and the staff outdid themselves. Not only were there hotel guests, but dignitaries and notables from the town were also present. Federica and George dined with Sophie and Jacques and thoroughly enjoyed the evening.

"I'm sorry, I have no more gifts for you," George said to Federica on Christmas morning.

"Just being here with you is gift enough," she said. "There were times in the war that I feared that you would never come back."

"There were occasions that I wondered if I would get back," he said.

"I cannot imagine what you all experienced," she said.

"What did you do for the Christmases that I was away?" he asked.

"We huddled together, me, Nastia, Giovanna and Sophia and tried to be brave and enjoy what we could," she replied. "For the people in the factories, we had Christmas parties for the children and even had Father Christmas come and hand out presents."

"I'm sure that was appreciated," he said.

"I think all the more because they knew that you and Will were away in Egypt or France," she said. "Somehow that made us part of the families."

"I'm sorry we missed so much," he said. "Perhaps this talk of a League of Nations will amount to something positive."

"One may only hope," she said. "But, for now, let us breakfast and laze away the day. I don't suppose Boxing Day is celebrated here, so today is the main holiday."

"What do you think of the proposal from Jacques to supply us with silk?" he asked.

"We should take advantage while we can," she thought. "People are still cautious so soon after the war, but it will not be long before confidence returns and the demand for new fashions increases. So, agreeing to a longer-term supply with Jacques will be beneficial to us. I just hope that Marie can do justice to the fabrics and create suitable designs that we can readily make."

"I'm sure she will," he said.

"Actually, so am I," she said. "So, instead of lying there, it is time to be up and time that we went down for breakfast, though looking at the late hour, it might almost be for lunch."

All too soon, it was time to begin the journey home, so Federica and George said goodbye to the hotel and to Sophie and Jacques and boarded the train to take them home. If the weather had been nicer, it would have been a very pleasant journey, but winter had set in, and there was rain to the south, and as they went further north, the rain turned to light snow. Nothing that would impede their progress, but enough to put a dusting on everything and turn the world white.

"I wonder what 1921 will bring," Federica said to George over dinner.

"Expect the Bolsheviks in Russia to expand their control over other countries," he said. "And look for industrial unrest in the country, I think beginning with the coal miners."

"Do we treat our people well enough to avoid that unpleasantness?" she asked.

"You would know better than me," he said, "You have had much closer contact in the past years than me."

"My instincts may be wrong, but I think we will avoid such unrest," she said. "We pay quite well, we listen to them when they have an idea and generally treat them like people. And for us, what do we do?"

"I think go back to the monoplane," he said. "The question is wood or metal."

"If wood, then a sandwich like we have been using," she said. "Sandwiches of different woods laid with the grains at angles to each other. We should run some tests to see what angle gives us the best stiffness and strength. At least where we are, there are plenty of people who understand wood. High Wycombe has been the centre of furniture making for some time. I was thinking of talking to Lucian Ercolani to see if I could interest him in a veneer peeler, or else buying the veneers from somewhere and glueing them together, as we do now."

"There's also Gommes, Bartlett, Birch and Dancer and Hearne," he reminded her.

"True," she said. "I was thinking of a fuselage that is made in two halves, then fixed together with some reinforcing ribs, rather like a shell boat, a monocoque structure."

"You've thought about this," he commented.

"Nastia and I have our ideas," she confirmed. "And if we can solve the problem of the cantilever wing, we can make it work. I thought we'd start with a two-seater, single-engine plane, then if that works, twelve seats and a twin."

"Well, a lot to think about and do," he said. "Would our own Andrew Coates be of help with the sandwich construction, after all, we do that a lot for our cars?"

"We plan to talk to him," she said. "We may be able to do all the work ourselves and not involve anyone else. The challenge will be to form the material into curved shapes, more curved than with our cars, so we have some investigating to do."

"I'm sure that between the three of you that you will do admirably," he said confidently. "Now, I believe it's time for lunch."

The balance of the journey was marked by ever-dropping temperatures, so that when they arrived at Victoria Station, it was below freezing and just downright cold.

"I wonder how long this cold spell will last," Federica said to George as they made the railway leg of their journey from Paddington.

"I just hope the car will start," he said. "We left at Maidenhead and it's had time to get really cold."

"It's a pity that the heater that Margaret Wilcox invented in the last century has no means of control," she said. "I wonder if we couldn't invent some form of heater exchanger that has controls on it to vary the volume of hot air and thus the temperature. I'll put it to Mr White and see if he has any notions."

"Did you ever imagine when you were in Hong Kong that you would be thinking of such matters?" he asked.

"No," she laughed. "I doubt that I thought about it any more than you did when you were soldiering in India and South Africa."

"Well, here we are at Maidenhead," he said. "Now to see if the car starts."

The car did start, but the journey home was chilly, and at least the enclosed body of the car kept them protected from the wind and the drizzle.

Anastasia and Will were back from the Lakes and invited Federica and George to a New Year's Eve party. There were notables there from the surrounding area, including the local member, a Conservative who enjoyed a substantial majority, even after the acts of 1918 that had widened the voting field to include all men over the age of 21 and women who met certain qualifications. The member, in Federica's opinion, was an idiot who had no business purporting to represent the people. He had been elected because his opponent had been an out-and-out socialist, verging on Bolshevism, which even among the working classes did not sit well. All the member wanted to talk about the Labour Party and their platform that included high tax rates and nationalisation of certain, if not all, industry. Federica and George both had an interest in that but felt that the member's arguments were going to fall flat with all but a few. A General Election would be held at some time either in 1921 or 1922, the latter being postponed because of the war. Still, it was useful to cultivate the local member, as he might be useful in the coming years.

At the start of 1921, Federica applied herself to cars and Sirius, and she and Anastasia made improvements, both to the design and the manufacture, so that they could meet rising demand and increased competition, including imported models. She also spent time with Marie Garnier, who was now installed at Windsor Garments and already producing new lines of dresses. George set himself the task of finding a photographer who would work for them, taking pictures of clothes, cars and other products. He interviewed 25 and finally found three who might serve and invited them to meet with Federica, Anastasia, Marie and Ian. The upshot of that was that they took on Helen Greene. She had the best portfolio and was the most open to suggestions about the style of photographs they were looking for. The fact that she was a woman did not count against her with the family, after all two of the main drivers in the enterprises were women, and the men who worked in the various companies had long since accepted them. Federica approached furniture companies, and although they had an academic interest, business at the moment was too good to take on a distraction like aircraft, even though some had produced fuselages during the late war. They did give her advice as to where to buy the best veneers and also what the different characteristics of the various woods were. Andrew Coates set us a test stand and glued panels, bent panels, broke panels, subjected them to water, ice, heat and salt and acquired mountains of data, all of which he gave to Federica. She mulled over the data and decided that the fuselage would be a sandwich of three-ply birch around a five-ply larch inner. Glue was the greatest challenge, finding a glue that would stand heat, sunlight, rain and cold. In the end, she settled on a urea-formaldehyde resin recently patented in Austria by one Hanns John. Making sure that appropriate time and pains were taken to apply the glue properly and clamp it well would be a manufacturing issue, but she was confident that she could do that.

George helped Helen set up a photographic studio and dark room and bought cameras, tripods, developing tanks, enlargers and the rest. She started out with dresses from Windsor, and it was soon apparent that they needed a model, someone who would wear the clothes to best advantage. They found the model at Windsor. One of the ladies who ran a sewing machine was singularly attractive and happy to earn the extra they paid her. For cars, the studio was not large enough, so George took to driving around to find suitable locations outdoors where they could photograph the car in natural surroundings. He posed by the cars, dressed in anything from shooting jackets to dinner jackets. Helen then added colour by hand and created the pages for the advertisements to be placed in *The Autocar*.

"Are you enjoying your jaunts with Helen?" Federica asked him after a long shoot in the beech woods.

"I had no idea it was such hard work," he said. "Stand there, stand here, move your arm this way, lean on the car, lean on your shooting stick, it's been quite an education. I'm thinking of resigning my post as the face of Sirius and hiring a young, handsome man to be the model."

"I think you're handsome," she protested.

"Yes, but you're biased and you don't see the age, the camera does," he said. "At least photographing electrical items and biscuits doesn't need any people, just clothes and cars."

"Do you think it is going to do us any good?" she asked.

"I think so," he said. "We need to advertise, and for that, artists' illustrations or photographs, I would rather stay with the photographs."

"Do you think Helen does a good job?" she asked.

"I think so," he said. "Certainly, Marie and Ian like her work. How soon before you start work on a new plane?"

"We still have to work out the cantilever wing and how we attach the fuselage to it, or them," she replied. "I'm favouring a wing that is in two parts, shoulder mounted to the fuselage."

"What is the span, wing tip to tip?" he asked.

"I'd say 47 feet," she said.

"And you'd make wooden spars for each of the mainplanes?" he asked.

"In the same way that laminated beams are made," she replied. "The spars would need special shaping to get thinner as they get closer to the tips, but I think we could manage that. We'll also need that new radial engine that Will has been working on."

"Would you brace the wing at all?" he asked.

"I'm thinking of struts that run from the wing to the bottom of the fuselage," she said.

"Is there anything I can do?" he asked.

"Help me find the right wood, I'd like it to be birch or larch, clear with no knots if we could find it," she said. "I'll set out some long tables in the hangar and lay out what the spars should be like, and we can build them up."

"And to cover the wings?" he asked.

"We'll make plywood panels the right size and shape," she said. "Do you think it's possible to bury a petrol tank inside the wing?"

"Possibly where they're thickest, at the shoulders where they attach to the fuselage, I think that's what Junkers did with their F13," he said. "Do you have any drawings to show you how much space there would be and how large a tank you could fit?"

"I'll take a look," she said. "With our old planes, it's not possible, the wings are just not built that way, but with a cantilever wing, they have to have some depth just to be stiff enough."

"If we did that, then we'd have to think carefully about the plumbing, where it goes, how we draw petrol from each tank, because I'm assuming you'd put one on each side," he said. "Then we'd have to add all that before we put the final skins on the wings."

"I think we can do all that," she said. "Nastia and I will put our heads together and finish the design and construction of the wing, I hope by March."

"How do we pay for this?" he asked. "I'm reluctant to raid Sirius and the other companies."

"I still have £10,000 or so left from the money your father willed to me to start Sirius," she replied. "I think that should be adequate."

"I have received a communication from Sam Higgins," George announced at breakfast in mid-January. "He has had the Andromeda rebuilt, and his son has flown it, and they are using it to fly guests from New York to a country hotel in Maine. He says it is performing well and that he may copy it and build another."

"That is good news," Federica said. "I wonder how they deal with the weather over there. I have read in the newspaper about storms, snow and all kinds of unpleasantness."

"I would presume that they know the weather and when not to attempt to fly," she said. "Nastia and I have a wing design that we'd like to try."

"So soon?" he asked.

"We were further along than we had thought, so now we are at the stage of building up the wings, and then we'd like to try some tests on them," she said. "What I would like to try is to build a small-scale model and see if we can get the opportunity to test it in the wind tunnel at Farnborough."

"Will a scale model reflect the behaviour of a full-size craft?" he asked.

"That I really don't know," she admitted. "But I think we would learn much, and if we are able to do it, I would like to try."

"I'll talk to people at the Royal Aircraft Establishment at Farnborough whom I know," he said.

"How big are the tunnels?" she asked.

"Seven feet in diameter," he replied.

"So, we would need to build a tenth-scale model," she thought. "So that it would fit easily into the tunnel. Does everyone do this?"

"I have no idea," he replied. "I would think not, or the demands on the tunnel for time would be too high."

"How do we test the model?" she asked.

"I think attach little wisps of fibre to the wings and parts of the fuselage and see if they stream out in the airstream or flutter wildly," he said. "I'm sure the scientists at the RAE can give us some guidance."

"Should we build our own tunnel?" she asked.

"Wenham did, so why shouldn't we. We would need a big fan, a building large enough to hold it and some means to hold the models and observe them. I think the Farnborough tunnels are more open wind channels than actual tunnels, we should try and visit and inspect them," he thought.

"What fun," she said. "I'll set about building the model, will you help me?"

"Of course," he said. "Do you have all the drawings done?"

"Most," she said. "I have the basic shape of the wings and the fuselage, but not yet the actual construction drawings, but for our purpose, that does not matter; we're looking at how the finished aircraft performs in the air."

"What about wheels?" he asked.

"I think one wheel on each side fixed to struts that come out from the bottom of the fuselage, I think also attached to the forward wing strut" she thought.

"And tailplanes and rudder?" he asked.

"I think simple," she said. "I have ideas for them already."

"Well, it sounds like we have work to do. I suppose we should get on with the day," he said.

Federica got to work and produced drawings from which she could make her scale model. She actually shaped it from solid pieces of wood, consulting some of the furniture makers as to how best to carve, shape and sand the shapes. For the struts, she used simple wire and soldered the pieces together to form the wing struts and the pyramids that the wheels sat on. For wheels, she had one of the machinists in the Sirius shop turn her little wheels to attach to the struts. The propeller, they had a big debate about, whether to use a two, three or four-bladed propeller. Variable pitch propellers had been around for a while, but they had to be adjusted on the ground. But developments by Baynes and Turnbull pointed to the ability to do this in the air; however, their systems were not reliable yet, so could not be used. So, for the moment, they would have to stay with a fixed pitch propeller. After much debate, they settled on a two-bladed design, which was actually simple to make as it was one continuous piece, pierced in the centre for the spinner. Meanwhile, George had been busy and had arranged for them to take their model to Farnborough and run some tests.

The tests turned out to be very instructive. Clearly, there were areas where things could be improved. Federica and George watched fascinated by the fibres attached to the model and how they behaved in the wind, and they watched the streams of coloured smoke that were directed over the wings and the fuselage and saw what flowed nicely and what was turbulent. They were somewhat constrained as the tunnel only produced wind speeds of 90 mph, so not as fast as they actually hoped to fly, but sufficient to point out potential problems. The scientists and engineers at the RAE cautioned about directly scaling the results and provided suggestions as to how best interpret the results.

"This is super," Federica said to George as they watched the tests. "Look there, at the wing tip, the way that vortex formed. Is that a result of the tunnel or the wings themselves?"

"Perhaps we could modify them a bit and see," he suggested.

"We could, but would they invite us back to take up more of their time?" she asked.

"I'm sure that there's a limit to what we can reasonably ask," he said. "I'm thinking that we could build something like this ourselves. We could also put models of the cars in it to see how they fare at speed. Looking at what they have here, I'm confident we could reproduce this."

"Who has big fans?" she asked.

"We do," he said. "The lead mine that we shut down in Derbyshire had ventilation fans, and I'm sure that one of them would be big enough. We would have to see if it would still work well blowing at much higher speeds, but it's worth the test. I'll get a couple of the miners that we had to put out to take one apart and bring it to Handy Cross. In fact, we had a young mining engineer who, apart from knowing about blasting out the lead ore, was the ventilation expert. I'll see what he is doing at the moment."

Mr Robin Hoppes, the mining engineer, had found employment with a coal mine, but was less than happy in his new job, so was delighted to come south and talk about the opportunity to build a wind tunnel. The fan taken from the mine arrived just after he did, and he set about designing a building that would house the fan and direct the air through a series of ducts and throats to where they would suspend the model. He was confident that he could give them wind speeds in excess of 100 mph, which would tell them a lot. The only drawback to Federica was that it would all take time, and she had models to test immediately. She had made two more models of the same plane, with some changes to each, so that she could see which gave the better performance.

"This will cost some money," Robin pointed out to her.

"How much?" she asked.

"At least £1,000," he said.

"Proceed," she said. "We can sell the two small planes we have in the hangar. We can probably get £500 apiece for them. I'll advertise them for sale and see what may occur."

Pegasus

The RAF surveyed and started a cross-desert route for mail from Cairo to Baghdad. Trial flights were made with flying boats from London to Paris using the Thames and the Seine, but it was determined that the idea was not practical due to payload limitations. Aviation was taking off around the world, but commercial passenger traffic was limited by the size and speed of the aircraft and by the costs.

Robin had the wind tunnel built by the end of March, a time that Federica and George thought remarkable. He tested it and reported wind speeds of up to 120 mph, a number that delighted Federica. There had been some concerns raised by one of the local farmers about the noise the fan made, so George invited him to come and see it in operation and promised to give him reasonable notice when they were going to operate it. Being in the area governed by the High Wycombe Rural District presented some issues, but they were really minor. Generally the Handy Cross operations had been left alone and in the period of the Great War, expediency and speed to produce aircraft for the war effort had meant that the council had essentially left them to their own devices, which had included installing their own electricity generation, but it was rumoured that electrical service was going to be extended from High Wycombe to Handy Cross. Federica and George tried their original aircraft model and saw that they could closely replicate the results from the Farnborough wind tunnel, so they then tried the two new models, noting the differences and marking which model seemed to give the best overall performance. Robin had some ideas about how to minimise the effects of the walls of the tunnel on the wing vortices, and they were tried and approved of. That set Robin onto a campaign of his own to learn more about airflow and fluid dynamics in general and the principles of flight. Federica also made a model of their Andromeda plane to see if the changes and assumptions she and Anastasia had made had been of value. The tunnel tests showed areas that she had not considered and pointed to some of the fundamental drawbacks of wings that were too flexible. After that, she was satisfied that it would fly well, but that it could have been improved upon if she had had access to a wind tunnel earlier.

"So, are you ready to start building your prototype plane?" George asked Federica as they studied the wind tunnel results.

"I need to modify the drawings to match the final model, then I may make a start," she replied. "What I would also like to do is go to the Paris Air Show and see what is new."

"I'll make arrangements," he promised. "What may I do to help you with the drawings?"

"Between Nastia and me, we can manage," Federica replied. "How are we doing with wood supplies?"

"There are still problems finding suitable spruce," he replied. "We may have to create our own laminates from spruce we can get and from birch. I also read that tropical conditions can deteriorate the spruce."

"Perhaps we should conduct some tests with our laminates in hot and humid conditions and in hot and dry and see what happens," she said. "It may serve our purposes to set Robin up with Mr White and expand upon the testing laboratory to investigate materials of all types that we might use in our cars, clothes, electrical items and planes."

"I'll talk to them both and see what we can do," he said. "I am curious to see how our cars might behave in high winds. Perhaps we can have someone make us a quarter-scale model and see."

"I like that idea," she said. "We should discuss it with Nastia, Will and Ian Stuart."

"Of course," he agreed.

The family met and talked about the businesses and the general condition of the economy. The 1920s were turning out, for them at least, to be a time of growth and success, but George was concerned that would not last, so insisted that they limit growth to that which they thought they sustain, and to create reserves so that if the economy worsened then they could weather a depression. Robin Hoppes was set up with Mr White, their in-house inventor and tester of materials, and they were given more space and equipment to conduct tests and experiments. Federica told them all that she had sold the Aquila and Auriga planes that they had for £1,500 and that that money would go to defraying the costs of the wind tunnel. Then she turned to the task of building a prototype of the new plane. She and George had asked Andrew Coates to join them, and he offered a suggestion about how to build up the fuselage panels, glueing the various veneers in place inside a mould that was shaped to the form of the fuselage, and to weight it down while the glue set. The veneers were thin enough that they had a degree of flexibility, even with the grain, as long as the radius was not too sharp. The radius would be essentially the diameter, or the major diameter of what was basically an elliptical shape, and would never be a tight curve, so it was worth trying. It was either that or steam the flat panels enough to be able to form them post-glueing. He also suggested a least one layer of linen fabric to add strength to the whole. For the openings in the fuselage, he suggested a series of shaped laminates that would be affixed around the opening to take the loads.

"How do we create the mould?" George asked.

"We can make one out of a steel frame and thin concrete shell," Andrew suggested. "In the manner that ferrocrete boats have been made, back as far as 1840, pioneered by the Frenchman, Lambot."

"So, we'd be essentially making an inside-out boat hull?" George asked.

"That's how I see it," Andrew replied.

"Let's try that," George said. "Who shall we find to make the moulds for us?"

"I know a boat builder who could do it," Andrew said. "Bonds of Cookham, I know David Bond, I'll talk to him and get a quotation, do you have some drawings that would give us the shape?"

"We do," Anastasia confirmed. "I have a set of drawings for both halves of the fuselage."

"What do we do for windows?" Will asked.

"We'll cut them out of the finished pieces and add reinforcing around the openings. For the glass, we'll either make our own or buy from Triplex Safety Glass," Federica replied. "Now, Andrew, let us know when we may meet with Mr Bond."

"I'll do that," he promised.

David Bond was quite enthusiastic about building a mould for them and also offered to help create the laminates themselves. He told them that he wanted to see if it would be applicable to boat building. He thought not, but it was worth the investigation. He had the moulds made in his boatyard, and Federica arranged for a lorry to carry them to Handy Cross. Meanwhile, George had been busy acquiring veneers and laths of spruce to make the laminated shell of the fuselage and the wing spars. It took David Bond two weeks to make and cure the moulds, and then they were ready to start. The next question was whether to place the layers allowing for the openings of the windows, or to create a solid shell and then cut the windows from it afterwards. David suggested making a solid form, then cutting the windows and doors and applying the reinforcing around the openings and adding stiffeners that ran around the whole periphery to attach the floor to, and adding another thin layer of laminate on the interior that was finished nicely, the gap between providing some degree of noise insulation. That fit well with the method that Federica had been leaning towards. Laying up the veneers took time as each addition was glued, then allowed to set properly before the next layer was added. While that was being done, George and Federica built up the wings and installed the cables that would control the ailerons and flaps. They also installed the petrol tanks and the plumbing needed to transfer fuel to the engine. George and Federica also built up what would become the wing box, the frame that the two wing halves attached to. The frame would go inside the finished fuselage, so it had to be ready before the halves were glued together. The stiffeners were going to have to be added from the inside, so they needed the doors cut to gain access.

"I wonder if we haven't made this more complicated than it needs to be," Federica commented to George as they looked at the chart that showed what had to go in first and so on.

"Perhaps," he said. "But it's either do this or build a conventional frame and clad it with the plywood. I like this method more as it gives us a lower weight in the end. I need to check with Will to see what we will need to mount the engine on the front of the fuselage. We'll certainly need a degree of reinforcing there."

When the two fuselage halves were ready, with door and window cutouts and reinforcing done, the reinforcing ribs were glued in, and the wing box fitted, then the mounting for the wheels and the wing strut. Then the moment of truth came when the second half was fitted and the whole was clamped together with straps that ran around the outside in a dozen places. They allowed two days for the glue to set properly, then they also set screws through the fuselage into the ribs. George went inside the plane and threaded the control lines for the rudder and tailplanes all the way from the cockpit aft. He also looked for gaps between the reinforcing ribs and the outer shell and could find none. Then he installed the floor and with the help of Will, the engine, the doors and windows and the pilot's controls and attached the plumbing for the fuel tanks to the engine.

"I think it's time to test the engine and see how much everything shakes," Will said after the inside was finished.

"Ready?" George asked.

"Ready," Will confirmed. They started the engine and ran it up, and started to look through the fuselage, looking for vibrations. There were some, but not quite as many as they had expected.

"Try the fuel tank switch," George suggested.

"Here goes," Will said. "I note a small hesitation there. I wonder if we shouldn't have a small reservoir that actually feeds the engine and fill that from the tanks."

"So, what's your best guess, estimate, or calculation about the range we'll get?" Federica asked.

"I'd say about six hours of flying, so with good wind conditions, 700 nautical miles, perhaps a little more," Will said. "I can probably add some extra tankage and get that to at least eight hours, but I'm not sure any passengers we'd take would want to be stuck for that long without a break."

"So, our route to the Cape would be, here to Rome, Cairo, Khartoum, Kisumu, Livingstone, Pretoria, then Cape Town, with stops in between for lunch, fuel and toilets," Federica thought. "I don't suppose there would be any issues with petrol on the way, except perhaps over Central Africa, we'd have to make sure that there was petrol there. The only hotel I have questions about would be Kisumu, but we can check on that fairly readily."

"Shall we try mounting the wings?" George asked.

"We should," she agreed. Will shut down the engine, and they turned their attention to the wings. Then they had a debate about how to do it, try and do both at once, or mount one, then the other. That led to some calculations about turning moments; they would not want the plane to tip on one side with only one wing mounted. Will suggested that they actually raise the wing with a small platform and let the platform carry the weight until the other wing was fitted.

"It looks well, doesn't it," Federica commented after the wings were attached.

"It does," George agreed. "Shall we try some taxi tests?"

"That is a good idea," she agreed. "Will, do you wish to sit in the front and observe?"

"Why don't George and I take it up and down the runway a few times, and you and Nastia observe from here and tell us what you see, then we'll trade and we'll watch from here," Will suggested.

"Let me first attach some ribbons to see how the air flows over the wings as you taxi," Federica said. "Nastia, what did you calculate the takeoff speed to be?"

"I calculated 60 knots," she replied. "At about 40 knots, the tail should lift. I also calculated that the takeoff run should be about 600 feet, so less than half the runway we have."

"Does our car go that fast?" Federica asked.

"Not one we have," Nastia replied. "But, I know of one that will easily do that and more, perhaps we should borrow it and travel down the runway, with one of us driving and one of us observing."

"I wonder if the War Office is selling off Aeroscope cameras," Federica said. "Perhaps we could purchase one and take moving pictures of the plane as it taxis. For today, let us just watch from partway down the runway and see how it performs."

They ran taxi tests, back and forth into the wind and with the wind. It looked as if Anastasia's calculations were quite good because at what they estimated to be 40 knots, they saw the tail lift and the plane level out.

"The engine performs well," Federica commented when they took a break.

"I'm happy with it," Will said. "It has more than enough power for this plane, and we should get a very good cruise speed."

"I noted that we lifted off very slightly on four runs into the wind at about 56 knots," George said. "I think that tomorrow we may try and take off and see how it handles in the air."

"Looking at the ribbons I attached, the airflow across the wings looks good," Federica said. "I noted some little eddies at the very tips of the wings, but I suppose that is normal."

"I wonder if we could borrow another plane and fly alongside and watch it in flight," Anastasia said. "Who has a plane fast enough?"

"It's a pity that the Siskin is only a single seat, because that's more than fast enough," George commented. "But, I do know a chap who has a Martinsyde F2 that is almost there in speed and does have two seats, I'll talk to him."

"What more do we have to do to get the airworthiness certificate?" Will asked.

"Trial flights with data," Federica replied. "We have the design data, we have the wind tunnel tests on the model, so now we need real flight data."

"So, we'd better get in the air and start," Will said. "Let's look at the weather for tomorrow and plan out our day."

The weather did not cooperate, and they were grounded for almost a week before the trial flights could begin. But that had given them the time to acquire an Aeroscope camera and the film to go with it and instructions on how to use it. Federica asked Helen Greene to become familiar with the camera, and also asked her if she felt that she could fly in a plane and operate it. Helen was quite excited by the notion, and Federica fitted her out with the proper clothes, so that she would not be cold sitting in the open cockpit. George also made arrangements with his friend, Angus Fraser, to join them for the day and fly as a chase plane to their new plane so that they could observe it in flight. It struck

Federica that the whole process was a lot more organised and scientific than their early forays into the air, where they had probably trusted to providence a little too much.

"Angus, this is my wife, Federica, my sister, Anastasia and her husband, William, and Helen Greene, she will be operating the camera taking moving pictures," George said as he introduced everyone when Angus arrived.

"Good morning," Angus said. "So, George tells me you have a new plane that you'd like to start air trials with and that you'd like to take some moving pictures of it in flight."

"That's correct," Federica confirmed. "We have designed and built planes in the past, but never a monoplane, so this is a first for us, and we'd like to see if our assumptions are correct. How close will you be able to fly to our plane?"

"As close as you want me to," Angus said. "Do you want me above, below or alongside?"

"I admit I had not thought of that," Federica said. "Is it too much of an imposition to ask for four flights, one slightly behind and slightly above, one behind and below, one directly astern and below and one alongside?"

"Not at all," Angus said. "This is most interesting. Helen, have you flown before?"

"No," she said. "I'm excited to be going, but I've never been before."

"Perhaps before we do the tests, we should take a short flight to see how you fare," he suggested. "Also, bring the camera and see if you can hold it while we fly. We'll first just fly a little for you to get used to it, then you can try with the camera."

"I'm ready," she said.

Federica and George watched her go with Angus and climb up into the cockpit. Will handed her the camera, and she grinned at them all. Angus started up, taxied out then took off. He flew around for about thirty minutes, then came back in to land.

"Did you enjoy that?" Federica asked Helen. The huge grin she got was reply enough.

"It was wonderful," she said. "We flew over High Wycombe and Marlow, and I could see all the houses below. I can't wait to go again."

"First, we should fill the petrol tanks," George said. "We don't want Angus running out of petrol."

"I've enough," Angus said.

"We're going to fill them anyway," George said. "You are doing us an enormous favour, so the least we can do is make sure you have enough petrol."

"Thanks," Angus said. "From what Helen told me, we'll have to come back and land between each run for her to change the film in the camera. So, do you want to come back in each time, or loiter?"

"We should probably come back in as well," George thought. "The more takeoffs and landings we get, the more we learn about the plane."

"Good, I'll go up first, circle back around in time to catch you taking off and climbing out," Angus suggested. "Then I'll come back in first each time, and if Helen has any film left, we can get you landing. Then, when we're done with the four runs in the air, Helen has suggested that she film you taking off and landing."

"Right," George said. "Fede, do you want to fly this time?"

"You take the first run, then Nastia, then me, then Will," she suggested.

Angus took off and started to circle around, so George started his takeoff run and was just lifting off as Angus came up behind him. From the ground, with her binoculars, Federica watched the planes and could see Helen pointing the camera at their new plane. The flight did not last that long, and Angus came back in to land, followed by George. Will went over and helped Helen down, and she scurried off into the hangar to the temporary dark room she had set up there and changed the film. Then she was back, eager to be off again. They went through all the flights, then Angus asked if he might try the controls. George went with him and briefed him on the controls, the engine speeds required, the takeoff and landing speeds, and answered the questions that Angus had. Federica, Anastasia and Will watched as they took off, went through all kinds of turns, banks, climbs and dives until they came back in.

"This plane truly handles well," Angus said when he joined them at the hangar. "Could I get one?"

"We hadn't yet thought of building another," George said. "But, if you really want one, I'm sure we could manage that."

"Just let me know how much," Angus said. "It has better speed, better handling than my F2 and the cockpit is enclosed with actually better visibility than the F2."

"So, Helen, how long to develop the films and arrange to view them?" Federica asked.

"Give me a day to do the developing and set everything up," Helen said.

"Fine," Federica said. "Meanwhile, we should all compare notes about what we felt, saw and heard."

"Why don't we all meet tomorrow at the Sirius offices?" Federica suggested. "Angus, are you able to stay at least until tomorrow?"

"I can stay for the next two days," he replied. "I am interested to see what the moving pictures of the plane show."

"We would be happy to have you as our guest," Federica said. "Is there anything that you need?"

"No, I came prepared for a few days," he replied. "I've learned to travel with some basic luggage to always be prepared."

"Splendid," she said. "We have our car here, would you like to put your plane in the hangar, there is room enough?"

"Better than leaving it out," he said.

"We have a small tractor that we can use to tow it in," George said. "We'll just attach a line to the wheels and pull it in."

"You've done this before," Angus commented as he watched George and Will attach a bridle to the wheels, then pull the aircraft into the shelter of the hangar.

"We built a fair number of aircraft during the late war," Federica said. "So, we looked for all ways to make our lives easier. The tractor is actually one of our Sirius cars that we modified for towing."

They met the next day in the meeting room that Sirius had, along with Mr White and Robin Hoppes, and each had their turn to talk about the way the plane felt and handled and if there were any changes that should be made. The consensus was that no changes to the wings, the fuselage or the tailplanes were required, but they all felt that the rudder could be a little larger. The overall impression of the plane was it was better than had been anticipated. It was certainly faster, it had a better climb rate, and it handled in the air as well, if not better than any of the other types they had all flown. The other item that was discussed at length was the insulation in the fuselage for cold and for noise. They had yet to install the heater that was planned, but felt that that would benefit from better insulation. Robin chimed in to say that he and Mr White had been working on a new sandwich material that should provide superior insulation both for sound and for temperature, be it heat or cold. He said that they could have enough made to replace the existing interior panels in about a week. He added that they thought they had a better heater with more control and were looking to also make a version for the Sirius cars. There was one last item: what to call the new plane.

"I think Pegasus would be good," Federica suggested. "It stays with the astronomical naming of all our planes and cars, I know that Vacuum Oil in South Africa use a flying horse, probably Pegasus, as their emblem, but it has not been copyrighted here in England."

"So, we see this as a flying workhorse," George said. "I like that. Then, if we do sell planes, it will make good advertising copy."

"What images are out there in the classics of Pegasus?" Federica asked.

"I would put that to Helen," Anastasia suggested.

"Do you always get into this much detail?" Angus asked.

"If we can," George replied. "We've found that it helps to discuss things, to tear apart our assumptions and see if we have been wrong. It has helped in the past with the cars and with the other enterprises that we have. The only one that Will and I missed was the Andromeda aircraft that Fede and Nastia designed and built while we were in France. They did a remarkable job, and we flew it on a number of long flights before we sold it to an American."

"Why did you sell?" Angus asked.

"It was a large biplane," Federica replied. "And it's our view that the real future lies with monoplanes, so we wanted to move in that direction, hence Pegasus."

"What's the chap in America using it for?" Angus asked.

"Apparently, he has hotels in New York and in other places, so he flies guests between them; his son is a pilot and does the actual flying," George replied.

"This has been very good," Federica said. "I'm looking forward to seeing the moving pictures tomorrow."

Helen had everything ready when they reconvened the next day, with a screen set up and the first reel of film already loaded into the projector. She and Alice had covered the windows with black crepe paper so that the room would be dark when the projector was run.

"Have you viewed this, Helen?" Federica asked.

"I have," she confirmed. "It is really interesting. I managed to get ten minutes of film of each flight and of the takeoff and landing."

"Splendid," Federica said. "Whenever you are ready."

"This is the first flight, taken from a little behind and above," Helen said.

"Look at the ribbons," George said. "It's interesting the inboard ones stream straight back, and as you move towards the wind tips, we get a little more flutter."

"That was what we expected," Anastasia said. "That's what we saw in the wind tunnel."

"So, this seems to confirm that the wind tunnel is a useful tool in the testing of concepts," Federica said.

"It does," Anastasia confirmed. They watched the other films and made notes on each. When it was all done, Helen turned on the lights and looked to them for comment.

"Super job, Helen," George said. "Thank you, Angus, for getting as close as you did."

"I didn't want to get too close," Angus said. "I didn't know if our being close would affect the airflow around your plane."

"Good thought," George said. "Did anyone see anything that really needs to change, apart from increasing the size of the rudder, which we've already talked about?"

"Nothing extra," Federica said. "You did a wonderful job on the design, Nastia. This is truly the best plane we have built yet."

"It would be better if there were some kind of special lens, like a telescope that would let me get closer pictures, but that might also increase the shake that you see sometimes with the camera. I tried resting it on the cockpit side, but the engine vibration caused it to shake a little, so had to hold it," Helen said.

"I think when we run tests in the wind tunnel in the future, that we should film the tests," Anastasia said.

"Good idea," Federica agreed. "This has been a very good morning. I think it's time for lunch."

The request for a certificate of airworthiness was submitted to the Air Ministry. They were told that it would be a few weeks before the examiner could be at their factory. In the interim however they were issued with a registration identifier for the plane, that they had painted on the sides of the fuselage, after they filled all the screw heads and painted the fuselage and the wings Sirius blue, paying a couple of painters from the car body shop to do it over a weekend.

"So, what do we do while we wait for this inspector from the Ministry?" Federica asked George.

"Why don't we do some longer test flights, say to Scotland and back," he replied. "We probably can't land at the RAF station again, but there is a field that a couple of fliers have near Carlisle that we could try. I don't know if they have petrol, so we should take enough to get us there and back."

"That should be a good test," she thought. "Let's check the weather and see what the next two or three days hold."

"I think Angus and Helen may see each other again," George said.

"Really?" Federica asked.

"I think so," he replied. "They were talking after we'd watched all the moving pictures, and there is definitely something there."

"Just as long as he doesn't whisk her away to parts unknown," Federica said. "Then we'd have to find another photographer."

"Is there anything we could give him to do?" George asked.

"I should think upon that," she said. "I wonder if he would be interested in biscuits. Mr Robertson is nearing the age when he might retire, and he has mentioned it once or twice."

"I'll talk to him and to Mr Robertson, perhaps arrange a luncheon with the three of us," George suggested.

"I'll leave that to you," she said. "What does Angus do now?"

"He has a confectioner's shop in Town in Knightsbridge, they make their own cakes and sweetmeats," George said. "He inherited it from his father, and he does have a younger brother who is also engaged in the business."

"Would it be a possibility for us to buy the business?" she asked.

"I'll talk to Angus and see what he says," George promised.

"The weather looks good tomorrow," George announced at breakfast time. "We should take a test flight north."

"I'll talk to Will and Nastia and see if they want to come," Federica said. "It may be that they're too busy at the moment. This December, should we exhibit cars in the *Salon de l'Automobile* in Paris?"

"Why not," he said. Anastasia and Will were busy for the next two days, working on improvements to the cars that would be offered for sale in 1922. Federica had a now familiar twinge of guilt as she was ready to go flying again while Anastasia and Will were attending to everyday matters of the car business. She did resolve that, weather permitting, she would take flights on weekends and devote the weekdays to the companies that they had. But, for the moment, the weather looked perfect for the next couple of days and horrible for the upcoming weekend.

"Ready?" she asked George as they went through the checks to make sure everything was in order on the plane.

"Ready," he confirmed. "Let's start up and see how we do on a longer flight."

"I wonder how long it will be before the government improves on the system we have today for controlling air traffic," she pondered.

"I suppose when wireless becomes better, when every plane is equipped with wireless and there is a better map that shows who is where," he thought.

"But how do you know who is who?" she asked.

"Well, I suppose we'd have to call on the wireless and say who we are, where we are and where we are going," he suggested. "And the chaps in Croydon could then mark it on their maps."

"Well, for the moment we don't have to worry about that, so let's taxi out and go," she said.

"I'll call Croydon and tell them we're on our way and where we're off to," he said. "Good, that's done, we can go now."

"I really like the way this plane handles," she said as they soared into the air. "It's better than any of those we built."

"It's almost as good as the fighter planes I flew in the War," he said. "I'm not sure I would want to throw it around the sky the way I did some of the fighters, but I'm sure that it would survive even that."

"It's fast, isn't it?" she said.

"Faster than I expected," he said. "I wonder what the range is at this speed. Should we climb a little higher?"

"Where are we now, 10,000 feet, let's go up to 12,000 feet, how far up can we go before there's not enough oxygen to breathe?" she asked.

"That seems to depend on the person," he said. "Some people even have problems here at 10,000, so for them going higher is not good. I've been up to 15,000, and I noticed that I was slower to react, so I came back down a little. In the War, it was often a race to see who could get the highest, then come out of the sun onto the enemies below. The Germans were very good at that."

"Look, we're passing over Birmingham now," she said. "Next Liverpool, then I thought we'd hug the coast up to Carlisle."

"It is a beautiful day for flying," he said. "When we try for the Cape, I was thinking of May or June, the weather here is not too bad then, and in the Southern Hemisphere, winter is setting in, so it's not too hot. We'd just have to check the rains over Kenya and Uganda and see when they're the worst."

"So, next year in May," she thought. "I like that, it gives us time to check on everything, it gives us time to gain more experience with this plane and decide whether it is reliable enough to get us there, or if we need to build another that has two engines."

"Part of me says that two engines would be better," he said. "But if this engine proves to be very reliable, then we could go with this."

"I wonder if on the way back we should fly over the fells and the lake,'" George said. "Did we bring a camera?"

"I did," Federica confirmed. "If you fly back, I'll try and get some pictures of the lakes as we fly over."

"It's a pity that the Windermere landing is only for seaplanes," he said. "But I suppose finding a long enough piece of flat land is hard in the Lakes, but at least Windermere is flat. Let's see, the field I was told about is a little west of Carlisle, just over the Eden."

"Is that it there?" she asked, pointing to a field.

"Looks like it is, wind sock, hangar, that's it, let's see the wind in off the Solway so we should circle around again and then go in," he said.

"This field is quite smooth," she said as they touched down. "It's close enough to the Eden. I wonder if it ever floods."

"Good question," he said. "Taxi over there, there are some chaps there waving to us."

"Good morning," one of them said as George opened the door.

"Good morning," George replied. "We hope you don't mind us dropping in on you like this. George Wheelwright, this is my wife, Federica."

"John Forster," the man said. "Henry Blake, David Gambles and James Scott. May we see your plane?"

"By all means," George said. "Come aboard."

"Do you happen to have a toilet?" Federica asked.

"At the back of the hanger," John said. "If you'd like tea, there's some just been brewed."

"Thank you," she said.

"We like your plane," David said when Federica rejoined them. "Your husband tells us that it handles well and has a good turn of speed."

"We flew up from High Wycombe, probably 227 nautical miles in a little under two hours," she replied.

"That is fast," James said. "This is your own design?"

"It is," George confirmed. "There are four of us in the design team, Federica and I, my sister and her husband. Her husband is the engine specialist."

"And you both fly?" Henry asked.

"We do," George said. "I was in the RFC, then the RAF, but before that we both went to school in France and at Brooklands."

"Wait, are you Lieutenant Colonel Wheelwright?" David asked.

"The same," George confirmed.

"When you showed up in Egypt, we were all jealous about how well you had been provisioned," David said.

"That was mainly Federica and my sister's doing," George said. "They made sure we had everything we could think of. We own Sirius Cars, so the lorries and a lot of the other equipment the company donated."

"They had everything," David told the others. "Camouflage nets, glasses to ward off the sun, petrol and water bowers and even a land leveller."

"Have you built planes before?" Henry asked.

"We built and flew some before the War and had two at the outbreak of hostilities," George replied. "While we were gone, Federica and my sister designed a built a behemoth that was fashioned after the craft made by Sikorskii. We flew that one to Cairo, then sold it to an American and shipped it to New York."

"I saw that in Cairo," David said. "Damn thing was huge, four engines, nice looking cabin from what I could see. Why did you sell?"

"We see a better future for monoplanes," George replied. "So, rather than keep taking funds from the company, we sold the Andromeda and the other two small planes we had and used the money to build the Pegasus, that's this one."

"Would you care to join us for an early luncheon?" James asked.

"That would be delightful," Federica said. "But we would insist on paying, we have, after all, trespassed upon your field."

John had a car, as did Henry, so they rode in convoy into the centre of Carlisle to a hotel near the castle. It was a little early for lunch, but

James knew the proprietor well, and he was happy to accommodate them. The conversation over lunch was about planes and flying, and Federica soon impressed them with her knowledge and understanding of the principles of flight and the mathematics behind it. They wanted to know how the fuselage and wings of the Pegasus were made. George gave them a brief description of the methods and processes they had used. There was a long discussion then about the merits of all-metal aeroplanes, which Federica and George thought would be the ultimate future, but only when the various aluminium alloys were strong enough to replace steel. They both felt that there would probably be some steel still, even with an almost all-aluminium aeroplane, but that it would not be much. Engines were the next big topic, radials or in-line engines. George told them that they had both and had Vee configuration engines that would exceed the horsepower of their radials, but at a greater weight. There was also the issue of cooling. The radials were air cooled, whereas the in-line engines were all water cooled, which led to radiators and piping and pumps.

After lunch, they all trooped back to the field and George and Federica were offered petrol for the plane, but they told the others they had more than enough to get them home. Goodbyes were said, and George and Federica took off and headed south over the fells and lakes.

"I'm getting some wonderful pictures," Federica said. "I just hope they will develop nicely. Can you come slightly to the east, I'd like to get a picture of the estate at Windermere."

"I could always drop down a little and circle it," George offered.

"That would be splendid," she said. They crossed over Keswick and Derwentwater, then the fells and on to Windermere.

"I see the estate," he said. "I'll just circle around, and you should be able to get a good photograph."

"That's good," she said. "I've just used the last of the film, so we can go straight home now."

"Let's climb back up a little and head straight home. Visibility is good enough that we can pick out landmarks easily, so when we get closer to home, we can orient ourselves. I've set the compass heading. When we get south and identify a significant landmark, we can then check the heading against a map and see how good the compass is," he said.

The rest of the flight home was quick; they had a good tailwind, so were tearing along over the ground. Landing was a little tricky as the wind was somewhat across the runway, not parallel to it, but George managed fine, and they were down and into the hangar in short order.

"That was a nice trip," Federica commented the George when they arrived home. "Did we get all the data we're looking for?"

"We did," he confirmed. "We have all the engine data and air speeds as we went. I saw nothing to raise concerns, I'll show it all to Will and see if he sees anything."

"How many more test flights do we need to do before airworthiness?" she asked.

"I think another three like today should be ample," he thought. "All the regulations say is that it should be fit to fly, and I think things are left largely up to the examiner. I'm sure that in time the Air Ministry will set more definitive requirements in terms of flight hours and data collected, but for the moment, I think we have enough, we have wind tunnel tests, we've got calculations, we've got actual flight data, so I don't foresee a problem."

"I wonder when the government will start issuing safety regulations for cars," she said. "I suppose that in time, with more cars on the roads, that will be inevitable."

The Air Ministry inspector came sooner than expected and reviewed all the data they had and then asked to go up in the plane. George took him up and let him take the controls for a while. When they landed, the inspector was all smiles and issued the certificate of airworthiness with congratulations on the design of the plane.

"So, now we're official," Federica said to George after the inspector had gone.

"One thing less to be concerned about," he said. "He really did like flying the plane and commented on the handling and how easy it is to fly."

"Now to Sirius matters," she said. "I've been talking to Nastia about the improvements she and Will came up with for the 1922 models, and I like what they've done. Better seats, better instruments and more horsepower from the same basic engines."

"Did you see the item recently about Austin going into receivership?" he asked. "I gather that they were spending quite a lot on planes and their airfield, and I think that their French venture is costing them more than they thought. I'm certain that they'll come up with financing to keep the company afloat, but it may cost them."

"I'm not surprised they went into receivership," she said. "The factory was old, and they've added all kinds of buildings and people, but nothing is laid out with efficiency in mind, and their control of parts is not as good as it should be, so I'm sure they have times when all kinds of machines and people are standing around idle. So, we should keep looking at where delays are and what doesn't fit right, to cut out unnecessary costs, and also be very circumspect about what we spend on planes," she said. "Our French factory, I'm not that concerned about, Philippe has that well in hand, and we started it early enough to benefit from wartime orders. Still, it would pay us to be careful."

"I agree on the planes," he said. "Indulging one's passion is all very well, but not at the expense of the companies we have."

"On that note, there are some investments we should make at Windsor and Abbey," she said. "I can arrange for some private financing on loans for that at advantageous rates. Then we have the larger investment to consider, presses to stamp out whole body sides for cars. We also need to look at which of the British steel producers can make a thin plate of the size we want. We may have to go to Germany, France or the United States to get what we want at the price we want to pay."

"I'll talk to Andrew and we'll come up with a plan that includes where we would put the presses and where we would get the power from," he said.

"It would be quite a shift for us to go from the sandwich we have now to all steel, but with the right dies we can have more streamlined bodies on the cars," she said. "It will be the future of car bodies for a while, mark my words, wood will be gone in ten to fifteen years."

"Did you happen to overhear that one of the chaps we saw in Carlisle worked for Carrs?" he asked.

"No, I missed that," she said. "Who?"

"David Gambles," he replied. "I think for him flying is a weekend hobby, and he likes the camaraderie that he shares with the others who also have his passion for flying."

"I wonder how many people know that apart from Sirius, we also own Abbey Biscuits," she said.

"Probably not many," he thought. "But, perhaps because Sirius is traded on the stock exchange, they could pick up a little from the annual reports."

"Perhaps," she said. "But we don't disclose much about the other businesses that we have, so perhaps not."

"Anyway," he said. "I've been checking on the hotel in Kisumu, and it seems quite adequate."

"And petrol?" she asked.

"The stops I would have concerns about would be Mongalla and Tabora," he replied. "The RAF laid in some supplies, but I've no idea if it's been used or even stolen. I'll check with the RAF and see if they know how much is there. We should take filters to clean the petrol wherever we get it, we don't want dirt in the engine."

"So, let's plan for June of next year," she said. "Weather permitting, leave here on the first and be in Cape Town on the seventh. Now, is Pegasus reliable enough to go, or do we need a twin-engine version?"

"Depends on how good we are with a toolbox," he said. "What we should do between now and then is get an engine and pull it apart, rebuild it, and do it all over again until we are thoroughly familiar with it."

"I'm sure Will can tell us what tools we would need," she said. "I'll talk to him. Do we take a mechanic with us?"

"If we become proficient enough, then I see no need," he said.

"Fine," she agreed. "I'll be studying what weather reports we can get for Central Africa this June so we'll have a sense of what to expect."

Motor shows

"This is going to be a busy autumn and early winter," Federica commented as the family met to discuss the calendar for the latter half of the year. "We've got the *Olympia Motor Show* next month and then the *Salon de l'Automobile* in Paris in December. I presume we'll take cars and vans from Orly for the Paris show at the Grand Palais."

"The Grand Palais, I've never been there," Anastasia said. "I suppose it is very posh, at least we can just drive our cars there from Orly."

"Shall we all go to both shows?" George asked.

"I think we should," Anastasia said. "I'll ask Mama to come south and see to Giovanna for a few days in October while we're in London and then again in December for the Paris show, and she can stay for Christmas. I thought we'd drive to Olympia and perhaps fly over to Paris. After all, Pegasus does have four seats."

"I agree," Federica said. "Do we stay in London for the *Olympia Motor Show*?"

"It might serve us better if we did," George thought. "Then we would not have to travel to London every day. For Paris, I'll make some hotel bookings close to the *Palais*. I think the Hôtel de Crillon would be as close as we could get. I'll also talk to Philippe about picking us up from Le Bourget and taking us to the hotel. In London, the Bailey's Hotel is on Gloucester Road, so then it's just a short District Line train to Addison Road and Olympia. I'll get Alice to make bookings for us, fifteen rooms in all."

"Fine, what cars and vans do we exhibit?" Federica asked.

"I think the Procyon, Regulus and Spica cars, and perhaps one of the vans," Anastasia suggested.

"Did we book large enough stands at both shows for that many?" Federica asked.

"It might be a little cramped, but we could manage," George said.

"I had wondered if we should get scale models made of each of our cars, vans and lorries, that way we could display all without taking too much space," Will suggested. "I was thinking of one twelfth scale."

"Who do we get to make them?" George asked.

"The chap who is building our quarter-scale model of the Procyon can just as easily build twelfth scale," Will said.

"How much will it cost?" Anastasia asked.

"I'd guess about £15 each," Will said.

"That's quite a bill for the whole line, £255," Federica said.

"I'll negotiate and see what can be done," Will promised..

"If we have the models in time for the *Olympia,* we can also ship them across the Channel afterwards to use at the *Salon de l'Automobile,*" George suggested.

"Good idea," Federica agreed.

"The plan is still the Cape in June?" George asked Federica later.

"I would like to," she confirmed. "I will have assuaged my conscience by then and have devoted all my energies to the businesses."

"You have no need for that," he said. "We have with Nastia and Will, and the managers, we found people very capable of managing things even without us."

"While that is true," she said. "I still feel some guilt about frittering away money on a personal ambition for flying. Flying to the Cape is not the same as flying on the weekend to enjoy a hobby. As a hobby, it is expensive enough, arranging a trip to the Cape could be as simple as flying from town to town, buying petrol and oil and food, or as costly as crashing the plane and having to make our way home having failed."

"Yes, but if we don't try, we will always regret the fact that we did not," he said. "We should go; if we fail, we fail, but it will not be for want of trying."

"Who do we have to ask to find out if there is petrol at the landing site down through Africa?" she asked.

"The RAF," he replied. "They set the landing sites up and put the petrol and oil there and have replenished what was used by the previous attempts at the Cape route.

"At least now I feel confident that I could tear apart the engine and repair it if something goes wrong," she said. "I'm very pleased we had the men from the factory go through all that with us."

"So, there are two of us that can now do that, so we have no need for a mechanic on board," he said. "That means we can take more supplies, tools and such for the journey."

"I asked you before about taking a gun with us, should we do that?" she asked.

"It might be advisable to take a pistol," he said. "In the event that we were to put down far from one of the landing sites, we might encounter less than friendly people."

"I have a packing list of clothes, tools, spare parts and such and have weighed everything so I know what the takeoff weight will be," she said. "We don't want to repeat the experience of van Ryneveld and crash at Bulawayo because the plane was too heavy for the altitude and temperature."

"We are aware of the possible issue, so are forewarned," he said. "Plus if we go in June, it will be winter and cooler."

"That is true," she agreed. "Well, let us see if we cannot sell more cars from these shows and show a handsome profit, then I will feel more at ease with taking time off to fly to the Cape and spending the money to do so."

"If we spend our own money and not take money from the company, then we should not be concerned," he said.

"Perhaps," she said. "But much of our money comes from the company, we should ensure that the two are quite separate."

"I'll talk to Douglas about that," he promised.

Will met with Walter Ferguson, the model builder and told him what they would like to have, and Walter agreed to a job lot of the whole line for £12 each. Will also asked him if he could make models of planes, and he confirmed that he could. He had just completed the Procyon model and gave it to Will to take with him. Walter promised to have all the models done in good time for the *Salon* in Paris, he also asked what colour Will would like the models to be, and Will told him the blue that Sirius used and asked him to paint the vans with signs that identified them as being used by Abbey, Windsor and Star. Will also had some small brooches that were used by those who went to the motor shows, and suggested that Walter pull them apart and fix them to the front of each model. They would be a little large from a scale point of view, but it would at least help to maintain the identities of the cars. Will then went to Robin Hoppes and Mr White and asked them to make simple plinths for the models, with signs on them identifying them, with specifications as well.

Federica and Anastasia took their plane, collected Helen Greene and flew over to Paris to talk about the *Salon* with Philippe. Federica introduced Helen to Philippe, and he was delighted to have a photographer who would accompany him to the *Salon*. He assured them that the cars and the van would be ready in time and that he would get them through Paris to the Grand Palais without getting them dirty. Federica was not sure how he would manage that, so he told them that he was going to use some Altair lorries, *camions* in his parlance, to transport them. He also had a number of people already identified to man the stand and was eagerly awaiting the models that Will had promised. He had all the signs ready, in French, that identified each model and listed all the specifications. He promised to be at Le Bourget when they flew over for the show and took them to the hotel to view the rooms they had booked. All that remained now was to finish the vehicles to be exhibited and then prepare the stand. That all done, Federica, Anastasia and Helen took Philippe, his wife, Yvette, and René Picard, the sales manager of Sirius France, and his wife Marie, to lunch and talked about fashions, food and finance with Federica and Anastasia taking turns translating for Helen, which made that less of a burden, before flying home.

The cars and vans that were destined to be exhibited at the *Olympia Motor Show* were identified, and when they were completed, were taken aside and given a thorough cleaning and polishing. The only concern was that the weather would be poor and that they might get wet and muddy on their way to London. Federica decided to follow the lead of Philippe and use a few Altair lorries to actually carry them to London so that mud might be avoided. She then sat down with everyone, including Helen Greene, Ian Stuart and Andrew Coates, and they went through each day the show would be on and who would be on the stand when. They recruited Alice, Robin, Douglas Wilson, their accountant, Arthur Dent, who ran their London showroom, and eight others drawn from Abbey Biscuits, Windsor Garments and Star Electrics to join the stand team, making sixteen in all, pairs taking two hour shifts through the day, which after all was long, running from ten in the morning to ten at night. Those picked from the other companies could all drive and commonly drove vans assigned to them, and were knowledgeable about the line in general. Federica had learned over the years that standing around at the shows was actually very tiring, so was trying to limit the amount of time each of them would have to spend on the stand. She would assess each day and see if there were peak periods when attendance was greatest, and have two pairs on the stand at those times. With sixteen people and six two-hour shifts, she did have some flexibility. Helen would not be assigned any stand duties, but would be free to wander the halls, photographing what she saw and what drew her interest.

Sophia journeyed south in early October to look after Giovanna while Anastasia and Will were at the motor show. Anastasia wondered how much work she would have to do afterwards to undo all the spoiling that Giovanna would receive from her grandmother. Still, it was worth it to all to have Sophia visit.

"Do I have to go to school?" Giovanna asked hopefully.

"You do," Anastasia confirmed. "Your grandmama will take you and help you with your homework if you need it."

"Will you bring me pictures of the other cars and vans at the show?" Giovanna asked.

"I will," Anastasia promised. "Mama, make sure she does her homework."

"I will," Sophia promised. "But, we'll also enjoy ourselves a little."

"I'm sure you will," Anastasia said. "For tonight, we'll just have dinner and see if Grandmama will tell us anything about her great novel."

"I have finished it," Sophia said. "Now it is in the hands of my editor, and I'm waiting to see what changes he suggests."

"I'm sure, not many," Anastasia said. "What will he know about Africa and what it was to live there?"

"He has an imagination," Sophia said.

"When can I see a book?" Giovanna asked.

"Soon, I hope," Sophia said.

"What is the title?" Giovanna asked.

"*I was a banker among the Boers*," Sophia replied.

"It sounds well," Anastasia commented.

"I would like to see what George has to say," Sophia said. "He lived the life, first as a child, then in the army."

"So, do we dress for dinner, or just stay as we are?" Anastasia asked.

"Let us stay as we are," Sophia suggested. "Just a simple family dinner."

Anastasia and Will left the following morning and joined Federica, George and the others for the trek into London and the motor show. Walter had been as good as his word, and they had all the models. Robin Hoppes and Mr White had also built the plinths and made up the placards that described each vehicle and listed the specifications. George suggested that if they ever exhibited in an air show, they should do the same thing and have models made of all the planes they had built. Federica liked the sound of that and asked Will to retain Walter to do that. These would not be models destined for wind tunnel testing, but models built to show all the details. In London, they went first to Bailey's and registered and deposited their luggage and then went to Olympia to view the stand. Ian had been up a few days before with a crew from the factory and had built the stand and placed the cars and the vans, and the models. Federica looked at it with a critical eye and studied the plan of the building, noting the entrances, the toilets and the restaurants so that she could gauge likely heavy traffic patterns.

"Could we move the models more that way so that when people pass to the restaurant, they walk by them?" she asked.

"Of course," Ian said. He, George and Will moved the plinths a little, directed by Federica and Anastasia.

"That is good, very good," Federica said. "It catches the eye and is hard to ignore. Good, this is a wonderful job, Ian, thank you and thank your workers for us. Now, I think we should repair to the hotel and dine and prepare for the show."

The show was a success, both from the point of view of the number of visitors, but also by the number of orders they actually received, which rather surprised them all as they thought of the show as rather more for looking than buying. Having enough people there to limit the hours standing around made it much easier on everyone, even though the days were long. What did surprise Federica was the number of enquiries they got for the car, van and lorry models. The enquiries came from garages, shops, transport companies and even a few car enthusiasts. They received 15 enquiries from shops who all wanted models of the vans with their names emblazoned on the sides, and another 12 from transport companies, who also wanted their names applied. Will suggested that they engage Walter to build more and charge £30 for car and van models and £40 for lorry models. Anastasia got a little concerned that they would run out of company brochures, but Alice assured her that they had a supply view that would be sufficient for the duration of the show. Anastasia collected brochures from the other exhibitors to study herself and to give to Giovanna. Some were glossy affairs full of art and verbose language, others were simple printed sheets with just the car particulars. Some used actual photographs, while others used artists' impressions. Their own brochures included photographs taken by Helen, all very artistically presented to give the best impression of the vehicles.

After the show, they all met again to discuss the show and what was good and what could be improved. Helen had photographs of the other stands and their cars, which helped in the discussions about their own stand. Federica made copious notes that she would pass on to Philippe for his consideration. Helen also had many photographs of their own stand and the people on it, and suggested that they might think of a company newspaper or magazine that could be sent out to employees to let them know what was happening in their part of the company and elsewhere. She also asked if she could go back to France to photograph the factory there and then be on hand for the Paris motor show. George told her that he would arrange it for her to take the train to Paris and then a hotel that was close to the Orly factory. Anastasia wondered if there would ever be a show for commercial vehicles, buses, tractors, lorries and larger vans. Vehicles really too large to be included in the Olympia Motor Show, but which could benefit from exposure to a wider audience. There had been interest at the show, and they had handed out many brochures to prospective buyers from all walks of industry. For larger lorries, they competed with AEC, Tilling, Foden, Thornycroft, and now the relative newcomer, Scammell, plus others. Federica and Anastasia had been toying with the idea of building a separate factory where they would make the lorries, as the sheer size of the various parts tended to complicate the workflow in the car factory. They were looking at factory designs and layouts and developing the costs which they would have to budget for.

"Is there anything else we need to consider before the Paris show?" Federica asked.

"Not that I can think of," George said.

"Good, then we'll go back to normal business until December when we go to France," she said.

Helen came out with the first edition of the company's quarterly magazine. It was a glossy affair with 20 full pages of captioned photographs and editorials. It covered all the companies, so there were car and people pictures from Burnham and Orly, and clothes pictures from Windsor, biscuit items from Abbey and even articles and pictures of the growing markets for electrical products. Helen had been in touch with Philippe, and he had arranged for an insert that gave a good French translation of all that was said in the magazine. Helen had also prevailed upon Federica, George and Anastasia to provide a message from the owners, so the other two had delegated that to Federica. Helen also worked with Alice to organise what had now become a fixture on the calendar, the company Christmas parties for the children of the employees. Mr White was again engaged to be Father Christmas and was a great success with the children.

Sophia journeyed south again in December to the delight of Giovanna, who looked forward to the spoiling that she would get from her grandmother. Federica, George, Anastasia and Will packed their bags and got ready for the off to Paris and the Salon. There was enough room in the plane for luggage behind the seats, so George took charge of stowing it while Will attended to petrol and oil.

"Who wants to fly us over today?" Federica asked.

"I'll fly," Anastasia said. "Fede, you can sit by me, and you two can sit and watch the world go by."

"Now remember, Paris is that way," Will teased Anastasia, pointing to the south.

"We did go there recently," she reminded him. "And we managed to find our way and not get lost. Now, I'm presuming this engine of yours will work today."

"Of course it will," he said. "I've been gratified at the reliability it is showing and the minimal wear we've been seeing. It bodes well for Fede and George's trip to the Cape."

"Are we all ready?" Anastasia asked as she took the controls of the plane.

"Ready," Will replied for the rest of them.

They taxied out, had a short conversation with the people at Croydon then took off for Paris. The weather was not the best, but they were able to get above the really low clouds and scud along, looking down on the whitish-grey blanket that covered southern England and the Channel. The northern part of France was not much better, but the clouds started to break up, and by the time they actually reached Paris, they could at least see glimpses of the ground. Federica talked by radio to the people at Le Bourget and learned that there was another plane ahead of them that was just landing, so they circled once over Paris, then went in to land themselves. A customs officer met them and stamped passports, and welcomed them back to France. It was the same officer that Federica and Anastasia had seen on their last recent trip to Paris. Philippe was there to meet them, along with René and Helen and three cars. Cramming five and luggage into one car would be uncomfortable, so Philippe had done the practical thing and brought the three cars. It took a little while to drive to the hotel, traffic in Paris was chaotic, with cars, buses, lorries, horse-drawn carriages and carts, men with hand carts all together, with pedestrians in the mix, all directed at some crossroads by gendarmes who were at times seemingly helpless to control things and at other times masterfully in control.

The Hôtel de Crillon was a grand edifice in the very centre of Paris. They were greeted effusively by the hotel staff and shown to their rooms, which were on the upper floor looking out over the Place de la Concorde. Helen had also been booked there, transferring from the hotel she had been staying at in Orly. The Crillon was much more convenient for the motor show.

"I suppose we should change for lunch," Federica said as she and George unpacked.

"I think so," he agreed. "Flying clothes would probably raise eyebrows in a fashion-conscious city."

"What should I wear?" she asked.

"The tweed skirt and the heather jacket, and the tam for a hat," he suggested. "Very English."

"At least they'll be warm enough," she said. "It's quite chilly outside. I wonder if the Grand Palais has heat."

"It's a huge building, so I'd be surprised," he said. "I would suppose that by the time there's a lot of people there, the temperatures will go up."

"I'm sure you're right," she agreed. "Shall we go down and join the others?"

Philippe already had a table for seven, and over lunch, he told them that the models had all arrived in plenty of time and were all in good condition. He described how the stand was set up and where, and mentioned a few other car makers who were also there. To Federica, they were, for the most part, to be expected; companies like Berliet, Bugatti, De Dion-Bouton, Hispano-Suiza, Renault and Lion-Peugeot were often represented. Citroën, a relative newcomer, was also there, as were Levassor, Talbot, and Hotchkiss. Alda and Minerva. She expected the greatest competition from Citroën, Renault and Lion-Peugeot, and she really wanted to see if anyone was following the lead of Budd from the United States to make all pressed-steel bodies. Budd had been producing steel bodies for Dodge and other companies and was building quite a large business. She suspected that Citroën would be among the first French companies to adopt the manufacturing system, as it was rumoured that they were in discussions with Budd. Citroën was already making 100 cars per day, and she thought that would increase if the manufacturing costs were kept down by the rapid pressing of car bodies. There were manufacturers of large steel presses at the *Salon,* and Federica thought that she might be able to buy one on advantageous terms from Germany, which were keen to rebuild their industries after the War, or perhaps she would have to go to Bliss of New York to buy one or more. She also wondered how many presses she might need, or if it would be possible to change the dies quickly so that one or two presses might suffice. Apart from car bodies, she also thought that it should be possible to press wheels from steel, or at least wheel halves that could then be welded together to form the whole. That would get them away from the spoked wheels they used and into something potentially more substantial.

"Shall we go and see the stand?" Philippe asked, dragging Federica back from her musings.

"Of course," she said. "You have been studying English, Philippe?"

"I have," he said. "René and I thought it would be of value to learn to be able to talk easily to English and American companies and customers."

"I'm sure you're right," Federica agreed. "When the *Salon* opens, do you expect many visitors?"

"I am expecting close to 250,000 over the days," Philippe said. "But I may be very wrong. Do you have an overcoat to wear? The nave of the *palais* has no heat, so it could be quite cold."

"I will go upstairs and get ours," George said. "Will, do you want me to collect yours?"

"I'll come with you," Will said. "It's as well we brought clothes for all weathers."

The stand at the motor show had a large sign above it advertising their attendance. The cars were placed in front of the van, and the models were neatly arranged where they could be easily seen. Federica was happy with what she saw and congratulated Philippe and René on their presentation. The whole of the space around them was crowded with stands filled with cars, motorcycles and vans and on the peripheries, there were the stands of the suppliers of oil, petrol, instruments, tyres and the various and sundry accessories that went with motoring. René gave them a catalogue that listed all the companies and what they had on display, and also included a map of the stands with a key as to who was on which. Federica looked at the map and where the doors were and the toilets, and restaurants, looking at likely traffic flow of people coming and going. There were companies from all the car-producing countries with the exception of Germany and Austria, bound by terms of the Treaty of Versailles, which limited what they could do; even so, companies like the Dutch Maybach did include Benz engines, so there was a subtle representation. They made a leisurely tour of the exhibit halls, marking down the stands they wanted to go back to view again.

"Is there anything we need to do before the show opens tomorrow?" Federica asked.

"I don't think so," Philippe said. "I will have some coffee and croissants early tomorrow morning. We have brochures to distribute for those who may be interested in purchasing our cars. I am also certain that our competitors will collect them as we will theirs."

"Thank you both for the time and attention you have given this," Federica said. "Let us hope that all goes well in the next few days and that we do not get snow."

"*Sacré bleu*, we do not need that," Philippe laughed.

"Helen, do you have all the photographs you need?" George asked.

"I do," she confirmed. "And more, we motored down to the Med and took some there that we can use in advertising materials. I've also been taking fashion pictures for Marie Garnier; she had asked me for certain lines to be looked at, and I believe I have just what she wants. Philippe and René have been very patient, and I'm also trying to improve the little French that I have."

197

"She does very well," Philippe said. "Yvette is quite enthralled by the interest in fashions and has been helping Helen a lot."

"So, shall we meet in the morning before coming to the *Salon?*" Federica asked.

"I think that would be wise," Philippe said. "René and I will be at the hotel at eight for breakfast."

They assembled at the Crillon and then walked over the Place de la Concorde to the Grand Palais. It was cold, but not raining or snowing. When they reached the *palais*, Philippe introduced them to those he had assigned to be on the stand. Helen had obviously met them all, and there were poses taken about the stand encouraging her to set up her camera and shoot them. When the doors opened and the public streamed in, Federica was surprised at the sheer number who came, but then France had become one of the premier centres for motoring, so perhaps it should have been expected. The Paris show followed the pattern of the Olympia show, and men rotated duties on the stand and talked to people, made note of interest, handed out brochures and even posed at times with potential customers while Helen took photographs. Federica and George took one side of the nave, while Anastasia and Will took the other, and they walked the halls and the stands looking and examining and asking questions. Federica was particularly interested in the stand of Farman, she knew them as a builder of aircraft and wanted to see what transfers of ideas they had used between planes and cars. Federica and Anastasia did take their turn on the stand and drew crowds as the only women representing car companies, surprising most by their knowledge of the cars and their design. It probably would have alarmed most if they had learned that they had actually designed the cars, and not just learned a script. Because the show ran until Boxing Day, Federica risked annoying the organisers by telling Philippe that if all his staff wanted to be home at Christmas, then they would shut down their stand early, removing everything the night before Christmas Eve. Philippe agreed with that and put it to his people an idea that was greeted with acclamation. So, late in the night of the day before Christmas Eve and early into the morning of the day, they removed the cars and the models and went home to be with families.

Federica also told Philippe that they would arrange taxis through the hotel to take them to Le Bourget, so he had no need to come and get them.

"Can we fit an extra seat into the plane?" George asked Federica. "I'd like to try and get Helen home on Christmas Eve."

"There is room," she said. "If we box up our luggage into trunks and have it shipped home, we can fit a seat at the back."

"I don't mind if I have to sit on the floor," Helen said. "It's not that long a flight."

"We'll find a seat that we can put in," Federica promised. "Let's talk to Philippe and see what we can contrive."

"I'll take the floor at the back," George said. "As Helen said, the flight is not that long, and I flew in some uncomfortable positions in Egypt and the Western Front, so this will not be a hardship at all. There's no need to bother Philippe, we should just go out to Le Bourget and go home."

"Are you sure?" Federica asked him.

"I'm sure," he replied. "I slept in a railway wagon full of boxes of rifles and ammunition in South Africa; this will be comfort in comparison."

"Fine, then let us all go home," Federica said. Luggage was dispatched to the railway, and the accounts settled at the hotel. They took taxis to the airport and loaded up the plane.

"Who's flying us home?" Anastasia asked.

"Why don't you let Will fly us? You can sit in the front with him and Helen, and I will take the back," Federica said. That settled, they let George get in first and make himself as comfortable as he could, then Will took them out onto the runway and they were off. The weather had not improved a lot, and it was clouds and rain all the way home. Will talked to the people at Croydon, and they reported that the weather in the south of England was cold with clouds broken by patches of clear sky with light winds from the west.

"Let's see if we can find Handy Cross," Will said to the rest. "Does anyone see the ground yet?"

"I do," Helen said. "That's Windsor below us, I can see the castle."

"Fine, I'll drop down a little and see if we can break through it all," he said. They dropped down to a mere 500 feet above the ground, following the Thames up to Bourne End, then the Wye and the railway to High Wycombe, from there it was an easy task to go south and west a little, then come back to the runway.

"There's a welcome sight," Anastasia said as they lined up for landing.

"I suppose in time we will work out a communication system so that people on the ground can tell us where we are and line us up for the runway," Federica said. "I wonder if we could afford to put some lights down the runway to make it easier to see in poor weather and at night."

"If we did that, we'd have to work out a system to either have someone turn them on, or if we were really clever, we could have a radio signal to do it," George said from the back of the plane.

"That's interesting," Anastasia said. "I'll investigate that and see if that's possible and if so, from how far away."

"How many lights do you think?" Federica asked.

"I'd think put them every 100 feet," George said. "Two lines, running down the sides of the runway, parallel to the centre line, so for 2,000 feet that we have 20 times two."

"Buried in the ground with just the glass showing?" Will asked.

"I don't think we'd have to bury them," George thought. "The runway is wide enough, and if we put the lights down the edges, they wouldn't even be on the tarmac. We'd have to be able to see them for both directions."

"How bright do the lights have to be to see them from a mile away?" Anastasia asked.

"That's an it depends answer," George said. "At night, you don't need a very bright light for it to be seen from quite a way. In Egypt, we used tins filled with rags and oil and burned them, and they were adequate for night landings. It was surprising sometimes how far away we could see the line of lights that showed us the runway."

"Well, for today we didn't need any," Will said. "We're down and home, are you all right back there, George?"

"I'm fine," he replied. "But I would like to get out, stretch, then go home for a soak in a bath."

They met their usual HM Customs agent, and all he wanted to know was whether the weather in Paris was any better than the weather there.

The rest of Christmas Eve, everyone went their separate ways to clean up after the trip and to prepare for Christmas Day.

"I don't think I'll be going to the Paris motor show again," Federica commented to George as they put up some Christmas decorations. "It's very inconvenient being right at Christmas, I wonder whose bright idea it was to have it at this time of the year."

"I wonder," he echoed. "We do need to be represented, though, so perhaps we should work with Philippe to find volunteers and provide for them some incentive and extra compensation."

"That is a splendid idea," she said. "When did Nastia suggest that we go to their house?"

"She said about ten tomorrow morning," he replied. "By then, Giovanna will have been up, ripped open presents and will be busy, so a quieter time for us to talk to Sophia."

"Do you ever think you should do the lord of the manor thing and go to the local church?" she asked.

"I don't think the vicar looks on us that way," he said. "There is the manor house and its current owner, and I think he rather expects them to show willing and be there."

"Good, because tomorrow I have a mind to sleep late," she said.

"Of course, you may not actually get much sleep," he joked.

"Oh, like that is it?" she laughed. "Well, there's no one here, we have nothing else pressing, so perhaps we could start now."

"Is that an invitation?" he asked.

"No, it's a strong suggestion, more of a royal command," she said.

"You two look very pleased with yourselves," Anastasia commented when they arrived at her house the next morning.

"Really?" Federica asked in feigned innocence.

"I won't tell Giovanna what you've been up to," Anastasia said. "Then I won't have to go into long explanations. Merry Christmas, by the way."

"Merry Christmas," Federica echoed.

"Let's go in, sherry and a mince pie?" Anastasia asked.

"That would be lovely," Federica replied. They ate, drank, laughed and admired the presents that Giovanna had received then Will brought something quite large in and told Federica and George to open it.

"It's wonderful," Federica said. It was a large map, a good six feet tall, of Africa with roads and railways marked and most importantly, the route to the Cape that had been mapped by the RAF.

"Look, it's like the ones in the Times Atlas, it shows the geography and I see it's got all the landing sites marked," George said. "And whether or not they have petrol and oil. Thank you for this."

"It will give you something to look at, dream about, and plan your trip in June," Anastasia said. "We have one similar and will mark your progress as we hear. We got it from Bartholomew and had them print up large wall maps for us."

"We promise to telegraph back reports," Federica said. "Again, as I already said, it's wonderful, thank you both."

"Thank all of us," Will said. "Mama helped, and even Giovanna gave up some of her savings for this."

"Now we need to find the best place to hang it," George said.

"Somewhere where we will be reminded often of the dream, so that we don't lose sight of it," Federica said. "Then, when we come back, we can mark where we were on the different days."

"I would like to see that," Giovanna said. "When I'm old enough to fly myself, I would like to do that as well."

"Well, when you're old enough, we'll teach you to fly and then work out what kind of plane would be best," Anastasia said. "I'm sure that by then all kinds of improvements and advancements will have been made, so that it will be just as easy for you as it will be for your Auntie Fede."'

"You will keep a journal that talks about the clouds, the winds and all the weather changes that you see?" Giovanna asked.

"We will," George replied. "It will make it easier for anyone following."

"I think a toast," Sophia said. "To the Cape!"

"The Cape," the others echoed.

Preparations

Early 1922 saw the introduction of uniforms for pilots and company officers of Instone Air Line; it also saw the beginning of a three-year subsidy scheme to assist British airlines trying to compete with Continental companies. Cross-channel traffic increased to 1,000 passengers in a week. The Imperial Airship Scheme, aiming for service with six airships from Britain to India and Australia, was proposed. The first collision between two civil airlines occurred in April, a Daimler Airways plane collided with a Cie des Grands Express Aériens plane over Poix in poor weather, and seven people were killed.

"I wonder what 1922 will hold for us?" Federica said to George as they celebrated the New Year.

"Well, we're going to the Cape, bar war or extreme pestilence," he replied.

"We need to make some longer flights to Rome and Cairo to get more engine data," she said. "We should plan for some trips, always weather permitting."

"We should see what kind of weather we can fly in," he said. "We might be in the air and run into rain or clouds, so should be prepared. We should also work out our procedures for what to do if the engine cuts out, from trying to restart it to making an emergency landing."

"I was thinking of adding some slightly larger wheels and better springing," she said. "That way, if we have to land somewhere other than a prepared field, we might fare a little better."

"Would that add much weight?" he asked.

"I'll see," she said. "If we have only the two seats and not the back seats and no passengers, then I don't see a problem."

"What about petrol?" he asked.

"We have enough for over six hours of flying," she said. "Without some toilet facilities on the plane, I don't think I want to be in the air that long. How did Alcock and Brown manage crossing the Atlantic?"

"I think they had what are called comfort tubes," he replied. "Easier for a man than a woman, but I agree with you, we're not going for endurance records, we just want to be able to get there in one journey."

"I wonder if we could fly over the Alps direct to Rome," she pondered.

"We would need to be at least 10,000 feet around Chamonix," he said. "I think preferably 12,000 feet in case our altimeter is in any way lacking in accuracy, but we wouldn't have to stay that high for long, once clear of the Alps, we could drop back down again to 10,000 feet."

"Do we need to take oxygen?" she asked.

"I don't think so," he said. "I've been up to 15,000 feet and noticed some loss of skills, but at 12,000 we should be fine. We'll see some drop in performance of the engine as we go up, but as we've found with our tests so far, not enough to really affect things."

"Good, let's keep an eye on the weather if there is promise of a couple of clear days, even if it's cold, we could try for Rome, here to Paris, then over the Alps," she suggested.

They got their opportunity in mid-January. There was a clear spell forecast, both for England and much of the Continent, so they told Anastasia and Will that they were going.

"Did you see the letter that we got from HM Customs?" George asked Federica.

"No, what did it say?" she asked.

"That they can no longer accommodate us with an officer to meet us at Handy Cross, in the future, we'll have to go through Croydon for passport controls and customs inspections," he explained.

"That's inconvenient," she said. "But I suppose inevitable."

"I think it's because they've appointed an immigration officer to deal with air traffic at Croydon and they want all international arrivals to go through there," he said. "It all has to do with the Aliens Act of 1920."

"I suppose jobs for the British first," she said. "That's understandable, we really don't need to have to support people who just show up. So, when we leave for Rome, we have to make a detour to Croydon, perhaps we should fill up with petrol there too."

"I had thought we would do that," he said.

"Is it too far to go straight to Rome?" she asked.

"It's about 770 nautical miles," he replied. "So, with a good tailwind, it would be possible, but I think it prudent to stop in Paris, then go on."

"You're right," she agreed. "Even at our speed of 120 knots, that's still almost six and a half hours of flying, right at the very limits we have with no room for errors or headwinds. We need another 40 knots at least. I wonder if Will can work more miracles and get us an engine that would do that."

"We should ask him," George suggested. "There aren't many planes out there that can even do what we do, let alone 150 to 160 knots, and all the large passenger planes are horribly slow, 90 to 100 knots."

"We should wind tunnel test our model up to 160 knots and see if it holds well," she said. "Will our fans give us that much?"

"I'm sure we can do that," he said. "We should talk to Robin and see what he can contrive and what problems he might foresee."

"You want how much?" Will asked when they put the question to him.

"Enough horsepower to cruise at 150 knots," George said.

"That's a tall order," Will thought. "I think it would have to be an inline engine, I'm not at all sure I could design a radial to give us enough."

"No hurry," George said. "We don't even know if our design would work well at those speeds."

"When I have a spare moment, I'll think about it," Will promised. "I can design an engine today that would give you enough horsepower, but it would weigh too much, and we would go round and around with the lift, mass, drag, thrust equations. When do you leave for Rome?"

"The weather is holding and looks good for the next four days, so tomorrow," George replied. "We're going to try Croydon to Paris, then direct to Rome over the Alps."

"Stay high enough," Will said. "Don't relish the idea of reading about you and Fede and bits of plane picked up off the Alps."

"We'll stay high enough," George replied. "One of the reasons we want to try with clear weather is to see how high we would have to go to safely clear the Alps, so that if we can't see the peaks, we know we won't run into one."

"Perish the thought," Will said. "Take a camera with you, I'd like to see some pictures of the Alps from the air."

"Good idea," George agreed. "I'm also going to get Fede to contact Franco to see if he wants to meet us in Rome."

Federica and George set out the following morning as soon as it was light enough to safely take off, and they made the short ten-minute hop to Croydon, where they took on petrol and informed the controller that they were bound for Paris, then Rome. He wished them well, and they were off. They had a wonderful view of the South of England and the Channel, and could see France as soon as they cleared the English side of the Channel. They actually saw three other planes and took care to avoid them.

"If one is coming straight towards you, how near does it have to be to actually see it?" Federica asked.

"Closer than you would think," he said. "If we're both going over 100 knots, then we're closing at 200 knots, so probably a minute, maybe two at the very most, depending on how good your eyes are."

"How do we know it's not a bird that's close, but a plane that's far away?" she asked.

"You get so that you can recognise the difference," he said. "To me, it would make sense to have one altitude for going north and another for going south so that we could avoid horrible collisions."

"I suppose that would mean the various governments would have to sit down and negotiate some kind of treaty or agreement," she said. "Given how governments work, that might take forever. Perhaps it would be better if the airlines all sat down together and made an agreement."

"Might be quicker," he agreed. "Could you see if you can raise Paris on the radio?"

"I have Paris," she said. "They advise that there is an Instone flight ahead of us and will land first, we should probably slow down as the Instone is emulating a snail."

"They probably wouldn't like to hear you say that," he laughed. "We'll slow a little, perhaps even circle once to give them time to land and clear the runway, I see them, there, ahead of us."

"Are you sure?" she asked. "I see what you're looking at, but how do you know it's them?"

"We're not gaining quickly enough for it to be a distant bird, so it's them and it's on the right path for Paris," he explained.

"Look, there's the airport and I can see a plane taking off," she said.

"That will be one of the French airlines on its run to London," he thought. "I suppose there is enough traffic for all these competing airlines."

"The taking off one is well clear and there goes the Instone," she said.

"We'll fly over and circle around and then come back in to land," he said.

"That's just what the chaps on the ground said to do," she added. "They report that the Instone has landed and is now clear of the runway."

"Fine, then we'll go around and line up to go in," he said.

They were on the ground ten minutes later and taxied over to where they could get petrol. They told the customs people that they were not staying, but were going on to Rome. Time was marching on. They had left with first light, but in January, that is actually quite late, so it was already eleven-thirty Paris time. Another four hours should see them in Rome, so after coffee and a toilet break, they checked the petrol and oil, checked and waggled all the movable surfaces on the wings and looked for anything untoward and then were off. They had to wait for an AT&T plane coming in from London to land, but then they were clear to go.

"Our first landmark city is Dijon," George said to Federica as she took command of the controls. "That way, heading 130 degrees."

"Let's see how good this compass is," she said. "At least it's a sunny day, nice and clear. As I calculate it, we should be over Dijon in just over an hour."

"I wonder when we'll first be able to see the city," he said. "Does Dijon have a big cathedral?"

"You're the one who spent time in France," she said.

"Yes, but that was mainly to the north of Dijon on the Flanders part of the Western Front," he said. "Leave we did get, rare though it was, was usually to Paris."

"It's very brown down there," she commented.

"We are in the middle of winter," he said. "When we get south of Dijon on the way to Geneva, I expect we'll see snow and lots of it."

"What's that dead ahead?" she asked. "Can you see with binoculars?"

"It's the spire of a church," he said. "That must be Dijon."

"It's interesting, is doesn't seem to be getting any closer," she said.

"I think that's because up here we can see for over a hundred miles, so we can see places far away," he said. "It's a nice smooth ride so far, don't be surprised if it gets a little rough going over the Alps, the updrafts and thermals will cause all kinds of different conditions."

"I was thinking, should we have some way to strap ourselves to our seats, so that we don't get bounced out of them?" she asked.

"That is a good idea," he thought. "The belts will be simple enough, but what kind of buckle should be used to make it easy to fasten and unfasten?"

"I'm glad we fixed the seats down, but we need some adjustment there, you and I are different heights, so what is good for me is cramped for you," she said.

"Let's look at that when we get back," he said. "We need to be as safe and comfortable as we can be when we fly to the Cape."

"That was Dijon, now Geneva, come right to 145 degrees," he said. "This is a shorter leg, forty-five minutes. Look, we can see the Alps ahead."

"All covered in snow as well," she said. "I wouldn't want to run into them. That would not be good. I wonder how countries will deal with people like us just flying over."

"I'm sure they're mostly like Britain, certain places are off limits, but I wonder how you are supposed to know that," he said.

"That is a good point, I suppose they all publish areas that are restricted like Britain does," she added.

"Well, at least on the way to the Cape we'll be flying over areas that are under British control until we get to South Africa," he commented.

"I'll check to see if there has been anything published about restricted areas in Africa, and I suppose we should for France, Italy and Greece," she said.

They flew on, over Geneva and then watched the ground rise steadily as they crossed into the Alps.

"I think climb a little to 12,000," he suggested.

"Twelve thousand it is," she confirmed. "It's bumpy up here."

"That's the mountains and the updrafts and air currents around them," he said. "We should expect more until we get clear of the Alps on the Italian side."

"We really do need to find a way to strap ourselves down," she said. "I was nearly bumped out of my seat there. How are you managing with the camera?"

"Just fine, I think I have managed to get some good shots of the peaks and the snow," he said. "We've passed the high peaks, there's nothing high ahead of us, so we can probably drop back down a little now, back to 10,000."

"Ten thousand it is," she confirmed. "That's better, now that we're clear of the really high mountains, things are smoothing out a little."

"There will still be a little," he said. "Until we're well clear of the Alps, there will be odd air currents."

They flew past Turin, then at Genoa crossed over the sea for a while until Livorno, and then it was all overland until Rome. Franco was there to meet them and was really interested in the new plane and wanted to know when he could get one. Federica suggested that he talk to Caproni and see if they would be interested in building one for him using her drawings. They told Franco all about the flight and about flying high over the Alps, taking photographs as they went. Franco had business in Rome, selling cars and vans that he sourced from the Orly factory. There was increasing competition from Italian companies like Fiat, Alfa-Romeo, Lancia and Bertone and a host of other smaller companies. Franco was interested in starting a factory locally to build their cars and vans, so Federica recommended that he go to Orly and see that factory there and talk to Philippe. If he felt there was a market of sufficient size in Italy, then she would fund a joint venture between Sirius and the trading company that Franco now ran.

After an overnight stay in Rome, Federica and George retraced their steps and flew back over the Alps to France and thence to England and Croydon.

"Did you have any issues?" Anastasia asked when they finally got home.

"With the plane and the engine, no," Federica replied. "But, we have concluded that we need to find a way to strap ourselves in; we were bounced around quite a bit as we flew over the Alps."

"Well, the belts should be simple enough," Anastasia said. "We make sure the seats are well secured and modify the seats to have attach points on them to take the belts, but what kind of buckle is easy to fasten and most importantly, unfasten?"

"That is what we see as the real challenge," George said in agreement.

"Cayley had a belt in his glider," Federica said. "I wonder if any of the museums have drawings of models that show that."

"We should get some of Cayley's papers and see if he talks about it," George suggested. "I recall that Foulois in America just used a leather strap buckled in, but that would not be easy to release if something went wrong."

"What if you had a tongue that went into a receiver with a tang that was lifted by a lever?" Will suggested.

"Could we try and make some ideas and test them?" Federica asked. "I really don't want to get bounced out of my seat if I'm trying to fly the plane."

With the help of Mr White and Robin Hoppes, they made half a dozen different ideas and started a test program. First, they tested the strength of the buckle itself by pulling on each end until it failed, looking to see whether it was the tang that broke or the machining done to allow the straps to be attached. Then they tested different kinds of leather and fabric to find a belt that would work. Finally, they tested the method of fastening the buckle to the belt to see whether sewing or riveting was better.

"So, which works best?" Federica asked Mr White.

"Number four, the buckle with the two tangs and the multiple layer three and a half inch wide canvas strap that is sewn back for three inches," he replied. "The buckle makes it easy to fasten and unfasten, just push the one end into the buckle until you hear the spring tangs engage, then lift the top of the buckle to undo it."

"Could we get those made for all the seats on the plane?" she asked.

"I'll have them ready by next week, and we'll have the modifications to the seats done by then as well, and we'll have an adjustment item in there as well to change the length of the belt," he promised.

"Should we have these in cars?" Robin asked.

"I think if we had a really fast racing car, then I would add them," Federica said. "In our usual cars and vans, I'm not sure. It would mean modifying all the seats and incurring the extra expense to include them. If we see a demand, then we should be ready with a plan, but for now, let's just leave it at the plane."

"When's your next test flight?" Anastasia asked.

"When we see a nice few days that would let us get to Cairo and back," Federica replied. "So, we'll be following the weather forecasts closely."

It was not until the middle of February that there was another cold, clear spell in the weather, with sunshine forecast for most of France and all of the Mediterranean. England was as usual for February, dreary with clouds, light sleet or snow at times.

"Do we go?" George asked Federica.

"We go," she said. "There's enough visibility to get us safely to Croydon and then the Channel, and things will improve over France."

"Stop in Paris again, then over the Alps again to Rome?" he asked.

"I think that would be good," she said.

"We have our new belts for the seats," he said. "Robin finished making the modifications to the seats, and we can test them over the Alps."

"Good," she said. "Tomorrow morning, as soon as there's light enough, we can hop over to Croydon, pick up petrol and leave for Cairo."

"I'll make us some coffee, and we can take a Thermos with us," he said.

"I should telephone Thomas Cook and get us bookings in Rome and Cairo," she said.

The flight was uneventful until they were approaching Geneva.

"Look, the Alps are covered in clouds," Federica said.

"We should climb to 12,000 now so that we'll be sure to pass safely over them," George said.

"Right, we wouldn't want to run into them," she said. "How long should we stay at 12,000?"

"Forty-five minutes to an hour to be safe," he said. "We should be almost over Turin by then."

"We must be getting close to the Alps," she said. "It's getting quite bumpy, I'm glad we put these straps in, that was a big bump. Should we try a little higher?"

"Let's try 14,000," he suggested.

"That's better," she said after they had climbed up to the higher altitude. "Look, it's clearing down there, the clouds must all be on the northwest side of the Alps," he said. "You can drop down at any time."

"You can see a long way from 14,000 feet," she said.

"About 200 miles on a clear day," he replied. "So we could probably see mountains that far away, but towns would be hard to see."

"As we fly down over Africa, I imagine we'll see the Ruwenzori mountains long before we see anything else then," she said.

"We could probably pick out Lake Victoria, it's big enough," he said. "And I imagine that following the Nile, even with its twists and turns, would be quite easy as the sun would reflect off the water."

"I'm excited to see that," she said. "There we've descended to 10,000 feet again, next stop Rome."

After a night's sleep in Rome, they were off early in the morning heading for Brindisi, then Athens, a flight of a little under five hours. The winds cooperated, and they were there in just four and a half hours, in time for lunch and a break before setting off on the longer overwater run to Cairo.

"Let's do this leg at 12,000 feet," Federica suggested. "You fly and I'll navigate and pass you coffee."

"Dinner in Cairo at Shepheard's?" he asked.

"Dinner at Shepheard's," she confirmed. "Then a whole day off before we fly back. This gets tiring, doesn't it, isn't there something we can do to help?"

"There is the system that the American Sperry invented in 1912," he said. "It uses a gyroscope and keeps heading and attitude, so would probably keep us straight and level."

"We should look into that," she said. "If nothing else, it would make things easier on these long, straight legs. As long as we stay alert, we can always take over if things drift a little or something goes wrong."

"We'll do that as soon as we get home," he promised. "Sperry had some spectacular demonstrations of his invention in Paris back before the War, so it has been proven, and there's no reason for us not to use it."

"I presume that it's not at the stage yet where we can just set a route and then go to sleep," she said.

"I wouldn't recommend that," he laughed. "But there are tales of Sperry indulging in romantic encounters while in the air, unfortunately, things went awry and he and the lady landed up in the drink and had to be rescued by duck hunters."

"When was that? I must have missed it," she said.

"1916, I believe," he replied.

"I don't think we'll be trying anything like that while we're in the air," she laughed. "That's what hotel beds are for."

"There's Crete," he said, changing the subject and pointing. "The next landfall will be Alexandria."

"Well, we're right on time," she said, consulting her chart. "Without trying to spoil things, all seems to be going well."

"It does, doesn't it," he agreed. "How's the petrol level?"

"We're only down to 85% of the tanks," she said. "So, petrol is good, if you wanted to go a little faster, we could, oil pressure and temperature both look good, we have no overheating problems."

"Let's not push things too far," he said. "This is a comfortable cruising speed. We might go a little faster, but it wouldn't get us there that much sooner, so why stress the engine."

"Coffee?" she asked.

"Thank you," he said. "If you put the cup there and take the controls for a minute, I'll drink it, then take over again."

"Here you are," she said. Pouring coffee and putting the cup between them, along with a plate of biscuits."

"Look down there," he said. "Is that birds?"

"I do believe it is," she said. "I suppose the migrations from Africa to Europe have started. We wouldn't want to fly into that lot."

"Amazing, isn't it," he said. "Here we are dependent on an engine and artificial wings, and yet there they are flying across the water, with nowhere to stop until they make landfall."

"When you were flying in Egypt and France, did you ever run into any birds?" she asked.

"I didn't," he replied. "But it happened, my pilots would run into gulls along the coast of Egypt. Fortunately, we were luckier than the American Rodgers, who in 1912 hit a gull over Long Beach in California, and the controls on his plane jammed and he crashed in the water and couldn't get out. In France, we had issues with birds around the airfield and had to scare them away when we wanted to take off."

"Well, I hope we don't run into any birds when we make our run to the Cape," she said. "I would not like to have to crash land in the middle of Africa. How high do birds fly?"

"There have been reports of birds higher than we normally fly," he replied. "I know that cranes go really high, so can swans and ducks, so we should see if we can find out when migrations happen."

"Another thing to check on," she said. "I'll add it to the list. We definitely wouldn't want to run into something as large as a crane."

"Alexandria," she said, pointing ahead.

"Good, not too far now," he said. "When we get back, we should see if we can modify the seats a little to make them more comfortable when we're sitting for hours on end."

"If you want, I'll take the controls and you can get up and stretch in the back," she offered.

"No, thank you, though," he said. "I'll be fine until we land. Can you raise Cairo?"

"I have them," she confirmed. "They tell me that there is no traffic at the moment, so we can go straight in, the wind is light and from the south."

They landed at Cairo and, after covering the engine intakes and the pitot tubes to stop sand getting in everything, got a taxi into Cairo and the hotel.

The trip back was uneventful until they got to Paris and learned that fog had formed over most of southern England, and Croydon was closed to traffic as visibility was down to a few yards. The Instone, AT&T, Daimler, Grands Express Aériens, Messageries Aériennes, Farman and Latécoère flights had all been cancelled, and people were resorting to trains and ferries to get back and forth.

"What do we do?" Federica asked George. "Wait a day or so until it clears, or leave the plane here and take the ferry back."

"I propose that we take the ferry back tonight and once in England, see how long this will last," he replied.

"We'll do that," she agreed. "We'll close up the plane here and come back and get it when the weather improves. I thought that we were due a longer clear spell, but clearly weather forecasting has its limitations."

"I wonder how long it will be before a system is invented that allows flights even in poor visibility," he mused. "But then, even if it may be somewhat safe to fly, you still have to be able to see the runway to take off and land, or perhaps one day even that may be automatic."

"I've been thinking that it may be safer for us to have two engines," she said.

"Will that mean a larger plane?" he asked.

"A little," she said. "I already have the basics of the design, I just want to do some wind tunnel testing to confirm things."

"How long will all that take?" he asked.

"I can have a plane to fly in late April," she said.

"So soon?" he asked.

"We have all the drawings, after we built Pegasus we know how to build the moulds for the fuselage, the wings will be a little different as the engines will hang from them, but I have the designs for that, it's now a matter of finishing the model I started and running the wind tunnel tests, then building the plane itself," she explained.

"It will be interesting to see if two engines work," he said. "I suppose if we lost one engine then the other might suffice, but we'd have to watch what it did to the flying characteristics, there would be asymmetric thrust, so we'd have to counter that."

"Unfortunately, our wind tunnel doesn't allow us to check for that," she said. "Anyway, we'll see what the model looks like."

"Any issues on the flights?" Anastasia asked when they finally arrived home.

"None, just the weather here," Federica replied.

"It's awful, isn't it?" Anastasia said.

"I suppose we'll just have to wait until it improves before we get the plane; meanwhile, we've decided to add the Sperry gyroscopic control system to the plane to help us fly straight and level," Federica said. "So, we have some research and studying to do. That and I want to see what I can find out about bird migrations and if we are likely to run into any on our way down Africa. I'm also thinking of increasing the wingspan a little, lengthening the fuselage and adding two engines, one under each wing, so that we've got three engines, not the two I was thinking of. I can either use the same engine that we have on Pegasus or use the smaller version that gives us 300 hp."

"I'd use that," Anastasia suggested. "Then you're not overloading the engines at all, and you should have a nice, reliable aircraft."

"I confess, I did sketch out the design a while ago," Federica said. "Perhaps you would check it for me."

"Of course," Anastasia said.

"I've also got a model I want to test," Federica said. "I think the wind tunnel tests will be fine, but I want to be sure. I've added the engines to the model, and I'll see what it does to the flight characteristics."

The weather cleared up a week later enough that Federica was able to go to France to see to the plane. She did decide that if Franco wanted to buy it he could do so, so she telegraphed him and he met her in Paris, handed over money and got a lesson in the handling of the plane from Federica. He was already a good pilot, so all that was new to him were the particular controls of the Pegasus and its idiosyncrasies, not that it had many. He was delighted with the plane and flew it back to Florence while Federica took the train and the ferry back to England. The money she got for Pegasus, she put towards building her new plane, the Condor. She would still have to add some of her own money to make up the costs of the Condor, but not too much. Franco had, of course haggled about the price, but they had reached agreement to the satisfaction of both. Then she set about the serious business of testing her designs using the model she had built.

The model tests done, Federica was happy with the wing design and the three-engine configuration. Little did she know that Fokker and Stout would both come out with similar designs only a couple of years later. Her new plane would have seats for eight passengers, if they carried any, and would have fuel tanks for 700 nautical miles. She used the smaller engines, which she calculated would give her a maximum speed of 150 knots and a cruise speed of 130 knots. She and Anastasia debated propellers and finally decided on a three-bladed one. They had investigated the variable pitch devices that Turnbull, Baynes and Levasseur had invented and demonstrated, but concluded that, for the moment, the reliability was not yet proven enough to use on the long flight to the Cape. Aviation was changing fast. They were barely twenty years past the first recorded and well-advertised powered flight, and the changes since the now crude and ungainly looking Wright Flyer to the almost sleek designs of the 1920s were amazing. To be able to plan for a sustained flight of over 600 nautical miles instead of the mere 120 feet that the Wrights flew, a multiplication factor of 3,000 was a feat not often seen, engine improvements had also been made and whereas the Wrights used a four cylinder in line engine that weighed 180 lbs and delivered 12 hp, giving 15 lbs per hp, in 1919 the Bristol Jupiter nine cylinder radial engine weighed 995 lbs, but delivered 550 hp, giving 1.8 lbs per hp.

Satisfied with the design, Federica commissioned David Bond to make moulds for her for the fuselage halves, and while he was doing that, she and her team of craftsmen that she retained set about building the wings. They used the same construction as they had with Pegasus and built up all the ribs, then covered the whole with thin plies of wood. Once the fuselage moulds were done, they set about glueing in the veneers of wood that would make up the laminate. The halves made, it was then just a question of adding the reinforcing ribs, the reinforcements around the doors and windows, then glueing the halves together, adding the wings, then fitting all the controls, fuel tanks and engines. They did include the Sperry system of control. They also fitted modified seats for the pilots and the passengers, seats that they felt would be more comfortable on a longer flight. The seats they secured to the floor and also added belts, so that if they encountered turbulence, they could strap themselves in.

The first test flight took place on the fifteenth of April and was a success. The plane flew and flew well, it was fast, it handled well and felt solid and sturdy in flight. They made improvements to the suspension of the landing wheels that gave them less of a jolt when they did touch down. But, apart from that, what they had learned with Pegasus translated easily to the bigger plane. They got their registration number and airworthiness certificate by the beginning of May and ran some longer-distance flights to Cairo and back to test the engines and the design. Things looked good, so then Federica and George picked a date and started to make serious preparations for the flight to the Cape.

"Should we ask Helen is she wants to come with us to document the flight with photographs?" Federica asked George.

"That is a splendid idea," he said. "I'll talk to her."

Helen was thrilled at the notion of flying down the length of Africa, and all she wanted to know was how much in weight of her camera gear she could take with her. As the passenger load was very light, there was really no limit to what she could take, so she set about acquiring film, both for the still cameras and for the Aeroscope. George advised her about clothes to wear, including shoes or boots, so that she would be comfortable on the long runs between stops. Federica asked Anastasia and Will if they wanted to come, but they declined, citing work and the risk, no matter how slight, that something catastrophic could leave Giovanna orphaned.

"Should we invite a member of the Press?" Federica asked George.

"I'm not sure," he said. "I know that *The Times* had a man aboard one of the first attempts to fly to the Cape, but they were also sponsoring the attempt, so that was logical. If we were to take anyone, it would be someone from *Flight* or *The Aeroplane*."

"Should we invite them?" she asked.

"I'll talk to them and see if they have an interest," he said.

Flight was definitely interested, as was *The Aeroplane*, so George invited both and Andrew Wilson of *Flight* and Gordon Dodd of *The Aeroplane* came to Handy Cross to see the plane and take a test flight before the long trek to the Cape. George and Will flew them to Windermere and back, which seemed to satisfy them that the plane was airworthy. Both said that their editors would pay for hotel accommodations along the way and that if the return trip was not to be immediate, then they would return by boat. The last thing George did was to contact the RAF and the various British authorities to let them know that they were going to fly Cairo to Cape Town and back, and essentially got permission to do so and a commitment from the RAF that there would be petrol at the various landing sites. George gave them their proposed route with stops and told them that he would confirm exactly when they would start. He also packaged up complete sets of spare parts for the engines and shipped them to South Africa in care of his cousin, Koos, so that they could overhaul the engines before thinking about a return flight.

The Cape

The second half of 1922 saw an expansion in air services from London's Croydon airport. Night flights between London and Paris were started. Flights were started between London and Ostend, then London, Paris, Lyons and Marseilles. A Daimler Airways plane, G-EBB, flew five single trips between London and Paris in one day. The British Civil Aviation Advisory Board reported on the Imperial Air Mail Service and made recommendations as to routes and planes as far as India. The London to Berlin route was surveyed, but service would not start until 1923. Instone Air Line had financial difficulties and ceased its London to Paris route in October. London to Rotterdam was opened up, as was the domestic flight from London to Manchester.

"Are we ready to go?" George asked Federica in early June.

"Ready," she confirmed. "I have made bookings in Brindisi, Cairo and Khartoum. I thought we'd confirm other bookings when we get to Cairo. I have filters on board for the petrol we'll buy along the way, and I have my bag packed."

"I talked to Helen and she is ready," he said. "If we load everything on the plane this afternoon, we can leave at first light in the morning. The reporters are here, bags in hand, they are staying at the White Hart in High Wycombe, so we'll pick them up on the way to the airfield."

"I presume they've got passports," she said.

"If they don't, then that's their problem," he said. "I'll leave a message at the White Hart to let them know that we'll collect them at five in the morning. I know it's early, but the dawn will already be up, so there will be plenty of light to fly by."

"It's a pity the long days don't hold in the lower latitudes," she said. "It would mean that we could go farther in one day."

"Until runways are lit, that will be an issue," he said. "Grands Express Aériens may have started night flights from Croydon to Le Bourget, but Khartoum and points south will not have lit runways."

"Let's not do what Messageries Aériènnes recently did and crash over the Channel," she said. "I wonder what happened. What was it, a Blériot-Spad?"

"I believe so," he replied. "The regulations for accident investigation that were included in the 1920 Air Navigation Act come into effect soon, so perhaps they will look back at some of the accidents and try and work out what went wrong."

On the way to Handy Cross, George stopped at the White Hart and collected the bags of the reporters, leaving them with just a very small bag each to take them through the night. He also told them that he would be picking them up at five the next morning, which, to some, meant moaning about early mornings, until he pointed out that flying conditions were better in the cool of the morning. An early morning start would have them in Geneva at about ten-thirty, well before the heat of the day. He also suggested that they abstain from drinking that evening so that they would not have any after effects the next morning. They took that in good part and even joked with each other about what they might drink instead. Helen stayed the night with Federica and George, so was ready when they were the next morning.

"What is the empty weight of this plane?" Andrew Wilson asked as they boarded the next morning.

"Five thousand four hundred and twenty pounds," Federica replied.

"How did you manage to get it so light?" he asked.

"The engines are only 775 lbs each, and the fuselage is a monocoque construction of wood; the wings are also wood. We would have used Duralumin if we could have found enough and learned how to shape it and weld it," she replied. "The plane in this configuration is about as light as we could make it. The gross weight is 9,880 lbs, of which 2,700 lbs is petrol; each engine burns about 125 lbs per hour."

"That's a good seven hours," Gordon commented.

"We know," she said. "Enough to get us to the stops we plan, plus a reserve in case things don't go well, or there's a strong headwind."

"Are we given to understand that you will be the pilot?" Andrew asked.

"I am," she confirmed.

"I will not go with you," he said. "No woman is capable of such a feat as to fly down the length of Africa."

"That goes for me as well," Gordon added.

"If you gentlemen feel that way, then you are not welcome on this trip," George said. "I will leave your bags here and you may find your own way back to High Wycombe."

"Idiots," Federica said as they taxied the plane out onto the runway. "Helen, do you have a problem with me flying?"

"I've flown with you to France," Helen replied. "I don't see the problem. I encounter some of the same stupidity, do I know how to operate a camera, do I know which chemicals to use when developing the film, all very frustrating and annoying as those men are the only ones with any brains."

"It's a cross we all have to bear," Federica said.

"Fede, do you want to fly us to Geneva or take Geneva to Brindisi?" George asked.

"I'll take Geneva to Brindisi," she said. "Helen, when we cross the Alps, there may be the chance for some good photographs."

"Let me know when we're getting close, and I'll be ready. Why do we stop in Geneva?" Helen said.

"It's a better split in times of time and distance than Paris," Federica said. "It's about halfway to Brindisi, so a good place to stop for a break and most importantly, petrol."

"All set?" George asked. With nods of confirmation, he took off for the short hop to Croydon, where they checked with the immigration people, then left for Geneva. It was a beautiful June day, not too hot yet, but warming up nicely, the kind of day that drew hordes to the seashore and had people picnicking in the countryside. Once over the Channel, they could see the French shore and were over it in under 15 minutes, then it was on to Paris and then Geneva. Their stop in Geneva at the new airport was short, enough time to visit the toilet, stretch their legs, fill the petrol tanks, get some coffee and croissants, and then off to Brindisi.

"We have to climb a little higher now," George told Helen. "Those are the Alps in front, and we need to be well above them, and it looks as if we have a nice clear day."

"Could I stand behind you and take some moving pictures?" she asked.

"Of course," he said. "We might hit a few bumps, so find a way to brace yourself so that you are not thrown around the cabin."

"I'll try," she said. "Is that still snow?" she asked.

"It is," he confirmed. "The Alps are high enough that the snow on the tops never melts, and there are even glaciers in places."

"This is super," Helen said as she filmed the Alps. "When we get back, I will try and put all this together to show the whole journey."

"The next large town we'll see will be Turin," George told Helen. "Then Genoa and we'll cross the Med briefly coming ashore again at Livorno, then on to Rome, then we'll go on down the length of Italy to Brindisi."

"Fancy that, Rome and beyond in a day," Helen said.

"We started early enough so that we could make Brindisi in a day," George commented. "But that only works in the summer months; in the winter, the days are so much shorter that until runways are lit, we're constrained to daylight hours, so we'd have to make more stops."

Rome was passed at three that afternoon, and they reached Brindisi at just before six that evening.

"What do you think of our journey thus far?" Federica asked Helen over dinner.

"It's so exciting," she replied. "This is my first visit to Italy. I should come back and spend some time here, there's so much history to explore and appreciate."

"I think you'll find Athens and Cairo the same," Federica said. "They're both old cities with so much that has influenced us."

"Will we see the pyramids when we get to Cairo?" Helen asked.

"We will," Federica confirmed. "I'm hoping that if we get an early start tomorrow that you'll have time to pay a brief visit there in the late afternoon, just before the sun goes down."

"What fun," Helen said. "And beyond Cairo?"

"For us, that is new territory," Federica said. "We have maps and all we need to navigate, but we've not been there before, so it will be exciting for us as well."

"We stop in Khartoum, don't we?" Helen asked.

"We do," Federica confirmed.

"Gordon of Khartoum, I presume it's safe today, no Mahdi or Fuzzy-Wuzzys to attack us," Helen said.

"That war was over in 1899 when Kitchener reoccupied Khartoum," George assured her.

"You didn't fight there?" Helen asked.

"No, I was on leave from India, and was recalled and sent to South Africa in 1900," he replied. "Khartoum today is a centre for river traffic on the Nile and boasts several swanky hotels."

"And, south of there?" Helen asked.

"Then we're into Central and Southern Africa, less Arabic and more Bantu," George explained. "We're hopping between British colonies. Uganda, Kenya, Tanganyika and the Rhodesias before heading down briefly into Bechuanaland and then South Africa."

"Tanganyika was German, though, wasn't it?" Helen asked.

"It was," George confirmed. "It was German East Africa until the Treaty of Versailles, when Germany relinquished all overseas territories, Britain took over, then renamed it the Tanganyika Territory in 1919, and the League of Nations gave a mandate to Britain to manage the territory in 1920."

"Such a lot for all the poor people there to go through," Helen commented. "First one European power, then another."

"Colonies are a mixed blessing," George said. "On the one hand, they may bring in mineral and agricultural wealth, but on the other hand, they are expensive to administer, and they rarely really consider the wishes of the indigenous peoples."

"That's a long political discussion to be had at another time," Federica said. "For now, we need to focus on navigation, weather and petrol."

They left Brindisi at six the following morning and crossed the Adriatic at Lece.

"Imagine, the Romans built roads all the way down here," Helen said as she took still and moving pictures.

"They built roads everywhere," Federica said. "I suppose it made moving their armies easier, but also it built up commerce and trading."

"Where do we enter Greece?" Helen asked.

"Close to Patras, then it's not far to Athens," George said. "We should be in Athens by nine-thirty at the latest."

"That's Greece," Federica said, pointing ahead.

"It's all very green, isn't it?" Helen commented.

"I imagine we'll see a lot of brown as we fly down Egypt and the Sudan," Federica said.

"There's Athens," George said, pointing.

"I suppose that once we leave Athens, then it's water all the way to Egypt?" Helen asked.

"It is," George confirmed. "We'll see Crete on the way, but there's nowhere there to stop."

"We'll stop in Athens, fill the tanks, then it's six hours to Cairo, so we should make sure we find a toilet," Federica said.

"There's a boat," Helen said, pointing down to the Mediterranean as they flew south of Crete towards Alexandria.

"I would imagine that we'd see boats quite often," George said. "When we get nearer to Egypt, there'll be the boats going to and leaving Suez."

"The canal makes a big difference to sailing to India and Australia, doesn't it," Helen commented.

"India, more so than Australia," George said.

"At least in a plane we can go where we want in a straight line," Helen said.

"Not quite," George said. "When we get to the southern part of Uganda, we'll have to go around the Ruwenzori; some of the peaks there are too high for us to fly over, and they haven't been mapped well enough to know where the passes through the mountains are."

"I hadn't thought of that," Helen said. "Look, there's another boat."

"Did you send off a progress report to Nastia and Will?" Federica asked George.

"I did," he confirmed. "I gave them times, fuel consumption, engine data and weather conditions."

"Good, so they can plot our position on the map," Federica said. "Helen, have you been noting where you take pictures so that we can place where they are on the map?"

"I've been noting times," she replied. "I'm relying on you to tell me where we were at those times."

"We can work out with reasonable accuracy based on heading and time," Federica confirmed. "We'll do that when we get home."

"This is the Nile Delta," George said, pointing to the green ahead. "It stretches from Port Said in the east to Alexandria in the west and south to Cairo."

"Is that the pyramids?" Helen asked, pointing ahead.

"It is," Federica confirmed. "You'll have plenty of light to see and photograph them, sunset isn't until almost eight, it might be an idea for you to take a taxi and go straight there, and then join us at the hotel later, Shepheard's."

"I will take your suggestion, will you take my luggage for me?" Helen asked.

"Of course," Federica said.

Once down at Cairo, they went their separate ways, Helen scurrying off to see the pyramids while there was yet light and Federica and George to the hotel to rest from the day and prepare for the next leg. George composed and despatched the daily telegraph to report on their progress, with a comment that thus far all was going well, really well.

"If we are ever to create a commercial route, it will be a challenge to fly this many hours with a reasonable break," Federica commented to George as they bathed.

"That same thought had occurred to me," he said. "Perhaps if we stay with Khartoum as the turnaround point for the pilots, we should build in a whole day of rest."

"When you were in Egypt and France, how many hours did you fly a day?" she asked.

"Of course, it depended on the weather, but if conditions were good, then two missions a day, each less than three hours, which is typically all the fuel we had, so six hours in all," he replied.

"So, our potential eight-hour days are long," she said.

"Yes, but with two pilots we trade so each only flies four hours at the most," he said.

"Something to think about," she said. "I wonder if Helen is back and if we should go down for dinner."

Helen was indeed back and already changed and ready for dinner.

"The pyramids are amazing," she said. "I didn't have time to climb to the top, but I took photographs with the sun setting behind them. It's a pity that there is no way to capture the colours on film, as it was truly beautiful."

"I imagine that one day, someone will invent a system for colour pictures," Federica said.

"Well, there is the French Autochrome process," George said. "I have seen some of the results and they are truly inspiring, but I understand that exposure times are long, and it uses pre-manufactured plates, so it may not be convenient for use on expeditions like this, but for fashion pictures, car pictures and such where the subject is still, then it would be worth investigating."

"I will do that on our return," Helen said. "Meanwhile, I can always hand-tint pictures, if I remember what the colours were."

"Well, the Alps would be easy," George laughed. "White and grey."

"Yes, but blue as well, plus other colours, it's a more complex picture than one would imagine," Helen said. "So tomorrow, Khartoum, so we just follow the Nile?"

"Essentially, but not absolutely," George replied. "The Nile twists and turns, and we can cut across many of the turns. At the altitude we fly, the Nile won't ever be far out of sight. We'll stop at Assuan for a break and petrol. I'll talk to the concierge and arrange for a packed breakfast and lunch for us to eat on the way."

They set off for Assuan well before dawn, so they got the cool of the day. Helen was excited to be able to see the sun come up, and she took photographs through the window, trying to capture the sight and fixing in her mind the colours she would add later. George was flying the first leg of the day, and he kept the Nile to his right as they flew straight over the Egyptian desert. Two hours into the flight, he pointed ahead to the Nile, now lit by the rising sun, that they were going to cross.

"It's so green right around the river," Federica commented. "But, look, you don't have to go far from the river before it gets brown and desert."

"We'll stay quite close to the river now," he said. "It swings back to the west just ahead, then east again, and then we fly almost overhead all the way into Assuan. As we get to Assuan, we'll see the lake formed by the dam the British built a few years ago. This will be our biggest test, because this is the hottest place we will land. Taking off, they must have a long runway because the Vimy took off from here."

"Why is that a problem?" Helen asked.

"As the air heats up, it becomes less dense, so we get less lift. The only condition that's worse is high temperatures and high altitudes; high altitude is not a problem here, we're only 295 feet above sea level," he replied. "But, we've got a light load, we'll calculate just how much petrol we'll need, and our engines will give us the speed we need to take off. For us, the challenge is to find a time of year when conditions are reasonable all throughout Africa. Now we're going from midsummer to midwinter, for Assuan, the winter months would be better as it's cooler, but for Southern Africa, we'd be into summer and the rains. That's why we left Cairo so early, to try and get in and out of here before the heat of the day."

Landing at Assuan was interesting; they had to come in quite quickly, so the rollout before they stopped was quite long. Fortunately, the runway was long, the RAF, or whoever had actually built it, had anticipated temperature issues and made sure that not only was it long enough, but there were no high objects to run into on the climb out.

"I'll take care of petrol," George said. "If you two want to find a toilet and perhaps some water. My God, it's hot, isn't it?"

"And going to get hotter," Federica said. "The sooner we're gone, the better."

There were ground staff to help with petrol, so he ran it through the filters he had and filled the tanks with the amount they had estimated they would need for the four hours to Khartoum, plus a reserve of forty-five minutes. That done, he found a toilet, which he was less than impressed with, but the heat probably made it difficult to maintain.

"All set?" Federica asked as she took the controls for the flight to Khartoum. She got nods of affirmation, so she started the engines and taxied to the very end of the runway. She stood on the brakes and ran the engines up, and then let everything go, and they accelerated down the runway. At Handy Cross, they could take off within 600 feet, but she estimated it was almost 1,000 feet before she could feel it start to lift, and she pulled back the stick. It took a while to climb up to 12,000 feet, where it was significantly cooler.

"We should let Will know that his engines performed superbly," she said to George.

"What will we see on the way to Khartoum?" Helen asked.

"Lots of desert," Federica replied. "The river makes a big curve out to the west, but we'll just go straight south until we cross the river for the second time, the first time is the river going back towards the east, then the second time it comes back towards the west, then we'll follow it the last little bit into Khartoum."

"Khartoum sounds so romantic," Helen said.

"It's probably had its moments," George said. "Now it's a tourist place where people come to see where the White Nile joins the Blue Nile. They take the train to Assuan and then a boat to Khartoum."

"There's the Nile," Helen said as they crossed it and ran back across the desert again.

"When we see it next, we turn slightly and follow it into Khartoum," George said. "That should be about an hour and a half."

"Look over there," Federica said. "That looks like a sandstorm."

"Let's see the wind is out of the north, so the storm is likely to stay over there and not come this way, the landing fields are all to the east of us here, so we'll have to try and outrun it if it comes this way," George said.

"It doesn't look as if it's getting any closer," Federica said after a while. "It's rather like watching a rain squall over the sea."

"I suppose getting caught in a sandstorm would not be good?" Helen asked.

"No," George said. "We'd probably lose the engines, which would not be good."

"One of the other things to consider for a service to the Cape," Federica commented.

"I have a list," George said. "I'm adding as we go."

They arrived in Khartoum without encountering the sandstorm. It was four in the afternoon, so still hot and likely to remain so until late in the evening. The hotel for the night was the Grand Hotel, a very nice-looking place on the river that catered to travellers and tourists. Helen was gratified to note that there was no antipathy towards them; in fact, the staff of the hotel were very attentive, without being servile.

"We should try and leave before dawn again," George said. "Let us take off before the day heats up."

"Where next?" Helen asked.

"Mongalla in the south of Sudan," George replied. "Five hours there, it's on the White Nile, which comes from Lake Victoria. There's some British administration there, but not a lot. Apparently, it's an important station for monitoring the water flow in the Nile. We climb a little from here; Khartoum is at about 1,250 feet, and Mongalla is at 1,500 feet. We'll have to watch for rain as June is one of the rainy months, but it's not as hot as Khartoum. I'll telegraph Mongalla later and see if they have a weather report, and then we'll decide whether to go tomorrow."

"Where do we stay tomorrow night?" Helen asked.

"Kisumu," George replied. "It's on a bay of Lake Victoria, it's served by the railway and ferries. Mongalla to Kisumu is not that long a flight, probably just under three hours. It's a lot higher than Mongalla, at about 3,900 feet, so a lot cooler."

"It strikes me that a commercial air service down Africa is fraught with issues," Helen said.

"It is," Federica agreed. "It's a dream, but perhaps we're just a little too soon for it to be a reality. That's why we're doing this, to fly the route and identify possible problems."

"We'll have to wait at least a day," George announced over dinner. "It's raining cats and dogs in Mongalla. It's expected to clear tomorrow afternoon, so I'll check again and see what conditions are like. I'd like to give the runway a little time to dry out. I've sent off the daily report to Nastia and Will and also told them that we're holding for a day because of the rain."

"So, what shall we do tomorrow?" Federica asked.

"I think first thing in the morning, check the plane, and make sure everything is in good order, the next few days will take us over territory where emergency landings might be difficult, then perhaps in the afternoon hire a boat and take a trip on the river."

"What fun," Federica said.

The maintenance checks found nothing untoward, but they changed the oil in the engines anyway, cleaned out all the petrol feed lines and then filled the fuel tanks, to be ready to go when the weather improved. Then there was the river trip, up the Blue Nile, because they would see more of the White Nile as they went south to Mongalla. They hired a felucca and sailed up the river for a while to an island that was teeming with ducks and other birds.

"I wonder if this area floods," Federica said as they watched the birds.

"I suppose it must from time to time," George said. "Heavy rain in the upper reaches of both Niles would all flow down here, my guess is that September has the higher risk of flood."

"Well, at least the aerodrome is well above the river," Federica said. "But that island we saw that sits right where the two Niles come together must be at risk at times."

"I'm sure it is," George said. "Helen, can you get any good pictures of the birds?"

"If they would sit still long enough," she laughed. "I think I may, we'll see when we get home."

The weather report that night was much better, so Federica and George had a discussion and elected to go on to Mongalla the next day. George telegraphed the Hotel Royale in Kisumu and made bookings for them, so that they would have a place to stay. The Grand Hotel provided a very nice packed breakfast and lunch for them to take in the morning, and they were off at five.

"We'll go by compass heading here," George said as they flew south. "The variation in this part of the world is apparently not that bad, but it gets greater as we go farther south. We'll lose the Nile to the west at about two hours and twenty minutes, then we'll pick it up again after another two and a half hours, which should put us very near Mongalla. Fortunately, the river is big enough that it'll be hard to miss."

"Ready then?" Federica asked. With nods of agreement from the others, she taxied out to the end of the runway and took off to the north, turning as she climbed to come back south.

"It's easy to follow the river here," Helen commented. "Just look for the green. I wonder when tropical Africa really starts and everything turns more green than brown."

"I would imagine that it's a time-of-year thing," George said. "When I was in South Africa during the dry months, things were brown, then after the rains, it all turned green almost overnight."

"There's the Nile going west," Federica said. "Now we'll look for it again after another two and a half hours, you said."

"That's it," George confirmed.

"There it is," Federica said as they picked up the Nile again. "Now let's look for the aerodrome."

"There," George said, pointing ahead. "Let's see the wind sock shows us that the wind is light and from the west, so let's come around and land upwind."

"Good morning," the British official said as he came out to meet them, accompanied by about 50 native Sudanese. "Archibald Robertson, I was told you were on your way from Khartoum, even mowed the grass and made sure the landing field was clear. What do you require of us?"

"George and Federica Wheelwright and Helen Greene. We need to buy some petrol," George replied. "And some oil while we're about it."

"How many gallons?" Archibald asked.

"One hundred and fifty gallons," George replied. "Do you have that much?"

"We have plenty," Archibald said. "We started out with 1,214 gallons here, and we had the draws from the other flights in 1920, so you'll make a dent in what's left, but not a large one. We've had no call for petrol since van Ryneveld came through. I must confess that, because we've had so little call for it, I've been using it for the car that I have. How have things been going for you?"

"It was really hot in Assuan and Khartoum," George replied. "Otherwise, apart from the delay because of the rain here, very well. We stop for the night at Kisumu, and then we'll go on to Tabora."

"Well, best of luck," Archibald said. "When you leave here, I'll telegraph Kisumu that you're on your way, at least get them to mow the grass, and I'll also telegraph London to say that you've been here."

"How long have you been here?" Federica asked.

"Four years now," Archibald replied. "I'm due a long leave soon, so I'm just waiting for my replacement. Must keep the office in order. Abdullah here will help you with the petrol."

"I'd like to filter it as we pump it in," George said. "We have filters here that we can use."

"Good idea," Archibald said. "It's been sitting a while, so don't know how clean it is. Would you care for some tea while we do that?"

"That would be delightful," Federica said. "That and somewhere where Helen and I may spend a penny."

"Of course," Archibald said. "This way, we have facilities here in the Native Administrator's office."

The plane refuelled, tea drunk and pennies spent, they said their goodbyes to Archibald and his staff and set off for Kisumu. The flight to Kisumu did only take the three hours that George had estimated, and navigation was simple: fly southeast until they hit the lake, then follow the coastline around the north to Kisumu.

"Good afternoon," the official there said when they got out of the plane, accompanied by his horde of followers. "Geoffrey Gilbey, Archie told me you were coming. You have a hotel?"

"We do," Federica replied. "The Royale, we'll check the weather and leave in the morning for Tabora. I'm sorry, I should have introduced us all, Federica and George Wheelwright and Helen Greene, who is along as our photographer."

"How many days has it been so far?" Geoffrey asked. "Who flies the plane?"

"George and I both fly," Federica replied. "We try to stop at about the mid-point of the day's stage if we can."

"And you've managed?" he asked.

"She does as well as I," George said. "As to how many days so far, let's see, first day Croydon to Brindisi, then Cairo, then Khartoum, and we had to wait a day there for the rain to clear in Mongalla, so three long days of flying and one day of maintenance and sightseeing."

"And you plan to go straight through to the Cape?" Geoffrey asked.

"If we can," Federica replied.

"Well, let's get you filled with petrol and oil and then we'll get you to your hotel," Geoffrey suggested.

"Would you care to join us for dinner?" Federica asked.

"That would be an honour," he replied.

Dinner was a delight, Geoffrey was full of stories about being the local administrator and had great sympathy for Archibald, who he saw as being stuck out in the back of beyond. He wanted to know how long Federica had been flying and was surprised when George let it slip that it was she and his sister who had designed the plane.

"A plane would be most useful for us here," Geoffrey said. "We have so much country to oversee, and travel by land takes time. But, the Colonial Office is its usual parsimonious self and getting them to pay for a plane is impossible."

"I'm afraid we can't offer you ours," George said. "We rather need it to get home."

"You'll be flying back then?" Geoffrey asked.

"We'll take a couple of days in the Cape to recover, then try and make it back in one piece," George said.

"That would be an amazing achievement," Geoffrey said. "Is anyone in England following your progress?"

"My sister and her husband are," George replied. "We telegraph back a report each day with data from the flight and comments about the weather and other things we encounter."

"Well, if there is anything we may do for you here, just tell me and I'll take care of it," Geoffrey offered.

"If the weather is good, we'd like to leave at about five for Tabora, then we thought we'd make quick stops in Abercorn and Broken Hill before flying on down to Livingstone," George said.

"That's a long day," Geoffrey commented. "I suppose with the three engines on your plane, you have some margin of safety. I'll alert Tabora and Abercorn that you're coming, please telegraph me when you get to Tabora."

"We'll do that," George promised. "And we'll let you know when we reach Livingstone."

"I envy you the trip," Geoffrey said. "Tell me, Miss Greene, have you been getting good photographs?"

"I hope so," she replied. "I am keen to get the films home and develop them all to see what we have."

"Would you take one with us all?" Geoffrey asked.

"Of course," Helen said. "Let me just find someone to press the shutter, if we gather over there by the reception desk."

Geoffrey had tea for them the next morning and saw them off before first light. They flew south, keeping the lake to their right until it was gone, then it was miles and miles of trees with the occasional town and here and there sightings of the railway that wound its way through the country north from Tabora. George had told Federica that the first leg of the journey should take about two hours and forty minutes, and he was right. They all saw the town at the same time and saw the runway that had been built. They landed and reported to the official there. He promised to telegraph Geoffrey and also said that he would alert Abercorn that they were on their way. They took on a little petrol and set out again for Abercorn.

"What do we look for particularly?" Federica asked George.

"Lake Rukwa, we should fly over it, not far from Abercorn, and if we're too far to the west, we'll hit Lake Tanganyika, then we should go south to Abercorn. Abercorn is high up, almost 5,500 feet, so look for an escarpment," he replied.

"You said before that taking off from high altitudes could be a problem," Helen said. "Will that be a problem for us?"

"No," George said. "We're south of the Equator now, so it's the winter months, so a little cooler, and the altitude cools it down anyway."

"When did we cross the Equator?" Helen asked.

"Just before we landed at Kisumu," George replied. "Sadly, from the air, there's nothing to indicate where it is, I'm not even sure if there are any signs of the roads that tell you."

"And the Tropics?" she asked.

"Cancer just south of Assuan and Capricorn will be between Palapye and Pretoria," he replied.

"That must be Lake Rukwa," Federica said. "It looks more like a huge marsh than a lake, and ahead, that's quite a range of mountains; it must be quite a climb from the lake to the tops."

"This map says that they're the Mbizi Mountains," Helen said, consulting the atlas she had brought with her. "Peaks up to 7,300 feet."

"There," George said as they passed over the peaks and watched the land drop down again. "There's Abercorn, can you see the aerodrome yet?"

"Over there," Helen said. She had been looking through her binoculars and pointed to the runway.

"I see it," Federica said. "I see the windsock too, winds light from the south, so we can go straight in."

"It's good that there are no trees around the runway," George said. "It looked to me like the whole of the surrounding country is covered with trees. I wonder who will be here to greet us."

There were two Europeans there to meet them, James Williams, the Native Administrator and Piet Cloete from the British South Africa Company, plus the now usual horde of onlookers and interested parties. Piet did most of the talking and explained that James had just been posted there and was getting his feet on the ground, while he, Piet, had been there for five years. George attended to buying petrol and then supervising its loading into the tanks while Federica and Helen chatted to James and Piet, spent their pennies and took photographs of the people, the place and the activities on the runway.

"Where next?" James asked.

"We'll try and hit the railway at Ndola then follow it south to Broken Hill," George replied.

"Your big landmark on the way will be Lake Bangweulu," Piet said. "If you're on track for Ndola, you should fly right over it, then you'll cross a part of the Congo before hitting Ndola. One thing about this time of year, it's cool, but skies are clear and there'll be no rain to deal with. We'll let Broken Hill know that you're on your way."

They flew over miles and miles of tree-covered land, with an occasional village, obvious because the trees had been cleared and land had been planted.

"There's the lake," Federica said, pointing ahead. "It's quite big, not the size of Lake Victoria, but hard to miss. I don't suppose the Congo will be any different to this."

"I see a railway," George said. "We should turn to the south and follow it to Broken Hill."

"This map shows the railway as being right on the border with the Congo," Helen said.

"Well, from here south, there'll be no more real wilderness," George said. "Now it will be railways, roads and towns all the way to the Cape."

"I don't know," Federica said. "Looking down there, it looks like the railway runs through miles of bush and trees."

"When do we get to Broken Hill?" Helen asked.

"We should be there by just after two," George replied. "Then we'll buy some petrol and head on to Livingstone and the Victoria Falls."

"I think we should take a stop there for a day and see the falls," Federica suggested. "I would like to see them and I'm sure Helen would like to take some photographs."

"We'll do that," George promised. "Now, that must be Broken Hill, look, you can see the headgear of the Broken Hill lead mine."

"I wonder if there'll be a welcoming committee here," Federica said.

"We'll find out soon enough," George said.

There was a welcoming committee, the Administrator for the district, managers from the mine and the railways and a horde of onlookers, larger than anywhere so far. The fact that Federica and Helen were on the plane was a matter for great discussion, and when it was learned that she was one of the pilots, that set off a huge buzz of chatter. Not wanting to delay too long, George made their apologies to the officials and attended to petrol, then after a suitable interval of interviews and breaks for visits to toilets, they were off again, following what had become known as the Iron Compass, the railway line that would take then all the way to Livingstone. The station master at Broken Hill said that he would telegraph the various stations along the way to let them know they were coming, and then also get progress reports as to where they were. They had done that with the van Ryneveld flight. Federica and Helen were keen to get on to see the Victoria Falls, so as soon as they politely could, they took their leave and took off. They flew south until they reached the Kafue River, then their route went more southeast, always roughly following the railway line, which twisted and turned beneath them. It was just past four in the afternoon when they saw the Zambezi and the spray thrown up by the Victoria Falls. George, who was flying that leg, dropped down so that they could see the falls and circled them, allowing Helen the opportunity to take photographs, then they looked for and found the landing field at Livingstone and went in to land.

"It looks like the whole town is here," Federica said, looking out of the cockpit window.

"I doubt that there have been many planes land here," George said. "And I read that when van Ryneveld landed, they were greeted by the Administrator and probably the whole town, white and black."

The Administrator, Sir Francis Chaplin, was there to meet them, as was Colonel Stephenson, who had been in charge of the Aviators Welcome Committee when van Ryneveld and his crew landed there. Federica and Helen were marvelled at, and newspapers and people wanted interviews and comments. They did their best, then pleaded exhaustion from the day and asked to go to a hotel. With profuse apologies, they were taken to the hotel. George did say that they planned to stay the next day to see the falls and would be available to discuss their flight so far, and he suggested to Sir Francis and to Colonel Stephenson that they and their spouses might join them for dinner. That invitation was accepted with alacrity as they were very interested to hear about the journey and the plane.

"Let's go and view the falls in the morning, then check out the plane," George suggested. "We wouldn't want a failure now, we've come so far without incident."
"I'm very happy that we went with the three air-cooled radials," she said. "They have given us no problems."
"That's true," he agreed. "But we also learned from the previous flights and their problems and wired bolts and nuts and taps so that things would not vibrate loose or open."
"Should we go for dinner?" she asked.
"We should," he agreed. "We won't be dressed for dinner, but I think they'll understand."
"Mrs Wheelwright, we understand that you have been flying the plane," the colonel said.
"I have," Federica confirmed. "I got my licence before the Great War and have been flying ever since."
"We got a telegraph from our man in Kisumu that you had a hand in the design of the plane," the colonel said.
"I did, my sister in law and I designed it, this is our twenty-third design, the others were single, twin and four-engined biplanes, this is our second monoplane, but the first with three engines, my brother-in-law is the engine designer," she replied.
"You've built twenty-three planes?" the colonel asked.
"We designed and built those; we also built others under contract during the war," she said. "We built the de Havilland DH-5, de Havilland DH-10, the Royal Aircraft Factory S.E.5, the Sopwith Camel, the Handley Page O/400 and the Vickers Vimy, so we were busy."
"Our main business is cars, vans and lorries," George added. "We own the Sirius Car Company, plus a couple of other businesses."
"Geoffrey Gilbey telegraphed that you were in the RFC, then the RAF," the colonel said to George.

"I was," he confirmed. "I was first in Egypt looking out for Suez, then went to the Western Front."

"Mrs Greene, how have you managed photographing things?" Sir Francis asked.

"Very well," she replied. "I have been taking both still and moving pictures and hope to splice it all together when we get back to make a film of the journey."

"What has been the greatest difficulty?" the colonel asked.

"The heat at Assuan and Khartoum," George said. "We have enough power, but takeoffs when it's that hot are always an issue. Abercorn is high and the runway fairly short, but again, we've enough power and we're flying with a light load, so that wasn't a problem for us. But, I gather from the reports that Lieutenant Colonel van Ryneveld's team threw out a lot to lighten their plane."

"Do you need a guide for tomorrow for your visit to our falls?" Sir Francis asked.

"That would be delightful," Federica said. "Perhaps we could do that in the morning because we wish to spend the afternoon checking out the plane and the engines."

"Who is your mechanic?" the colonel asked.

"George and I share duties," she said. "We built the plane ourselves so know it intimately, and we've pulled apart and rebuilt the engines a few times."

"Remarkable," Sir Francis said. "Well, here's a toast to you all, may you reach Cape Town soon and safely."

The Victoria Falls were awe-inspiring, looking down into the chasm below with the water tumbling and roiling as it fell the 355 feet. The bridge over the river gorge was also an impressive sight, not that old, having been opened in 1905. It allowed railway and other traffic to cross the Zambezi without having to go upstream to where a ferry could operate. Helen took pictures, both still and moving and began to worry that she would run out of film. Federica and George spent the afternoon looking over every inch of the plane, searching for items that showed wear or chaffing, for nuts, bolts and screws that might have come loose, and finally they checked out the engines completely and satisfied themselves that they were in good order. George telegraphed Will and Nastia with the progress report and included details of their inspection of the plane and the engines. He also telegraphed Will's parents, who lived in Kimberley and told them that they would be in Cape Town in two days' time. They replied, saying that they would meet them there. His last telegraph was to his cousin, Koos Englebrecht, who was ageing now, but who also said that he would be in Cape Town.

They took off for Bulawayo at six the next morning and followed the railway, which made navigation very easy. They were in Bulawayo by seven forty and were surprised to see another plane there. Apparently, an enterprising soul by the name of Major Miller was offering Rhodesian Aerial tours in an Avro 504K plane. He was about to take off for his first tour of the day and waved to them as they taxied up to where they could buy petrol. Talking to the ground staff, George learned that the runway had been made a little safer by clearing another 150 feet of trees so that the climb out would not be so hazardous. They left Bulawayo after only a short stop and were in Palapye by ten and Pretoria by one-thirty in the afternoon, landing at the new Zwartkop airfield.

"Tomorrow, Cape Town," Federica said. "It will be nice to get there at last. Today was one of the shortest, if not the shortest day we had."

"Tomorrow will be fairly short too," George said. "I thought we'd leave at six, put down in Johannesburg briefly, then go on to Beaufort West, and Cape Town."

"You were in Beaufort West in the Boer War, weren't you?" Federica said. "I remember getting letters that were franked Beaufort West."

"I was only there briefly," he said. "Mainly to get my marching orders and to report."

"How long a flight will it be to this Beaufort West?" Helen asked.

"Four hours," George replied. "And then another two to the Cape."

"Are there any more mountains to cross?" Helen asked.

"We're pretty high here," he replied. "We're almost up at 6,000 feet, so it's downhill from here. There are the Witteberg Mountains, and on the coastal ranges of the Langeberg, we might actually see snow."

"Fancy, snow in June," Helen said. "That would be nice to see, then I can have pictures of snow on the Alps and on the Langeberg."

Their hotel in Pretoria, the Royal, did them proud for dinner and packed breakfast and lunch. Then it was off to Cape Town, after a very brief stop in Johannesburg, landing on a golf course of all places. After all the flying over vast areas of East and Central Africa with little in the way of European-style development, it was different to fly over towns, farms, roads and railways. Their route took them over Welkom and down between Bloemfontein and Kimberley and on into Beaufort West, where they touched down at eleven. They took time to eat their lunch, drink water and tea, spend their pennies, take on more petrol and then left for Cape Town at noon.

"Look, over there," Helen said excitedly. "That's snow, it's hard to comprehend that only a few days ago we were looking at snow on the Alps, and now we're here the other side of the world, looking at more snow."

"Air travel will definitely shrink the globe," Federica said. "I wonder if that's such a good thing, making people rush around and not enjoy the journey."

"I have certainly enjoyed this journey," Helen said. "It has given me a long list of places I would like to go back to to see properly. Have you been to South Africa, Fede?"

"I have," she replied. "I came with George in 1903, we sailed south on the Kildonan Castle and were entertained by a cousin of George, we saw elephants and all kinds of animals."

"Who is meeting us in Cape Town?" Helen asked.

"George's cousin Koos Englebrecht, and Hamish and Fiona McIntosh, they're Will's parents, they live in Kimberley and represent Sirius Cars in most of South Africa," Federica replied. "George's cousin handles Cape Town and imports, and Hamish manages everything else."

"Kimberley is where the big diamond mine is, isn't it?" Helen asked.

"It is," George confirmed. "A huge hole in the ground that men have dug through the years. We're coming up on the mountains and hills that surround Cape Town, and we'll start descending soon."

"There's the sea," Federica said. "That must be the Indian Ocean and that the Atlantic, is that right?"

"Not quite," George said. "The officially recognised spot is Cape Agulhas, which is back that way a little, it's the southernmost point of Africa."

They landed at Cape Town at two and were met by Koos, Hamish and Fiona, Colonel van Ryneveld and an army of reporters and government officials. The reporters wanted pictures of them and the plane, and interviews describing the journey. They had actually made the journey in seven days of flying and had added two days, one for weather and one for sightseeing, so nine days in all, far faster than the ships of the day. Colonel van Ryneveld wanted to see the plane, so Federica invited him aboard and gave him a complete description of the plane, its design, its manufacture and its handling characteristics. As the Colonel headed up the South African Air Force, he was really interested to see if it had any military use. Clearly, it was not designed as a bomber, nor a fighter, so it would have very limited use except as a transport. But for all that he had an interest, as did several others, and there were requests for flights. George said that he would consider flights after they had had a day or two to rest after their long journey.

Koos had booked them all rooms at the Mount Nelson and Federica, for one was looking forward to a bath and some dinner. Dinner was a time for recounting the events of the journey and for catching up on Sirius and family matters. Koos said that he had received the boxes of spare parts for the engines and that he had a garage in Cape Town that had room enough to overhaul the engines. After a night's sleep, George went back to the airport and gave rides to the South African Air Force people and to several other aviators and businessmen. That generated a lot of interest in the plane, and he actually received four offers to buy it then and there. He said that he would consider it and told them all that their first mission in Cape Town was to tear the engines apart and examine them for wear and then rebuild them, using the parts that he had shipped earlier. That also generated interest to see how the engines had stood up to the rigours of the long flights. George committed to providing the data when he had them. Meanwhile, Helen had found a laboratory that would develop her pictures, both moving and still, so she was working with them to get that done to give some to the local press. Federica got tea and sat on the terrace with paper and pen, and set about detailing the costs of the trip. The costs included petrol and oil, maintenance, most yet to be expended, but which she knew was necessary and for which they already had the parts, and then depreciation of the aircraft itself and what would be the salaries of the pilots and the mechanics that they would need if a commercial venture was to be undertaken. Plus, they would need some ground staff at the various stations where they made overnight stops and accounts at the hotels and a booking agent. She worked out the essential operating costs of the plane in terms of pounds per hour, then constructed a fare schedule from that and from the hotel bills they had paid. Then she made other notes about the conditions of the airfields that had been found and issues that might arise.

Harsh Reality

Early 1923 saw consolidation of French airlines, work on a scheme for the best method of subsidising British airlines crossing the Channel and the first night flights.

"I've been looking at numbers," Federica told George. "They don't paint a very pretty picture. If we took passengers, then the fares would have to be quite a bit more than the first-class fare on the Union Castle boats, and luggage allowance would be very small. There might be some who would want to get here in under ten days, which would be much of the time if the weather cooperated, but is that a large enough number to make a service viable?"

"I'm sure that you have the answer to that," he said. "That's what you've been scribbling away at for the last couple of days."

"We have shown that the route can be flown with good, reliable engines, but the unknowns are how reliable would a timetable be given the vagaries of the weather and how many people would use the service," she said. "If we have to build time into the timetable to accommodate for weather, then the arrival times would only be a little better than the ships."

"So, this is all leading up to something," he said.

"I think we are just a little too soon," she said. "And there's another thing, I've been hearing rumours about changes in the Air Ministry. I heard that Samuel Hoare is likely to be the next Air Minister. He's likely to look at the mess that British airlines are in and try and make some kind of sense of it all, particularly the long routes to India and Australia and to here."

"So, what do you see happening?" he asked.

"I think look for someone to be given the task of examining the whole structure, and if I were the government, I would consolidate all the little competing companies into one national airline," she said.

"So, if we had Sirius Airlines flying to the Cape, you'd see that being absorbed into a national entity?" he asked.

"I do," she said. "If we look at cross-Channel traffic, between each other and the Continentals, the British airlines competed each other into almost bankruptcy, until the government stepped in with subsidies."

"So, your dream is dead?" he asked.

"Sadly, I don't see it as viable at the moment," she said. "If we also consider the state of the aerodromes and landing fields we flew into, they need some serious work before we could safely take fare-paying passengers into them. They've been rather abandoned, and as an airline we should not have to bear the expense of keeping up the fields and storing petrol and oil."

"I had wondered who was maintaining them," he said. "Archibald and Geoffrey both commented that once in a while, they mow the grass, but they use the fields more as cricket pitches than airfields. I suppose if there were more local aviation, that would change, but the only place I see that happening is here in South Africa. In East and Central Africa, it would be most useful, but who pays, as Geoffrey said, a plane for him would be a godsend as he has such a large territory to administer, and he's right, the Colonial Office is known to be parsimonious when it comes to spending."

"It was apparent too at Assuan, Khartoum, Abercorn and Bulawayo that whoever decided on runway length really didn't understand what altitude and temperature would mean, so the runways are too short to be really safe for commercial flying, even Johannesburg was close to the limits," she added. "I also see further issues at Assuan and Khartoum when it gets too hot, and we couldn't get enough lift without limiting the takeoff weight, even with a longer runway. It might be an idea to break up the route and use river steamers on the Nile where it's really hot, that would add time, but it might be less risk."

"So, if I look at all we've talked about, first the basic structure of aerodromes is not ready and it's not at all certain who would pay for that, second the weather will be a limiting factor more often than we would like, either too hot or too wet, plus throw in the odd sandstorm that might come up, third the operating costs are such that the fares would need to be probably more than the steamer fares, fourth, luggage will be really limited because of takeoff weight issues at Assuan and Khartoum and at Abercorn, Bulawayo and Johannesburg, and lastly we don't know how many passengers we might get, is that about right?" he asked.

"That's what I see," she confirmed. "The harsh reality is that at this time it's not really feasible."

"You've thought about this a lot. What's your proposal?" he asked.

"I think for us we build another Pegasus, we sell the Condor we have here and use the funds for the new Pegasus," she said. "I know I had a dream, but having flown the route and seen what it entails, there is much that needs to happen before a service can be started."

"I have received several offers for the plane," he said. "What if we sell it here and take a boat home?"

"Like we did before," she said. "That would be fun, we'd have to buy some clothes, the boat people might frown on us showing up decked out for flying."

"We can do that," he said. "I should check with Union Castle and book berths for us and for Helen."

"That's a load off my mind," she said. "I've been wondering what to do. Now, I think we should spend some time with Koos and Hamish and discuss Sirius Cars' business."

They met with Hamish and Koos, and Koos told them that he was of an age that he wanted to just hand everything over to Hamish. Hamish agreed to that and also mentioned that he was readying his son, Robert, to take over the business from him. It was a sad reality that none of them were getting any younger; in fact, Koos was now 62, not really old, but approaching that age when most made changes in their lives. George and Federica were not old, but at 51 and 49, they were probably unusual pilots, but they could still stay active in the car business and the other enterprises that they had. Hamish was a contemporary, so it was good that he was making sure that Robert would be capable of running the business. He also had his daughter, Elizabeth, involved, and she was essentially managing all the accounts and the finances while Robert saw to sales, parts and service. Koos and Hamish both commented that the best sellers were the vans and lorries, followed by the Arcturus line of four-wheel drive cars that were popular with farmers and safari outfitters as they went just about anywhere. Federica took notes to pass on to Anastasia and asked if there were any changes that they would like to see. Both Koos and Hamish commented that larger petrol tanks would be useful, distances in South Africa were large, and petrol stations scattered. They also asked when a diesel engine might be available for the lorries. Federica said that she would investigate that, but she knew that one of the problems with diesel engines was reliability, not that people were not working on that. She promised to put it to Will to see if he could develop a working diesel engine that would not break down as often as some engines had been.

George met with those who had expressed an interest in buying their aircraft and actually got four offers. None were conditional on anything, except that all wanted the spares that had come and the manuals that would tell them how to overhaul the engines. George consulted with Will, and Will gave approval to release the manuals to interested parties. He then sat down with each bidder and negotiated the best deal he could get.

"I got £14,500 for the plane," he told Federica when it was all done.

"That's marvellous," she said. "It cost us £12,575 to build, add in the spares for the engines at another £1,500, and we've done quite well; that will also give us enough for boat passages."

"I've arranged that," he said. "I met with the Union Castle people and we have two first-class berths on the Windsor Castle, which they tell me is one of the newer boats, only having gone into service in April of this year."

"What did Will have to say about selling the plane?" she asked.

"All he asked was whether we were sure and did we want another engine for a new single-engine Pegasus," George replied. "I told him we did, so he said he would have it ready for us."

"I suppose we should go shopping and buy some clothes for the voyage," she said. "I'll take Helen and Fiona with me and we'll see what we can find, perhaps you can go with Koos and Hamish and get some suitable gentlemen's suitings."

"First, though, I need to take Andrew Forster, the buyer of the plane, up for a lesson on the controls," George said. "He's a pilot and has flown a few different models, so I don't imagine it will take him long to adapt to our plane."

"Perhaps I'll come with you as a passenger," she thought.

Andrew Forster proved to be a skilled pilot who quickly learned the controls, instruments and handling characteristics of the plane and who landed it neatly on their first outing. They took off again for a little longer trip and actually flew over Cape Agulhas so that Federica could see the Indian and Atlantic Oceans. Andrew had plans to start an air service between Cape Town and Johannesburg and wanted to hear about any difficulties they had had with the altitude. Both George and Federica assured him that the plane had had power enough to take off safely at Pretoria and Johannesburg, but suggested that he check with the authorities there to see if the runway could be lengthened as an investment against future larger-sized aircraft that would need a longer runway. They had landed briefly at Johannesburg, but that had been on the Germiston Golf Course, something that was probably not practical in the longer term. The other factor that needed to be considered was the use of the Zwartkop airfield at Pretoria, the South African government had purchased the farm for an air force station and probably would cavil at too much use by commercial traffic, plus whereas Pretoria was the government centre, Johannesburg was the commercial centre so would likely see more demand for air traffic than Pretoria. Andrew had work to do organising things for the future, but he was confident he would prevail. George suggested to Andrew that he look at offering air trips to Victoria Falls, he suggested Cape Town to Bloemfontein, then Palapye and finally Livingstone, which would take a day. There were already excursion trains that connected with the docking ocean liners that took people to the falls, so why not air. Andrew thought that a splendid plan and said that after he had overhauled the engines and done a couple of test flights, he would fly the route and make note of landmarks on the way. The ultimate destination should be easier enough to find as the Zambezi was a big river; the only thing to watch out for was cutting across the river above or below the falls, even that was made easier by the fact that the river ran in a gorge below the falls.

George and Federica then went their separate ways, but both ended up on Adderley Street in the same shops, just different departments. George bought two new suits and shirts, ties and shoes, and Federica and Helen both bought what would seem to George later as an innumerable number of dresses for all occasions. They also bought steamer trunks to pack everything into. Helen had her pictures, moving and still, back from the developer, so George invited interested parties to a reception at the Mount Nelson, where Helen displayed her photographs and also borrowed a projector to show the moving pictures she had taken. In all, they had almost a hundred people come, some from the Air Force, some from the government, but most from either the press or the fledgling aviation industry, many with their spouses. It was obvious from the pictures that both George and Federica shared flying duties, which put to bed speculation that Federica had just been along for the ride. Members of the press asked for copies of photographs, and Helen took down a list and promised to get prints made for them. After all the moving pictures had been shown, George asked if there were any questions. There were questions galore. Some about flying conditions, some about runways, and some about food at the hotels they had stayed at. There were even some about the design of the plane and why they had selected a monoplane rather than the more common biplane. Between them, Federica and George answered all the questions, some of which led to more questions. There were also photographers in the group who had questions for Helen, some of which were quite technical, and Federica wondered if they were not trying to trip Helen up in a typically male fashion. However, Helen acquitted herself marvellously and impressed those there with her knowledge and expertise. Both Federica and Helen were asked if they were afraid to fly down Africa, and both replied that they saw it as an adventure, which endeared them to most of the men and condemned them with many of the women who saw it as quite unseemly that women should be involved in such an enterprise.

"Do you regret not to be flying back?" George asked Federica as they boarded the Windsor Castle.

"Yes and no," she replied. "Yes, because there are parts of Africa I am unlikely to see again, and no because we have shown that our plane will make the trip in one go, and discovered that things are just not ready for a commercial air service yet, so my dream of a commercial service to the Cape is a little premature. When we get home, I will build another Pegasus. I'm not giving up flying, but I will devote more time to car, van and lorry development, and perhaps even something else that we haven't looked at yet. What about you, any regrets?"

"None," he said. "We made the trip and made it in good time, with decent weather, we could have been here in seven days, but it was apparent that inclement weather could add days to the trip. I'm looking forward now to a few days of doing nothing and letting someone else worry about the navigation and the engines."

"We really do have to congratulate Will when we get home," she said. "His radials did a tremendous job, with no breakdowns; that is a remarkable achievement."

"I wonder if we can make the inline engines for Sirius Cars as reliable," he said. "We should look carefully at what failures there are and how we can design things so that we remove the failure possibilities."

"Should we build and sell the radials to other aircraft builders?" she asked.

"It might be an idea," he said. "We've got all the data from the trip so we can advertise the fact that we flew from Croydon to Cape Town with no problems with the three engines. That's a good testament to their reliability."

"Pierre van Ryneveld and Quintin Brand were both knighted after their trip down Africa and being the first to fly all the way from Cairo to Cape Town," she said. "Will anyone note our trip?"

"I'm sure they will," he said. "We gave enough interviews here and at Livingstone that something will get reported, plus you were one of the pilots, so that's a first, first woman to fly to the Cape, and we're the first to fly all the way in one plane, we're the first to fly here in a monoplane, all kinds of firsts."

"There's Helen, we should make sure she gets settled in her cabin," Federica said.

"This is super," Helen said as she stowed her bags in her cabin. "I've got a porthole, I can see outside, and I've even got my own washing facilities. I will miss the adventure of the flying, but this is another adventure."

"I think when we get home, you should put on an exhibition of your photographs of the journey," Federica suggested.

"Add to the flight pictures some taken on the boat here and that will give people a sense of the differences between to two modes of travel," George suggested.

"I have already taken pictures of our steamer trunks that I can compare with the small bags we had for the plane," Helen said. "I wonder if the captain would let me take pictures of the boiler room and the steam turbines."

"We can only ask," Federica said. "Now we should find out where we are seated for dinner, the ship departs at four, so in another half an hour."

"This is a nicer boat than the one we went on before," George said.

"It's a lot newer," Federica said.

"Which one were you on before?" Helen asked.

"We came south on the Kildonan Castle and the Walmer Castle north," George replied. "I had previously been on the Walmer Castle returning from the war in South Africa, and that voyage was crowded as they tried to get as many men on each boat as they could."

"There's the second hooter," George said. "We're leaving now, the first blast was to tell people not sailing to leave the boat. We should go out on deck and watch."

"It's quite chilly, isn't it?" Helen said. "I suppose it's midwinter, so no great surprise. Let me get some pictures of you posed with Table Mountain in the background."

"Let's see if we can persuade someone to take a picture of the three of us," Federica said. "You can't always be behind the camera, Helen."

"May I be of service?" a man offered. He also had a camera and had been busy taking pictures of the boat, the harbour and the passengers.

"That would be very kind of you," Federica said. "Perhaps with us posed against the mountain."

"Of course," he said. "This is a nice camera."

"It's a Zeiss, it has seen us well," Helen said. "I have some interesting pictures of the Alps."

"Do you work as a photographer?" he asked.

"I do," she replied. "I work for the Sirius Car Company and other companies, and you?"

"I'm a freelance photographer doing jobs for newspapers and magazines," he said. "Basil Rowe, at your service."

"Helen Greene and this is Federica and George Wheelwright," Helen said.

"So nice to meet you," he said. "I was reading about your adventure in the Argus the other day, did you really make it all the way from Croydon in nine days?"

"We did," Helen confirmed. "It would have been seven, but we lost a day because of rain at Mongalla, and we took a day off to see the Victoria Falls."

"Would it be presumptuous to ask if I might join you for a drink before dinner?" he asked. "I would be fascinated to hear about flying down Africa."

"We would be delighted," Federica said for the three of them.

"Until six in the lounge, then," he said.

"You have an admirer," Federica teased Helen.

"I'm seeing Angus still," Helen said. "So, this Basil is rather a non-starter."

"I checked the dinner room and we're at table number one with the captain and four others," George said.

"We've never been invited to sit at the captain's table," Federica said. "I wonder what we did to deserve that."

"We flew all the way from Cairo without incident," Helen said. "That's a first, even though there will be many who will not believe you and I had any part in it."

"That is true," Federica agreed. "When we started the Sirius Car Company, we faced many obstacles from men who thought us incapable of designing a car."

"Do we have to change for dinner?" Helen asked.

"The tradition is that on the first night out, it is not necessary to dress for dinner," Federica said. "The rest of the way, we're supposed to show the flag and be icons of fashion."

"Shall we go inside and meet again at six in the lounge?" George asked.

"I shall go and deposit my camera and be ready for dinner," Helen said.

"I just need to go and comb my hair," Federica said.

They reconvened in the lounge, and Basil ordered drinks for them and then asked to hear all about the flight from Cairo. George gave him the basics and just said that it had been very tiring, even with two of them flying the plane. He added that Helen had taken many photographs along the way and had also taken a series of moving pictures of places they had seen from the air and from the ground. Federica then turned the tables and asked Basil what he had been doing in South Africa, and he told them that he had been on an assignment for the London Illustrated News, taking pictures of animals and the various peoples of South Africa. He had travelled extensively in South Africa from the Limpopo to the Cape and from the Indian Ocean near Durban to the Atlantic miles north of Cape Town. He was glad to be going home, looking forward to a few weeks off before his next assignment.

The dinner gong sounded, and they went to the dining room and found their table. Basil was with them as was the captain, Thomas Bremner and chief engineer, Neil McPherson, and a Mr Michael and Mrs June Walton. The Waltons were wool merchants and had been in South Africa looking at Dorper sheep for sheepskin to make coats and the like from. Neil knew who George and Federica were and wanted to know all about the design of the plane and put questions to George, who deferred to Federica to answer them. That rather surprised the others at the table, but it became very clear to Neil and Thomas that she really did know what she was talking about. Later in the dinner, Helen asked if she could take some pictures of the engine room with the boilers and the steam turbines, which Thomas agreed to if they would give a talk to interested passengers about their flight down Africa. Federica and George agreed and suggested that Helen display some of the pictures she had taken. There was no projector on board the ship, so she could not show her moving pictures, which was a shame.

"You should get some recognition from the government for your feat," Thomas said. "To have gone so far in such a short time is remarkable."

"The credit really goes to William McIntosh, my brother-in-law," George said. "He designed the engines that performed so well on the journey."

"How many hours did they actually run?" Neil asked.

"Fifty-three hours all told," Federica said. "The longest single run was five hours and twenty minutes. We have yet to get to the reliability of marine engines that run for days on end."

"When we first went to steam turbines, there were problems," Neil said. "But over time we learned and improved the designs, I'm sure that in time the internal combustion engines you use will improve."

"The greatest constraint we had was the use of a toilet," George said. "We had no facilities on the plane; otherwise, we could have made longer flights and cut down the journey time, but the five hours and twenty minutes were long enough. We marvelled at the fortitude of Alcock and Brown flying across the Atlantic in an open cockpit with the minimum of conveniences."

"Your cockpit is not open then?" Neil asked.

"No," George replied. "Ours is enclosed with the rest of the fuselage."

"What were the greatest challenges?" Michael asked.

"Taking off from Assuan and Abercorn," Federica replied. "Assuan because it was hot and Abercorn because it was high and the runway short."

"Why are those issues?" Michael asked.

"Without getting into a long technical explanation of the forces that influence flight, temperature and altitude both are important factors in our ability to generate enough lift to take off," Federica replied. "In some ways, it's similar to the Plimsoll line; temperature and altitude affect air density, which affects lift, in the same way that temperature affects water density."

"So, for you, a nice cool day at sea level is better than 90 degrees at 5,000 feet?" Neil asked.

"Much," Federica confirmed. "At Assuan, temperatures were over a hundred, and Abercorn was over 5,500 feet, and Johannesburg was even higher at 6,000 feet. Fortunately for us, we came in the Southern Hemisphere winter, so temperatures in Abercorn and Johannesburg were very mild."

"Forgive me, Mrs Wheelwright, where do you get your education that you know so much?" June asked.

"I grew up in Hong Kong," Federica replied. "And my father provided me with tutors in everything from mathematics to language."

"And you, Miss Greene, how did you become a photographer?" June asked.

"My father is a chemist," Helen replied. "I would help him in the shop compounding medicines that were prescribed, so became interested in chemistry. Sadly, the school I attended did not offer chemistry, so I taught myself, and I also investigated the physics of light and lenses and then put it all together and took up photography."

"And you, Mr Wheelwright?" Michael asked.

"I was an army officer, serving in India, then South Africa," George replied. "I resigned my commission after the Boer War to concentrate on the family estate and the companies we have, the Sirius Car Company, Abbey Biscuits and Windsor Garments. I was called up in the last war and served in the RFC in Egypt and the RAF on the Western Front."

"You have Windsor Garments, perhaps at some time we might discuss sheepskin coats and other items," Michael said.

"I'm sure that in the next twenty days or so there will be time," George agreed.

Their talk about the trip down Africa was well attended, and there were questions afterwards, questions about the people they had seen, the food they had eaten, the weather they had encountered and even a few about the design of the plane and the engines. Helen got her photographs of the boiler room and the steam turbines, and was invited to the bridge and took pictures there as well. For the rest of the voyage north, they were plied with drinks and treated as celebrities by many of the passengers. Most found it incredible that Federica and Helen had undertaken the flight; it was something that women just did not do. The day before they docked the Captain Bremner told them that there would be a reception committee in Southampton and that they would be expected to make some kind of statement about their flight. It was good to be forewarned, so the three of them huddled in the lounge and concocted a bald statement that described the flight and also gave credit to all the local officials they had met on the way and thanked them for their support. They decided not to mention the deficiencies of the various airfields they had landed at, which could come later in a longer, more detailed report. They gave credit to Will and his engine design and essentially threw in an advertisement for the engines.

Captain Bremner had been right, there were people from the Air Ministry, from the RAF, from the Colonial Office to meet them, all wanting to take credit for the flight and all full of congratulations for the achievement and yet all with questions about who had actually been flying the plane, none really accepting that Federica had done her share of the flying. George told them that they had their log books that would show who flew which leg and that they would share that in due time. There were also members of the Press, all keen to get interviews and all vying for attention to get the scoop on the others. As the Cape Argus had already published a long article on the flight, it was hardly news, but not many people in Britain took the Argus, so the story did bear repeating. When they finally made it through the throng of officials and reporters, Anastasia and Will were there to meet them and take them home. They had each driven a car down, so there was room enough for the three travellers and luggage.

"Glad to be home?" Anastasia asked when they arrived at the house.
"Very," Federica said. "The voyage was nice enough, but being polite to so many people for three weeks was a challenge."
"Who did you sell the plane to?" Will asked.

"A chap who wants to start a commercial service in South Africa," George said. "We think he may start with trips from Cape Town to the Victoria Falls. Your engines are what did the trick for us on the flight; not a single problem all the way there. More of an issue than the plane and the engines were the runways. The RAF might have built them in 1919, and they were used by the various teams that went in 1920, but since then, they've been rather neglected and are usable, but barely. Any thought of commercial service down Africa is first going to have to address the infrastructure to support flights."

"We filed reports with *Flight* and *The Aeroplane* as you went," Will said. "We kept the papers so you could read them. I'm sure that both would like to get a story from you, with photographs that Helen took."

"Helen has lots of photographs and moving pictures," George said. "We should set up the projector here and show them."

"I'll invite the factory managers," Anastasia said. "Then I know it will be a burden, but I think it would be good to show them to all the people in our companies,"

"We met some people on the boat who want to talk to Windsor about sheepskin coats and other items," Federica said.

"What next?" Anastasia asked.

"I'm not sure," Federica said. "New cars, I think, but then you have that well in hand, I may look for another venture, something that is less of a dream than a commercial service to the Cape and more practical."

"Well, take your time," Anastasia said. "We're doing well enough at the moment. Perhaps you could think about what the next few years will hold for us and if we are likely to see problems in the next ten years, and if we do, how do we prepare. I see problems brewing in the coal mines. We didn't export coal in the last war, so mines in Europe and America filled that gap, and there is no going back, so the mines here will face challenges. I also see the heavy industries cutting back as the demand for artillery, ships, and tanks goes away, so problems there, too."

"I might just do that, I'll think about those industries and how it may affect us," Federica said. "But for now, I plan to enjoy the summer, and perhaps we'll take Giovanna to the Lakes when she has her school holidays, and I'm going to build a new Pegasus."

"I have your engine for you," Will said. "We have bench-tested it and it runs better than any we have made to date, so it should serve you well."

The picture shows were a success, and Helen received employment offers from half a dozen studios and magazines, but she declined all, stating that she enjoyed what she was doing. George made sure that she had time and the resources to explore the world of photography and did not discourage freelance work that she might take, as long as the companies had first call on her time. The editors and reporters from *Flight* and *The Aeroplane* came to see them, unapologetic about their withdrawal from participating in the actual flight, but keen to hear about any issues with the plane of the engines. George and Federica had their map of Africa with progress marked on it and talked about each leg of the flight and what they saw. They provided both publications with the flight logs and all the measurements taken along the way, and also commented on the state of the runways and the issues of temperature and altitude. That gave the papers something to write about and to editorialise on, decrying the attitude of the government towards encouraging the new air transport industry.

Federica and George took August off and took Giovanna to the Lakes as promised. They stayed with Sophia, who had enjoyed considerable success with her novel and was being encouraged by her editor to write another. They hired a small yacht for the summer and learned to sail on Windermere, teaching Giovanna as they learned. Federica also bought copies of books and papers written by various economists through the years and read the works of people like Robert Giffen, David Ricardo. Adam Smith, John Hobson, James Steuart and Thomas Malthus, agreeing and disagreeing as she went. She felt that much of what they wrote was purely theoretical, but she brought her own experience in running businesses and all that that brought with it. Their thoughts were though always challenging, even when she did not agree, because she had to explain to herself why she did not agree.

George received invitations to speak at meetings of the Royal Aeronautical Society and the Royal Geographical Society, and he accepted, provided that Federica and Helen would be welcome and could speak as well. He was sure that that led to all kinds of discussions, but their curiosity must have outweighed their prejudices as they both agreed. Helen was also asked if she would speak at the Royal Photographic Society, a chance she jumped at. Their first meeting was with the aeronautical people, and they were introduced as Lieutenant Colonel George Wheelwright, DSO and bar, DFC and Mrs Wheelwright, MBE and Miss Helen Greene. George structured things in three parts: the journey that he talked about, the plane and engines that Federica talked about and the pictures taken along the way that Helen displayed with technical details about the cameras and lenses she used and the films and their development. There were some questions about the plane design being adequate, but the flight logs rather spoke for themselves, and the questioners sat down feeling rather foolish, and General Harris was there and he spoke out for Federica and praised the work she and Anastasia had done in the War building aircraft. Then her body of supporters, Angus Fraser, Richard Collins and Stephen Walker, all chimed in as pilots who had flown planes that Federica had designed and built, and all were fulsome in their praise of her designs. As George said to Federica later, the very idea that a woman would design and build a plane and then fly it was such a challenge to their perceived superiority as men that they just had to challenge the notion. They were surprised when the society announced that they had both been awarded the society's Gold Medal for contributions to the science and industry of aeronautics. The geographers were more interested in weather, mountains, rivers and such and were all intrigued by Helen's pictures, still and moving. They awarded no medals as Federica and George had not explored new territories nor broken new ground in the science of geography; they had merely flown over ground previously surveyed. The last meeting was with the photographers, and Helen displayed her still and moving pictures, now spliced together to show a 90-minute film of the journey. Her work was greeted with unanimous acclamation, and she was given an Honorary Fellowship in the society.

In time, the public interest died down, and they were no longer objects of curiosity and marvel, which suited all of them. Still, they would go down in the history books as the first to fly the same plane from Cairo to Cape Town, and the first woman to do so. Public accolades were there, though, from the various societies awarding medals, to towns and cities wanting to name things after them. The final accolade came in the 1923 New Year's Honours List, and it named George as a Knight Commander of the British Empire, Federica as a Dame Commander of the British Empire and Helen as a Member of the British Empire. They all dutifully trooped off to Buckingham Palace to receive their awards, and henceforth, George was now Sir George, which delighted Anastasia. Federica, as Dame Federica had to live with the fact that most people did not know what that really meant, the award had only been given to women since 1917, so it was not yet part of the long tradition of honours.

"So, Sir George," Federica said after the ceremony. "What now?"

"Find the next venture," he said. "For now, I think wind up the airline companies, keep the aircraft company, spend some more time with Abbey, Windsor and Star as well as Sirius Cars and the foundry, then look at what opportunities and businesses arise that might fit with what we're good at doing."

"I think concentrate on the basics of living if we can," she said. "Large capital goods like ships will be subject to the vagaries of the world economy, so stay with things that people really need and can afford. My readings in the field of economics lead me to believe that the effects of the last war will be felt for some time, and we will see hard times in the future, perhaps in five to ten years."

"My fear is that there will be another war," he said. "The Treaty of Versailles is harsh on the Germans, and I can see that causing problems. If I were a German, I would be looking for ways to circumvent the terms of the treaty and strike back at the French, particularly those who clearly wanted to only punish the Germans."

"Let's hope it will not be in our lifetimes," she said. "I don't relish the idea of another war."

"Nor I," he said. "I've been in two major wars and also actions in India, I don't need to see another. But, enough of that Dame Federica, let's go and find ourselves a nice restaurant and see if Sir George and Dame Federica means anything to the hosts."